A marriage ha **KT-221-632**

Springtime
Betrothals

Two heartwarming tales of
romance and family!

Elizabeth Beacon lives in the beautiful English West Country and is finally putting her insatiable curiosity about the past to good use. Over the years Elizabeth has worked in her family's horticultural business, became a mature student, qualified as an English teacher, worked as a secretary and, briefly, tried to be a civil servant. She is now happily ensconced behind her computer, when not trying to exhaust her bouncy rescue dog with as many walks as the Inexhaustible Lurcher can finagle. Elizabeth can't bring herself to call researching the wonderfully diverse, scandalous Regency period and creating charismatic heroes and feisty heroines work, and she is waiting for someone to find out how much fun she is having and tell her to stop it.

Kathryn Leigh Albright, the daughter of a naval officer and a doll doctor, grew up in San Diego. Her journey to publication has included graduating from college, writing magazine articles and reading voraciously. She currently resides in the Midwest with her husband and three sons.

Springtime
Betrothals

ELIZABETH BEACON
KATHRYN ALBRIGHT

M&B™ and M&B™ with the Rose Device
are trademarks of the publisher.
Harlequin Mills & Boon Limited, Eton House,
18-24 Paradise Road, Richmond, Surrey TW9 1SR

SPRINGTIME BETROTHALS © by Harlequin Books SA 2010

Captain Langthorne's Proposal © Elizabeth Beacon 2009
Texas Wedding for their Baby's Sake © Kathryn Albright 2009

ISBN: 978 0 263 88025 0

11-0410

Harlequin Mills & Boon policy is to use papers that are
natural, renewable and recyclable products and made from
wood grown in sustainable forests. The logging and
manufacturing processes conform to the legal environmental
regulations of the country of origin.

Printed and bound in Spain
by Litografia Rosés S.A., Barcelona

Captain Langthorne's Proposal

ELIZABETH BEACON

To the two Di's,
Diana Russell and Diana Singelton,
the best friends any author could wish for.

Chapter One

Countesses didn't hide in damp woods from handsome baronets, Serena Cambray told herself sternly. Once she had been too proud to hide from anyone—how her current cowardice would have been reviled. Well, people changed, and the widowed Lady Summerton perhaps more than most, Serena informed herself stoutly, and tried to sit as still and cool as an ice-sculpture on her slightly damp tree stump. Even as she tried to tell herself she was quite calm, her thoughts drifted to the man she was avoiding so assiduously. If only she had seen beneath his youthful arrogance and that annoying air of omnipotence to the man he would one day become, how different her life might have been.

The first time she had met Adam Langthorne he had threatened to tan her hide and send her home to her father, with a message informing him that his daughter would never be permitted contact with his sister again.

'Only my grandfather's sense of chivalry prevents me from packing you off right now, even if you have to travel all night,' he had told her, and looked down his nose at her from the superiority of his lanky height and his new commission in His Majesty's army.

Serena had glared back at him and refused to admit she had anything to apologise for—even if she and Rachel Langthorne *had* been within a whisker of causing a scandal and had put themselves in deadly peril. To be labelled ungovernable hoydens given to outrageous pranks like dressing up as coachman and postilion and stealing his grandfather's carriage to go to a mill would have blighted their reputations for life, even though they had only been fourteen at the time, but how she had hated him that day, she recalled with a wry smile. Probably all the more so because she had known he was right. It struck her that if he had published her infamy to the world, George Cambray would never have tainted his great name with such a hoydenish wife. Only think of the danger of passing on such bad blood to the docile and dutiful daughters he had expected her to bear him as the inevitable side effect of breeding his heirs.

Shaking off such unwelcome thoughts, she listened for Sir Adam's soft footfall on the unpromising surface of the ancient woodland floor and wondered about that first meeting. Even at fourteen to his nineteen had she already been secretly in thrall to the tall ensign of dragoons? If so, she'd stoutly refused to allow the idea room in her silly head—and that would have been one secret she would never have confided in her best friend even if she'd known it herself. So much as a whiff of a match between Serena and her adored elder brother would have turned Rachel into a hardened matchmaker on the spot. In fact, now she came to think about it… Could that explain Sir Adam's uncanny knack of knowing where Serena was before she'd hardly thought of being there herself?

She shook her head absently and acquitted her friend of such perfidy; Rachel knew everything about her but that one almost unformed secret, and wouldn't serve Sir Adam such a backhand turn even if she had a suspicion of it. Yet Serena's stubborn thoughts lingered on what might have been, and she drifted into a fantasy of meeting the by then Lieutenant Langthorne at her come-out ball instead of the rather awesome Earl of Summerton. If only that dashing and dangerous gentleman had presented himself to be danced with, dined with, and even perhaps mildly flirted with, could she have seen a truly nobleman from the outward pattern of one?

Who knew? She had been ungovernably silly in her debutante days, so it would probably have been in the lap of the gods. So goodness alone knew why the wretched man was intent on getting her alone now. Once upon a time she would have assumed he wanted to make her an offer and preened herself on another conquest. Now she dreaded it. And he could hardly find himself a less suitable wife if he combed every assembly room in the British Isles.

'Good day, Lady Summerton,' the wretched man greeted her, as if he had no idea she was attempting to hide from him yet again.

Serena jumped at the sound of the deep voice she had been trying not to hear in her dreams, and turned to watch Sir Adam Langthorne effortlessly close the gap between them with a long, easy stride. She told herself it was foreboding that was making her heart beat faster.

'Oh, dear—I mean…good day, Sir Adam,' she said, and felt herself blush like a green girl instead of a respectable widow of four and twenty. 'I felt unaccountably tired for a few moments,' she explained feebly, trying not to see the hint of laughter and something even more dangerous in his dark gaze as one dark eyebrow rose in polite incredulity at her limp excuse for behaving like a fainting young miss with considerably more hair than sense. 'It's unseasonably mild today is it not?' she heard herself ask with an internal groan, thinking she sounded very much like the vicar's spinster sister, who was one of the silliest women in England.

'Last week you were sheltering in that tumbledown barn because you informed me it was too chilly in the open air,' he responded solemnly, and she wondered if she had been right as a girl to think she would quite like to strangle Rachel's superior and insufferable brother. Then he grinned at her, and she knew it would have been a grievous waste of both their lives, and a smile trembled on her own lips before she controlled it and looked back at him rather severely.

'And so it was. Such are the vagaries of the English weather, Sir Adam, in case you have quite forgot them during your sojourn in the Peninsula.'

'Indeed I have not. This is the only country I ever came across where we have all our seasons in one day, but at least this one is fine and, as I never seem to see anything other than the hem of your pelisse disappearing over the horizon of late, my lady, it must be ranked an especially clement one for me,' he added with a sardonic smile, and her stupid heart raced all over again.

'I have been—that is to say, I *am* very busy,' she told him solemnly. 'Very busy indeed,' she added, and took her late father's half-hunter watch out of her pocket and inspected it as if every second of her day were precious.

'Then we mustn't waste your valuable time,' he said, taking her gloved hand and raising her to her feet as if she was made of spun glass, then fitting it into the crook of his elbow as if it belonged there. 'A lady of your advancing years should learn to take life a little more easily,' he chided wickedly as he led her inexorably back onto the footpath that led away from her brother-in-law's acreage and onto Sir Adam's even larger estates.

It felt like venturing onto dangerous ground, but Serena told herself not to be silly for perhaps the thousandth time since she had met him again. It had only taken one look to know the infuriating, arrogant youth who had given her a tongue lashing that had bitten all the deeper for being well deserved, was now an infuriating, arrogant mature and potent gentleman she had endless trouble dismissing as merely her best friend's brother.

'And a gentleman of yours should learn better manners,' she snapped back, before she had time to put a guard on her tongue. Catching a glint of satisfaction in his brown eyes, as temper robbed her of the starchy dignity she was forever striving for in his company, Serena decided she was an idiot to secretly prefer his provocation to the smoothest compliment.

'I wonder if the objects of your inexhaustible charity know you are a spitfire of the first order,' he mused, but this time she refused the bait.

'They are my friends,' she countered, mildly enough, 'and as such aware of my faults without you taking the trouble to point them out, Sir Adam.'

'No doubt,' he replied amiably, and proceeded to guide her past a particularly persistent puddle.

Infuriating wretch! How dared he be so irritating and look so devastatingly handsome while he did it? Yet she suspected that even if he had been born as plain and homely as a man could rightly be, he would still have commanded the attention of any room he walked into—and why on earth wouldn't he take the hint and turn his charm and wit and undoubted looks on some other unfortunate woman and stop plaguing *her* with them?

She had resolved to avoid the man when she noticed how his eyes heated whenever she met them, but he now seemed determined to force a meeting on her. A craven part of her wanted to wrench her hand from the warm contact on his russet coat sleeve and run away before she let herself consider the flesh-and-blood man underneath it, and reawakened some of the wicked fantasies that had been disturbing her dreams since he had come home. If she had ever met a man who inspired such contrary emotions in her she was very certain she would have recalled him, and a seductive voice whispered how very satisfying it might be to be constantly surprised, exasperated and seduced by such a faulty and unforgettable gentleman for the rest of her days.

Utter rubbish, of course, and the sooner her life returned to its usual mundane serenity the better. Until Sir Adam had come home from the wars the unchanging routine at Windham had been so soothingly predictable—and novelty, Serena decided huffily, was vastly overrated.

'The news from Spain is decidedly mixed, is it not?' she finally asked, in the hope of introducing a topic even he couldn't bend to his own ends. The storming of Badajos by Lord Wellington's Peninsular army had cost so many deaths Serena wasn't sure whether to cheer or weep, and felt vaguely ashamed of herself for using it as a means to deflect a possible proposal and the discomfort and distress it would cost her to refuse him.

'Very,' he replied, seriously enough to make her feel much better, so it was a shame she merely felt guilty for reminding a former soldier of what his comrades had so recently endured. 'Old Nosey's not that good at sieges, I'm afraid,' he added, and she had little doubt he was one of those who saw past the glowing accounts of victory to the long lists of dead and injured.

'I dare say you know his strengths and weaknesses better than most, Sir Adam,' she replied.

The mere mention of his service in the Peninsular reminded her of her first sight of him as a fully adult male, in the prime of his life and power, instead of the annoying brother of her best friend she remembered from that humiliating encounter as a rebellious girl. Captain Sir Adam Langthorne, dark-haired, dark-eyed and breathtakingly handsome, in silver-laced blue coat and all the attendant glory of a cavalry officer's uniform, had still had the power to disturb her six months later. It ought to be made illegal for any man not blessed with a squint, or a figure akin to the Prince Regent's portly one, to go abroad so decked out in the presence of susceptible ladies. Now he had sold out of the Queen's Light Dragoons she would get over the memory, of course—if she contrived to avoid him a little more successfully in future.

Today his russet coat fitted loosely, and his shabby leathers shouldn't enhance his powerful figure. But neither did anything to disguise the latent strength in his broad shoulders and those long and sleekly muscled legs. Put her brother-in-law in such a ramshackle outfit and he would look like a carter instead of an earl, yet Sir Adam looked just as dangerous as ever.

'Your brother-in-law has just informed me the war is costing too much and our army should be brought home— to do nothing, presumably,' he now informed her rather shortly, as if he was still restraining himself from telling his most powerful neighbour and fellow magistrate exactly what he thought of such waverers.

'Henry has no concept of military strategy or battle tactics, I'm afraid,' Serena said apologetically. Her brother-in-law probably had no idea how offensive such second-hand ideas were to a man who had seen what price the expeditionary forces were paying for keeping some of Bonaparte's most battle-hardened generals so unsuccessfully occupied.

'If he paid more attention to you and regarded his wife's arrant nonsense a little less, I dare say he might speak a little sense once in a while,' Adam said ruefully, and there was laughter and something more disturbing back in his fascinating eyes.

They were too complex to be categorised as just brown, she decided dreamily. His pupils were rayed with gold, as if permanently touched with sunlight, and there was a depth of rich colour to the rest that had nothing simple about it—although she really shouldn't be intimately acquainted with them. Oh dear, now she was cataloguing his assets like a besotted schoolgirl! She looked away swiftly, but heat still surged through her in an embarrassing tide, and made her wish him distinctly less acute, for there was amusement and a little too much understanding of her confused feelings in his eyes now.

Having had six months to consider his graces, and one or two of his faults, she already knew he was tall enough to make her feel less lanky than usual. And she really must stop meeting his eyes in this coming fashion—just because she had met a gentleman who could look down at her without standing on a box! He was quick of thought and action for a tall man too, she remembered dreamily, picturing him exerting iron strength to stop a bolting horse stampeding through Marclecombe village and threatening to crush a child under its deadly hooves…

Reminding herself he was also impatient and domineering, and as irritating and persistent as a burr, she slanted a minatory glare at him, adding 'managing' to his list of faults. One benefit of widowhood was her freedom from being *managed,* she reminded herself sharply. And of course being excused marital duties. Given her late husband's outspoken disgust with a wife who could not even give him a daughter in four years of marriage, that was a decided advantage.

Guilty that she couldn't mourn a man who had changed from a light-hearted and carelessly charming fiancé into a spendthrift husband with a foul temper and worse habits, she ordered herself to be more dutiful. It hadn't been George's fault she had been too young to tell love from infatuation—although he had killed any lingering enchantment stone dead by the time he had died. She shivered even in the bright sunlight and turned her attention to the present. Even with the conundrum that was Sir Adam Langthorne in it, now was much more pleasant time in her life.

'I can think of nothing more likely to cause trouble,' she said, with a shudder at the thought of Henry being silly enough to listen to her views over his wife's. 'But pray tell me, is Rachel still busy with her spring cleaning?' she added brightly, once more intent on finding a neutral topic of conversation.

'Indeed, my house is not my own. I might wish myself back in Spain and enduring the rigours of campaign if not for certain compensations,' he replied, with a warmth in his deep voice that shouldn't make her senses sit up and take notice.

Drat the man! She should have known he could bend

any subject to his own ends, and there it was again—that fascinating softening of his acute gaze she was determined to resist. If she once let him get the words out it would be the end to so much, and Rachel Langthorne's friendship was too precious to lose because her brother refused to be set at a proper distance.

'I suppose Burgess wishes to consult you about the lambing, Sir Adam?' she asked, still trying to keep their conversation impersonal, despite his lazily amused gaze telling her he knew exactly what she was about.

'I expect Burgess is all but finished with that,' he replied, obligingly for once, 'and at least he won't talk me half to death while Mrs Burgess provides you with a list of her ailments and those of her numerous brood.'

'Bearing twelve children and keeping ten alive is an achievement in itself,' Serena told him, as she fought back a smile at this all-too-accurate description of Mrs Burgess's preoccupations.

'You'd think she would realise what was causing them by now, wouldn't you, though?' he asked with a wicked grin.

'Well, really, Sir Adam!'

He raised one dark eyebrow and his eyes were alight with laughter. 'I hope you're not turning into a prig, Lady Summerton?'

'Pray confine such comments to the gentlemen in future,' she said stiffly, trying to remove her hand from the crook of his arm.

He bowed briefly, but placed his other hand over hers. She stilled immediately. 'I beg your pardon. I thought you were beyond the series of hypocrisies and evasions that commonly make up polite conversation,' he told her, and she couldn't tell if he was teasing or deadly serious.

'Then you thought wrongly.'

'Perhaps,' he replied enigmatically, releasing her hand at last—only to clasp it again as he helped her over a stile and onto the footpath that led to Red Bridge Farm.

'I'm a conventional creature, Sir Adam. Despite any rumours you might have heard to the contrary,' she made herself say airily, over the thundering of her heartbeat as she leant on his strength as briefly as she could without tripping over.

'I don't listen to rumour, my lady. Instead I like to gather facts and make an informed judgement for myself.'

'If only more of our kind did that,' she replied impulsively, and risked undoing all the good she had managed to do herself by smiling up at him as if they were more than the mere acquaintances she had assured herself they were.

Luckily he resisted such an obvious opening, and returned her look with a quizzical one of his own. 'It has often occurred to me that most of the nobility and gentry don't have nearly enough to do—unlike you, my lady.'

'I hate being idle,' she told him earnestly.

She didn't have it in her to be as elegantly useless as her sister-in-law, although Amelia *was* increasing, and had an excuse at the moment, and the Dowager Countess was a martyr to rheumatics. As the only Countess of Summerton currently willing and able to carry out her duties, there was little risk of Serena becoming bored. Yet at four and twenty should her life really be so settled, so relentlessly unchanging? The suspicion that it shouldn't had been driving her harder than ever of late, and she was almost sure Adam Langthorne had nothing to do with that unease.

'How fortunate you married a Cambray, then,' he now said brusquely. 'But if your neighbours had their way,

Countess Amelia and the Dowager would do more, and you would wear yourself to a wraith considerably less.'

'The Dowager is ill and my sister-in-law in an interesting condition, Sir Adam,' she replied, and told herself that 'wraith' was a gross exaggeration of her natural slenderness. She tried not to stare down at her person as if checking for too much skin and bone.

'Since the other Ladies Summerton spend their time lying on sofas countermanding one another's orders, it would do them a great deal of good to exert themselves now and again before the furniture collapses under their indolence,' he observed sardonically, as if he had no idea why she was frowning down at her faded morning gown as if she had never seen it before.

If he dared to mock her preoccupation with his suggestion she was too thin she would turn on her heel and walk away, Mrs Burgess or no Mrs Burgess. Anyway, the Burgesses were Sir Adam's tenants, and not Henry's, so why she was here in the first place was beyond her. Tradition, the Dowager had claimed, since Burgess's mother had been head housemaid up at the Hall, and at Windham tradition was everything.

'It would do them both good to be more active,' he went on, either oblivious to her frown or indifferent to it. 'Then you could find a better use for your time.'

'I'm happy as I am,' she told him, dangerous ground shifting under her feet as a possible alternative presented itself.

'No, you're not unhappy,' he insisted. 'Which is a vastly different state from being truly happy. You spend your life waiting for the party to start.'

'I have no liking for parties,' she told him crossly.

Was he about to make her a very improper suggestion that *she* should spend lots of time lying about on the furniture with him, somewhere louche and forbidden? Or an honourable offer of marriage? Not to be thought of, she decided, impatient with herself for even momentarily lingering on the image of herself as a sinful houri, much too available for a gentleman's pleasure, or an active and much appreciated wife. According to George she'd had no talent for either position and, considering how mistaken she had been about their marriage, she would be twenty times a fool to contemplate another— even if Sir Adam were ever so willing to put his head in the parson's mousetrap, which she very much doubted from the slightly feral gleam in his eyes just at the moment.

'Only because you lack the nerve to enjoy them,' he told her inexcusably. 'I've watched you sitting with the chaperones nobody else has the time or inclination to bother with, and playing the piano for the so-called "young people" to dance to. What happened to the eager young girl you used to be? The one I recall whispering mischief with my sister when you were schoolgirls together, and refusing to be awed by any threat or stratagem I could think up to keep you in line before you landed yourself and Rachel in Newgate? You do your best to fade into the furniture, and people have the devil of a job recalling if you were even at the few social engagements you attend. When you made your debuts my sister used to write about your mutual misdeeds so joyfully that I could tell you were doing her a great deal of good. Where did the headlong miss who danced every dance on her card and still found the energy to drive herself about the town in her own curricle and pair the next day and set the tabbies by the ears get off to, my lady?'

'None of your business,' she told him shortly, and glared

at him as she wrestled for possession of her hand in a most unladylike fashion, winning at last only because she knew he would never knowingly hurt her.

'Rachel's letters used to come alive with the misdeeds the two of you perpetrated,' he continued relentlessly. 'Despite her terrible grief when poor Tom Hollard died, I thought such a lively neighbour would cheer her in time. Instead my sister is intent on becoming an antidote, and if the pair of you went to town for the season, I dare say you'd only attend Blue Stocking soirees and church.'

'That we shouldn't. We'd dance 'til dawn to prove you wrong, Sir Adam, even if we wore our poor feet raw,' she snapped. 'You should thank your stars we're so conventional nowadays.'

'Never!' he vowed, and there was no mistaking the resolution in his steadfast gaze now, even if it did seem very different from the one she'd thought. 'You might be happy to watch Rachel dwindle into a reclusive old maid who'll soon start breeding lapdogs, but I'm not. I want the eager young woman Rachel was before Tom died back, and you're going to help me.'

'Even though you just pointed out how staid I am?' she asked coldly.

'You think this good enough for my sister? This not unhappy state you have fallen into as if you were both four and sixty instead of four and twenty? Well, I think it only half a life. Yes, Rachel suffered a terrible tragedy, and you endured an unhappy marriage, but life didn't stop because of it.'

'My marriage is none of your business,' she informed him very stiffly, as she did her best to retrieve her hand once more from the firm, warm clasp he had taken it in while she was preoccupied with his incendiary words.

He obviously despised her for losing the reckless spirit she had faced life with once upon a time. Just as well she didn't need his approval nor want it. No longer being the thoughtless creature he had contrarily admired, she checked her temper, unclenched her teeth and forced herself to consider his words. *Was* this life enough? Not for her—she had taken her gamble on life and lost—but for Rachel?

'You know Rachel loved Lieutenant Hollard very deeply,' she said carefully, despising herself for the hesitant words issuing from her own lips.

'You mean to warn me that my sister's feelings run deep, my lady?' he asked more gently.

She marvelled that he could go so quickly from stern commander to gentleman, whose reassuring presence invited confidence. And why was it that when he called her 'my lady' like that it suddenly seemed more like a promise than a rather archaic form of address? For a moment it seemed the most natural thing in the world to unburden herself, but then she decided it was a useful trick developed after years commanding troops.

'Rachel may have put a brave face on her grief in her letters to you, but she was devastated when Lieutenant Hollard was killed.'

'I read between the lines. But she was nineteen when Tom Hollard went down with his ship, and he would not have wanted her to wear the willow.'

'Rachel could never cast his memory aside,' Serena said with a frown. Yet at least Rachel had the lodestone of true love to measure her feelings against. So, yes, perhaps she *could* be happy with another man.

'Tom wouldn't want this state of not quite content for her,' he said, with a flash of something in his golden-brown eyes that she couldn't read. 'It's time my sister had another chance, Lady Summerton. Are you friend enough to help her take it?'

'She'll have my unflagging support once I'm convinced it's for the best,' she said, 'but Rachel didn't enjoy her debut very much.'

'No, and she's a stubborn minx,' Sir Adam agreed philosophically. 'But although she can't be pushed she can be led—if one goes about it the right way.'

'Which is?' she asked, offended by the idea of his manipulating her friend, even with the best of intentions.

'You sound every inch a countess when you put on that cut-glass voice and look down your inadequate nose at me, my dear.'

'I'm not your dear, and it's a perfectly good nose,' she exclaimed, then frowned at him for provoking such childishness.

'It is a perfect little nose—just not very well suited to looking down,' he replied outrageously.

Serena wondered how Rachel had resisted the urge to murder him when they were in their nursery, for he must have been the most exasperating of brothers then, however considerate he was now. 'My nose is irrelevant, Sir Adam, and if you're so worried, why don't you do something about it?'

'What? Your nose? I like it very well as it is,' he replied with an infuriating grin.

'How flattering. But unfortunately your opinion of myself and my features is a matter of indifference to me. Confine yourself to your sister's affairs,' she informed him with frigid dignity.

'She doesn't have any,' he informed her unrepentantly.

'Something most brothers would be profoundly grateful for.'

'I *knew* you hadn't really become missish in your old age, Lady Summerton,' he said, with every appearance of satisfaction.

Recognising his tactic of infuriating her to the point of indiscretion, she took a very deep breath and counted to ten. 'Either stick to the subject in hand, Sir Adam, or I'll drop my basket on your toe,' she informed him coolly.

'It's really is most ungallant of me not to be carrying it in the first place. Whatever will Mrs Burgess say?'

'I don't care a straw what the wretched woman says. Give it back,' she demanded, as he whisked the offending article out of her hand and put it on the grass at his side.

'No. Now, stop distracting me and stick to our sheep,' he goaded her, that wicked, compelling smile warming his gaze once more.

'Pot calling kettle black, Sir Adam? You're the one whose attention keeps wandering from the subject under discussion.'

'With very good reason,' he said with apparent satisfaction as his gaze dwelt on her animated face.

'For no reason at all, so far as I can see,' she countered smartly. Only to be confounded as he raised his eyebrows and gave her another of those warmly approving looks.

'No,' he replied softly, 'I dare say you can't.'

'Oh, pray stop treating me like an idiot, and tell me how you plan to get Rachel to change her mind about marriage?' she demanded impatiently.

Wrongfoot her and charm her as he would, she refused to succumb to the potent spell of a tall and handsome gentleman blessed with a wicked sense of humour and a very

astute mind. Then there was his strength and integrity—
qualities that would outlive mere bodily vigour, she
reminded herself distractedly.

'Very well, then, I shall take her to town—suitably chaperoned, of course.'

As his intent gaze fixed on her, Serena could hardly
mistake the chaperon he had in mind. So that was why he
had been conspiring to get her alone for so long. It was all
she could do not to stamp her feet and fall into strong hysterics. All this time she had avoided him and he wanted her
to chaperon his sister! She was delighted not to have to
refuse a discreet affair between two untrammelled adults,
of course, and need no longer call on Rachel when he was
out. Except if he had his way she wouldn't need to call on
Rachel. She would be living with her.

Chapter Two

Serena had decided years ago that not even Sir Charles Grandison and brave young Lochinvar rolled into one dashingly perfect gentleman could persuade her to marry again. Not that Sir Adam had marriage in mind. No, even if he *had* been attempting to get her alone, he had a very different proposition to make her. Anyway, although he looked like a hero, Sir Adam Langthorne would probably tell a damsel in distress to pull herself together and fight her own dragons before he rode to her rescue. For some reason that sounded a wickedly tempting combination in a suitor, so it was just as well he had no intention of courting her.

'That chaperon certainly won't be me,' she snapped, taken by surprise both by his determination to turn her into Rachel's duenna and her own unwavering opposition.

Half an hour ago she might have found the idea of being removed from her monotonous routine and a distinctly unpromising future alluring—and in Rachel's company as well. So why was she about to refuse such an escape from her responsibilities?

'I should wait to be asked if I were you, my lady,' he

reproved, that infuriating smile once again making her palm itch to slap it off his lips.

'I still won't do it,' she insisted implacably.

'Well, that settles that, then,' he said. And if he was trying to appear cast down he was failing dismally.

The wretched man was confident of getting his way; she could see it by the unwavering determination of his firm mouth and his golden-brown eyes had a glint in them she deeply mistrusted.

'Unlucky Rachel, to possess such a fair weather friend,' he said mournfully, and this time her wrist actually swung out before she sharply ordered it back to her side, and glared at him with infuriated ferocity instead.

'We have no need to prove our friendship, sir, so I suggest you save your tricks for those who might be taken in by them,' she told him, with a glare that should tell him she was too polite to say what she really felt about his stubborn aim of getting his own way, whatever the consequences.

'If I ever find another lady so perfectly suited to bear my sister company I shall seek your advice,' he said blandly, and she could see no lessening of his iron resolve whatsoever. 'I'm determined to turn her thoughts into more hopeful channels, and she trusts you, my lady,' he insisted relentlessly. 'Rachel won't put her confidence in a stranger.'

'Perhaps, but she needs someone older to reintroduce her to the ton,' she countered.

'Indeed,' he agreed meekly. 'But such a hardened cynic might misjudge my sister and try to shuffle her onto someone rich and titled but totally unsuitable in every other way, don't you think? While Rachel's capable of fending off such an insensitive soul herself, it would probably ruin her stay, and you would let her pick out her own suitors.'

'Rachel's chaperon will be in for a surprise if you let her expect meek agreement with her every whim,' Serena persisted.

'No, she won't. You know her too well for that.' He held up his hand when she gathered breath to condemn his high-handed assumption that she would agree to his scheme. 'I don't want Rachel to be upset by battling over every detail from the cut and colour of her gown to how many steps she can take in the park with a beau without causing a scandal. Together you can both ease yourselves back into the polite world and actually enjoy yourselves,' he replied, so reasonably that Serena had to remind herself she was in danger of being manipulated by a master.

'I refuse to tell my best friend how to run her life,' she said doggedly.

'Little chance of that—which is why this arrangement will suit so well, if I can bring it about,' he said with a wry smile.

'Do you always arrange the lives of your family and friends in the way you feel is most likely to do them good, Sir Adam?'

'Whenever I can,' he replied, with an unrepentant shrug.

'Lord, how I pity them.'

'Lady, you have no need to,' he told her, and suddenly there was an infinity of promises in those intriguing eyes of his, and she felt a shiver run down her spine that had to be apprehension—didn't it?

'So you say,' she managed to reply, steadily enough.

'So I *know,*' he said quietly, and this time there was a steadfast intent in his gaze that worried her more than anything that had passed between them so far.

Serena made a determined effort to put everything else aside and concentrate on Rachel's well-being. 'I'm not sure I could stop the staidest two-in-hand racing out of control,' she admitted ruefully, 'let alone keep Rachel from being overwhelmed by unsuitable gentlemen.'

Rachel Langthorne was a considerable heiress and, even if she was far too shrewd to fall for a fortune-hunter, would find the ton at play intimidating after so long at Marclecombe, caring for her grandparents and more lately her ungrateful brother. For Rachel's sake Serena supposed she had to take this idea seriously, even if going to London for the season in Sir Adam's company was the last thing she should do if she had any sense at all.

'You'd soon get back into the way of it,' he said with remarkable gentleness. And Serena didn't make the mistake of thinking he was referring to driving a pair of spirited Welsh greys around Hyde Park.

'Not if I stay here, I won't,' she replied stubbornly.

'Faint heart,' he accused her lightly, as if he was supremely confident she would see things his way if he persisted long enough.

'If you like,' she told him steadily, striving for the appearance of indifference, even if she couldn't quite manage the fact.

'I'm not one to meekly give up on an enterprise likely to succeed so well, Lady Summerton,' he warned her, with a mildness she refused to mistake for wavering of purpose—he was altogether too dangerous to her peace of mind for such leeway.

'And that enterprise is?' she demanded frostily.

He had the effrontery to laugh at her imitation of an affronted aristocrat before sobering. 'My sister's future happiness, of course,' he told her seriously. An underhand statement if ever she'd heard one—for how could she argue with such a motive?

'I'm not convinced going to London would enhance it,' she argued stubbornly.

'We'll see who's right when we get there, then.'

'No, for I'm staying here, remember?'

'Of course,' he agreed, with a smug smile that was enough to try the most patient of saints as they approached Burgesses' rather perfunctory front garden at last, and Serena was forced to swallow a less than polite reply.

'Oh, my lady *and* Sir Adam—what a pleasure to see you both,' Mrs Burgess declared rather breathlessly as she bustled out of the front door.

'Good afternoon, Mrs Burgess, and how are you today?'

'None too stout, I fear, Lady Summerton.' The worthy lady faltered, and Serena sent Sir Adam a reproving look when she saw his broad shoulders shake—for Mrs Burgess was very far from slender after her many pregnancies.

'I'm very sorry to hear it. Perhaps we could all take a glass of your delicious cowslip wine while you tell us all about it, Mrs Burgess?' said Serena.

Which would serve him right, she decided. The idea of Sir Adam Langthorne choking down this good lady's home-made wine when he was reputed to have the finest cellar in the county made her long to laugh out loud.

'None of that potent brew for me thank you, ma'am, I need to keep a clear head for whatever business your husband has with me,' he informed their hostess with an engaging smile—the slippery rogue. 'But there's no reason you and her ladyship can't have a comfortable coze before I see her home.'

'I can find my own way, thank you, Sir Adam.'

'Normally I'm sure you would, Lady Summerton, but after indulging in Mrs Burgess's famous cowslip you might go astray. We can't have her ladyship spending the night in a ditch, can we, Mrs Burgess?'

Serena might have been tempted to argue for the ditch if her hostess's eager ears had not been taking in every word. Instead she sent Sir Adam a pallid smile that promised revenge, and allowed herself to be led into the parlour and fed plum cake and gossip while she cautiously sampled her wine. It really was quite pleasant, she decided, and she *was* thirsty. But when Mrs Burgess would have topped up her glass she managed to refuse.

'I have no wish to become tipsy and prove Sir Adam right—delicious as this is, Mrs Burgess,' she excused herself, and sipped gratefully at the cup of tea she was offered instead. 'Now, tell me all about this ghost the sexton saw the other night. It sounds a most unlikely tale to me, and I can't help but wonder if he hadn't been at your excellent wine.'

'I wouldn't waste it on the likes of him,' Mrs Burgess declared with a disgusted sniff. 'That ne'er do well would drink the dregs out of the chalice of a Sunday if he could get hold of them. The drink has got to him well and truly at long last, and I dare say he'll be found laid in one of his own graves one morning, stone-dead. I'll believe in that there ghost when I set eyes on it and not before, my lady.'

'I'm pleased to hear it, as all sorts of wild tales are doing the rounds. A voice against it is most welcome.'

If rather surprising, Serena added in her head. Mrs Burgess usually believed every wild rumour that went around, and added a few embellishments before passing them on. She had several times told Serena that the French were stealing Burgess's turnips and the eggs from her hen-house, despite the fact that Red Bridge Farm was seventy miles from the sea.

'And that daft besom he's married to has spread tales as would make your hair curl,' Mrs Burgess went on indignantly.

'Has she indeed?'

'Said this ghost of his rose up out of the Canderton vault and that Lady Canderton was walking, she did, my lady. I told her sharpish that my old mistress was as respectable a woman as ever walked God's good earth. She would no more come back to haunt us than the King himself would—if he was dead, of course, which he ain't. Might just as well be, the poor mad soul, but that's neither here nor there. I'm not having that baggage putting it about that my poor late lady's unquiet in her grave, for she was as decent a woman as you could find in the whole of England.'

Serena vaguely remembered hearing Mrs Burgess had been in service before she'd wed. The family had died out with Sir William Canderton's death twenty years before, just a few months after his formidable mother went to her own eternal rest. The land had been sold off to pay wild Sir William's debts, and the ancient house demolished as a danger to anyone rash enough to venture inside its rotten shell.

Mrs Burgess was probably the only one who cared if the Candertons were at peace or not, and that seemed rather sad. Serena set herself to soothe her with such a liberal helping of sympathy and flattery that by the time Sir Adam reappeared her head was reeling with our Liza's hives, the shocking price Mrs Burgess's remaining eggs had fetched at market, and the French spies who were ruining the country from within.

'You should have kept on with the wine,' her escort informed her unsympathetically when they finally got away from the voluble farmer's wife. 'No doubt the infernal woman talked you into a headache anyway. More alcohol might have blurred her confounded rigmarole.'

'I doubt I could keep sufficient guard on my tongue.'

'There's that, of course, but once she's in full flow I doubt she hears what anyone else has to say.'

'Probably not. But she *was* in a rare state over the rumour Wharton is putting about. I've never heard her as voluble as she was today.'

'Whereas Burgess is as close mouthed as she is loose-tongued—which may explain why they go on so well together. He's the ideal audience, and she saves him the effort of thinking of aught to say.'

'So far as I can tell Mrs Burgess is upset that the sexton said he saw a ghost coming from the vault where her late mistress is laid. She takes offence that so virtuous and generous a mistress should be thought to trouble the living instead of staying respectably dead.'

'I hope time will deal so well with my reputation after I'm gone, then. Lady Canderton was a complete tartar. They had the pew behind ours in church, and she used to clip me round the ear whenever she felt I wasn't paying enough attention to the sermon. She once got me a fine beating for stealing cherries out of her kitchen garden as well.'

'Deserved, I suspect,' she said unsympathetically.

'Rachel was the culprit. But maybe Lady Canderton thought I should take her punishment as I shared her booty.'

'None of which gives reason for her ghost to walk. Indeed, it sounds like a mare's nest to me, and I dare say Mrs Burgess is right.'

'That seems unlikely. But about what?'

'The sexton is addicted to the bottle—and not her cowslip wine neither, "for he ain't worthy to so much as taste it."'

'Are you sure you didn't have too much yourself?' he asked, grinning at her imitation of the voluble woman.

'Not nearly enough, I assure you, Sir Adam. Now our ways must diverge, as I need to see Janet Partridge and I doubt she wants to see a gentleman when she's so near her time.'

'I dare say you're right, but I'll escort you to her door nonetheless. Gadding about the countryside alone with all those light-fingered Frenchmen and restless ghosts running about is pure folly, my lady.'

Sensing a serious note under his teasing, she wondered fleetingly what it might feel like to be ruthlessly bullied for her own good by Sir Adam Langthorne for the rest of her life. She had undoubtedly drunk too much of that wine after all, because it seemed a seductively attractive notion—and that would never do.

'I doubt if either are bold enough to venture abroad in daylight, and I have no wish to visit the churchyard or Hangar Woods during the hours of darkness, I assure you.'

'You have no taste for the gothic, my lady?'

'None whatsoever—which shows a sad want of sensibility I dare say. Indeed, I can imagine nothing more horrid than coming across a headless spectre or a restless spirit while I'm busily minding my own business and harming nobody.'

'I suspect one or two of them might like to come across such an appealing quarry as yourself, though. But it's my belief Wharton is hiding something in that churchyard and means to frighten everyone away from it—especially after dark.'

'So you intend to go there just to confound him?' she asked sharply.

'Maybe I'm foolish enough to wonder what a supernatural encounter might be like,' he admitted laconically. Why did she think he was serious about this odd business? Surely there weren't really French spies running about rural Herefordshire for want of something better to do?

'Trust a man to be curious,' she accused, knowing she had no right to protest his determination to run headlong into the first danger that presented itself because he might be bored after his adventures in Spain.

'And trust a woman to know best,' he parried infuriatingly.

'Not two minutes ago you were warning *me* to be careful, and it's commonly held to be the other way about.'

'Have you never wanted to break out of the role you were allotted in life, Lady Summerton?'

'Frequently. But then I grew up.'

'Ah, so that explains it! Women grow up and men just learn to hide their curiosity a little better.'

'Or we pique your curiosity, so you satisfy it at no cost to ourselves.'

'Then you want to know about the ghost after all?'

'No, but I should like to know just what Wharton is hiding in that vault.'

'Meet me there tonight and find out, then,' he challenged her, and for a reckless moment she was sorely tempted.

Sharing outrageous midnight adventures with Sir Adam Langthorne seemed the ideal way of proving to both of them that she wasn't as staid and colourless as he thought. Glimmers of the wild young girl she had once been, up for any mischief on offer, must still lie under Countess Serena's sober façade after all. She reminded herself that reckless actions led to uncomfortable consequences and managed to crush her inner hoyden for the time being.

'Not even if I consumed a whole bottle of Mrs Burgess's wine. You're a former soldier, and used to alarms and night watches. It's probably your job to satisfy the curiosity of your neighbours while we sleep safely.'

'I hope I know better than to go looking for trouble, but I'm also a churchwarden, and duty must outweigh caution.'

'Good luck, then, Sir Adam,' she managed to say, cheerfully enough, and offered him her hand in farewell as she opened the Partridges' front gate.

He bowed over it like a beau from a previous age, and kissed it lightly instead of shaking it. Fire shot through her, as if he had touched his lips to bare flesh instead of her supple leather glove. She snatched her hand back and looked about her. Luckily the men were at work and the women busy cooking. This time she had been lucky, but she must avoid him in future.

'Thomas will meet me here with the gig,' she lied brightly.

'He must have learnt the dark art of being in two places at the same time, then. When I met him not half an hour ago he was on his way to Hereford. Either he's a top sawyer and that old grey nag a phenomenon, or you're guilty of shameless untruth, my lady.'

'It's not at all the thing for a gentleman to argue with a lady,' she said hotly, squirming at being caught out under his amused gaze.

'Dear me, what a hard furrow such paragons choose to plough.'

'How would you know?' she muttered under her breath, but his sharp ears caught her words and he gave her an unrepentant grin.

'I wouldn't, of course. But I'll meet you here after I've seen the smith. Shall we say half an hour, my lady?'

'You can say what you like, Sir Adam,' she replied with a shrug she hoped looked as pettish as she felt. 'I'll go my own way.'

'I can't tell you how glad I am about the first part of that statement. Half an hour and no longer,' he ordered, and turned away, as certain of being obeyed as if she were a subaltern under his command.

She'd see about that, she decided militantly, tapping at the front door.

'Lady Serena—how lovely,' her once properly reserved ladies' maid exclaimed. 'Come on in off the street, do,' she ordered as they embraced with a lack of reserve Serena's sister-in-law would have found profoundly distasteful between one-time maid and mistress.

How that neat, coolly efficient maid had once intimidated her, Serena recalled ruefully. Yet since coming to Windham as the new Lady Summerton she and her personal maid had become firm friends. Indeed, Janet knew a great deal about her that Serena had trusted in nobody else. Over the last five years the aloof little Londoner had blossomed, and become as staunch a convert to country life as you could find anywhere—especially since succumbing to Zachary Partridge's heartfelt pleas to become his wife.

'Marriage suits you, Janet,' she told her.

'Ruined my figure, but I dare say Partridge'll not stray far.'

'He can't take his eyes off you long enough to look elsewhere, and well you know it.'

'I'd never have married him otherwise, Lady Serena,' Janet said, and sent her a speculative look. 'Time you found yourself a good man who loves *you,* Lady Serena. It's two years since himself died, and not even the Countess Almighty could object.'

'I like my independence too well to give it up.'

'Independence? Those other two countesses don't let you rest from sunrise to sunset—and I never took you for a coward, my lady,' Janet told her sternly.

Serena wondered why her words never seemed to carry weight. 'I'm not made for domesticity, and prefer to stay as I am.'

'I did say you must find a *good* man this time,' Janet chided, more gently, and Serena knew they could stand here arguing all day and never agree. Janet was like a dog at a bone when she was trying to organise the life of one of the select band of people she truly loved.

'Well, your Zach might live under the cat's paw nowadays, but I cunningly escaped you when you married him, and fully intend to follow my own path from now on,' she teased, and a militant light came into her old friend's eyes.

'Cat's paw, my foot,' Janet snorted. 'Sir Adam Langthorne is a fine man,' she continued, as if she had not heard a single word Serena said.

'Yes? And what has that to do with the price of fish?'

'He'll make some lucky lady a fine husband.'

'I'm sure he will, but he certainly won't be mine.'

'Strong men don't have anything to prove, so he'll treat his lady like a queen, I'm thinking.'

'I dare say. I'll dance at his wedding when it comes.'

'Happen you'll do it with a heavy heart, then,' Janet insisted.

'Nonsense. I'll wish him very happy.'

'Aye, and so will I—supposing he weds the right lady,' Janet agreed, with a significant look at her former mistress.

'Today, however, I wish him at Jericho. So, unless you have any other plans for the rest of my life to discuss, I'll take myself off and be in good time for my dinner for once.'

'Sir Adam has the look of a very determined gentleman,' Janet observed with some satisfaction.

'And I'm an equally determined lady,' Serena declared firmly, hoping that was the last she would hear of the subject. Sir Adam had taken up too much of her day already, and she didn't care to grant him any more of it.

'There now—even you admit how well matched you are, Lady Serena. Fate. That's what it is.'

'It's wishful thinking, and next time I come I hope you're thinking straighter.'

Janet put her head on one side, as if to deliberate better—a sign that a pearl of wisdom was about to fall. 'With respect, my lady, it's your thoughts that have got out of the way of running true, and we both know why.'

'Maybe, but luckily I'm in too much haste to stay and argue with you today, Janet. So, if there is nothing else you want to lecture me about, we can have a really good dispute about it another day.'

Giving her tenacious ex-maid a quick peck on the cheek, Serena hurried out of the neat house on the village green before Janet could regroup. Only twenty minutes had gone by, so she could set out for Windham with impunity. She had never asked Sir Adam to treat her as if she were a young miss just out of the schoolroom, so a few minutes cooling his heels outside Janet's house might prevent him repeating that particular error.

Chapter Three

⟨ornament⟩

One more turn in the village street and Serena would be alone in open country. Or at least she would be, had Sir Adam not been sitting in his curricle, waiting for her to appear, like a rather handsome spider in the midst of a well-spun web. How had the wretched man managed to summon up such a neat equipage at short notice? she wondered crossly.

'You're late, Lady Summerton,' he said, by way of greeting.

'I'm ten minutes early,' she was flustered into saying. Then could have kicked herself for making it sound as if their assignation existed anywhere but in his head.

'On the contrary, you're at least five minutes after I expected you,' he argued. 'If you wanted to confound me, you should have slipped out of your friend's back door.'

It was quite true; the shortcut across the fields would have got her to Windham much more quickly and he would never have seen her. Whatever had she been thinking of not to use it? Did a secret, rebellious part of her really want his company so badly that quarrelling with him was preferable to not seeing him at all? Next time there was the least chance of avoiding him she must seize it determinedly— if only to prove to herself he meant nothing to her. Maybe then he would take the hint and stop plaguing her.

She was so sunk in gloom at this happy notion that she let him hand her into his curricle before she noticed she was doing as he had planned all along.

'I haven't the least wish to ride home with you,' she protested idiotically, and she didn't need his amused grin to feel a fool when she was doing such a good job by herself.

'Your reluctance is duly noted,' he said solemnly, and set his team in motion.

'And you fully intend to ignore it?'

'Precisely. The fact that you're here speaks for itself.'

'You are ungallant, Sir Adam.'

'And you're in the mood to argue with your own nose today, my lady.'

'I'm not considered in the least contrary by anyone else I know,' she told him between clenched teeth.

'Of course not. You're far too busy trying to please them all to argue with anybody. Which makes me wonder why you resist my perfectly natural wish to make your life more comfortable so stubbornly.'

'I have an aversion to being managed, and milk-and-water misses get trampled all over,' she said with an audible sniff.

'How would you know?'

'I have observed it,' she said, and shivered.

'Cold, my dear?'

'No, and I'm *not* your dear.'

'Even you can't police my thoughts, Lady Summerton,' he said, with that wicked glint back in eyes she had no intention of meeting, despite the shiver of awareness that shot through her at the intriguing idea of reading those thoughts there.

'Then pray govern your tongue, Sir Adam,' she said primly, fervently hoping her waspishness would divert him from the silly blush that had stolen over every exposed inch of skin.

'I'll endeavour to do so, my lady,' he said smoothly, sounding not in the least bit chastened as he gave his pair the office to trot.

Something told her their thoughts were in a most embarrassing harmony on the forbidden subject of her finding out just what it might be like to be mercilessly ravished by the handsome, intelligent and uniquely intriguing gentleman who was Sir Adam Langthorne. She felt ridiculously ignorant of such sensual delights, and she was quite certain they would indeed be almost too delightful. He might be arrogant, and far too certain that he knew best, but she suspected he'd be a lover to eclipse all others. Not that she intended taking any more. Appalled at the direction of her own unwary thoughts, she mentally corrected herself. No, she never intended taking *any* lovers.

Not that he wouldn't be a magnificent lover, she conceded silently. It was there in his heated appreciation of her, the way his eyes lingered on her slender curves and played over her slightly too generous mouth, as if intent on reassuring her that their pleasure would be absolutely mutual when she finally yielded to him. She believed it emphatically. It had been quite a revelation when she'd first caught the feral gleam in his dark and light eyes, and a warm shudder shook her at the memory of the flowering of heat it had awakened in her wilful body. Considering they could never be more than neighbours, however he might persuade her, such thoughts really were no help in her battle with her baser impulses. And neither was he, she decided militantly, as she once more caught that look of sensual amusement on his far too fascinating mouth, as if he could read her struggle with the ultimate temptation in her stormy eyes.

'We're going the wrong way,' she informed him stiffly.

'Not if we intend going via Thornfield Churchyard.'

'Well, I certainly have no wish to visit the wretched place.'

'It's not dark, and you have told me many other things I intend to disprove today, my lady, so we might as well start with Thornfield and work our way down the list.'

'No, let's go to Windham Dower House instead, so I can take my leave of you, Sir Adam. Once I'm home you can chase ghosts all day and night with my heartfelt blessing. Take half the neighbourhood with you, as long as you leave me out of it.'

'Shush. We're nearly there, and you really shouldn't be so uncivil to your neighbours—myself included.'

'I won't hush, and I like being uncivil. I didn't want to come and I have no desire to racket about the countryside with a person who never listens to a single word I say,' she said smartly, fervently wishing it were true. Something told her she might go with him to the ends of the earth if he asked with just the right pitch of need and hunger in his dark voice.

'Coward. But why not just humour me for once? I would never have brought you if I thought you were in the slightest danger.'

'Then your definition of danger and mine must be wildly out of kilter,' she muttered darkly, then subsided into silence as he halted the curricle well short of the church and passed her the reins.

'If I'm not back within a quarter of an hour fetch my head groom from the smithy, then go home,' he ordered quietly, before jumping lithely down and ghosting off into the shadows himself, before she could think up a sufficiently indignant and crushing protest.

'Insufferable, ungovernable, insensitive man,' she muttered under her breath, but she sat and kept the pair as quiet as she could even so.

If it hadn't been for her nagging fear that Sir Adam might end up lying disabled and hurt in the ancient churchyard, she might even have found this peaceful interlude quite pleasant, she decided, as she listened to the triumphant fugue of birdsong. Instead she had to force herself not to imagine ruthless villains lying in wait for him, and reluctantly considered his ridiculous scheme to find Rachel a husband to distract herself.

Her friend might be happier, more fulfilled than she was now if she were married to a good man. But after so many years of longing for her dead love, would a mere everyday one ever satisfy her? In such a mundane marriage Rachel might crave the unconventional life of an officer's wife she would have had with Tom, if only he had survived long enough to live it with her. Excitement, Serena decided with a stern frown at an ancient yew tree that had done her no harm at all, was vastly overrated. Yet if she was strictly truthful she had been bored and restless with her own life for some time now. The question was, had she got to the point where she would grasp any opportunity to escape. Especially if Sir Adam were the one offering it to her, and with her best friend the supposed beneficiary?

Looked at dispassionately, she supposed a season in London with Rachel should be an offer seized on with delight, rather than regarded as a gift horse of the most suspicious variety. Yet she suspected Sir Adam had more in mind than diverting his sister's thoughts from her lost love. The headlong Serena of her debutante days, that impulsive idiot he had just waxed so lyrical about, would have accepted his offer without a second thought, and worried about any consequences when they came along. Which was precisely why she refused to let the little ninny command her life now. If he thought to influence her by comparing her current lack of spirit with her overabundance of it during her youth, then he was very wide of his mark.

Indeed, if she could go back in time she would settle for one of the worthy young gentlemen who had laid their all at Lady Serena's elegantly shod feet, instead of the more outwardly fascinating Lord Summerton. And if Sir Adam Langthorne considered her poor-spirited for choosing safety over risk with the benefit of hindsight, then he'd better find someone closer to her former self to confuse with his hot glances and arrogant certainty. A picture of a heady what-might-have-been slotted into her head. If only the then Lieutenant Langthorne had attended the same balls and parties as her younger self had, only to be ruthlessly dismissed. She knew the full treachery of air dreams nowadays, and reality invariably failed to live up to such fool's gold promises.

She heard the church clock strike the quarter and could hardly believe only ten minutes had ticked by since he had left her sitting here, doing just what she had told herself she wouldn't and thinking only of him. Even by considering his plan she was giving it credence. Janet's coming baby was a much more attractive topic to dwell on, she decided resolutely, and spent five minutes wondering how much influence a godmother had over a child's life, and if she was worthy of such a role.

All the time she was straining to hear the softest of footfalls on the mossy grass that grew under the yew grove at the churchyard perimeter. She felt she was fast becoming part of it. If only he would hurry back, he could drive his restless pair to Windham, restore her to her rightful place, and the world would settle back into its allotted course. By sitting here on pins, as if Sir Adam Langthorne's safety was of prime importance to her, she was being drawn further and further away from her place of safety and deeper into the dangerous land of make-believe.

Tomorrow she would go and see Rachel, and between them they would circumvent the almighty Sir Adam and his ridiculous schemes. Unfortunately there was today to be got through first, and a cold fear was settling like ice in her belly, almost convincing her that he was lying in the graveyard gravely injured and in dire need of help. She shifted on seat cushions that were somehow becoming harder by the second, and began to seriously contemplate tying the reins to the rail and creeping to the rescue.

If he didn't need rescuing, or was lying in wait for some nameless villain, she would spoil everything, of course. She would count to a hundred, and if he hadn't put in an appearance by then, she would drive boldly up to the church and put paid to this whole ridiculous episode. Serve him right if she *did* put his quarry to flight, she decided militantly, for treating her like some inanimate parcel that could be left here until he was ready to deliver it. When she lost count and had to start again for the third time she gave up, and diverted herself by contriving fitting punishments for such a faulty gentleman.

'Good girl.' His deep voice seemed to arrive before he did, and she jumped several inches in the air.

'I'm not a spaniel. And don't creep up on people in such a fashion, Sir Adam. Unless you wish to see off your entire acquaintance from the apoplexy,' she chided furiously. 'It would serve you right if I was of a vapourish persuasion, just so you would have to cope with my delicate nerves after giving me such a shock.'

'Believe me, Lady Serena, if they were that finely strung you wouldn't be here in the first place. Your nerves are as stout as Mrs Burgess's are wasted,' he replied, looking infuriatingly unrepentant.

'Then I must spend more time in her company in the hope of acquiring some sensibility.'

'Pray do not. I'd hate to be deprived of your delightful companionship for such a flimsy reason—and even you must admit the good lady's nerves are the only insubstantial thing about her.'

On the verge of a betraying chuckle, she forced her mouth into a straight line, 'Stop it, Adam,' she said with a stern look. 'It's not kind to mock a good woman.'

'I promise never to do it again if you'll call me by my name and not my title more often.'

'That I won't! I never meant such a coming piece of over-familiarity to slip out in the first place.'

'A pity. As we'll be seeing so much of each other in town, I thought we might consider ourselves friends and be comfortable together.'

Which was the very last thing she would ever be with disturbing Sir Adam Langthorne, Serena decided darkly.

'You know very well only close family members are so familiar with each other. Anyway, I'm not coming to town, so the need won't arise for us to call one another anything for several months.'

'Don't celebrate your escape too soon, my lady. I learnt strategy from a master, and I'm not so patriotic I can't watch and learn from Boney's tactics either. A skirmish is never over until the last shot is fired.'

'Except your foe might refuse battle.'

'You never ran from a fight in your life, my lady,' he said softly, and the steady understanding in his eyes made her shiver.

At least she somehow convinced herself it was a shiver, even as she was held by his gaze, warmed by a host of wonderful possibilities even as her sensible self was telling her to break eye contact and shore up her faltering defences immediately. Torn by two contrary urges, she felt the true power of sensual temptation for the first time in her life.

'On the contrary, I shall retreat to fight another day. It may just be that you haven't observed the enemy, Sir Adam.'

'You're not my enemy, and it's high time we went—unless you'd like me to compromise you irredeemably, of course?'

Carefully relinquishing the reins to him, with as little contact as possible, she preserved what she hoped was a chillingly dignified silence from then on and tried hard not to admire his easy mastery of the pair. They were highly trained and well mannered, but spirited enough to prove a handful to a less experienced whip. He had good hands as well, she conceded, slanting a look at them— long-fingered and elegant, despite his size and all too evident strength. They would be sure of touch but gentle, she decided, and shivered once more as she guiltily imagined them touching her in the most shockingly intimate fashion. She blushed and turned an apparently intent gaze on the spring barley rushing to fresh green life in a nearby field.

Watching him like some besotted schoolgirl gloating over her hero wouldn't do at all. She was a widow of four and twenty, not some dazed child, greedy to experience all the forbidden delights the world had to offer.

'Are you going to enlighten me about your discoveries, Sir Adam?' she asked, hoping he was too occupied with his pair to notice that betraying flush.

'Oh, that feminine curiosity you all share—however strikingly you differ in other ways,' he said, with a secretive smile that probably meant he missed nothing. 'I found some things I expected and others I certainly did not.'

'Well, now I know. Pray don't be more infuriating than you can help, Sir Adam—even if you are a man and therefore can't avoid it.'

'Well, that's put me in my place,' he lied blithely. 'But if you must know the vault had been opened lately, as I'm sure you suspected after hearing Wharton's fanciful tale. The grass around it was torn, as if something heavy was dragged over it. Why anyone should disturb the dead when there must be so many less macabre hiding places in the neighbourhood is currently beyond me, but I did find this,' he told her, taking the reins in one hand while he dug in his pocket. He handed a small object to her with yet another frisson of shock when their fingers touched.

Serena wondered if he felt it too, but if he did nothing showed on his face as he concentrated on his pair once more and she forced herself to look coolly composed as she examined the object he had passed her. It was a button of distinctive design, still attached to a piece of dark grey cloth.

An elusive memory stirred at the back of Serena's mind, but however hard she tried she couldn't make it tangible.

'It looks vaguely familiar,' she finally admitted, 'but anyone we know could have lost it in the village churchyard.'

'It has been torn off in some sort of accident—or an argument, perhaps. No man would have a button wrenched off like that and not notice unless he were preoccupied with something very urgent indeed.'

'Yet until we discover something illegal has taken place we're as guilty of flying at phantoms as any gothic heroine.'

'Speak for yourself, my lady. Nobody ever accused me of being a heroine before.'

And nobody ever would, she decided, with considerable exasperation at his wilful misunderstanding. 'It amazes me that Rachel never pushed you into the lake when you were children, Sir Adam.'

'Not for want of trying. But, being five years younger than I am, she was always too small to manage it on her own.'

'What a shame I didn't know you both better then; somehow we could have soaked you between us.'

'In your presence I would have been on my best behaviour even in my unregenerate days,' he said, with such a mix of teasing and admiration that she felt the breath catch in her throat.

'You regarded me as a scrawny and irritating chit, not worth knowing because I couldn't play cricket. Believe me, I'm liberally supplied with male cousins who left me in no doubt as to the general inferiority of the female half of the population when they were home for the holidays, so there's no need to pretend you were any different,' she managed, coolly enough.

'Scrubby brats!' he said, with apparent amusement and

far too much understanding of her contrary emotions in that teasing smile. 'Point them out to me when we're in town and I'll dunk them in the Serpentine.'

Serena couldn't suppress a delighted chuckle over her mental picture of the scapegrace Marquis of Helvelin, immaculate Mr Julius Brafford and the very dashing Lieutenant the Honourable Nicholas Prestbury picking mud and pondweed off their normally resplendent persons. 'Well, you could try,' she said with a smile, as she reckoned up the combined strength of her three tall and muscular relatives.

'You should laugh more often, your ladyship. It makes you young and carefree instead of overburdened and old before your time.'

So he thought she looked haggish, did he? Her smile wiped effectively off her face, Serena frowned, then gazed haughtily at the distant Welsh Hills to prove he meant nothing to her whatsoever.

'I *am* a widow,' she informed him majestically. 'And I live a very comfortable life, thank you very much.'

'That you do not,' he replied, as if he would like to shake her for taking such an optimistic view of her situation. 'You're exploited by your mother-in-law, and when not relieving *her* of her duties or fussing over her you're at the mercy of a sister-in-law who delights in setting your consequence at nought and her own A1 at Lloyd's. What I quite fail to fathom in the face of such wilful self-abasement is why on earth you endure it and what Helvelin is about to let you, considering he's head of your family. If you're truly content with such a lot you're far more poor-spirited than I ever thought you.'

'I'm nothing of the sort,' she snapped furiously, trying hard not to let him see how that brutal assessment of her character had hurt. 'And I'll thank you to leave my cousin out of this and mind your own business.'

'No. You're Rachel's best friend, and it concerns her deeply that you let yourself be trampled on by a family who don't really appreciate you. Even if you won't allow me to be concerned on my own account, you can't forbid me to worry about my sister's friend.'

His voice was gruff with emotions she dared not examine too closely. Her breathing threatened to stall in the face of any chances she might be about to throw away—the main one being the possibility Adam Langthorne might care about her. That could not, *must* not be. There was no future in such thoughts on either side. Even if she loved him—and so far she'd managed to avoid that trap—she couldn't marry him. Come to think about it, she couldn't consider it *especially* if she loved him.

'I suppose I could always join my aunt in Bath for a while,' she said without enthusiasm.

'Where you'll run her household and look after Helvelin's tribe of sisters instead of being at the beck and call of your family by marriage, I suppose? You have a way of humbling a man with your choices to avoid him that is without parallel, Lady Summerton,' he replied austerely.

Inflicting pain on Sir Adam Langthorne was difficult, but less unthinkable than seeing him grow restless and bored with her. 'I feel very real affection for my cousins, as I believe they do for me. But they have a doting mama and little need of me, and I do like to be busy.'

'Yet you just made it sound as if your boxes are packed and your farewells all but complete. Could it be that you are less convinced than you sound, my lady?'

'I have no wish to be a burden.'

'Anyone less likely to be a charge on any household she became part of I find it hard to imagine. You overflow with misplaced loyalty to those who don't deserve it, and begrudge yourself to those who'd value it way above rubies.'

'That I don't. I value true affection and consideration far above duty,' she said stiffly.

'Then prove it and come to London with Rachel, who surely deserves your friendship and loyalty even if I don't. Prove you mean it, Lady Summerton, instead of revelling in the heady delights of sacrificing yourself on the altar of family duty in Bath instead of Herefordshire.'

'I can't,' she replied in a hard little voice, trying not to slavishly watch for his reaction to her denial.

She knew without looking that his eyes would be flinty now, and his sensuous mouth set in a disapproving line. It was an effect she had been striving for these many weeks, after all, but she couldn't resist a sideways glance at him, despite destroying any admiration he had for her once and for all. To her amazement he was smiling at her as warmly as if she had agreed to his ridiculous scheme as eagerly as a schoolgirl.

'You mean you won't let yourself, however strong the temptation?' he asked with considerable satisfaction, and seemed to require no answer. 'You have no idea how flattering it is to be regarded as so dangerously irresistible that a lady of character dares not risk my company lest she succumb to my fatal charm.'

'Pray don't congratulate yourself on reaching that ridiculous conclusion, Sir Adam,' she replied stoically, although of course it was true. Trust him to deduce exactly why she was refusing such a tempting offer. 'You must have every single one of your attics to let to truly believe no lady dares spend time in your company lest she falls at your feet in a frenzy of gratitude and infatuation.'

'Well that's properly put me in my place. If I might suggest you take a few lessons in rebuffing a gentleman's hopes and dreams with finesse before you brave London society once more, Lady Summerton? Or perhaps it should be the other way about and your potential suitors are the ones who need their courage honed by an expert? At least giving lessons to them will help me pass any tedious moments during our stay, and I feel uniquely placed to offer such forlorn hopes my wise counsel.'

'You can't possibly live with us!' she heard herself say, as if everything was settled and nothing left to do but decide where they would reside.

'I really don't see why not. Even the most exacting chaperon would trust your reputation to Cousin Estelle and my sister.'

'Your cousin wouldn't notice if you held an orgy under her very nose!'

'An interesting notion, but I think I can restrain myself. And my sister would be justly furious if we abandoned her to Cousin Estelle's tender mercies. She would never see the outside of the nearest library or Hatchards.'

'You would be there,' Serena protested, but her resolution was faltering.

She recalled the circus that was the London season for debutantes such as she and Rachel had once been with a shudder. To leave Rachel to face all that in the care of bookish, otherworldly Miss Langthorne would be distinctly unfriendly, and she knew she couldn't do it.

'My presence will make matters worse,' she defended

herself weakly, feeling she was leading a forlorn hope against a superior tactician.

'Rubbish. Nothing could be worse than poor Rachel spending months being carted from one blue-stocking salon to another on my cousin's coattails, and you know it—unless you've become as blue as my esteemed relative.'

'You know perfectly well I haven't,' she told him, 'and nobody could call Miss Langthorne formidable,' she added lamely, quite ruining her effect.

'I prefer to call her a force of nature,' her undutiful cousin said with a surprisingly affectionate smile for a relative who benignly ignored him and everyone else most of the time.

'That's one alternative, I suppose.'

'It is the only description I ever found that fitted her.'

'As she has a reputation for speaking her mind, I can't think why you consider her a suitable chaperon for myself *or* your sister, given that she will doubtless refuse to attend any event that's unlikely to amuse or interest her.'

'Which is precisely why I need your presence. Cousin Estelle, eccentric though she might be, would never permit immorality to flourish under any roof where she was residing,' he replied, with every appearance of shocked virtue himself. 'Any more than I would dream of suggesting it.'

'I should stop right there, Sir Adam. You were doing so well until you got carried away,' she said, with a frown that was only partly in jest.

'Then ignore my pleas and come for Rachel's sake. It could be a bigger disaster than her first season if you don't support her.'

'I really don't see what I can do that any other widowed lady might not do better,' she protested.

'You have the sophistication of taste to see my sister is dressed to suit her own looks, rather than those of whichever blonde beauty the dressmakers are promoting this season—or you have when you choose to employ it,' he said, with a disapproving glance at her very plain gown and shabby cloak.

'You have a way of flattering a lady that is almost unparalleled, Sir Adam,' she forced herself to parry lightly, but he had given her pause for thought and she suspected he knew it.

'What do you think the Bond Street Beaux would say about my sister if she turned up in the salons of the ton in her current guise?' he challenged her.

'Poor Rachel,' she said unwarily, as she considered her friend as she had last seen her clad in a tobacco-brown stuff gown that had never been fashionable, even in the dim and distant past when the village dressmaker had made it up for her.

'Then you'll do it?'

'I'll talk to Rachel, and if she truly wishes to go I'll support her in any way I can.'

'Hmm, an admirably evasive reply. You'll support her, but is that to be from a distance or at her side, where she needs you?'

'Where she needs me, of course. It's time I returned the favour.'

Chapter Four

Sir Adam gave her a sharp look, but Serena focused her attention on the east lodge of Windham looming on the horizon as if she had never seen it before. She had never discussed the darkest days of her marriage and widowhood with anyone but Janet and Rachel, from whom it had been impossible to hide her unhappiness, and she refused to start now.

'Thank you,' he finally said quietly, and she turned to look at him at last.

She could see nothing on his face but relief that she had agreed to his scheme. He was a good and thoughtful brother, yet she couldn't dismiss the idea that she had just conceded the first round of a match that was more important than she knew—and to a master of strategy as well.

'Unless you wish to be invited for dinner at Windham tonight, I suggest you set me down by the picket gate into the park, Sir Adam, so I can walk to the Dower House unremarked,' she said, rather helpfully for someone who had been so neatly outmanoeuvred.

'Will you be there?' he asked, and she tried not to care that he asked as if his enjoyment depended on her company.

'Luckily my sister-in-law takes my no for an answer, but *you* wouldn't be so fortunate, I dare say,' she said lightly.

'Then I shall do as you say, my lady, and trust such humility will lead you to greet me with a little more than bare civility when next we meet.'

'I hope you don't think me so rude as to ignore my neighbours, sir?'

'Well, that is good. I must put myself forward more often,' he replied, with a decided twinkle back in those rather fascinating eyes.

She really must concentrate harder on winning their battle of words and wills if she was to see him every day when they went to London, she decided. Refusing to dwell on his victory, she graciously allowed him to tie the reins to the kickboard once more and hand her down with due ceremony.

'Thank you, Sir Adam. You have saved me from arriving home all aglow from walking home on a warm day.'

'I have, haven't I? What a splendid gentleman I am,' he said, in a self-satisfied tone that had her hiding a smile despite her resolution to be all dignity and propriety with him from now on.

'That you're not. I'm too much the lady to say what you really are.'

'Very commendable, my dear,' he replied, then gave her such a warm smile before he touched his hat brim with his whip and drove away that he left her feeling as flustered as if she had run all the way home after all.

When she reached the Dower House her flushed cheeks and windblown hair led the Dowager to inform her that she looked like a milkmaid, which gave Serena a good excuse to seek out the privacy of her chamber while she restored her appearance to suitably subdued order. A quiet evening at the Dower House with a cosy fire and a good book was, she decided, just what a female under siege from a determined gentleman and her own wayward inclinations needed to restore her peace of mind.

Sir Adam made sure the whole household knew he would be busy with his account books and correspondence that evening. He even managed to give them some attention—until his sister came in to inform him he was very poor company and she was going to bed. He murmured something suitably infuriating, before going back to his figuring as if lost in concentration, then sat back in his comfortable chair, feeling vaguely guilty as she wished him an impatient goodnight and left with a sharp click of the door that told him she would have slammed it if she wasn't too much of a lady nowadays.

If he let Rachel get so much as a sniff of his planned trip to Thornfield churchyard in the middle of the night she would attach herself to his coattails like a burr. He grinned as he recalled their youthful misdeeds, and decided their neighbours must have windmills in their heads to think the outwardly proper Miss Langthorne bore the slightest resemblance to the real woman under that false image. Frowning now, he thought of another deceptively proper young woman, and wondered what on earth he had been about to encourage Lady Serena to join him on this midnight adventure. At least now he was away from her incendiary presence and thinking rationally again. What would he have done if she had taken him at his word? Although, given the impulsive nature he was certain only lay dormant under all that propriety, it was better to know where she was and what she was up to, it had been pure folly to even hint he would welcome her presence tonight.

He lay back in his chair and contemplated the youthful widow Lady Summerton until his glower gave way to a wolfish smile that would probably have given Serena palpitations had she only seen it. She thought herself so different from the spirited young woman she had once been, before George Cambray had convinced her that all that made her unique was deplorable. What a pompous dolt the man had been! To win such a wife, then fail to realise his extraordinary luck confirmed every doubt Adam ever had about the Cambrays' collective intelligence—and George's lack of it in particular.

Yet perhaps he had the late Earl to thank for giving his wife such a disgust of marriage that she was still widowed now, when Adam had come home. The very idea of another man coming between him and his fate made his fists clench and the heady passions he had been holding in check since the day he came home threaten to slip their leash at long last, so that he might march over to Windham Dower House and drag the stubborn female home to his bed, will she nil she.

For the thousandth time he ordered those untamed longings back to their kennel and told them to stop there until they could have their day. If it took years, somehow he would get her to trust the reckless passion that slumbered under her prim exterior. At least Summerton hadn't quite managed to stifle the warm, sensuous woman he still caught a tantalising glimpse of now and again under all that protective starch, but he must give her ladyship room to realise that what she now considered the shady side of her nature could be set free after all, without disaster inevitably following.

There had been one or two cracks in her determination to hold him at arm's length lately, and he planned to widen them at every opportunity. Perhaps he should give her a little longer to accustom herself to being wanted as he wanted her, but he wasn't a plaster saint and his patience was beginning to wear out. There had been a spark of very feminine interest in her lovely azure eyes today, before she'd retreated behind her proper façade and pretended they were little more than strangers.

It was high time he fanned the sparks into flame. If he hesitated she might take herself off to Bath after all, just to make their lives difficult. Fighting the surge of primitive, possessive emotion threatening to put everything else out of his head, he reminded himself he had other business to deal with tonight. Somehow he had to forget the lovely Serena, Countess of Summerton, and give his full attention to the task in hand. He could spare tonight for whoever was using such a grisly hiding place, but woe betide them if they got between him and his true quarry too often.

Shrugging out of his well-cut evening coat and elegant waistcoat, he swiftly replaced his snowy linen with a dark shirt and stock he had hidden in the window seat earlier, then flung his grandfather's old cloak over it all, listening for any sign of wakefulness. Nothing indicated anyone was stirring, so the household must have left him to his figuring and gone to bed as ordered. Carrying the soft-soled boots he had secreted here for midnight wanderings, he raised the sash on the nearest window and silently closed it after himself before ghosting out into the night.

Even as he rode towards Thornfield, fugitive thoughts of Lady Serena wouldn't quite lie. Surely she wouldn't take him at his word and join him after her vehement denial and her current love affair with propriety? Or would she? He shook his head impatiently. Of course she wouldn't. If she loved him Serena might find it impossible to stay safe and warm in her bed while he took the mild risk of watching for the unwary miscreants using the Canderton vault, but at the moment he didn't think she knew what love was. He stifled the thought that if she turned up after all it might show that she cared more than she knew, and tried to dismiss the idea that even the best of women were devilish unpredictable at times.

There was only one thing wrong with Serena's plan to spend an evening in splendid solitude—and he was well over six feet tall and possibly the most infuriating gentleman she had ever met. She knew Sir Adam would go to Thornfield Church at dead of night to find out what was going on, and that he would probably do so alone. The thought of him lying there injured and needy until he was found in the morning, after some mysterious attacker had done his worst against that magnificent body by some foul means, ruined her longed-for respite.

At last she put aside the book that had failed to capture her attention and tried to think about the whole business logically. She considered the macabre idea of body-snatchers coming this far into the country to ply their gruesome trade, and concluded that nothing in that particular vault was fresh enough to interest them even if they did. With a shudder at the very idea, she told herself she had no wish to set foot in a churchyard at any hour of the night, and parted the heavy curtains to stare out into the darkness and carefully consider how she could get there undetected.

Suddenly there was no question of her staying here,

and all there was left to do was to get out of the house without anyone knowing she had gone. Telling the butler she would retire early, then waiting impatiently for the nightly rituals to roll inexorably on, she knew she should be feeling guilty at such deception. Instead she was impatient at having to wait so long before she could safely slip back downstairs. Having to undress and get into bed was a confounded nuisance, of course, but she managed a few artistic yawns before ordering her maid off to bed too.

Somehow Serena made herself wait, listening to the soft sounds of an occasional footfall on a creaking board as everyone finally went to bed. At last it seemed safe to get up and dress in an old black round gown she usually wore to walk the dogs, before draping a black crepe shawl over her unfortunate hair. Carrying kid half boots soft enough not to make much noise when she ran across the cobbled stable yard, she left her room, feeling as exhilarated as an errant schoolgirl escaping her stern governess.

Long ago she and her cousins had crept about Heron House in the dark when they were supposed to be in bed. Practising their staff work, her cousin Nick had called it at the time. According to her father's household they needed no practice, already being limbs of Satan who would rather make mischief all night long than sleep quietly in their beds like good Christian children. Serena smiled and felt that childhood daredevilry rise on a shiver of pure rebellion as the dignified propriety George had insisted on his countess assuming at all times cracked irreversibly. Looking back, she realised it had just been easier to comply with his demands than argue with them and she was suddenly ashamed of what her marriage had made of her.

She could think of few things George would have

hated more than to see her now. He would have been furious, she decided, with an impish grin her childhood partners in crime would have recognised with glee. She briefly wondered if she was really worried about Sir Adam's fate, or just intent on enjoying her unaccustomed freedom. A bit of both she concluded, as that unwelcome picture of him lying injured in the darkness forced itself into her mind once more. Bracing her shoulders, and telling herself not to be a pessimist, she slipped the key to the garden door out of her pocket and turned it so stealthily it moved the mechanisms without so much as a click. At least good housekeeping occasionally paid off, she decided wryly, relocking the door and slipping the key onto a chain round her neck before she set off across the garden, blessing her night eyes for rapidly adjusting to the darkness.

It had all been much too easy, she decided a few minutes later, as she finally allowed her mare to break into a trot. The Dowager's ancient coachman and groom were at the Hall with the equally ancient carriage her ladyship considered superior to any modern conveyance. Her own groom, Toby, was walking out with a girl from the village, and so the stables had been deserted. She frowned briefly, deciding she must have words with him about leaving the horses unattended when she was done with her own nocturnal adventures. No self-respecting horse thief would steal the Dowager's stubborn old mare, of course, but Serena didn't want to lose her lovely Donna, the one present she had received from George she had truly appreciated.

'Gently, lovely girl,' she murmured, as the fretting thoroughbred grew frustrated with the slow pace. 'It's much too dark to risk our necks tonight, but next time it's clear moonlight we'll have a good gallop, and to the devil with propriety,' she promised recklessly.

Donna shook her dark head sagely, as if she understood every word, and suddenly Serena felt like laughing out loud. In the darkness, with nobody awake for miles around to see her, she felt young and carefree again for a few precious moments. Maybe the fact that she was still only four and twenty was breaking through the pall of respectability George had insisted on at last. Indeed, she was enjoying herself so much that she might have let her horse find her way as she chose until dawn came if not for Sir Adam's lone watch for villains unscrupulous enough to disturb the dead.

Nagging concern finally nipped away her euphoria in the most disturbing fashion, and if Sir Adam had been nearby he might have received a mighty scold for his recklessness even as she managed to ignore her own. Such a protest might be interpreted as caring for the wretch's well-being, of course, so she would just make sure he was safe, then go home without him ever knowing she had been there. She checked Donna and wondered how on earth she could conceal her from any watchful ears and eyes.

Farmer Grey's barn was far enough away from both farm and village for her to leave Donna there in safety and walk the rest of the way in silence. When they got there she found it already tenanted by Sir Adam's raking grey, and Serena sighed even as her mare pushed impatiently at her shoulder. Donna might not get a gallop tonight, but the exclusive company of her beloved Silver Birch was probably even better to her way of thinking.

Serena unsaddled her mare and rubbed her down. No doubt she would have a job catching her when it was time to persuade her to leave her favourite companion behind, but that was a problem for later.

Afterwards she would have no idea how she'd managed that walk through the dark countryside. Before she had had the warm breathing presence of her horse to keep her company, but now she suddenly felt horribly alone in the deserted lane. Or at least she fervently hoped it was deserted. All of a sudden her imagination was ready to believe almost anything was lurking just beyond the limits of night vision. The furtive movement of some living thing off to her right made her freeze in her tracks, almost expecting a heavy hand to fall on her shoulder, or an angry fist to club down on her head. She softly cursed herself for an over-imaginative fool when she heard the sharp, hoarse call of a vixen and forced herself to carry on, despite the shiver of primitive fright it gave her.

Once a hunting barn owl went past her on pale wings and she recalled the country superstition insisted that they were omens of death. Yes—death for some small creature going unwarily about its business, she told herself hardily, and ordered her racing heartbeat to slow down. The creatures of the night were not to be feared in this safe corner of England; it was the human beings who might be in it that she should be wary of.

She managed to reach the churchyard wall in safety, and once she'd furtively clambered over it there were a whole new parcel of fears and superstitions to overcome.

Luckily Serena had never been terrified of the peaceful dead. To her way of thinking a churchyard set in a sunny countryside was far too quiet a place for the dead to bother haunting. If they walked at all, they would look for more promising places than hallowed ground, and she quite enjoyed a stroll among the gravestones while she was awaiting the Dowager after church on Sundays. Fortunately George was interred in the Cambray mausoleum at Windham—which reminded her, she must make sure nobody ever put her with him when she reached the end of her earthly span.

She reassured herself that her fascination with the worthy inhabitants of the village in days past didn't make her morbid, as the Dowager insisted, but this place certainly had no horrors for her by daylight. Now it felt curiously alien, though, and the sweep of a furtive breeze in the yew and holly trees sounded like someone whispering dark mischief to an imagination that had suddenly grown annoyingly vivid. There was nobody here, she assured herself. Well, nobody but Sir Adam Langthorne, and she might well give him a large piece of her mind when she finally tracked him down and found him perfectly hale and hearty.

Annoyed by the fact that she really would welcome him with open arms if he stepped forward and declared his presence like a good Christian gentleman, she forced herself to keep to the shadows and stay as silent as he was being. Surely this was all a mare's nest? Not even the drunken sexton would venture out on such a night. It was probably a ruse to keep people from finding him fast asleep by the vestry furnace whenever he was too drunk to go home. There could be nothing more sinister than that behind the reported hauntings, and if one of the crypts was disturbed they need look no further than Wharton seeking silver or brass to sell in order to feed his cravings. However repulsive such a theft might be, it was hardly a grand mystery, or even much of a surprise.

When Sir Adam finally appeared at her side as if by magic, clamped a gloved hand over her mouth and held her in an iron grip before she could even think about struggling, she was strongly tempted to bite him. She knew it was him as surely as if he had announced the fact with the clarion call of a town crier, and she told herself it wasn't in the least bit pleasurable to be clasped so securely in his strong arms. Unlucky, then, that her body wasn't listening, and moulded against him as if being locked in his arms was both her sanctuary and her dearest desire.

'Ridiculous, impulsive, reckless female,' he whispered furiously into the rebellious golden curls that had somehow escaped, despite all her efforts to bind them tight to her head.

'Mumph, grrh!' she told him, equally angrily, and he relaxed his grip a little so she could gasp in a much-needed breath.

'Now you *are* here, kindly keep quiet before you ruin everything,' he muttered, in the same intimate undertone that sent a quiver of something she dared not name through her.

This was decidedly not the time or the place to find his strong body so emphatically pressed against hers infinitely appealing. Nor was it a good idea to listen to his mumbled words with the fascination of a befuddled schoolgirl. In fact, now she came to think about it, no time was appropriate for that, and she would get as far from him as she could, when he finally released her.

'Promise to be silent?' he whispered, and she felt his breath stir the feathery curls against her neck. She gave a shiver that had nothing at all to do with the cold.

She nodded emphatically, deciding anything was worth submitting to if it put a safe distance between them. He took his hand away just far enough to gently turn her head and direct her gaze to where his had been resting before she'd distracted them both so effectively. It took all her self-control not to make a liar of herself and gasp out loud, for in a sudden shaft of moonlight she could see two burly figures, crouched over the entrance to the Canderton vault. She vaguely remembered that some difference of doctrine had led the family to build their vault out here rather than in the church itself, and watched as the pair wrestled with the slab that should have sealed the entrance to the living. Serena heard the grate of metal as a heavy mechanism closed, then the click of a lock tumbling into place.

The significance of that sound occurred to her even as she strained her ears to try and hear what the two men were saying. One of them had to be Wharton, the village sexton, for Serena quite refused to believe that the elderly vicar or his churchwardens would stoop to such underhand deeds.

'I ain't happy, Alfie,' Wharton rumbled gruffly to his shadowy companion, and Serena froze into an even more statue-like pose under the yew tree as she strained every sense to pick up his words.

'I don't pay you to be happy, and I won't pay you at all if you don't manage to forget my name and the fact that you ever knew me,' a second, lighter, clearer and much better-educated voice replied coldly.

'No need for that, guv,' Wharton snuffled, and even from here Serena could tell how much he wanted the comfort of a bottle in his shaking hands, for even his voice gave it away by its tremor.

'Every need for that. Whisper so much as a word of me in your cups and I'll soon know of it and kill you. You know I will, don't you?'

'Aye, I know it. You're the spawn of the devil—always was an' always will be.'

'Maybe, and as such you'd best beware of me. You know nothing of what was discussed tonight any more than you do what was done last night or the one before that.'

'Course not, Alfie, but I don't think he'll ever sign that bit o' paper you keeps waving under his nose.'

'By tomorrow he'll be so desperate he'll sign anything.'

'By tomorrow he could be dog's meat.'

'Then I'll get someone else to sign it for him, and his precious brother can pay over my money.'

'Our money,' Wharton reproached his confederate, and if he hadn't the sense to shudder at the chill in the second man's reply, Serena did it for him.

'Indeed. I haven't forgotten you, my friend,' he assured his partner in whatever crime they were engaged upon. If Wharton had any sense he might well wish he had.

'Thing is, we need a body,' he mumbled on blithely.

'Why?' the silky, chilly second voice asked, as if more interested in the addled workings of Wharton's mind than in any sensible answer.

'Inheritance. Men of the church like me knows a lot about inheritance—has to when we're dealing with the dead all the time. No body, no titles and no monies.'

'Well, then, we'll have one.'

'Aye, in the wrong place.'

'Not after he's dead. We have his horse and his pack and saddle. What more natural than we let all three wander the countryside until someone finds the confounded nag? Then the hue and cry will lead to his master's body. The poor stupid animal has no interest in any other man on earth after all.'

'If he leads them here, they'll know something's gone bad,' Wharton said sagely.

'Oh, what it is to witness such a brain in action,' the coldly sarcastic gentleman retorted, and Serena suspected he only answered Wharton to satisfy himself of his own infinite superiority of mind. 'When the deluded idiot is finally dead, you will take him deep into the woods and leave him there, artistically posed to look as if he fell from his unrideable nag and met an untimely end, out of sight and sound of any human help.'

'Might work, I suppose,' Wharton agreed grudgingly— and who could blame him for sounding disgruntled as *he* would have to carry out that macabre task?

Well, Serena thought upon closer consideration, she could do so quite easily. She could blame him for not protesting the proposed death of the poor soul they were discussing as if he were an inanimate object instead of a suffering human being, whatever he had done to bring down the wrath of a pair of conscienceless rogues on his head.

'Of course it'll work. After the beating you gave him to get him off that horse and into our hands, anyone would believe he died from a crashing fall and exposure. But it's high time we made ourselves scarce, before some of your fellow drunkards start to forsake that stinking hole you frequent and roll into the nearest ditch and see one of us.'

'Won't think nothing of seein' me about,' Wharton said with some satisfaction.

'They will if you're sober,' the second man told him with weary patience.

'Well then I won't be—or leastways not for much longer.'

'Say anything of this and I'll put a bullet in you and yonder fool and leave you both in the woods,' the other threatened, and this time the menace in his silky tones broke through even Wharton's dim perception of the world outside the nearest cider vat.

'I won't say nothing. You know you can trust me, Alfie. You always could, even when we was boys, and you'll always be able to so long as we're both alive.'

'Make sure you don't let me down now, then.'

'Silent as the grave,' Wharton promised, and on that feeble joke ghosted off into the darkness. After a short pause, when it felt to Serena as if every occupant of the graveyard, living and dead, listened tensely, the second conspirator turned to glare at the crypt he had just quitted, before finally nodding, as if making up his mind, and following Wharton off into the gloom.

Chapter Five

Serena and Sir Adam stood silent and listened for long moments before hearing the lichgate click very faintly and the softest betraying slide of boots on stone. Serena let out a long breath of relief. A squeeze of the warm hand that was now resting on her shoulder as if it had every right to be there captured her attention, and Sir Adam pointed emphatically at the tree where they were standing and then at her. Serena nodded her head, knowing he would feel the faint movement as much as see it. She had to trust him to know what he was about, and part of her acknowledged she would be more of a liability than a help to him if it came to a fight with those furtive intruders. Two against one it might be, but at least Sir Adam knew any blow he landed would find an enemy, whilst they would be hampered by their complicity.

If her senses had been alert for danger before, now they were directed so acutely at the action in front of her that a bear might have walked out of the shadows behind her and she would probably not have noticed it. So far she could discern very little. Then she heard the sound of a single horse in the lane. The faint noise of hooves on hard-packed ground receded, and the night settled once more into a wary silence. Serena eyed the vault suspiciously, for it seemed to her in the solitude that the faint wind groaned even more eerily than usual. If the dead were ever to walk it would be after such a rude awakening, she decided fancifully, and wondered if she dared leave her appointed place in order to find out if Sir Adam was about to join them or no.

The awful quiet of not knowing seemed like a physical thing—a presence whispering round her like another mourning veil. She was in danger of becoming vapourish, she decided, and ordered her common sense to the fore. Gentlemen who had held a commission in a crack regiment, and survived it for as many years as the annoying baronet, would not quit life without putting up a bitter fight, and she would certainly have heard that. Even so, her breathing was short and her heartbeat erratic as the seconds stretched into minutes and then what seemed like hours before she heard a stealthy footfall on the soft grass nearby at long last.

'Our mysterious gentleman's long gone, and I followed Wharton until I could be certain he was well on the way to the nearest flagon of cider,' Sir Adam's deep tones informed her succinctly from out of the darkness.

Serena threw down the heavy stone she had purloined from the churchyard wall with an audible gasp of pent up breath. Really, he was the most infuriating man she had ever come across, she decided, for maybe the thousandth time since she first met him. 'So we can talk now?' she whispered furiously.

'If you don't screech and bring half the village down on us.'

'Thank you,' she said, with great restraint, 'but I'm not given to *screeching,* as you so politely call it.'

'You're not accustomed to creeping about the country-side in the middle of the night either—or at least I hope not.'

'Certainly not, sir. How could you even think such a thing of me?'

'Easily—considering that you turned up here tonight when you most emphatically said you would not, and then proceeded to get in the way and poke your nose in where it's neither wanted nor needed.'

'And yours is, I suppose?'

'Yes, the other churchwardens have asked me to find out what's going on, if you recall? Thinking that I have had plenty of experience of creeping about the countryside in the dark I dare say, they had more trust in my discretion than you seem to. And they didn't want to call in the constables until they were sure something was afoot, so I was the obvious solution. If they knew you'd come here alone, I'm sure they would think me quite justified in tying you face down across your horse and sending you home in disgrace, whatever my military experience.'

Breathing very deeply, to calm the temper that wanted to explode in a childish but deeply satisfying storm of words and blows, Serena made herself recognise diversionary tactics when she met them head on.

'Very good, sir. Now, shall we get on with finding out what they have been about, or do you propose to keep ranting on at me until daybreak?'

'Tempting though it might be to be caught in such a compromising situation with you, I have a mission to perform, my lady. So I suggest you just turn tail about and get yourself back to Windham Dower House before someone realises you're gone.'

'Well, really, Sir Adam, how could you imply anyone might come looking for me in the little hours? I live in a very respectable household, I will have you know.'

'Very respectable indeed when you can get out of it with such consummate ease,' he replied disgustedly.

'Irony is wasted on me. I grew up with half a dozen male cousins even more rude than you are,' she told him with an audible sniff.

'There, you see? Now you're taking cold, my lady, and obviously those manly relatives of yours failed to teach you any sense.'

'I certainly *will* take cold if we don't get on and find out what those two rogues were up to—and anyway, my definition of sense and yours seem to be wildly out of kilter.'

'Indeed they do,' he rasped out with an exasperated sigh, and bent down to heft a pack from the ground that she hadn't even noticed until now in her anxiety over the ungrateful wretch. 'Since you lack all traces of proper conduct, madam, I suppose you might as well risk seeing whatever lies in yonder crypt, despite my efforts to spare you. If only the sight will put you off careering about the countryside in such a scrambling fashion in future, it'll be worth all the shocks that might await you.'

Even in the heavy darkness Serena thought he looked rigidly furious as he strode towards the grave without a backward look to see if she was following him. He was quite right, as it happened. She was following him so closely she might be some faithful if misguided hound. Doubtless he could feel her body heat, and even the hurry of the breathing she was doing her best to control as they got nearer to whoever was hidden in that musty old tomb. Trying hard to ignore his dire warnings, she gave an involuntary shudder as they stopped by the disturbed tomb nevertheless.

Now even the night was co-operating with his attempts to scare her into turning tail and running. A breeze had got up and was scudding clouds across the half-moon. She only stopped herself starting at shadows with a severe effort. She would not give him the satisfaction of gasping with fright at the sudden shrill call of a screech owl in one of the churchyard's venerable yew trees, although it sent her heartbeat into a wild tattoo that thankfully only she could hear.

Throwing his pack to the ground again, Sir Adam extracted a lantern and a tinderbox, then thrust them impatiently at her while he delved in his coat pocket for the keys he must have been given by the vicar. With a philosophical shrug that should have informed him she had too much dignity to thrust them back at him and tell him to light the lantern himself, unless he asked for her help like a civilised gentleman, Serena took the tinderbox and struck the flint. In the rising breeze she had to shelter the box with her body before she got a good spark at last, and could hold the burning tinder to the candle's wick. With a sigh she felt her nerves calm as the task was done at last, and squared her shoulders in preparation for what was to come. After all, she wanted to know what was going on inside that vault too, didn't she?

It wasn't just because she hadn't been able to rest when he might be in danger that she had come here, or at least she hoped not. No, if that should be so, then the rest of her life would be fraught with sleepless nights, and she couldn't admit such a revolutionary notion just now. Pondering it all the same, she tucked herself behind Sir Adam's reassuring bulk as he started down the steps, and supposed she ought to be grateful when he managed to spare her a preoccupied grunt of acknowledgement as she handed him the lit lamp.

He really was furious with her, and she was a little surprised to find herself a little in awe of that fury. In awe, maybe, but she felt not the slightest hint of fear. Somehow Serena knew she had no need to fear Adam's angry fists, however much she infuriated him. George had laid about her very freely when he'd been in a rage, or drunk, and sometimes even both together. Two years after her husband's death she knew in her head that most men wouldn't dream of venting their violent impulses out on their womenfolk. In her heart as well as her head she now acknowledged that Sir Adam would never hit anyone not mighty enough to give as good as they got. Having put that straight in her mind, she should give her full attention to whatever was going on in Thornfield churchyard and stop getting side-tracked by her consciousness of the powerful man in front of her in this ridiculous fashion.

She reminded herself that the Canderton vault had been opened recently as the lock clicked once more and the heavy door swung reluctantly on a neat counter-mechanism she couldn't begin to fathom. Somehow it still smelt of dust and damp and death, even though logic told her the place must hold recent air in its cold and stony depths. The dead couldn't hurt her—a fact she had reminded herself of a good many times already tonight—and she wasn't about to let that reassuring idea go now, not when she was peering into the inevitable darkness that would meet all souls one day, until they came to be judged at the last trump.

Peering over Sir Adam's shoulder, she could see footsteps in the light powder of dust, and curiosity began to overtake her instinctive unease with the place. It was nothing like she'd expected, of course, so maybe she really had read too many far-fetched gothic tales in her youth. There were no cobweb-draped skeletons, no glowing red rat's eyes reflected back from the light of their lamp, thank heaven. Instead there were various ancient coffins set into their appointed slots with an unexpected neatness nobody had disturbed in decades, if not centuries. Around some the wood had rotted, and lead showed dull beneath, but the most recent interments looked as if they might have taken place last week or perhaps the one before. The silver was barely tarnished on the elaborate fittings visible under velvet palls, yet the occupants of those opulent looking coffins were just as dead as the lowliest pauper consigned to a common grave.

She shuddered as she considered the levelling hand of death, and tried to look for anything out of place here except the two living breathing creatures in this chilly underworld, of course.

Normally she prided herself on her stalwart nerves, but Serena nearly succumbed to a good old-fashioned attack of the vapours when what she had taken to be a shroud shifted on one of the coffins. She squeaked with shock. Reminding herself that Sir Adam expected spineless behaviour from females, and must therefore be disappointed, she looked again, dreading what she might see but still reluctantly fascinated.

'In there,' she said at last, pointing a decidedly shaky hand at the slot occupied by a coffin covered in rotting purple velvet. The dark shroud on top of it on a second look seemed more like a carriage rug than anything one would normally find in such a place.

'Here—hold this,' Sir Adam ordered brusquely and thrust the lantern at her.

Beyond reproaching him for his ill manners by now, she meekly did as she was told. After all, he was the one putting his hands into that niche and not her, and just then she would have put up with a great deal worse than his short-tempered orders to avoid touching anything that belonged in *that* particular darkness. She had to shift her position to light Adam's way and, robbed of his reassuring shoulder to peer around, could see more of their surroundings than she altogether wished to. Her breath drew in with almost a sob and he turned to look at her, some of the irritation leaving his dark gaze at long last as his eyes thawed into the familiar golden warmth that turned her knees to water once again.

'You needn't stay if you don't want to,' he said, in a more gentle voice than he had used toward her all night.

'Yes, I do. You couldn't see what you were doing if I turned tail and ran, and I'm not that chicken-hearted, Sir Adam, whatever else I may be.'

'Indeed you're not, my lady. You remind me of a reckless lioness rather than such a timid common fowl. You would be halfway back to your warm bed and safety by now if you weren't rackety to a fault. So stay, if you must, but for goodness' sake hold that lantern steady if you intend being of any use at all while you do so.'

'You really are the most infuriating man I ever met, you know.'

'Very likely,' he told her in a preoccupied voice. She heard his indrawn breath as he touched the shrouded mass, and then, of all things, a murmur of satisfaction. 'There's more life in this crypt than there ought to be Lady Summerton,' he said very quietly, as if reassuring a restless horse.

'Yes—there's us for one,' she said, with fine disregard for grammar and accuracy.

'And here's another, unless I'm very much mistaken,' he replied, and with a mighty effort hefted a substantial form out of the dark resting place it had been thrust into.

There was a moan as if of a soul in torment, and it took all Serena's stubborn resolution to hold the light still as Adam laid his burden on the floor and stood back to inspect it more closely. He peeled back the blanket to reveal an aquiline masculine face that looked quite pale enough for death, but even from where she was trying to throw light without getting in the way Serena saw faint breath stir the man's pallid lips. He looked to be somewhere between thirty and perhaps thirty-five, she decided, and while not strictly handsome he would be an attractive man when well. But he certainly looked very far from well now.

A great bruise marred his brow and extended down over his hollow cheek, so that one eye would have stayed closed even if he were conscious. She watched with instinctive horror as Sir Adam ran a gentle hand through the man's tangled mat of curly brown hair and came away with sticky blood on his fingers. Wiping it off on the already filthy blanket, he continued to feel his patient's limbs with a sensitivity that shouldn't have surprised her but did. He showed himself so different from her late husband that the more she knew Sir Adam Langthorne the more she expected of him, but she hadn't thought a man could be so gentle and compassionate until now.

'He's taken a mighty blow on the head and his arm is

broken. I think his ankle may be dislocated as well, if no worse, and he looks half-starved into the bargain,' he finally told her absently, almost as if he had forgotten her presence and was just summing up the poor man's condition out loud.

'If not for the blow on the head, one might indeed think he had fallen from his horse,' she observed thoughtfully, remembering one of her cousins taking such injuries from a particularly reckless day out hunting.

'He certainly didn't get himself locked in here by accident.'

'True,' Serena responded with a shiver of horror at the very idea of such merciless brutality. 'To choose such a place argues desperation on his enemies' part, but what on earth has he done to deserve all this?'

'Who can say? If sufficiently deranged, even the cut of another man's coat has been known to send a lunatic into a frenzy, but from the sound of the conversation we heard tonight there was something cold and very calculating about this attack,' Adam said thoughtfully.

Serena could almost see his mind working out scenarios, and either filing them for future reference or discarding them as impossible. Feeling rather forgotten and redundant, she looked at the pale face of the man at her feet and felt an upsurge of protective fury. If there was anything she could do to save him and circumvent such cruel villainy she resolved to do it.

'I doubt they'll risk coming back tonight, considering they heard nothing to alarm them,' she told Adam, although she knew he would never have let her come in here with him if he'd thought there was the slightest risk of the callous wretches returning. Sometimes saying the words out loud was more reassuring than repeatedly telling herself they were safe. 'Even so,' she persisted, 'we can't let the poor man spend another night down here. I dare say a couple of hours in this infernal darkness would kill any normal person from sheer fright. But should we move him without medical advice, do you think?'

'Probably not. But he stands more chance of surviving above ground and out of harm's way. I propose we get him into the church and lock him in the vestry for his own safety whilst I go for help. Meanwhile, you had best slip away before you're discovered and we're properly in the suds, your ladyship.'

'And leave him to the mercy of an attacker who has shown none of that quality so far? That I shall not.'

'Stay here much longer and you risk your reputation as well as your safety,' he warned her with a frown.

'Better than his life. Now, are we going to move him or do you intend standing here arguing with me until daylight makes it academic?'

'I know a lost cause when I see one, so you can hold the lamp,' he informed her brusquely, leaving her in very little doubt of his displeasure over her refusal to do as she was bid.

Muttering her opinion of high-handed, bad-tempered gentlemen who thought everyone should run about at their bidding, she backed out of the door and up the stone steps with a long, careful look for any possible enemies lurking in the darkness. Once more she tried hard not to be impressed by Adam's mighty strength when he picked up the stranger and carried him in his arms as if he was a mere fly-weight, which he quite obviously was not.

'Bring the keys,' he ordered, and strode off towards the church without any assistance from her faltering lamp.

She muttered rebelliously under her breath, but did as

he bade her all the same, telling herself she only did so because she didn't care to be alone in such a place at night.

Closing the dark shutter on her lantern as soon as she could wrestle the keys out of the door, she left the long dead Candertons to their unaccustomed fresh air and scurried towards the bulky darkness that was all she could currently see of Thornfield church. If General Langthorne wanted to cover their traces, then he would just have to come back and close the place up himself; she had seen quite enough of it, and lacked the strength to swing the heavy door shut on her own.

He was waiting at the church door by the time she caught up with him, of course, and she had to risk opening the side of the lantern and placing it on the floor in order to fit the key into the great lock with both hands. Trying not to let him see how much those hands wanted to shake as she turned the key, she finally managed it and stood back to let Sir Adam go first with his burden. Then she shut the massive door behind them with an audible sigh of relief and locked it from the inside. She spared a quick prayer for the familiar sanctity of their refuge, and then hastily scurried after Sir Adam as he strode towards the vestry. Fumbling through the keys again, she found the smaller one that opened the door to it at last, and let them into the cool silence of the vicar's sanctum at long last.

Now they must risk the light again, irrespective of returning enemies and terrified villagers, should they wake and see ghostly lights flitting about their church. Luckily the vicar kept an old day bed in his vestry—in case anyone needed it when relatives were keeping vigil over their beloved departed, he claimed. Serena had always suspected he found it useful to have a snooze here in more peace than his wife allowed him at home, but whatever the reason she blessed it now.

Hastily clearing the lumpy couch of prayer books and the vicar's faded old cloak, she stood back so that Sir Adam could lay down his burden at long last. He was tight-lipped as he did so, and she could see from the way he flexed his powerful shoulders what a mighty effort it had cost him to bear the strange man so steadily, for all his great strength.

'Somehow we must get him warm before he dies of sheer cold, for God alone knows how long he's been locked in that hellish vault,' he told her, and she hurried back into the body of the church to look for anything they could add to the dirty blanket and the moth eaten old cloak.

As she ruthlessly stripped the box pews of all the comforts the aristocracy and gentry had added to them and hurried back, Serena tried not to think of her sister-in-law's fury if she could see her robbing the Windham Place pew. Back in the vestry, she found Adam busy lighting the brazier normally saved for the bitterest days of mid-winter, and realised he was more worried about the stranger's survival than he had wanted her to know. If the gleam of the lamp failed to draw the attention of any waking soul in the district, the red glow of charcoal would soon bring them running. Hoping fervently that everyone else in the area was virtuously asleep in their beds, she peered anxiously at the sufferer in the uncertain light.

He was a tall and well-set-up gentleman, just as she had suspected, and Serena frowned in bewilderment that such a man should have let himself be overpowered and imprisoned in the first place. His coat was of fine dark cloth, even if it was not cut in the first stare of fashion, his linen had doubtless once been spotless, and all in all he looked like a well to do country squire. Such men didn't often attract the attention of desperate rogues and bullies. They were too powerful in their own right, and yet not rich enough to be worth the risk of demanding a ransom at the cost of one's neck.

Looking up from her study of the injured stranger, she encountered a rather enigmatic look in Adam's dark eyes, and handed over her haul of cushions and rugs as she watched him re-cover his patient with infinite gentleness. Underneath his care he was as angry as she had ever seen him, but something told her he would never let fury influence his treatment of a helpless man. She threw one of the unwanted cushions onto the floor and plumped down on it before he could argue once more that she should leave this poor soul alone and unprotected while he went for help.

'He'll be safe enough here,' he protested, all the same.

'I can't agree with you. Wharton has as many keys as you have, Sir Adam, and therefore could get in here with impunity once we are both gone. I refuse to risk this poor soul being spirited off to some new and perhaps even worse place whilst I slink off and cosset my reputation.'

'Sometimes I think it's your purpose in life never to agree with me about anything, Lady Summerton, but it's sheer folly to put your reputation in danger on the mere off chance of Wharton being sober enough to return.'

'Then make sure you only bring yourself and someone you really trust inside when you bring help. Then I might stand some chance of getting home without a grand fuss and this poor man will be safe at last.'

'If you think I'm going to let you dance round the countryside on your own with at least one ruthless villain on the loose, then you're even more headstrong and deluded than I thought you, Lady Summerton.'

'Why not? You were ordering me to do exactly that just now.'

He let out a heartfelt sigh of frustration and she saw his knuckles whiten by the light of the warming brazier. 'Unless you actually wish to marry me in very short order, Lady Serena, I suggest you take more interest in your reputation and a little less in scoring points off me in the pettiest of fashions.'

Chapter Six

Serena paled at the thought of being forced up the aisle by her own efforts, after promising herself she would never trust her fate to any man again, however charming and handsome he might seem. Eyeing him cautiously, she thought she saw hurt as well as anger behind his condemning gaze. No doubt her thoughts were written all over her face in her horror at the very idea. But the young, reckless and ridiculously romantic Serena she had once been seemed to be awake again at last, and whispering contrarily that becoming Sir Adam's lady sounded like a wondrous adventure to her. Serena told her she was no longer in charge, and furthermore not to be ridiculous. Refusing to let herself feel the full weight of her confused emotions as she evaded Adam's eyes, she made herself watch the unconscious man they were arguing over as if he was the most interesting person she had ever come across.

'What should I do for him while you are gone?' she asked in a tight little voice she had a job to recognise as her own.

'Keep him warm, make sure he stays as still as you can keep him, and if anyone tries to break in you had best shoot them with this,' he informed her succinctly, and there was no mistaking the chill in his deep voice as he rapped out orders like the officer he had so recently been.

'This' was an evil looking little pistol that he pulled out of that capacious pack of his, and Serena recognised it as the kind ladies sometimes carried in their muffs or reticules on long and dangerous journeys.

'It's loaded, so kindly do your best not to kill yourself,' he warned her brusquely.

'Thank you, but I do know how to shoot a pistol, Sir Adam. My father was reckoned to be the finest shot in England, and he taught me everything he knew about firearms—for all the good it has ever done me.'

'I doubt you ever tried to kill anyone, though, and that toy is too small to be very accurate, so if the need arises you had best aim for the body. That will give you a bigger target. But please try not to shoot me when I get back here.'

She sniffed at his appalling lack of both manners and faith in her abilities, and held out her hand for the lethal little weapon.

'Be very certain, Sir Adam, that when I shoot you it will be exactly where and when I intend to do so,' she told him, in a gruff voice that should have warned him she was very close to the limits of her self-control.

'Try it, vixen, and I'll wound you straight back,' he warned, and for some contrary reason this latest conflict seemed to cheer him up, for he gave her that extraordinary smile of his before stalking off into the darkness, whistling rather tunelessly under his breath.

'And kindly be quiet,' she called after him.

'Likewise, my angel,' he replied from the darkness, and

she heard the key grate in the lock of the vestry with nigh ungovernable fury.

The wretch had locked her in! If they were to talk about compromising situations, he had left her in one of the worst she could think of. Locked in a room with a complete stranger in the middle of the night. Who would believe any good of either of them if that tale ever got out? Nobody, she decided, as she glared down at her patient with disgust.

'And I haven't the least desire to find myself leg-shackled to *you* either,' she informed the prone gentleman she had insisted on being left alone with accusingly.

'Sorry to hear it,' was his weak and very unexpected reply.

Forgetting her justified ire with the man's principal rescuer, she plumped down onto her knees and examined his face with suddenly gentle eyes. 'I had no notion that you were awake, sir,' she explained unnecessarily, and watched pain-filled sky blue eyes do their best to focus on her face.

'Died and gone to heaven,' he joked weakly, and she realised he was half serious.

'No, you're very much alive and inside Thornfield church.'

'Am I? Wonder where that is,' he replied weakly, and Serena could see how gallantly he was hanging on to consciousness.

'I shouldn't worry about it just now,' she urged him with an encouraging smile. 'You're with friends, and we'll do our very best to be sure you recover from your injuries in very short order. Now, is there anything you wish for?'

She thought she saw a gleam of humour in his pain-shadowed eyes for a moment, but if she did it was gone in a moment.

'Drink?' he requested, as if he was sorry to cause her so much trouble.

'That I can manage,' she replied lightly, and scrambled to her feet to retrieve the carafe that was always kept filled with sweet water from the vicarage. Wary of hurting his poor head, she found yet another cushion and lifted him gently against it. Watching with considerable respect as he bit down on his bottom lip at the pain even that slight movement caused, she wondered if he would remain conscious long enough to take the drink he must be desperate for to endure such hurt.

'Ready,' he finally murmured, and she gently tipped the glass until he could sip from it.

Some dribbled out of the corner of his mouth, but at last she saw his throat work and knew he had swallowed more than they had spilt between them. She really was not a very good nurse she decided ruefully, and wished Rachel was here—either to tell her what to do, or preferably to do it for her. Her friend had nursed her grandfather with infinite skill and patience throughout his last illness, and knew as much about herbs and healing as anyone Serena had ever come across.

'But I'm the best there is until *he* deigns to come back,' she muttered under her breath, as she eased the glass back so they could both have a rest.

'You set great store by my other rescuer, I think,' the man whispered.

'And you have extremely acute hearing, sir,' she informed him rather crossly. 'Sir Adam is no more to me than a neighbour and my best friend's brother, I can assure you,' she added stiffly for good measure.

Indeed, she set no more store by Sir Adam Langthorne than she did by any other gentleman who had proved his courage and resourcefulness time and again in service of his country. Given that vow she had made to herself not to marry again, she could never let herself do more than admire his courage, his humour, and the grace with which he got his way with the more traditional folk on his estates without them ever realising he had done so. Oh, and his easy manner with Rachel, and the way he handled his eccentric cousin with such patience.

She sat back on her heels and contemplated the altogether too shrewd stranger in front of her. He was quite right, of course, she *did* set far too much store by Sir Adam Langthorne's good opinion and would do well to remember it; if only in order to make herself quarrel with him more often.

'Maybe we should introduce ourselves?' she forced herself to say lightly.

'Safer not to know,' he muttered, and she could see his gallant efforts at staying conscious were doomed to fail very shortly.

'Maybe, but anyway I'm Serena Cambray,' she told him gently, thinking that perhaps knowing her name would reassure him that he did not need to stay awake to make sure she didn't do something unspeakable to his poor suffering body, as his enemies had already done.

'Are you, by God? Summerton must have his wits out for an airing then, to be letting you out of his bed long enough to wander about alone with another man in the middle of the night,' he observed faintly, and slipped back into unconsciousness again, leaving Serena deeply frustrated that he now knew a great deal more about her than she did about him.

'And that's not at all polite,' she told her sleeping patient sternly.

He obviously knew of the family she had married into, even if not enough to know that she was the current Earl of Summerton's widowed sister-in-law, rather than one of his sisters or—heaven forfend—his wife. That fact alone told her very little about the mystery man lying so close to her. He was obviously a gentleman, and might know the Cambrays from any variety of sources. George and Henry would have been ahead of him if he went to Eton or Oxford, of course, but they might still have met there, or in wider society at any time since. It was useless to speculate, she decided, but as she had very little else to do but dwell on Sir Adam Langthorne's virtues and iniquities while she awaited his return, she might as well carry on doing so, if only to keep the cold at bay.

Adam too was attempting to attend to his duties as if his thoughts were *not* stubbornly lingering on the feel of Serena's soft curves brought hard against him when he had held her clamped to his side in the churchyard. Torn between a need of her that nigh unmanned him and a barely contained fury at her recklessness, he'd told himself it was as well that he had to leave her behind after all. Then nagging anxiety for her broke through his anger and he lengthened his stride despite the darkness.

Reaching the barn where he had left Silver Birch at long last, his firmed his mouth into a tense line as he saw Serena's mare flirting with the rogue through the gloom. Was there a single risk Serena had failed to take tonight? he wondered, with brooding exasperation.

He should have trusted his instincts this afternoon, and he felt fifty times a fool for believing her when she'd disclaimed all interest in being present tonight. Instead he had smothered his unease and told himself that not even the reckless young girl she had once been would embark on such a quest alone. How much more wrong could he have been? Not very much. And yet he suddenly remembered his wayward thought that if she did turn up after all perhaps she was less indifferent to him than she pretended.

Despite the danger she had merrily strolled into, he couldn't hold back a broad smile as he untied Birch's reins and managed to drag him away from his lady love without too much fuss on either side. He might have planned to watch over and protect Serena every step of the way if she had openly agreed to join him in his vigil, but he doubted that would have got him any further in his campaign to make her see sense, at long last, and at least let him kiss her gently, just to show her that such things weren't the scourge to be avoided that she appeared to believe them to be. This way at least he had finally got her into his arms, even if he'd had the devil of a struggle to let her go again once she was in them.

After all, he had been trying to get her close to him without her skittering away like a spooked thoroughbred for months now. Admittedly it might not have been the best move he had ever made to scare her half out of her skin first—but, considering he was still burning with need and frustration half an hour afterwards, that was a mere detail.

One thing he intended to make damned sure of was that if she were forced to marry anyone after tonight's ridiculous escapade it wouldn't be some chance-met stranger who didn't appreciate the honour. He would value every silken inch of that exquisite skin of hers, kiss each glowing curl on her lovely head in gloating detail to show her not all men were fool enough to despise such perfection, and as for her glorious body… Best if he avoided the very thought of that at present, lest he run mad from bitter frustration.

He needed to turn his thoughts to extricating all three of them from this mess without the need for any marriage at all—for he was fairly certain her ladyship would balk, even if her reputation was in shreds for the lack of one. What that sly-tongued, evil-minded devil had done to her he hated to think, but George Cambray should consider himself lucky he was already dead, so his bitterest rival couldn't kill him out of hand for poisoning Serena's view of herself so deeply she no longer trusted her essential self. Not that he wanted to rival the idle wastrel who had been the last Earl of Summerton on any other front. Only in his choice of bride had the fool shown even the slightest hint of intelligence, but the way he had treated her argued against that choice being anything but chance.

At eighteen, Lady Serena Verlaine had had the ill luck to be lovely, rich, noble, and available at just the wrong time. Any other season and Cambray would probably have fallen in with a female as shallow and heartless as he himself, but he had decided to go in pursuit of an heir at just the wrong time, and had won himself a wife most men would have given their eye teeth for. If the fool hadn't been killed while taking a recklessly ill-advised jump out hunting Adam might have felt like doing it himself, and he had no wish to hang for his sins or anyone else's.

Adam's mouth tightened, and he had to force his hands to relax on the reins before he spooked Silver Birch into as black a mood as he was now struggling with himself. At times it seemed more like torture than pleasure, being in thrall to a woman so wary of trusting a man that she would rather live her life alone than give in to the powerful drag of attraction that sang between them. But then he would see her again, and know that she should be cherished and seduced by a man who would value her as the unique, intelligent and infinitely desirable creature she was, and that *he* was uniquely suited to be that man. Holding back was becoming downright painful, though, and he wasn't sure he could risk being alone with her again—not when he needed to feel her go wild with passion in his arms and damn the daylight.

His thoughts wandered, despite his determination to keep his mind on his task and not the Countess Summerton. The second time he had laid eyes on her as a man instead of an unknowing boy she had eclipsed even herself. He recalled seeing her as he left a ballroom for his regiment and his duty, and felt something of the shock and the longing she had provoked in him then. How he had suddenly regretted ripping up at her years earlier, out of anxiety and fury with his sister and her reckless friend. He must have given her such a disgust of him that four years later she would doubtless have refused to dance with him if he'd begged her to on bended knee—even if he had been leaving for Portugal the next day and therefore unable to beg anything of a woman he must leave behind.

For years he had held the lovely, vibrant young Serena Verlaine in his heart as an unattainable image of what might have been—if only he hadn't been bound for battle and hardship, and if only she hadn't married a man he knew to be a blockhead and a bully incapable of appreciating her. She had been consigned to the past, regretted and occasionally remembered when about to risk his life in battle, searching desperately for a distraction that would conceal his terror from both his men and himself. Then, six months ago, a primitive voice had insisted deep within him as soon as he set eyes on her again that there was no *maybe* about it this time—even as his everyday self went about the polite business of introduction and greeting as if it were just a day like any other. Weeks and then months had gone past since then, and he had learnt new feats of self-control, but what had those months taught *her?*

His expression was grim in the darkness as he contemplated failure and then dismissed it as impossible. With every day that went past he discovered new depths to her, went beyond that initial passionate possessiveness into areas he refused to name even to himself. But what about Serena, Lady Summerton? She wasn't indifferent to him. If she had been she wouldn't avoid him as assiduously as she had been doing lately. He didn't repulse her. He knew that as surely as he knew his own powerful feelings for her puzzled and plagued her—mainly because she didn't understand them. Yet if she were truly revolted, or fearful of him, he would have removed himself from the neighbourhood and set about forgetting her by taking a wife as cynically as George Cambray had done just for the sake of an heir.

What he knew of the last Earl told him that his taking of her would not have been gentle. The less than noble George had had a reputation amongst the demi-monde for paying for his pleasure and giving nothing at all in return. Adam's mouth tightened as he contemplated the very idea of that boor not treasuring Serena's every breath and nerve, until she lost all sense of where she ended and he began. He ordered himself to forget such notions before he fell off Silver Birch and landed them all in the suds.

Yet the very idea that he might be similar in any way to George Cambray made him long to shout his displeasure at the fitful moon, but he suppressed it with a grin and wondered what on earth his former troop would make of the passion-led fool he seemed to have become. And it wasn't as if he hadn't tried to fight it. After Christmas, when all she'd done over that generous festive season was avoid any whisper of intimacy between them and pretend he was just another neighbour, he had ridden off to London and tried very hard to forget her in almost any dissipation he could think of. It had only taken him a fortnight to come to his senses and give up, when he had looked at the female he had set up as his paramour and found he was mentally listing the ways in which the suspiciously golden-haired wench would never resemble lovely Serena. Then he had cursed and sunk the idea in brandy that it would be far better for all concerned if he had never set eyes on the youngest Lady Summerton in the first place.

He had paid off the disgruntled ladybird and put his head under the pump, before hastily packing up and going to stay with friends in Kent while he recovered from that bout of despairing debauchery and plotted a new campaign. All in all it was going reasonably well, he comforted himself, as he rode as swiftly through the deadest hour of the night as Silver Birch could safely take him. Well, if not exactly well, then not disastrously either. Indeed, he thought he might very easily be anticipating a welcome release from this perpetual state of frustrated arousal in her deliciously formed arms by now.

For a moment he thought of the very willing ladybird, and wondered if he should have kept her after all, but his dismal failure to slake his need for one unique, wondrous woman who was no more than a pastiche of her told him otherwise. After the first driven flush of possession and blessed release he hadn't even been able to take the little houri fully, and her freely expressed disgust at the failure of his fabled ability to satisfy his current lady had probably done his reputation among the rakes and Cyprians of the demi-monde no good at all.

His mouth tightened into a line, and a frown almost knitted his dark brows together as he contemplated what his obsession with his sister's best friend had nearly reduced him to. Well, never again. Somehow he had to convince her that it was time to end this bitter frustration, and his well-honed instincts were telling him that need was mutual, if not likely to weigh as heavily on her as it did on him.

After all, his poor Serena had only had George Cambray's bungling rutting to gauge the tender arts of love against, and he knew that crass fool had had no finesse whatsoever. No, he had to remember that whenever his patience was close to snapping, and carry on winding a gossamer web of enchantment about her until she finally realised not all men were clumsy and self-obsessed. Even so, attaining his rightful place as her lover seemed far too distant tonight, as frustration rode him and his needy body threatened to rebel against the iron control he had learnt to impose on it whenever he was in proximity to the woman.

And there he was thinking about her ladyship again, like some lovesick youth, which would do naught to keep her safe or himself under control. With a predatory smile, he contemplated the ultimate reward for such a Herculean feat, and faced the next ordeal with something closer to resignation. His prize was tougher to gain than he had ever contemplated when he'd begun this siege, but she would be so winning he would never regret the struggle once he had her in his bed.

Coming back to his right senses just in time to be cautious again, he discovered that he was nearly at Marclecombe, and reined in the mighty grey in order not to wake the whole household with his approach at the gallop—or at least as close to a gallop as any sane man could go in this damned darkness.

Now he would have to wake Rachel and his stalwart head groom without rousing the whole house. He hoped his staff were all sleeping the sleep of the just tonight, for he certainly would not be. He led Birch in through the paddock, where his hooves would be muffled, and then to a barn where he once more tended to his sweating mount and left him munching contentedly on a generous measure of oats. It would take a reckless horse-thief to risk Silver Birch's ironclad hooves when he was tired and not inclined to be obliging, so no doubt he would be safe there until morning. Adam crept into the stables and woke Joseph, with a whispered imprecation not to rouse anyone else while he saddled Miss Rachel's mare and the chestnut gelding, and then woke his most discreet under-groom to help him improvise a litter. Really he should take the carriage, and be damned to waking the neighbourhood, but this was a dark and sinister business, and the fewer people who knew of their visitor, the less chance they would have to betray him to his enemies.

It took one of the longest half-hours he had ever spent to get ready for his unexpected guest and convince his sister to dress and fetch her box of medicines from the stillroom. All the time his mind would keep relaying the most unlikely scenario of Serena fighting off the returning attacker and putting her own life in peril. He told it to be sensible and logical, but even so an edge of tension nearly drove him to be clumsy and over hasty. He made himself empty his mind of such possibilities and deal with the task in hand. At last it was done, and he signalled Rachel and Joseph and the groom to follow him through the paddock as he bent his mind to saving Serena's reputation, despite her own careless indifference to it.

'Peace time too flat for you, Sir Adam?' Joseph taunted him as soon as they were out of earshot of the hopefully still sleeping household.

'Not any more,' he replied shortly.

'Well, I haven't had so much excitement in years,' his sister observed rather breathlessly, and Adam forced himself to abate the rash pace he had set in the fading moonlight.

He struggled with a wish not to tell anyone the full story, but at last decided he would be a fool to hide the truth from these two, who had never revealed a secret he had confided in them in their lives and surely never would. So he ordered the other man to circle round the church and check for anything untoward, then filled the others in on tonight's events as they tied their horses' bridles to the rings lined up by the churchyard walls for the purpose, and fed them the nosebags of good oats Joseph had attached to their saddles to keep them quiet.

'Heavens, poor Serena must be terrified,' Rachel said faintly and bustled into the church ahead of him as soon as he had the door unlocked.

'We haven't much time before dawn breaks,' Adam cautioned.

'Then the sooner we get on with it the better.'

Wondering if it was his fate to be surrounded by ungovernable females, Adam unlocked the vestry door and turned to his head groom as soon as he saw all was well with Serena and the stranger.

'Hurry along to Farmer Grey's barn as silently as you can, and saddle up her ladyship's mare, Josh. Then bring her round to the back of the churchyard, where she stands less chance of being seen. Her ladyship will be along shortly to collect her, and I want to you to see her home before scouring the area for any signs of the rogue who caused tonight's dramatics. He took the Malvern road rather than the Hereford one, but that could have been a ruse in case he was seen.'

'Aye, sir. You can trust me to look after your lady and then act the bloodhound for you,' the man replied with a cheeky salute, and marched off at the double.

'Now I come to think of it, *he's* pretty ungovernable as well,' Adam muttered under his breath, and followed his sister into the vestry at last.

'Ah, Sir Adam—I thought you had forgotten us both, you took so long. Although I haven't had to shoot anyone so far,' was the facetious greeting he got from the female he was going to so much trouble to both seduce and protect, and for a moment he wondered why he let her dance all over his heart in such a moonstruck fashion.

Then she gave him that enchanting smile of hers and he remembered all too well, cursing the ready response of his rebellious body to her artless greeting. Every time he thought he had himself under stern control she did that—or something equally, innocently arousing. Luckily she had no idea what a superhuman effort it cost him to resist this terrible urge to carry her off to his lair and make her his in every way that mattered, and keep doing it until she faithfully promised to be his and his alone. She really was the most contrary, wilful and exasperating female he had ever come across, he decided, keeping in the shadows as he watched the tableau in front of him with a peculiar sense of detachment.

Chapter Seven

He could hesitate, Adam mused, bungle this attempt at rescuing her good name. Then she would have to wed him by the time the local gossips had finished with the story. Temptation clawed at him as he recalled the feel and scent of her so close against him as they had waited under that tree in the darkness. No. She would come to him willingly or not at all. The thought of being racked by this heady, grinding need for much longer made him wonder if he was altogether sane. He certainly wouldn't be by the time she was finally in his bed, but he nobly determined to put his plan into action before his baser nature tripped him up, for he was fast discovering he wasn't a patient man.

'Joseph will escort you home,' he announced stiffly, encountering an odd look from her wonderful deep blue eyes that once more threatened his iron composure.

'He'll be missed,' she protested softly, and he silently blessed their hapless patient. If not for her determination not to disturb him, she would undoubtedly be yelling at him like a fishwife by now, and he didn't think his much-tried temper would survive it intact.

'Not he. Joseph has the stables too well ordered for anyone to question his movements, and would that I had his gift. But please don't delay him once you reach home. I want him to scour the neighbourhood for any sign of where the villain behind all this has gone.'

'He'll be far away by now—at least he will be if he has any sense.'

'Then we'll just have to hope he hasn't,' he argued, with what he considered admirable patience, even if the mulish look that now firmed her lips argued that she did not agree. 'And even if he has decamped, we might as well find any trace of him before the world is awake and blithely obliterating them,' he explained, only just controlling a powerful urge to kiss that look off her luscious mouth.

'But if word of any interest in him gets out, we'll never trap whoever is responsible for this outrage,' she protested.

'I dare say our man here will have a good idea who attacked him—so long as his brains aren't addled by that blow,' he argued, with rather less patience.

Surely even Serena must admit he had more experience of men of violence than she did? Aside from her wretched husband, he recalled with a frown. No, George had been more of a blustering bully than a cold user of whatever force it took to achieve his end. Not that he could imagine that one saving grace had brought her much comfort during their ill-starred marriage.

'He was perfectly sensible when he regained consciousness just now, the poor soul,' she declared, and his gaze sharpened on the recumbent figure he would have sworn was unconscious.

Either the fellow was a rogue after all, and a very fine actor with it, or the sight of his lovely Serena had revived him as surely as it would have done Sir Adam Langthorne in even more dire circumstances. He frowned again, more tried by the idea of another smitten suitor getting in his way after six months of patient stalking than he cared to be. Lately he had sensed that he was closer to his goal, but this poor wretch, if victim he was, and not an unwary thief who had fallen out with his brotherhood, might well queer his pitch more effectively than the most accomplished Corinthian.

'What did he say, Serena?' Rachel asked urgently, and stopped fussing over her new patient long enough to watch them with a little too much awareness in her eyes.

Serena decided that, although she loved her friend like the sister she had always wanted, sometimes she could wish her a little less acute. 'That Henry has his attics to let—which proved to me that he is as sensible as any man I ever met,' she muttered darkly. Recalling the rest of that odd conversation she blushed, avoiding what she mentally categorised as the baronet's examining magistrate look as she did so.

'If he said anything improper to you, I'll give him a matching pair of black eyes as soon as he's capable of fighting back,' Adam threatened darkly.

'Well, he didn't, and as he's going to be a guest under your roof you really have the most appalling notions of hospitality, Sir Adam.'

'I dare say by the time that lot have healed,' he said, with a comprehensive gesture at the stranger's many injuries, 'even my temper will have had time to cool.'

How could he think so ill of her, with the poor man only semi-conscious on the daybed and incapable of compromising even the most willing of females? And she was hardly that, even in the presence of the one man on earth who set her heart racing like a Derby winner.

'And bank on this, then, your ladyship,' he continued, in a hard, flat voice so unlike his usual deep and vibrant tone that she flinched, then glared furiously at him. 'If you don't get yourself out of the side door and up the path to Windham very rapidly indeed, then you will be caught stealing home with the dawn. All my attempts at preserving your undeservedly spotless reputation will be wasted and I shall be obliged to marry you myself.'

With that bombshell, he grasped her hand and tugged her impatiently to her feet, as she obviously had no intention of getting up of her own accord. Unable to bring herself to wrench her slender hand from his strong one, as propriety and temper dictated, Serena let him manhandle her while she frantically looked for any sign of her occupancy and tried to pretend she was perfectly com posed and had no need of a strong, manly shoulder to support her. She didn't, of course. But how pleasant to lean into his stalwart shoulders for protection if she ever needed to.

Rubbish. She liked her independence too well to let go of it so completely, and he would demand even more of her life than George had ever managed to dominate. She had no intention of putting herself under another man's thumb—not even if it came attached to a wickedly handsome baronet who had the most devastating smile she had ever witnessed on a man. Not that she had seen very much of it tonight, she reminded herself stalwartly, and hardened her heart against the strangely appealing notion of becoming the next Lady Langthorne.

'Heaven forbid!' she informed him militantly, and gave him a long, cool look to demonstrate her revulsion at the very idea as she made herself remove her hand from his large, warm and possessive one, where it had been worry-ingly comfortable once more.

To Adam, the faint scent of rosewater and the rosemary Serena used to rinse her hair was unmistakable, and as much of a give-away as if she had written a notice and left it pinned to the church door saying, The youngest Lady Summerton was here, in the most scandalous circum-stances, *and* in the middle of the night as well! While part of him was exulting at the fact that she had taken so long to refuse his wrathful offer, the rest was trying hard to remember his honour. Apparently there was a trace of the officer of dragoon still there somewhere under respectable Squire Langthorne's more staid duties, and that rather wild young gentleman rebelled at becoming shackled for life to a female who wouldn't even admit the powerful attraction between them to herself, let alone to him. Yet still his body was imprinted with the heady proximity of her, the fact of her pressed warm and somehow right against him in the shadowed gloom of this bizarre refuge.

No, if he moved too soon she would bolt as fast as her legs could carry her out of his reach on some plausible pretext. He must hope the rest of the world was less sen-sitive to her ladyship's presence than he was. The thought of any other man stalking the youngest Lady Summerton made his empty-feeling hand tighten into a furious fist at his side. Then he caught her looking at him, as if not quite sure of his sanity, and forced himself to loosen it and give her what he hoped was a politely social smile, and an inter-rogating look to ask what was amiss. It was either that or pull her into his arms and kiss her senseless in front of his sister and an unconscious stranger, in a church of all places.

'Tuck that pistol in your pocket, would you, Rachel?' he said at last, with a wave at the weapon Serena had abandoned as soon as they arrived. 'It's loaded,' he cautioned, then tugged her ladyship out of the room and through the silent church before she could argue with him again.

'Kindly unhand me,' Serena gasped as soon as they were outside, just as if she were the heroine of a melodrama.

'I'll let go when you see sense, you exasperating female. Do you actually *want* us to get caught here in the little hours of the morning?'

'Of course I don't. But I'm well beyond the age of needing a chaperon, even if we were—as well as being a respectable widow of good character.'

'I never heard anything so ridiculous. You stand in need of a keeper, my lady, not a chaperon,' he informed her through gritted teeth.

Then he added insult to injury by ruthlessly tugging her towards the dark tunnel of yew that led to the ancient coffin trail over the hills, disused after a properly made road had been built fifty years ago. Serena forgot to be furious for a moment, and shivered as they entered an even more profound darkness under those ancient trees. Suddenly she was glad of his disturbing warmth, as all sorts of superstitious nonsense rose up to haunt her. This was certainly not the time to give in to her fears, she decided, or to her nagging desire to fling herself into Sir Adam's arms and stop there until someone disapproving came along. With a shudder of relief or regret—she wasn't quite sure—she saw the darkness lighten a little, and told herself to be glad they had reached the gate onto the fields. At last there was just enough light to discern Joseph and a restless Donna, impatient for her own comfortable stable.

'Take care,' Adam ordered, in that low, driven growl he had used towards her ever since their first encounter in the churchyard tonight.

Then he resumed his managing ways by seizing her by her narrow waist and pressing a brief, hard, frustrated kiss on her surprised mouth, before boosting her into Donna's saddle as if he was longing to end their latest encounter.

'Goodnight, Sir Adam,' she gasped breathlessly, surprised she could still talk after the heady effect his kiss had wrought on her wretched, reeling senses.

Wrapping a leg securely around the pommel, she found the stirrup with her other foot, then turned the eager mare towards home, without looking back to see if he bothered to watch her go. She told herself she was glad to be free of him at long last and tried her best to mean it. How dared he kiss her as if he had every right? And in front of his groom as well. She visualised Sir Adam forgetting all about her as he stalked off to deal with more pressing matters, as if that hot, hungry kiss had been a mere interlude to an unusually busy night. Meanwhile her mouth was burning with the evidence of his firm mouth on hers, and yet it felt softened and needy after that hasty salute. She tried to tell herself that she was only thinking about it because she was still fuming over his temerity, but she suspected a little more of that quality would have been very…very—well, yes, exceedingly interesting, she finally concluded.

Purely on the basis of comparing his kiss to the only other ones she had ever received, Adam's rough salute had rendered *her* hungry and hot and oddly intrigued. Which was perfectly ridiculous, she decided, as she shifted Donna's reins to one hand and raised the other to her lips to explore that wistful longing for more. She had been a married woman, after all, and knew exactly what such careless caresses led up to. So why on earth she should want more of any man's kisses was quite beyond her. She shuddered in the early dawn air and wondered if she would ever be warm again as the memory of George's impatient fumbling haunted her all too vividly. Then she recalled the novelty of that brief branding from Adam and found that, yes, she could become very warm indeed between one breath and the next.

Sir Adam's kiss, rough, frustrated, and even a little rasping from fine dark stubble in need of a razor, had the power to blot out every perfunctory, meaningless salute George had bestowed on her during their entire marriage. So what did that make her? Needy? Too easy to seduce? Or just plain enthralled by the first handsome man who came along and paid her some attention? Or perhaps what she had feared from the first moment she'd laid eyes on him again six months before was finally coming true, despite all she had done to armour herself against him? Could she be falling in love with him, despite every barrier she had thrown up against that most unwelcome possibility, and thereby forgetting every heartfelt resolution never to take such a risk again?

'Slow down, my lady,' Joseph protested as he raced to catch up with her. 'Himself will have my hide if you kill yourself or the mare.'

'Quite right, Joseph. It's ridiculous to endanger you and Donna in the dark, even if I'm foolish enough to risk my own neck.'

'I always thought you was quite sensible for a female until tonight, your ladyship,' he told her, with a frown of disfavour that quite took the shine off that rare compliment.

'Oh, don't you start as well,' she ordered furiously, and concentrated all her energies on finding their way from then on, for the moon had set and the profound dark of pre-dawn was taking its place.

Consigning Sir Adam Langthorne to somewhere a little too warm for comfort, she set about the serious business of getting home without being seen. As an antidote to any more disturbing internal debates on the nature of instinctive passion versus that odd emotion some called love, it occupied her very well.

Once they were within sight of the Dower House she ordered her unwanted and thoroughly unsuitable chaperon to leave her, then cautiously led Donna through the park on foot. Suddenly she didn't want to go in, and found the very idea of returning to life at the beck and call of others oddly depressing. An impatient snort told her Donna wanted her comfortable stable, even if she *had* rediscovered the pleasures of nefarious night excursions in the right company, so Serena concentrated on getting her mare home as smoothly as possible, and did her best to ignore the lure of the dawn.

'My lady, I was scared you'd broke your neck.' An urgent whisper came out of the darkness when she finally led Donna into her box.

'Hush, you'll wake the stable lads—and whatever can you be doing up at such an hour, Toby?' she murmured at her henchman.

'I slept down here.'

'Did you, now?' She could have sworn she saw him blush, despite the darkness, and decided her groom had secrets of his own. 'I hope you're not leading that poor girl astray,' Serena remarked softly, as she urged Donna in and he unsaddled the mare while she began to rub her down.

'Banns bein' read for the first time this Sunday,' he confided, pride and shy wonder in every line of him as he furtively delved into the bran tub for the feed he had already mixed for his favourite charge.

'Oh, congratulations, Toby. I wish you so very happy,' she whispered.

'Thank you kindly, your ladyship. Now, you'd best get back indoors afore the old lady catches you and there's hell to pay.'

'And we'll have a little more respect for my mama-in-law, if you please,' she chided, half seriously.

'When she deserves it, she can 'ave it,' he replied stoutly.

Serena swallowed hard, telling herself she must be tired indeed to turn into a watering pot just because her loyal groom didn't blindly adore the Dowager.

Toby's unquestioning loyalty to her, and the memory of the silly young thing she had been when she first came here, excitedly accompanying the Dowager Countess to church to hear her own banns read for the first time, combined with that sudden weariness to threaten to overset her. Sighing faintly, Serena silently let herself back into the house and crept up the stairs to her own ancient wing of the house, remembering to tread only on the stairs that didn't squeak from habit alone. Very likely Toby would be as happy with his Susan as her former maid was with her beloved Zach—but then, maybe the grooms and maids of this world had a stronger grasp on love than the aristocracy, who so often were paired more like breeding cattle in a stud book than sentient human beings.

Or perhaps their expectations were more realistic? Hers could hardly have been less so when she'd blithely wed George, as if he were the prince out of the fairytale she had foolishly woven around him. Had she really been so naïve as to think love would grow out of the careless affection he had shown his betrothed until then? She winced as she recalled her awe and delight that such a handsome charmer had chosen her, out of all the eager debutantes he could have asked to marry him. Stubbornly cocooned in her haze of schoolgirl dreams, no wonder it had hurt her so much to come down to earth. Instead of hero to her heroine, she had woken up to find herself wed to a man with whom she had next to nothing in common. The shock had nearly broken her at the time, but at least she had finally grown up. Perhaps the children they'd failed to have would have bound them together, but the lack of them had driven herself and George further apart with every childless day that passed.

Serena shook her head to dispel her unhappy memories, and told herself there were many good reasons not to linger on Sir Adam's searing kiss. Yet the tears she had blinked away such a short time ago now threatened again as she tried to forget the feel and scent of him as he'd briefly savoured her lips, then torn his mouth away as if lingering there held all the temptations of hell for him. Where her eyes had fumbled for the full likeness of him, hot-eyed and needy in the darkness, her other senses had greedily filled the gaps and now wormed their way into her memory with extraordinary recall of his every word and deed. It was no good; weariness was making her maudlin.

She held her breath as she tiptoed into her own room at long last. Half expecting to find her mother-in-law's dresser sitting in the chair by the empty hearth, like a gorgon in curl papers waiting to challenge her with indignant satisfaction, it was wonderful to be alone in the grey light of the coming dawn.

Serena let out a sigh of relief as she warily closed the heavy oak door and sank down in that chair, to contemplate the extraordinary night she had passed. If the tale ever got out it would surpass her girlish pranks in London many times over, but somehow she wouldn't have missed it for a chaperons' bench full of propriety.

Having adventures with Sir Adam Langthorne was rather a heady experience, and since she refused to embark on a more intimate partnership with him, this one must serve to enliven her days instead. One midnight excursion to leaven goodness knew how many years of mundane propriety seemed a very slender reward. Especially when considered at the end of a long day spent guarding her heart against a man who might undermine her stoutest defences if she abandoned them for a second. She would resist the temptation to let him, but what on earth had possessed her to agree to accompany Rachel to London and place herself under his roof?

Undressing once again, she resumed her very proper nightdress, put away her disguise, and plaited her hair. Fighting tiredness that threatened to sweep over her in a great wave, she glanced about for any clue as to her scandalous adventure and, seeing none, she just managed to dive under the chilly covers before she tumbled into a deep sleep. At first she must have slept heavily, but in time her dreams were so haunted by nightmares that she was glad to be jolted out of them by a concerned maidservant as the stable clock struck eleven. Dreams where moments of indescribable joy were interspersed with abject terror; as corpses walked and unnamed horrors grasped at Sir Adam

Langthorne's muscular limbs from the grave, pulling him beyond her help for ever, were certainly best forgotten in the bright light of a new day, she decided with a reminiscent shudder.

'I thought you might like some tea, my lady,' the little maid offered timidly, looking as if she quite expected the sky to fall on her after such a failure to be up with the lark on her younger mistress's part.

'Oh, indeed I should, Jenny, thank you,' she gasped, as she tried hard to pretend she was her usual calm self. Grasping the cup with both hands to warm them, she took a deep breath and decided if that was sleeping late, she had already had quite enough of it to last her several months, thank you very much. It had all been nonsense, of course, and if there was one man she had ever encountered perfectly capable of fighting his own battles it was Sir Adam.

'Only her other ladyship keeps asking for you, my lady.'

'Oh, confound it—does she, indeed?' she replied unwarily, and the girl's eyes widened, as if she was waiting for a thunderbolt to strike Serena down for such language. 'Anyway my headache has quite gone now,' she improvised, knowing she had to find some rational explanation for oversleeping so disgracefully, 'and I really mustn't lie here luxuriating any longer. So, bring me some hot water and something I can eat quickly, would you, Jenny? I must be up and doing as soon as I can now, before her ladyship takes me to task for becoming a disgraceful slug-a-bed.'

It turned out that her ladyship was tired and a little fretful after the sedate dissipation of an evening at Windham Hall *en famille,* and remained so for several days afterwards, as if she somehow sensed some difference about her daughter-in-law. One that had nothing at all to do with the Cambray family and was therefore dangerous and to be deeply deplored.

Afraid she might be right, Serena fervently tried to forget that ridiculously brief kiss in the darkness of Thornfield churchyard and its disturbing after-effect on her misguided senses. Only a besotted idiot would dwell on such a fleeting and furious caress from a rake who had probably forgotten it the instant he turned his back on her and stormed away. Not that she had any sound evidence that Sir Adam Langthorne was a rake of course, except for his behaviour that night—and surely a rake would have lingered over his pleasures a little more appreciatively? Instead he had flung away from her as if she had some deadly contagion, and maybe that was why her wretched thoughts insisted on wistfully lingering on the memory? She was suffering from pique that he could so swiftly dismiss her from his thoughts, she assured herself, and tried to concentrate on the household accounts.

And suffering anxiety, of course—for how could she not brood on the events of that night and worry about the unfortunate stranger and his rescuers, all housed so close and yet so ludicrously distanced from her by custom and propriety? The poor man could be dead of his ordeal, for all she knew, or discovered by the man's attackers and Sir Adam and his household under siege from unscrupulous villains capable of the ultimate brutality. Realising how ridiculous such wild imaginings were, Serena tried hard to ignore them in the cause of common sense. They weren't living in the Dark Ages, and it was highly unlikely that anyone would dare to threaten so powerful a gentleman as Sir Adam Langthorne in his own home. Even less likely that such a sensational attack would pass unreported and unremarked by their neighbours.

No, she told herself, absently biting the end of her quill as she fought an awful feeling of hollow panic at the pit of her stomach, while her imagination threatened to fly all over the place, all was still well at Marclecombe. So far the gossips were just mincing the small, everyday scandals of country life as finely as they could for want of better fodder. A brief knock at the door interrupted her thought and heralded the overworked Jenny, with a message from the Dowager.

'Her ladyship says to come to the parlour when you're properly dressed, Lady Serena. There's visitors come,' she informed her breathlessly, before dashing out again.

Left with no idea who those visitors might be, Serena tried hard to ignore the pit-pat of her increased heartbeat as she contemplated meeting Sir Adam for the first time since that disturbing, distracting kiss had changed everything between them. It took all her will-power not to array herself in her best morning gown and fuss over her hair, so she could look her best while she was rigidly polite to him. She soon gave up on trying to appear the very correct and superbly attired young countess she had become under George's stern eye. If Sir Adam didn't like her in her practical dark gown, and the lawn cap covering her ridiculous hair, maybe he would turn his attention to one of the ridiculously susceptible younger ladies the district abounded in and relieve her of a dilemma.

The shaft of instant jealousy that knifed through her at the very thought was, she decided, understandable. Even if she had always considered her looks a mixed blessing, it wasn't easy to be seen as a doddering antidote by the younger generation—although where that put Sir Adam, at five years her senior, heaven only knew!

Chapter Eight

'How delightful to see you looking so well, dear Lady Serena,' the vicar's wife greeted her with an interested gleam in her eye.

'Yes, indeed, most delightful,' echoed Miss Pringle, her devoted lieutenant.

Refusing to meet either Sir Adam's or Rachel's amused eyes, Serena returned their greeting with regal dignity—for there was no point in being a countess if you couldn't trade on it now and again.

'Very delightful indeed, dear lady,' the wretched man informed her outrageously, and kissed her hand, provoking a delighted nudge from Miss Pringle to her bosom bow, who nearly strained her neck to catch a glimpse of Serena's face. Luckily that was impossible, without actually getting to her feet and staring in an ill-bred fashion she would consider most undignified.

'Good day, Sir Adam,' Serena greeted him repressively, and wished she could box his ears instead of slanting the impossible man a militant look that just made him smile as if she had greeted him effusively. 'What a pleasant surprise to see you all,' she added blandly, and smiled at the ladies as if she had no idea they were all speculating furiously about herself and Sir Adam.

It was a barefaced lie. She was anxious enough to discover the fate of the gentleman they rescued the other night, but had no wish whatsoever to cause endless speculation over the teacups of the Windham villages. Thanks to Sir Adam, that was now inevitable. She felt more like meeting him for pistols at dawn than for the trysts the ladies would now be eagerly inventing in their fertile minds. Suddenly she was in danger of grinning back at him with that ludicrous thought on her mind, until she met Miss Pringle's avid gaze and only just managed to greet it with the required mix of puzzlement and surprise in her eyes.

'Shall I ring for tea?' Serena offered brightly, hoping the prospect would send Sir Adam off to plague some other unfortunate with his ill-timed sense of the ridiculous.

'Her ladyship has already ordered it, along with something more substantial to help me keep body and soul together. Her ladyship always being infinitely kinder to me than her daughter-in-law,' he parried, with a charming smile that nearly had Miss Pringle swooning into her smelling salts and even led the usually sensible Dowager to simper a little.

He was a reprehensible rogue, Serena thought, torn between disgust at the ease with which he charmed any female he chose to bend to his iron will and a renegade urge to laugh along with him at a talent he wore so lightly. If he had been a little more in thrall to himself it would have made him so much less dangerous, she decided with a quick frown, then made herself discuss flower rotas and church sales with the ladies in revenge on him for failing to be a light-minded flirt.

When the refreshments were ushered in by the rather harassed-looking butler, Rachel managed to move over to sit by her friend under cover of all the fuss of passing cups and ratafia biscuits.

'He always was the most dreadful tease,' her friend murmured as she took Miss Pringle's tea from Serena and passed it to that lady, with an innocent smile that almost rivalled her brother's for bland charm.

'So I should imagine,' Serena whispered back as she bent over another teacup to pour Rachel herself some of the fragrant China tea.

Not for the world would she have either Langthorne know that she had dreamt of Sir Adam every night since their rackety adventure under the stars. Particularly considering the very disturbing farewell he had forced on her. Yes, that chimed much better with her hope that he was just a rake in search of light diversion until he was back amidst the sophisticated delights of the capital. She slanted him a sidelong glance in the hope that might indeed be all he was, and hoped the vicar's wife was too absorbed in her soliloquy on the impossibility of retaining good servants to note it. Unfortunately Sir Adam was not similarly enthralled, and she saw his firm mouth lift in a wicked smile. Both challenge and mischief flashed in the brief glance he sent her before carrying on with the impressive feat of seeming to listen attentively to every word that was said, while probably attending with less than a quarter of his acute mind to the general conversation.

Alerted to the truth of the matter by that quick look of complicity, Serena thought there was a danger he might know what she was thinking before she had time to consider it herself. Torn between horror at the idea that he could plumb her deepest preoccupations, and exasperation with such acute perceptions put to such use, she fought to stop her own attention wandering from the trials of life at the vicarage.

'Oh, is this not of all things delightful?' Miss Pringle exclaimed archly at last. 'My late father could never abide what he called our "women's nonsense", but here you are listening so attentively to our little concerns, and you such a hero as well, Sir Adam.'

He had the grace to blush just a little under such undeserved praise, and Serena was torn between gloating over his discomfiture at being stigmatised a hero and pity for Miss Pringle for enduring so many years under the thumb of such an unsympathetic parent. She supposed she might turn to gossip and flower arranging herself if she had been forced to put up with forty years of pandering to such a curmudgeonly old misogynist as the late Mr Pringle must have been.

'Delightful, indeed. But I am hardly a hero, Miss Pringle. Just another old soldier who managed to do his duty without falling flat on his face,' Sir Adam rallied enough to reply smoothly, then gave Miss Pringle the full benefit of a charming smile.

The little lady flushed and looked rather ruffled and pleased with life, and Serena suddenly glimpsed the rather pretty and eager young girl she must have been, before disappointment and the late Mr Pringle took a toll on her looks and her available choices. Feeling more warmly towards Sir Adam than she had since she entered the room and found him in such an infuriating mood, she hastily returned to her teacups and finally poured a cup for herself as the conversation continued.

George would never have endured Miss Pringle's amiable fluttering with such good will, and suddenly the possibility that her late husband had been the exact opposite of Sir Adam Langthorne occurred to her and refused to go away. It was just as well she was resolved never to remarry, she decided hastily, even if the wretched man had the least intention of making her an honourable proposal—which she doubted more than ever. Why would such a man even consider settling for a faded and disillusioned widow when he could pick and choose from among the most sparkling debutantes the ton had to offer? No question that with his wealth and charm and lineage he could look as high as he cared for a bride. And then there were his looks, she added with an inward sigh. Those alone would guarantee him the attention of any young lady anxiously casting about her for a husband unlikely to bore her to flinders. In their shoes she would have been about as resistant to his manly attractions as rapidly melting butter left in the sun, she concluded bitterly, and frowned down at her teacup as if she had found a caterpillar at the bottom of it at the very least.

'A penny for them,' Rachel murmured, with an amused smile that told Serena too much of her friend's thoughts about her preoccupation.

'You know very well who and what I'm concerned over,' she returned crossly, and then managed to smile enquiringly as the Dowager appealed to her for the name of some remote relative by marriage, whom she couldn't recall ever having heard of just at the moment. Having finally understood the question and supplied the name, she returned her attention to her friend.

'All's well,' Rachel told her uninformatively.

Serena turned an interrogating look on her friend, and belatedly noted something different about her. Rachel's defences against a prying world had become unconscious over the last few years, as she'd sought to put off pity or curiosity for the tragic loss of her fiancé. Serena could quite understand her reluctance to parade her emotions to the world, but was still relieved to see that faint air of defiance gone and a new vitality set in its place. In fact Rachel looked as Serena hadn't seen her appear for far too long. There was an indefinable air of possibilities about her—a sense that four and twenty was the perfect age to reassess the chances life had to offer a lady of character and independent means. Serena had liked the mysterious stranger from the first, but now she could have kissed him for giving her friend's thoughts a new and very welcome turn, even if she wasn't yet aware of it herself.

'He's stubborn as a field full of donkeys,' Rachel added darkly and Serena only just managed not to laugh out loud, for if ever there was a fine example of pot calling kettle black that was it.

'And you're not, I suppose?' she asked.

'I'm a perfectly sensible human being—unlike some I could mention,' Rachel told her indignantly.

Before Serena could reply a fluster of movement and the sound of Amelia's rather high-pitched voice came from the hall. The Dowager and Serena exchanged resigned, apprehensive glances, and wondered what the Countess in possession wanted with them this time. Now she was in an interesting condition once more, Amelia was inclined to impose on the goodwill of her relations quite shockingly at times, knowing full well that they cared too much about the welfare of her coming child to upset its mama.

This time Amelia obviously had something more in her

mind than an abiding belief that she was somehow hard done by, in a world where one of her predecessors had had a reputation for determined common sense and earnest good works, and the other had been a beauty in a style she could never even hope to rival. Despite all Serena's attempts not to upstage her successor in any aspect of her new life, Amelia stubbornly persisted in the notion that she was forever being weighed in the balance and found wanting, but just now she was too eager for an audience to trumpet her own superiority for once.

'The most dreadful news!' she proclaimed eagerly as soon as she had been persuaded to sit and the butler had been dispatched for more tea.

'Not Henry?' the Dowager immediately demanded, rather painfully, and Serena could have shaken Amelia for her penchant for the dramatic when the Dowager had already lost one son in the most unexpected way and dreaded losing her remaining one.

'Of course not. Hal is perfectly well, apart from being worried half to death by what has happened,' Amelia replied impatiently, and if there had ever been the slightest risk of Mrs Brakespeare and Miss Pringle leaving after the accustomed twenty minutes it subsided in the face of such thrills as her ladyship was hinting at so broadly.

'Whatever can it be, Lady Summerton?' the vicar's wife demanded breathlessly, her second in command obviously being too overwhelmed by wild speculation to even give voice to it.

'Yes, pray do tell us what has occurred, my dear,' the Dowager added, with rather more dignity and a little colour back in her cheeks, much to Serena's relief, even if Amelia was too big with news to notice such trivial details.

'The most shocking thing!' she declaimed in a voice Mrs Siddons would probably have been proud of.

'Yes, I believe we had all gathered that,' Serena couldn't help saying rather sharply. 'Whatever can be so urgent that it has brought you here so hastily and in such a state of agitation, Amelia?' she managed to add a little more tactfully. After all they would get to the heart of the matter more quickly if she pandered to her sister-in-law's sense of the dramatic, rather than telling her to take a deep breath and gather what wits the good Lord had given her, as Serena was so tempted to do.

'I should think I am agitated, and it can do me no good in the circumstances,' came the coy reply.

Serena repressed a most unworthy desire to either slap her sister-in-law, or shake her briskly until her teeth rattled in her silly skull.

'You show yourself to be a woman of character to hurry here in such a case, your ladyship,' Sir Adam put in solemnly, before Serena could take more drastic measures, and he sent her a stern look as if he could read her mind and had every right to override her impatience.

'I know my duty,' Amelia said stalwartly, and Serena had the distinct impression that Mrs Brakespeare might shake Amelia herself if her story was delayed much longer.

'Very laudable,' Sir Adam managed to reply encouragingly, and at last Amelia took a deep breath and launched her bombshell.

'Three break-ins!' she told them with a sharp nod, as if to pre-empt any skepticism. 'Henry has been so busy dealing with it all that he quite failed to tell me about it until just now,' she said, and none of them doubted her freely expressed displeasure at such tardiness and most quietly sympathised with the headache he was probably developing as a result.

'Three?' Serena echoed hollowly. 'Where did they take place?'

'Pullborough House, Red Bridge Farm and the Willows, of all places.' Amelia sounded almost insulted that such humdrum places had been broken into and the splendours of Windham Place ignored.

'But they are all churchwardens to my husband!' Mrs Brakespeare protested shrilly, and with the sound of rising panic in her own voice that the felons had struck so close to home. 'Why was he not informed straight away?'

'Henry would have been off to consult him before he'd even thought to tell his wife what had occurred if I had not heard the sound of a disturbance and discovered what was afoot,' Amelia informed them, almost forgetting to be overcome in her indignation. 'You may be very sure that I informed him his first duty was to his family, and that in his absence I would inform you of such dreadful deeds.'

'I expect he thought it best to shield you from such a nasty shock, my dear,' the Dowager managed to say soothingly, and cast Serena a pleading look.

'Indeed, we all know how delicate your nerves can be at present, and I'm quite sure Henry doesn't want you to be agitated in any way, Amelia,' she managed, rather half-heartedly.

In truth Serena was fully occupied with the frantic thoughts only Sir Adam and Rachel could share. Three churchwardens from the parishes of Nether Windham, Marclecombe and Thornfield had been burgled, which left only Sir Adam Langthorne to complete the set. Their rescue must have been discovered, and it must be quite obvious to the poor man's captors that it could only have been carried out by someone with access to the church keys or a herd of obliging elephants at their disposal—for she did not think anything less would get them into the Canderton vault. As his kidnappers could hardly march up to the front door of Marclecombe and demand their captive back, only stealth would get them anywhere, and she would be a fool to question their ruthlessness. After seeing the state the unfortunate man had been left in, she doubted they would stop at anything to gain their own ends, considering what they had already done. Even the vicar might have been in danger, except Wharton knew perfectly well he was as vague as he was good, and would probably not notice if the Candertons opened their own vault and walked about the churchyard in broad daylight. One reason it had been such a good hiding place for the stranger in the first place, she realized, and she fought back a shudder at such a macabre scenario.

Under cover of Amelia staging an artistic attack of the vapours, Serena let her glance meet Sir Adam's for a long moment and saw all she dreaded mirrored in his gold-shot brown eyes for once. Robbed of his usual teasing humour, they seemed more acutely alive and compelling than ever, and she fought a ridiculous urge to cross the room and seek refuge in his undoubted strength. Of course his touch couldn't keep the wicked world at bay, and not even a former soldier could save Marclecombe from a furtive visitation sooner or later. Suddenly she saw a spark of something challenging and infinitely masculine in his steady gaze, and instinctively knew he agreed and was actually looking forward to it. Renouncing all desire to go to him, she sent him a fiery look and turned back to heroine of the moment.

Regretfully abandoning the idea of throwing a pitcher of water over Amelia, Serena made herself admire her well-judged moans of recovering consciousness and rubbed her hands as if she believed in her faint as any dutiful relation should. Unless she was very much mistaken, Rachel was as eager for a confrontation with the ruthless villain behind the whole business as her reckless brother. Never had she admired their headlong courage less, Serena concluded, with a straight look for her friend that should have told her she knew exactly what she had in mind and thought her utterly misguided.

'We must leave you to tend Lady Summerton.' Sir Adam interrupted the scene smoothly—and how could she argue, kneeling by Amelia's side and seconding her very credible imitation of a delicate lady recovering from her fraught nerves as she was?

'How very thoughtful of you both,' she replied, with a touch of irony that made the Dowager slant her a thoughtful look. 'And of course you must have concerns of your own to deal with, Sir Adam,' she added, and could practically feel her mother-in-law speculating about the unspoken challenge behind her words from across the room.

'One does one's poor best,' he returned, with an outrageous smile and an easy bow, before he bade them all farewell and ushered his sister from the room with a final exhortation that none of "you dear ladies" should worry, and he would send the vicarage carriage over to fetch Mrs Brakespeare and Miss Pringle, as no lady should go abroad unaccompanied at such perilous times.

Swallowing a very pithy retort, Serena smiled weakly and stubbornly followed the Langthornes from the room. She wasn't finished with them or their unexpected guest by a country mile. When Sir Adam's curricle had been sent for, she pulled her shawl about her shoulders and insisted on waiting until it was brought round, like an ambitious hostess unwilling to part with a prime social catch.

'Well?' she demanded of Sir Adam, as Rachel took one look at her friend's resolute face and wandered off to study the hyacinths blooming at the base of the mellow south wall of the Dower House. Not appreciating her supposed tact, Serena glared at her friend before turning a steely gaze on Sir Adam. 'Am I to hear anything about what has or has not happened these last few days, or must I break into Marclecombe to find out what's afoot there myself?'

'I shouldn't do that. I should never forgive myself if I shot you by accident, and it would be devilish inconvenient for Rachel to have more than one patient to save at a time,' he drawled provokingly, and she was hard pushed not to scowl at him furiously and storm off forthwith.

Which, she decided, was probably just what he intended. He would use any means at his disposal in order to divert her from the mystery man he was sheltering under his roof. 'You would have to hit me first—and you still haven't told me anything, Sir Adam.'

'No, I haven't, have I? What a looby I am, to be sure.'

'I have a great many annoying male relatives, sir, and they hardened me against pretend obtuseness many years ago. So you won't put me off the scent as easily as that.'

'Then I shall just have to try harder,' he replied with an unrepentant grin, and Serena found herself actually stamping her foot in displeasure, despite all those irritating masculine cousins teaching her that most males would only see that as an irresistible invitation to taunt her even further. 'I believe I warned you about your fate if you looked down your nose at me like that the other day,' he added helpfully, and this time she gritted her teeth to force back the reaction he was determined to invoke.

'And I believe I told you that my nose, like the rest of me, is nothing to do with you whatsoever,' she said evenly, and challenged him with a straight stare he only returned with a look of limpid innocence.

'Yet that's not quite the impression you gave me later that night,' he told her unforgivably, and she wondered if it was safe to box his ears on her mother-in-law's carriage sweep after all.

'I had more pressing problems to consider at the time,' she told him regally, just managing to convince herself there was no rightful venue for that, or his likely reaction to her efforts to make him take this business seriously.

'I was too enchanted to even think what day it was,' he claimed outrageously, and, quite wrong-footed all of a sudden, she floundered like a beached salmon at the suddenly blazing heat in his gaze. 'I should give it up, Lady Serena. You don't have it in you to be a formidable *grande dame,* however elevated your birth and connections might be,' he added, with a rueful smile that told her he understood her confusion too well for comfort.

She eyed him sceptically and decided he was succeeding in his quest to confuse and deflect her too well. She was busy framing a question he couldn't slide round when she was interrupted by the sound of hooves and wheels on gravel as his curricle and pair at last rounded the sweep from the stableyard.

'Saved by your groom,' Sir Adam said lightly. 'Now you will have to join us after church on Sunday for the day, your ladyship, or remain forever curious about our mutual friends. My sister's duenna has returned from her inter-minable visit to York at long last. Is that not so, Rachel?' He raised his voice to recall his sister from her botanical studies.

'Is what not so?'

'Oh, dear—after all that expensive education as well,' he teased, and shook his head mournfully. 'I have been telling Lady Serena that Cousin Estelle is home from her latest odyssey, and that she will be correctly chaperoned if she joins us after Matins on Sunday for the day.'

'Well, Cousin Estelle is certainly home, although whether that means much when she has only the vaguest interest in anything outside the cover of a book I can hardly say, Serena dear. But you are very welcome to her profound uninterest.'

'Sometimes I think her lack of interest in the everyday world the only reason you can tolerate any female lending you countenance, sister dear,' Sir Adam observed, with an edge of steel in his deep voice that made both of them look at him twice.

Serena realised he was deadly serious in his quest to give his sister another chance at marriage, whether Rachel liked it or not, and was not quite sure if she should applaud or abhor his determination.

'Sorry about the delay, Sir Adam,' Toby interrupted cheerfully, before either lady could summon a suitably crushing reply.

'Think nothing of it. I should have brought one of our own grooms to attend to my horses rather than trouble her ladyship,' Sir Adam replied easily, and in front of Toby Rachel held her peace until brother and sister were safely ensconced in the curricle and Serena's groom had run back to his duties.

'Say you'll come, Serena?' her friend pleaded as Sir Adam gathered the reins and prepared to move off. 'I should love to have some agreeable company for the day. At least then I shall be excused the exclusive attention of a domestic tyrant of the worst kind.'

'Yes, do grant us your company to save us quarrelling disgracefully for at least one afternoon, Lady Summerton,' her unscrupulous brother said, with another one of those laughing, intimate looks in her direction that Serena knew she ought to deplore.

Deciding that to refuse would be cutting off her nose to spite her face, Serena tried to glare back at him and failed dismally. 'I certainly cannot undertake to achieve that, Sir Adam, but I should be very glad to spend the day at Marclecombe nevertheless.'

'Excellent. Then we will extract our cousin from the library for the occasion and dust her off,' he replied outrageously, and left her with the echo of his cheerful farewell and Rachel's splutter of suppressed mirth in her ears.

Torn between exasperation and laughter, she turned round and saw that the Dowager was beckoning her urgently.

'Pray help me take Amelia back to the Place, Serena dear. I fear she will embark on a tour of the neighbours with her news if we don't go with her, and it really can't be good for the baby for her to upset herself so.'

Cursing her sister-in-law for her total lack of consideration for anyone but herself and her preoccupations, Serena gave up the nagging temptation to order Donna to be saddled and ride after the Langthornes to demand an account of their unexpected guest and anything else Sir Adam was withholding from her. Just as well if he *was* keeping at least part of his thoughts from her, if the glow of amusement and something much warmer and more dangerous in his eyes as he bade her that impudent farewell were anything to go by.

'Of course. And I dare say you will feel better after you have consulted Henry about these burglaries,' she agreed in the face of the Dowager's concern. After all she had no idea that Windham Place was probably the last house in the area the villains would concern themselves with.

Chapter Nine

'And all these break-ins occurred on the same night, brother dear,' Rachel observed thoughtfully to her brother, once his curricle had pulled out of the Dower House drive and there was no danger of being overheard. 'That seems most singular, does it not? Considering that we have had no such disturbances for years and then three in one go.'

'Yes, indeed,' Adam replied, calmly enough.

Eyeing him without much favour, Rachel considered those burglaries for another few moments. 'When you think that they come in the wake of such an outrage as well,' she added quizzically.

'Indeed. One might almost think they were connected.'

'Hah! So you think our Mr Invisible's escape is what's really stirring up the neighbourhood too,' Rachel observed, as soon as her brother had turned the curricle out of the drive and set the greys into a smart trot.

'And whatever has the poor man done to earn your disfavour this time?' Adam asked, with all the attention he could spare from his horses and his thoughts. Conscious that he owed his sister more, he did his best to forget his preoccupation and concentrate harder on what she *wasn't* saying about their enforced visitor.

'Oh, nothing out of the ordinary,' she said airily. 'But I'm more convinced than ever that he knows perfectly well who he is, despite his disclaimers, and that he's quite aware of the identity of his enemy into the bargain.'

'Maybe you're right. But he could be protecting someone else by his silence.'

'Surely not the wretch who left him in that tomb to die?' Rachel asked incredulously.

'That would rather depend on their identity, don't you think?'

'No. Whoever it was, they richly deserve to hang.'

'Even if it were someone very close to him indeed?'

'Even then,' she insisted implacably.

'Then maybe you have never truly been in love after all, Rachel,' Adam replied very quietly, and felt his sister's intent scrutiny on his face.

Inclined to fire up at such an accusation, when she had thought herself ready to die in his stead when Tom Hollard was killed, Rachel eyed her brother very thoughtfully instead.

'Ah, but my love was a kind and honourable man,' she finally replied, and surprised them both by smiling joyously at the very thought of her lost love, who truly had been too transparently honest to hide anything much from those who loved him. 'I fail to see how a supposedly rational human being could go through such an appalling experience with his feelings towards such an unscrupulous person intact.'

'True, but I doubt it would be easy to see them exposed to public justice and a very unpleasant death. I don't think I could do it to you, even if you did turn out to be a murderous villainess after all.'

'After all what?' she asked indignantly, then took a sidelong look at his grim expression. Her eyes took on a wicked sparkle. 'But we are not speaking of sisters, are we?' Rachel asked, with a smug look Adam tried hard to find amusing.

'Who knows? I make no claim to be privy to your patient's innermost thoughts and feelings. I'm just pointing out possibilities.'

'How could any woman countenance such a scheme? Do you think he could have abused her in some way? Supposing you're right and there is a "she" involved?'

'Do you?'

Rachel sat and thought about that for a while, and seemed to come to a conclusion about their enforced guest that surprised her. It was Adam's turn to hide a smile.

'No,' she said with her attention clearly elsewhere, 'I think he would die rather than hurt anyone he loved.'

'Precisely,' he replied, a little grimly.

'You mean he would...?' Rachel sounded horrified as her voice tailed off, then she remembered her faith in the stranger's integrity and shook her head. 'Surely he wouldn't meekly wait to die or be abused again just for the want of trusting us?'

'No, but I think he will do anything he can to keep the identity of whoever he is protecting from us—at least until he is well enough to arrange matters to his own satisfaction.'

'Then he evidently doesn't trust us,' she said flatly.

'Would you?' he asked with a wry smile. 'We could be in league with his tormentors, for all he knows. In his place, would you confide in us?'

'No, I would keep quiet and recruit my strength,' she finally admitted reluctantly. 'But I should also try and find out all I could about the strangers I had fallen among while I did so.'

'Then I dare say we had best let him find out as much as he can about us. Unless you have some dark secret you would rather hide from the rest of the world, little sister?'

'You know very well that I haven't,' she said, not without regret, and he sympathised—although as her brother he probably should not. After all, Rachel had loved and lost, and that had to bring regrets at opportunities untaken and risks not run. 'Anyway,' she went on, 'the man would be an even bigger idiot than he appears if he failed to plumb yours, considering the ridiculous way you reacted the other night when Serena just smiled at him.'

Rachel cast her brother a sly glance, only to encounter a bland look that made her want to shake him.

'Oh, I don't think that's a secret at all,' he said calmly. 'Except from Lady Serena herself.' And brother and sister fell into a thoughtful silence for the rest of the journey.

Serena spent all afternoon at the Place, and by the end of it remembered very well why she had been so glad to quit it. No Cambray wife had succeeded in making it a comfortable home rather than a rigidly classical mausoleum, and Amelia's addition of excitable wall-coverings and numerous small objects only made her feel dizzy. Excusing herself on the grounds of a headache she hadn't altogether imagined, Serena indulged in the luxury of a bath and supper in her room on the Dowager's orders, and tried to remember the last time she had allowed herself such shameless self-indulgence. Once upon a time she had gone her own way a little too determinedly, but surely that was no reason to wear a hair shirt for the rest of her life? Just because she had made a foolish marriage?

She was damned if she would sit at home twiddling her thumbs just because her brother-in-law Henry said so. Surely she could be in no danger visiting the tenants and pensioners of Windham, as she had always done? It would be far more suspicious if she stopped doing so. As far as the world was aware Countess Serena had no reason to think herself a target, and she could take Toby with her—he would be glad of a change of routine. Somehow visiting the tenants appealed much more strongly than staying in the dower house, pretending to be content. The new possibilities offered by Sir Adam's London scheme seemed rather exciting, and she wondered what had come over her to make her crave change so restlessly. No, she would go out and about as usual. With Toby's stalwart presence at her side it would be seen that she took the presence of felons in the neighbourhood seriously, but had no cause to feel more fearful than anyone else.

As for feeling out of sorts with her current life, that was only to be expected when her relative youth finally reasserted itself, she reassured herself. It had nothing whatsoever to do with Sir Adam Langthorne. Spending weeks in proximity to such a dangerously handsome rake might try her nerves and her resolve to keep him at arm's length, but the idea made her feel abundantly alive—and hadn't she once revelled in sparring with such gentlemen and evading their dishonourable intentions? At first George's young countess hadn't been anything like the pale shadow he'd eventually made her, and, contrarily, he had been rather proud when other men had lusted after his wife but couldn't have her. Before he had decided he didn't much want her himself because she hadn't fulfilled her primary purpose in his life, of course.

She shuddered at the very thought of the travesty their marriage had been before George broke his neck. Maybe one day she would forgive herself for arguing with him until he was on the edge of fury before he rode out that morning.

To distract herself from those unhappy memories she collected Toby, and they set off on foot for Windham Regis—only to find it close to uproar when they got there.

'What's to do?' Toby asked the middle-aged village blacksmith, who was striding towards them with a huge hammer over his shoulder and a very stern expression on his face.

'Footpads,' he explained tersely, and went to join the knot of equally grim-looking men gathering by the village pond.

'Don't mind 'im, your ladyship,' his wife remarked from her shady seat at the side of the forge, and patted the bench encouragingly. 'No fool like an old un, milady,' she observed laconically, as she sucked on the short-stemmed pipe so many of the older women locally found an indispensable accompaniment to a good gossip. Intrigued, Serena sent Toby off to find out whatever he could, then obediently sat on the worn bench to do the same.

'What is going on, Mrs Hexham?' she asked, intrigued by whatever could have fetched the men out of the fields and their workshops when there was so much to be done.

'A break-in at the Home Farm this time, lady, and Farmer Buller wants a search made for any sign of the culprits. If you ask me it's a plain waste of time, as they'll be long gone by now—not that some excitement ain't welcome. You can see that by the way they'm behaving like a pack of dogs at a fair.'

'What was taken this time?' Serena asked, her thoughts

turning to Sir Adam's reluctant guest and the previous burglaries.

'Not much, but Mrs Buller was scared half to death when they heard someone creeping about the house in the middle of the night, poor soul.'

'And who wouldn't be?' Serena said, and shivered at the thought of what, or rather who, the so-called footpads were seeking.

If whoever had committed that vile act against an innocent man was now bold enough to begin searching for his victim so openly, not even mighty Sir Adam Langthorne and his independent sister could be considered entirely safe any more. Should she stay where she was and try to discover some clue to the villains' identities? Or hasten back to the dower house? Serena hastily decided on the former the instant she spotted a familiar broad-shouldered figure ride into the village. She should have known Sir Adam would hear of this business before Henry, who was Buller's landlord and the local justice.

Sitting in the shade with Mrs Hexham as she was, Serena decided she should be more or less invisible to Sir Adam. So why was she having to fight a ridiculous urge to run to him and express her profound relief at seeing him safe and sound, given the hideous spectres being offered up by her over-active imagination? Then, even across such a distance, and even seated in the shadows as she was, Sir Adam raised his hat in her direction and made a slight bow from his saddle. Drat the man. It seemed his sharp eyes always found her.

'Yon's a very fine gentleman,' her companion observed shrewdly.

'Sir Adam Langthorne's service as a soldier must always mark him out as a fine gentleman.'

'Don't hurt as how he's a handsome young devil, though—do it, my lady?'

'I suppose Sir Adam *is* a little out of the common way,' Serena managed, with an indifference she suspected wouldn't fool the shrewd woman.

'Only a little, your ladyship?'

Serena chose not to reply, although she knew her companion was secretly amused as they watched the uncommon Sir Adam Langthorne question the villagers about the events of last night. She managed to divert Mrs Hexham to the safer subject of her vast tribe of relatives, but all the time she was marvelling or condoling over their deeds and misfortunes she was conscious of Sir Adam's presence.

At last the knot of men moved out of sight up the road to Buller's Farm, and she could make her escape without being hauled back and examined on her every move. Part of her might want to spend every moment with him, but she intended to ignore it.

If only Sir Adam were a suitably dishonourable gentleman he might be persuaded to lightly seduce her—even if it would take ingenuity to do it discreetly in the presence of so many eager onlookers. Then at least she could taste paradise in his mighty arms for a few stolen nights. She smiled wryly at her own eagerness to embrace scandal. Unfortunately Sir Adam would never seduce a lady lightly, however shamelessly she wanted him to. She sighed and supposed that if he had been an easy seducer of women she wouldn't like him half so well. Liking was understandable—but loving? That was the most ludicrous of follies, and she refused to risk such utter disillusionment twice.

Snapping her thoughts from such ridiculous ideas, Serena tried hard to concentrate on the present, and decided that one burglary could be put down to a gang of opportunists from the city. Two inside a week argued a more daring purpose, and nobody would blame her if she stayed at home after this latest news. Yet as she and Toby walked home in preoccupied silence her thoughts were on Sir Adam rather than the potential danger she could no longer ignore and still appear a sensible woman.

He was infuriating and stubborn and all too certain of his own omnipotence, but to wish him other than the very masculine man he was seemed unthinkable. One day he would make some lucky girl a very fine husband indeed, if only she wasn't so sweet and biddable that he rapidly became bored with matrimony. She stopped in her tracks as she considered what a truly wonderful marriage Adam Langthorne might have with a woman of spirit and intelligence, then forced herself to walk on as she reminded herself she had no more intention of being that woman than she had of swimming to France.

On that bracing thought, she stalwartly resisted an urge to burst into tears, and stepped out so briskly that even stalwart Toby puffed a little and eventually asked her if they were having a race.

'The Dowager will worry if this news gets home before we do,' she improvised weakly, and from the shrewd look he gave her Toby doubted her altruism as much as she did.

'Not much chance of that,' he muttered under his breath, and Serena slackened her pace just a little and tried to concentrate on the here and now.

The ardent new Serena that Adam Langthorne had coaxed into being with just a fleeting kiss had a habit of taking over whenever her thoughts began to wander. That Serena wondered what it might be like to make love with

such a passionate man, and a shiver of irresistible anticipation shook her as the very idea threatened to render her
heavy-eyed and weak-limbed. Her steps faltered to a stop
again as she recalled a certain hot look in his gold-flecked
eyes, and suddenly she longed to behave very badly indeed
in Sir Adam's strong arms.

'What is it, your ladyship?' Toby's concerned voice
reached through her preoccupation. 'Have you hurt yourself with all that hurrying?'

'No, I was just wool-gathering,' she told him, with a
self-deprecating shrug that conveyed her despair at her
own wandering thoughts better than words.

'I've been doing a fair bit of that just lately an' all,' he
told her with a grin.

'You at least have just cause,' she told him briskly, and
picked up her pace again in the nick of time, as the sound
of a horse's hooves behind her banished any desire to linger
on ridiculous fantasies any longer.

It would never do to let Sir Adam catch her staring into
space like some dreamy-eyed girl. Somehow she knew the
rider's identity without the need for Toby's confirmation,
and the speculative look that accompanied it. She just
hoped Adam had left without letting the men know he was
following her.

Speculation ran like wildfire around the Windham
villages at the best of times, and she had no wish for it to
be noised about that Sir Adam made assignations with
Countess Serena behind her mama-in-law's back. She
wondered what he would say if she offered to become his
mistress and smiled wryly. He would say no, of course, and
haughtily inform her that he was a man of honour, and even
when he wasn't he preferred to make his own indecent pro-

posals, thank you very much. She glanced sideways at him as he reined his horse to her pace and gave Toby a curt nod, before turning his fearsome frown on her. Even after such an unpromising greeting, the wanton houri within her responded eagerly.

'Good morning, Sir Adam,' she made herself greet him blandly, even as her pulse raced and every one of her senses leapt. Stalwartly ignoring them, she strolled on, trying to pretend a cool composure she was far from feeling.

'It might be,' he replied impatiently, 'if you weren't being more idiotic than usual.'

Despite the flaring temper in his eyes, and the hard set of his other features, part of her longed to raise a hand to his face and wipe away the fierce mix of concern and snapping temper there. Stepping onto the broad grass verge to put more distance between them instead, she raised her eyebrows. 'Fortunately for me I can do as I please without reference to you,' she informed him stiffly.

'Not when you are running headlong into danger you can't,' he insisted roughly.

'How can my walking about my brother-in-law's estates be considered dangerous, Sir Adam?'

'No sensible female would ask that when a gang of felons is running loose in the neighbourhood,' he said in a bitter undertone, as if out here in broad daylight he was afraid they might be overheard by more hostile ears than Toby's.

'They won't risk being seen in broad daylight,' she replied lightly, for all she had to fight a sudden feeling of being watched by hard and hostile eyes from the wooded dell they were passing through. Moments before she had been revelling in the sight of primroses and budding bluebells all around her, and now even that small pleasure was denied her because of the stranger's cold-hearted attacker. She stiffened her shoulders and tried to march on regardless, but Adam's hand on her arm stayed her as if she had walked into an invisible wall. Her body reacted to his touch with eager anticipation instead of rigid indignation, and she ordered her inner wanton into an imaginary coal cellar and did her best to slam the door. Then she eyed his gloved hand coldly until he withdrew it as if the contact might burn him.

'Desperate men take desperate actions, my lady,' he told her in a clipped voice. 'You might not be so arrogant if you had seen what I have in Spain. There, women and children are raped, beaten and tortured before they died hideously, and all because they happen to be in the wrong place at the wrong time. So please don't prattle about dangers you know little of.'

The anguish in his deep voice made her ashamed of her own ignorance. 'But surely that is in the midst of a brutal struggle for freedom, Sir Adam?' she objected tentatively, and managed to meet the golden-brown eyes, still haunted by terrible memories. She had to restrain her hand from reaching up to brush his lean cheek and offer consolation.

He watched her in brooding silence for a moment. 'Once a man has breached a certain line in this so-called civilised country of ours, he will hang whatever he does, Lady Summerton,' he told her with a sigh. 'What is one more crime to a desperate villain on the wrong side of it?'

'But what use would I be to a man with another target in mind?' she asked, and almost sympathised with Adam's frustration as she heard him swear under his breath.

She wasn't a fool, but neither was she one of his troopers, bound to obey his orders without question or face stern military discipline. Distracted by that idea, she wondered how he had liked handing out punishment for breaches of discipline. Very ill, she suddenly knew, although he would have done it to ensure future orders were obeyed.

'You would be a hostage to offer in return for their quarry. They must know I am sheltering their man as they have explored all alternatives,' he rasped, as if the conclusion had been reached very much against his will. 'Now they have searched the neighbourhood and found no trace of him, they are sure to concentrate on me and mine.'

'So any lady in the area is in danger of kidnap?' she asked incredulously.

'No,' he informed her, anger and frustration once again flaring in his compelling gaze. 'Only you.'

'Why?'

'Guess,' he rasped, as if she was an idiot.

Blushing furiously, Serena felt her wanton self snap free, defiantly jubilant at the furious admission under that gruff invitation. If he had paid particular attention to the local belles, the feral Serena might well have turned on him like a tigress, furious with her mate for looking in the wrong direction. Quite ridiculous, of course. She had no right to count his smiles or begrudge the warm approval in his remarkable eyes to other women. Which didn't stop her temper rising whenever he turned them elsewhere, she suddenly realised.

'Your reputation will suffer if you take to broadcasting your favours wholesale, Sir Adam,' she managed to reply primly. Just as if she wasn't recalling that hasty encounter in Thornfield churchyard in too much detail, and the chaos his kiss had wrought on her wayward senses.

'Would you be jealous if I did, my lady?' he asked silkily.

'Er, me... No, why should I be?' she gasped, then

blushed and got back on her high horse. 'We mean nothing to each other.'

'If you believe that you're an even bigger idiot than I thought,' he replied, as if he was having the greatest difficulty restraining himself from kissing her once more, despite Toby who was standing twenty yards away, discreetly dreaming of his Susan.

For a long moment Serena met those fascinating golden-brown eyes and silently admitted there could be more between them than was wise, then she looked away and saw her own hands were restlessly fidgeting and giving far too much away. With a stern effort she stilled them, and looked carefully past Adam's left ear, trying hard to pretend his words hadn't affected her.

'I believe we owe it to Rachel to be polite together, Sir Adam.'

'Do we? As I'm not as faint-hearted as you, I hope we'll *never* be merely "polite" to each other.'

'A true gentleman accepts his congé with grace,' she made herself say, in the cool, drawling tone of a sophisticated society beauty—although she couldn't manufacture the requisite titter to go with it.

'Such a paragon might do so if you practised that ridiculous simper more often,' he replied solemnly, as if he was trying not to laugh.

'Then I shall certainly do so,' she told him crossly, and tried to step past him, only to be stopped in her tracks once more by his hold on her upper arm. 'Really Sir Adam, this habit you have of mauling me is preposterous!' she snapped, fervently hoping he had no idea how his touch made her knees wobble so much she was incapable of taking another step if he let her go.

'When you learn some sense, Serena, I'll have no reason to manhandle you,' he snapped back, any hint of humour quite gone.

Tears stung for a ridiculous moment; he wasn't even conscious of using her given name, so why did it sound so right on his lips? 'Then what would you call sensible?' she asked wearily.

'Walking back to the village with me while Toby fetches your carriage, and staying there until he returns with it. At least then I'll know you're not offering my enemy an open invitation to hold you hostage.'

Relieved that he didn't expect her to endure his protective presence at all times, she nodded with reluctant agreement. Something in her rebelled at giving the heartless villain behind all this any right to govern her life, but Adam was right. There was calculated evil behind the stranger's imprisonment and she would hate it to triumph through her.

'You promise?' Adam insisted brusquely, understanding her all too well.

Serena nodded again, and met raw anxiety in his frowning gaze. When it wavered not one jot she reluctantly did as he asked. 'I promise not to go out alone until the villain is caught,' she conceded. 'Although I would add that I am not alone, and Toby is large enough to put off the most determined footpad.'

'Maybe he is, but this is no ordinary rogue on the lookout for mischief,' he informed her, although the tightness around his mouth relaxed. 'At least I have your word on that much,' he said with a sigh, and stood back to give her so much room to avoid him she immediately felt insulted. 'It's best if we're not seen much together until he's brought to justice,' he added, as if he could read her mind and his voice was rough with emotions she refused to fathom.

The instant they stood apart, she felt a curious rapid force echo about her, then a fraction of a second later heard the bark of a shot fired from close range echo in her shocked ears. She stood dazed for the brief moment it took her to realize that yes, a gunshot really had just passed very close to her left ear indeed. It only took that iota of time before Adam threw himself at her and bowled her to the ground with the full force of his powerful body. Winded, and still floundering to understand what had happened, Serena gasped in much needed air as he finally realised how heavily he was lying on her and eased his weight onto his muscular arms. Shock and something less understandable surged through her as the pump of her own blood sounded loud in her ears and she discovered she was shamefully aroused by the feel of him so close they could each feel every breath the other took.

Chapter Ten

The silence was broken only by the rapidly fading sound of Adam's horse galloping back to his stable in panic and the agitated clap-clap of pigeons' wings, Serena stigmatised herself a disgraceful wanton to feel heady aches in places she had never known *could* ache for fulfilment at such a ridiculous time. As her body responded to the overwhelming sense of warm, seductive entanglement with Adam's, she tried to tell herself it was just the after-effects of shock that made her cling to him like a limpet. Her senses were amazed by the intimacy of their contact. Silly senses, she informed them sternly, and finally opened her eyes to look into warm, gold-flared brown ones, full of as many contradictions as she was.

'Be you still alive, my lady?' Toby's painfully anxious voice reached her almost as if it came from another world, and Serena tried to gather the few senses she had left.

'Perfectly, thank you, Toby. Are you?' she replied, with a mighty effort at some sort of normality.

'Aye, ma'am. Though I thought one of us was sure to be dead,' he replied roughly, and Serena closed her ears to

the addition of some succinct swear-words roundly condemning whoever had shot at them, along with several
generations of his forebears.

'Quite,' Adam agreed calmly, once Toby had run out of
breath and words, and then rose from their hiding place as
if gentlemen threw themselves and any available ladies
into ditches on a whim whenever they felt like it.

A wave of fury tore through Serena at his nonchalant
reply—for how could he pretend nothing much had happened when someone had just tried to kill her? And after all
that flattering anxiety over her welfare as well, she fumed.
Then she met his eyes once more and saw her mistake.

Raw fear fought with ferocious rage in his dark eyes, and
she marvelled at his self-control as her own anger gave way
to shocked reaction at last and she stumbled as he helped
her out of their ditch. Reluctantly freeing her hand from his
sure grip, Serena risked a glance down at her dishevelled
person and gave a shaky laugh as she tried to brush the
worst of the mud and dead leaves off her shabby skirts.

'At least nobody could accuse me of being faint-
hearted,' she joked. 'Both of you will bear witness to the
fact that I didn't even whimper, let alone scream.'

'Most admirable,' Adam said, looking as if he would
like to shake her. He doubted her self-control would stand
it, so he barked orders at Toby instead. 'Catch my confounded horse, or borrow another, then ride to Windham
Place and fetch his lordship,' he commanded brusquely.
'Then fetch the Dowager's coach and meet us with it in
Windham Regis, where even her ladyship can hardly get
herself into any more trouble.'

'I didn't make any of it this time,' Serena protested
indignantly.

'Yet somehow it found you so easily,' Adam muttered darkly.

Toby gave him a sympathetic man-to-man grin that made her fume even more, then bade them a cheery farewell and went off to do as he was bid.

'That was most unfair of you, Sir Adam,' Serena protested as soon as Toby was safely out of earshot.

'Yes, wasn't it?' he replied sardonically, then snapped her into his arms and held her to him as if he might never let her go.

'I swear one day you'll be the death of me, Serena Verlaine,' he groaned against her riotously curling blonde hair.

She shuddered in shock at his rather unfortunate choice of words, and wrestled her arms from between their bodies to lock them round his neck as if she never intended letting go. After all, she knew better than most that a man might be full of life and vigour one minute and dead as the nail in a coffin the next, and in the agony of even considering his death she knew Adam meant more to her than George ever had. Guilt threatened, but sheer panic flooded it out, and she wriggled disgracefully closer to Adam's very alive, very vigorous body.

'Don't you dare die,' she railed frantically at him, and raised herself a few crucial inches so she could close his mouth with her own and prevent more heart-stopping declarations like that one.

He groaned and deepened their kiss, before raising his head and muttering a few curses. Shockingly, she merely chuckled at his inventiveness as he abandoned the English language and took to remarkably idiomatic Spanish. Fire and something stronger and deeper was running through her in such a tide of sure heat that her heart was singing when she finally came back to at least some of her senses to take in their surroundings.

Reluctant to acknowledge the violence that had precipitated such an earth-shattering affirmation of life, she loosened her hold a little and allowed him to put himself between her and the rest of the world by pushing her against the nearest broad tree trunk, sheltering her body with his own. Even through a haze of sensuous pleasure she knew he was offering himself as a target to deflect the slightest chance of another bullet finding her.

'How dare you risk so much for me?' she reproached shakily, yet once more melded her wanton mouth against his, as if only such contact could reassure her they were both alive.

'He's long gone now, dearest girl.' He broke their contact long enough to reassure her, then returned to their kiss as if it was crucial to his continuing well-being after all.

Serena didn't have the chance to protest that she didn't feel the least bit girlish, but on the contrary very womanly indeed. His firm mouth gentled on hers as he drank in her over-eager response and soothed it, settled it, before firing her to a new, fiercer conjunction of their senses. She felt her heartbeat slow to a sensual tattoo after the panicked gallop that had been goading it, all the time terrified a second shot might slam into his mighty body. He was quite right, of course. Their enemy was too cowardly to face his own enemies, and would be planning some other nefarious enterprise as he skulked off to whatever hiding place he had slunk out of to remind them of his presence.

Even as Adam held her, protected and secure between him and the smooth beech trunk at her back, his mouth opened on hers and all thought of concealed gunmen and ghastly conspiracies faded away. It was unlike any kiss she had ever experienced even from him; his lips were warm, leisured, and yet so sure and arousing. Her mouth opened of its own accord and she gasped as he sipped at her lips, then nudged them further apart with his tongue and penetrated the softness within. A fleeting memory of George suffocating her with open mouthed, invading kisses flickered then died away as Adam's mouth seduced hers with hot tenderness. His lingering caress was nothing like that choking, alien probing she had so guiltily hated in the teeth of her marital duty—and who would have thought such a truly intimate kiss from Adam Langthorne could be so sweet and deep that her breath stuttered in her lungs so that they threatened to seize up altogether?

She sighed and let instinct dictate her response. Her mouth stirred and demanded under his while her fingers gently explored his features, as they had longed to from the first moment she had set eyes on Captain Sir Adam Langthorne. Oh, this was so far beyond anything she had known that she might have laughed with the bubbling joy rising within her if she'd only had breath to spare. Then, shocking herself with her own daring, she dipped her tongue into his mouth and felt curls of warmth pool at the heart of her as he welcomed it, then tangled his own with hers as if to explore each other and wonder at the richness of it was enough for now. Well, it might be for him, experienced as he obviously was in the finer arts of love, but she wanted more. In fact she wanted to know everything he had to teach her right now.

Bold again, she lifted an unsteady hand and pulled his dark head even closer, sought an even deeper intimacy. He granted it with a groan against her eager lips, plunging his tongue deeper into her heated depths, locking their mouths together as desperately as even this new, wanton Serena could wish.

Then even that was not enough as he let his hands wander in search of further delights and found them. Her breath caught on his as his hand closed on a breast so eager and aroused she felt every nuance of his touch through her pelisse and the cambric morning gown underneath. Indeed, her clothes might just as well have been made of tissue for all the barrier they offered to his fiery touch. She moaned as he rubbed and enjoyed her heated response, before he sought and then found the buttons of her pelisse to part it and settled his arousing, wondering mouth on the nipple that stood proud through her gown and the chemise underneath. Squirming with the intensity of the heat that shot through her as the moist warmth of his mouth settled and surrounded the needy nub through newly damp cotton, she muffled another groan of need against his dusky curls and felt him smile against her. It was such a poignant intimacy that for a moment it transcended the fiercely demanding heat building almost to pain at the crux of her.

'Come back to me,' she murmured, and he came away from his heating, tormenting arousal of her already very aroused body, as if his mouth wanted to be in two places at once if only he could manage such an impossibility.

'Demanding woman,' he chided as he eyed her.

Hot blue eyes met his, and rosy pouting lips parted invitingly. She felt colour tint her cheeks with heat and had never felt more beautiful. 'Discerning woman,' she corrected softly, and licked her lips. 'Although I'll be a demented one if you don't kiss me again very soon.'

'Well, we can't have that. An insane Lady Summerton

would never do when all I must do to prevent it is this,' he murmured against her mouth, and she squirmed against his mighty chest as the echo of his words found a home in hers.

Then he was as hotly demanding, as ruthlessly dominating as she suddenly wanted him to be. The past faded to nothing as Adam branded her with fire and feeling and mutual passion. For life, a tiny voice murmured at the back of her mind; she was his for the rest of her days after this wondrous encounter.

She tried to drown it out by writhing shamelessly, invitingly, against his incredibly aroused body, revelling in the strength of him as he let her feel the full force of that arousal. It was awesome, should probably frighten her into propriety, but she felt only sensual satisfaction as she stretched cat-like against the muscular length of him and savoured the inescapable reality of his physical response to her. The scent of him, the rasping sound of his breathing, the urgency of his touch as he explored her body under the soft cotton, was somehow more seductive than the most finessed undressing would have been.

He brought his hands up to caress the silky curls at her nape. Then he framed her face and gazed hungrily down at her, as if he sought to stamp an image of her as a wanton, wild woman on his memory for ever. Seemingly fascinated, he rubbed a wondering finger along one elegant dark gold brow, delicately feathered it over long lashes, then down one silken cheek to outline her full, very well-kissed mouth as he learned her face by feel as well as sight.

'I know so much more about you than I did this morning, but what goes on in here, my lovely Lady Serena?' he murmured softly as his touch swept past her lips along her chin and settled against the intimate curve at the back of her neck to cradle her head.

'A great deal of nonsense, Sir Adam,' she joked, but the evasion was enough to recall them both to the everyday realities of who they really were and what was afoot.

She gave a muffled squeak of protest against his familiar brown coat as his hand moved to a particular golden curl and he gently pulled her so close that she was in danger of being smothered by the roughly durable wool. He gave her a little space to breathe, and this time looked down at her with an odd mix of fading wonder and frustrated fury in his eyes.

'Look on this, if you still refuse to believe he was serious,' he urged gruffly as he plunged his hand in his pocket and pulled out the rest of that lock of guinea-gold hair for her inspection in a hand that shook for one betraying instant, before he clamped down on such a display of emotion and held it out implacably for her to acknowledge.

Serena let her questing hand meet his among her ridiculous curls and felt the place where that hank had been shorn about six inches shorter than the rest. She looked incredulously at that bright lock for a startled moment, and her eyes met his in shock. There was both pain and anger in his gaze as they contemplated what might have been. One bullet, she reassured herself, and felt her lips move on the words. He could not have been hurt unless there had been two, but he still looked like a man in mortal agony.

'A lucky shot?' she offered tentatively, only to falter into shaken silence at his fury that she would even try to diminish what had just happened to her.

'A fearsomely accurate shot,' he snapped. 'Meant as a warning not to cross him any further. I'd rather he put a bullet in me.'

'No!' she protested frantically, her heart thudding so he must feel it race against his powerful torso. 'Don't say that. I won't have you die.'

Although she had been estranged from George at the end, she had never wanted him dead—was thankful that even in her head she had never once wished it. One moment her husband had been all abundant, impatient life and vigour as she watched him lead off the hunt; an hour later he had returned with a broken neck, already cold and lifeless. She shuddered, but somehow scouted that last image of her husband from her thoughts to reassure herself once again that this man was very much alive. She couldn't pull away from him at that moment if her life depended on it, though, so instead she insinuated herself even closer to his warmth, to make sure none of it was in the slightest risk of draining away.

A shadow of his usual wry smile quirked Adam's firm mouth and she felt a terrible yearning to feel it on hers again, to let fire and passion blot out the newly terrifying world outside the circle of his arms. 'Never?' he asked with an attempt at lightness that warmed and exasperated her all at once. 'I have no yearning for immortality—unless you intend to bestow god-like status on both of us, my lady?'

'Of course I don't,' she informed him crossly, then felt a deep chuckle rumble though the heavily muscled torso she was snuggling into in a wanton fashion for a lady who had just declared so firm a no.

'Just say the word and we'll go in front of the vicar and say our yeas before God,' he teased unforgivably.

'Don't be ridiculous,' she snapped back. Trust a man to lapse into misplaced humour at exactly the wrong moment!

'I have to be,' he informed her huskily. 'It's either that

or ravish you on the spot, and I don't think the rest of the neighbourhood would approve if I did that just now.'

Becoming startlingly aware that a certain part of his anatomy was still giving him good reason to tease her into an unresponsive frame of mind, she was shaken by his ability to hold a part of his mind aloof from the fierce emotions that were still ruling their bodies. Contrarily, she wished him a little less scrupulous as the sneaky idea occurred to her that if he did ravish her in so unconventional a location, at least she would then be obliged to marry him and rescue his shattered reputation.

Amused in her turn by such a scandalous, rakish notion in a formerly proper countess, she smiled, and he quirked a questioning eyebrow at her.

'It would do untold damage to your gentlemanly character if we were to be discovered thus, Sir Adam,' she said demurely.

'I could live with it, minx, but I promise you that I will have you very soon. Furthermore, you'll cry out for my so gentlemanly attentions until you're hoarse, so then we'll do it all again until you can't speak at all. At least that way I can be sure of winning at least one argument with you.'

His intent gaze was a molten golden-brown with passion, and what looked ominously like more lasting feelings. Serena thought he was probably right about their fiery need of each other proving too much to withstand sooner or later, but she would find some way to keep her independence at the same time, thank you very much!

'Too much self-assurance is unbecoming in a gentleman,' she informed him, with a sceptical sniff that turned to an outraged glare when she realised he was only half listening.

'Rescue at last,' he muttered, his hands busily doing up

the buttons he had so hastily undone a few short minutes ago. He even had the effrontery to sound as if whoever was coming so hastily had been inexcusably tardy, instead of far too eager to interrupt them for her obviously depraved taste.

'Indeed,' she observed coolly as she pushed herself away from the tree and brushed herself down, giving him a stern look as he let her go with unflattering alacrity.

'Much can be excused a lady who has just been shot at, thrust unceremoniously into a ditch and almost ravished by her would-be rescuer,' he told her sagely, and she felt a nigh overwhelming urge to box his ears.

Instead she sniffed loudly. 'A true gentleman would not notice a lady's appearance at such a time, and certainly would not comment upon it,' she informed him regally.

'More fool him,' he observed succinctly, and the glint in his eyes informed her he had no intention of pretending today's more glorious revelations had never happened, even if she tried to do so.

By the time Henry and half the inhabitants of Windham were close enough to see them properly, young Lady Summerton and Sir Adam Langthorne were standing several yards apart by the roadside, looking as cool and un-affected by the past half-hour as their rather wild appear-ance would allow. Admittedly, Lady Summerton had grass stains on her walking dress, and a higher colour than might be expected of a lady in such a dire situation, but that might have been caused by ladylike embarrassment at being found in such a predicament. Luckily only Serena knew it was because, try as she might, she couldn't be properly ashamed of herself for hating their intrusion on her shameful interlude in Sir Adam's strong arms.

At first Henry was inclined to dismiss the whole

business as a careless shot by some hunter intent on taking down vermin. 'Pigeon, I expect,' he said sagely. 'Wrong time of year for anything else. Breeding season,' he explained—unnecessarily, as his listeners were all country people and knew very well that even poachers left the game alone while they were raising more to fill the pot.

The throng looked uncertain as they pondered this theory. Perhaps a foolish boy, who aimed at a pigeon and nearly shot a countess instead, might make himself scarce and never breathe a word of such idiotic cowhandedness to a living soul. Their expression said how unlikely that scenario actually was, and Sir Adam considered the men in front of him for a moment, then seemed to come to a decision.

'A private word if you please, Summerton,' he finally said abruptly, and they moved away from the crowd to murmur at each other in what Serena crossly categorised as a manly huddle.

It didn't need the sight of Sir Adam delving in his inside pocket for her curl to tell her he was informing Henry of the attack on her. How he would explain its probable cause she neither knew nor cared. Standing here, trying to look as if she hadn't a care in the world under the interested gaze of half the countryside, she would cheerfully have shot a curl off at least one of the titled gentlemen present herself, if she had only had a Manton available to assure the accuracy she had learnt early from her unconventional sire.

'Glad we came upon you, m'dear,' Henry assured her clumsily when they rejoined the bystanders again, and Serena was rather touched by the shock and pallor evident on his face. 'Amelia and I won't be able to rest content with you and m'mother alone at the Dower House and a parcel of rogues ransacking the countryside. Maltby and young

George Brooks can take turn and turn about with Mama's footman and the butler at guarding the Dower House from now on, and I'll get some new locks fitted as well.'

He sounded so anxious that Serena's tender heart melted, despite her fury at Sir Adam's managing ways. 'They will be quite dreadfully bored, but at least their presence should make your mother feel safe,' she conceded.

She spared a frown for the architect of it all, but wasn't in the least surprised to receive an unrepentant grin in return. Adam looked altogether too satisfied with his scheming, and she flounced towards the coach, as Toby finally drove it down the road, like an offended, if rather unkempt, queen.

If she were an innocent young lady, Serena supposed that she and Sir Adam would have to announce their engagement. As a widow, she was either considered automatically fast, or prudent enough to behave herself in the face of temptation. Too optimistic an expectation, as it happened, she decided, with a reminiscent smile she banished hastily as soon as she realised it was on her lips. She seemed no more able to behave in a suitably ladylike fashion around Sir Adam than walk on water.

Heady thoughts of her recent scandalous encounter with Sir Adam preoccupied her while Toby drove her back to the Dower House, with a guard behind and an outrider at either side, as if she were royalty or a very rich and very nervous merchant, and she marvelled at Adam's excellent staff work even as she tried to swallow her ire at his ridiculous over-protectiveness.

What a fine officer Lord Wellington must miss in him, she decided, and fell into a silly reverie. If only he had met her and begged her to elope with him all those years ago.

Surely her young and silly self would have seen the difference between gold and dross when it was so plainly put in front of her? She liked to think that even then she would have chosen well, and that everything about her life would have been radically different.

As the proud wife of the then Lieutenant Langthorne, she would have followed the drum with a far lighter heart than the one with which she had endured marriage to a man who, as it had turned out, had only wanted her to breed sufficiently noble heirs upon. Something told her Adam would never have treated her with the contempt George had too often displayed once it became clear she would bear him no little viscount, or even the odd noble young lady to fill his echoing nurseries.

All of which was building castles in the air. It had to be when she was chaperoned every moment of the day and quite unable to jump into any more ditches with him.

'We're here, my lady.' Toby opened the door and prompted her, and Serena finally realised she had been sitting in a stationary carriage, staring blankly at nothing.

'Thank you, Toby—as it seems that you have been picked out as my nursemaid for the next few weeks, I shall quite understand if you do not relish the task and would rather avoid it. His lordship values a good horseman, and will take you on in an instant if the idea irks you.'

'Never, my lady,' Toby said reproachfully, 'I'm your personal groom and I'll only leave your service if you come right out and tell me to.'

'I can very easily undertake not to do that, but what if I decide to leave Windham one day? Your Susan might be loath to leave her family.'

'Sometimes family can be a bit too close, like, and Sir

Adam would have my hide if I left you high and dry, my lady—quite right too,' he ended, with a knowing grin she refused to understand.

'Then thank you for your loyalty, Toby, and of course I would rather have you care for Donna than any man in England—and so would she, needless to say,' Serena replied, and added being cocksure to her list of complaints against Sir Adam Langthorne.

If she lived long enough maybe one day she might manage to look back on those hot kisses and caresses of his as a moment of mutual madness. Depressed by the very thought, she turned to greet the rather agitated Dowager, with soothing reassurances as to her welfare and the folly of local boys now trembling in their boots after shooting a lady instead of a rabbit.

Chapter Eleven

'Do you think we should get a landau, Serena? On clement days like today, it would probably do us good to take the air,' the Dowager said wistfully as they pulled up in the wake of the Langthornes' carriage the following Sunday.

Serena sighed with relief that her mama-in-law had at forgotten her anxiety long enough to think about something other than how many villains might be hiding behind each tree they drove past.

'Yes,' Serena agreed, 'if only we had more of them.'

'True. But it does disarrange one's hair so.'

'There is that of course,' Serena agreed absently, her thoughts on her half-promise to accompany Rachel to London. If she went, she would miss her mama-in-law, and even the quiet life they had created together at the Dower House. She hoped her defection would not leave too large a gap in the Dowager's life, but, though it grieved her to admit it, Adam was right. It was high time both she and Rachel broke out of the uneventful routine they had fallen into—whether they wanted to or no.

'Good morning, Lady Summerton—Serena.' A familiar

voice interrupted her guilty thoughts. 'And another lovely one it promises to be, does it not?'

Serena turned to greet her best friend with a smile that was carefully aimed at the Marclecombe party, yet designed so she did not have to meet Adam's disturbing gaze.

'Indeed it does, my dear. But I believe you are intent upon depriving me of my daughter-in-law's company for the rest of the day?' the Dowager asked, with a smile to take the sting out of her words.

'Yes, I have in mind for us to sketch by the lake as it promises to be such a lovely afternoon—if Serena is agreeable, of course.'

'Well, be careful neither of you catch cold,' the Dowager warned, with an anxious glance at Serena's best cambric and her dark blue velvet spencer as if it might not prove covering enough for a healthy young woman on a sunny spring day. 'This breeze is deceptive, despite the sunshine.

'We will look after her, ma'am,' Rachel promised brightly. 'And even if Serena and I prove careless, you can trust my brother to make sure neither of us takes cold.'

'I dare say she'll be safe enough with a former officer overlooking her welfare for the day. That dreadful attack on her was such a shock, although she insists it was a mere accident. I hope *you* will excuse an anxious old woman her fussing, Rachel, even if my daughter-in-law thinks I'm a worrywart,' her ladyship replied ruefully. 'Now, perhaps we had best go in before we make Brakespeare late with his sermon. The man has no sense of passing time once he is in that pulpit, and I don't intend to endure a scorched dinner at my time of life if I can help it.'

As Amelia arrived after the start of the service, and made sure it was held up for her convenience while she settled in the Windham pew, her ladyship's dinner and everyone else's seemed to be in jeopardy for a while. Her sister-in-law's superior smile when she finally took her seat made Serena wonder guiltily if her children would grow up as annoying as their mama, and even the Dowager shook her head sadly over such rag manners.

'Is it to be parasols at dawn, Lady Summerton?' Adam asked lightly as the Marclecombe carriage gathered pace and they left the church and her family behind.

He had taken the seat with his back to the horses, of course, which set him exactly opposite her. Seated thus, she had to meet his eyes when he asked that idle question, or appear as if she was avoiding them, and it would never do for Rachel to get wind of any change in her friend's relations with her brother. Yet after the other day how could she blithely pretend they were polite acquaintances?

'My mama-in-law is an equable soul, when her rheumatics are not plaguing her, and she would hate to fall out with Henry's wife and the mother of her grandchildren,' she replied, glad of any distraction.

'She's more patient than I am, for I shouldn't mind pulling caps with the current Countess in the least,' Rachel said.

'No doubt,' her brother replied, with a quizzical look for his fiery-tempered sister, 'but I would prefer to remain on good terms with my neighbours, sister dear.'

'You know very well I will—if only because Amelia would like nothing better than to provoke a good quarrel and I have no mind to oblige her.'

'You really ought to marry a diplomat, you know,' he suggested solemnly, and Serena managed to turn a chuckle into an unconvincing cough under Rachel's reproachful eye.

'Only if he no longer wanted a career,' she admitted ruefully.

'Perhaps it would be better if you considered a man who didn't need one, then,' he replied, and Serena suddenly realised she was about to take part in a family discussion she would far rather avoid after all.

'It's another lovely day, is it not?' she asked, in a determined effort to do so. But it did her no good.

'What ridiculous plot is he hatching this time, Serena?' Rachel demanded, with a sharp look for her brother and a reproachful one for her friend.

'Ah…well…' Serena managed guiltily.

'Don't drag her ladyship into this, Rachel. It's my plan and I'll take any blame for it as well as any glory,' her brother admitted, with a conscious air of nobility that made Serena long to give him the rough side of her tongue and caused Rachel's gloved hand to momentarily tighten into a fist.

'What plan?' his sister demanded.

'Just that we should spend a few weeks in town,' he replied soothingly.

'Why? Are you trying to get rid of me?'

'Perish the thought.'

'You are, aren't you? And you're intent on helping him, Serena. And I thought you were my friend,' this last was said with such reproach that Serena felt as if she had just been caught kicking puppies, and blushed consciously.

'Firstly, and most importantly, I don't wish to be rid of you—despite your naggy temper and shrewish ways, little sister,' Adam told her, with a grin that at least seemed to disarm her a little.

'Then what on earth *are* you talking about?' Rachel asked stiffly.

'I would just like to see you happy,' he admitted, and Serena silently wondered how even his sister could resist him when he looked at her with such open affection and concern.

'Then stop plotting behind my back with my best friend,' she snapped brusquely.

'I will—if you can come up with one good reason why we should not all enjoy a few weeks meeting old friends and making new ones in the capital,' he replied, reasonably enough.

'Because I'm antiquated and plain and spinsterish,' she said gruffly.

'Not true, and not a good enough reason to stay home even if it were,' he insisted with gentle ruthlessness.

'Besides being ridiculous,' Serena put in impulsively, and immediately wished she hadn't.

'You keep out of this, you traitor,' Rachel said, with enough seriousness behind her words to make Serena's heart ache for a friendship that seemed in danger. After all they had been through to test it, as well.

'I told you to leave Lady Serena out of this particular argument, Rachel. I can assure you that she's every bit as reluctant to agree to my idea as you are yourself. I'm sure I never met such a pair of faint-hearted females as you two are proving to be,' Adam said, with enough exasperation in his deep voice at both of them to convince his sister of Serena's reluctance to plot behind her back.

'Which shows her good sense,' Rachel murmured, with an apologetic glance at Serena. 'Just what idea are you referring to?' she suddenly demanded as his words sank in. 'And why does Serena need to agree to it?'

Now there was eagerness in her voice and a sparkle in her dark eyes that made Serena's heart sink for a very dif-

ferent reason. She could practically see wrong-headed con-
clusions flying through her friend's inventive mind and
stubbornly taking up residence there.

'Because you need a chaperon,' her brother informed
her, before Rachel could put her matchmaking schemes into
words and make all three of them deeply uncomfortable.

'Rubbish—of course I don't. And as I'm not going
anyway, that's an academic argument at the best of times.'

'Not even if Lady Serena agrees to act as your duenna?'

That seemed to give her friend another problem to
chew over, and Serena felt her heart sink as Rachel cast
a significant glance from her brother to herself, as if
wondering whether such a golden opportunity to throw
them together might just be worth making a few sacri-
fices after all.

'Whatever would Cousin Estelle say to such an odd
notion?' was all Rachel actually said, but Serena could feel
her friend's speculative gaze on her person again as she
glanced out at the landscape and tried to pretend she was deaf.

'Thank heaven for that, I should imagine,' Adam replied.

'True, she doesn't relish being dragged out of her library
to lend me respectability at the best of times.'

'Oh, she will have to come too, for Lady Serena needs
a certain amount of chaperonage herself if we are all to
share a roof, but if we whisper the magical name of
Hatchards, or mention a few of her bluestocking friends
often enough, I dare say she'll warm to the idea in time.'

'Just as you hope I shall, if you cozen me with it often
enough,' Rachel told her brother sharply, and Serena tried
not to wince.

'Exactly,' Adam said smugly, and his sister eyed him
militantly.

'One day you'll grow sharp enough to cut yourself,' she informed him sternly. 'Anyway, I have a patient to attend to—one you dragged home yourself, as well you recall,' she ended triumphantly.

'A patient who is daily gathering strength, now you have succeeded in breaking his fever,' he retorted, and gave Serena an indication of how the stranger was without encountering any more suspicious looks from his host if she enquired as to his welfare again.

'Hah! And he's just about as infuriating as you are,' Rachel informed him roundly.

'Surely that's impossible? You have told me at regular enough intervals over the years that I'm the most irritating male you ever had the misfortune to meet.'

'Well, I was wrong. He's stubborn, secretive, manipulative *and* utterly maddening.'

Serena thought he must be good company for Adam then, but once more decided silence was golden.

'He might as well come with us,' he countered imperturbably, and waited to trump any more cards his sister might attempt to play.

'I don't want to go,' she finally admitted flatly.

'You can't mourn Tom Hollard for ever, Rachel,' he said gently. 'He would hate the very idea of you wearing the willow for him for the rest of your life. He loved you far too much for that.'

'Well, I certainly don't want to marry anyone else,' she answered abruptly, but Serena thought she had nearly argued herself to a standstill.

'Spending a few weeks of frivolous pleasure-seeking hardly requires you to do so,' Adam countered reasonably.

'And how do I know you haven't got another ridiculous

plan up your sleeve to throw me at some unfortunate man who will doubtless run in the opposite direction?'

'I consider this mythical man would be very fortunate to wed my sister,' Adam told her seriously, and Serena had to admire his strategy, even if watching it in action made her more wary of him than ever. 'I promise you that I have no suitor in mind primed and ready to carry you off across his saddle-brow, Rachel. I just want you to enjoy a few weeks of aimless pleasure before you decide to join Cousin Estelle in her library and wall out the world with books for the rest of your life.'

'What a dread thought,' Rachel said ruefully, and then remembered her distrust of his motives. 'I dare say if I meet any suitable gentlemen in town you'll throw me at them until they hardly know which way to avoid me best,' she carped, but her resistance was obviously wearing thin.

'More likely I'll spend most of my time trying to prevent them getting their poor hearts broken, you little shrew. But even you must admit you're unlikely to meet anyone you would seriously care to wed if you stay here. Unless you have a mind to nurse Squire Battleby through his latest attack of the gout, or take on Brakespeare's scrawny curate as a tenant for life.'

'What a thought,' Rachel said, with a laugh for the very idea of assisting either limping gentleman down the aisle.

'At least say you'll think about the idea, then?' Adam asked.

'Very well, I will consider it—so long as you promise not to make any more plots behind my back with my best friend.'

'Of course. But I didn't want to raise your hopes without having the least idea if Lady Serena would consider coming with us,' he countered virtuously.

'How very worthy,' Serena said ironically. 'I believe we have arrived,' she added helpfully, as both turned to stare at her.

She indicated the fine prospect of Marclecombe Hall's neo-classical portico before them, and the head footman waiting patiently to hand the ladies down once the carriage door finally opened. The coach had halted while they were in mid-quarrel, and brother and sister shared a look of rueful mischief. What a wicked pair they must have been as children, Serena decided, and was almost sorry they had not entered her and her cousins' orbit early enough for them to have joined forces. The resultant anarchy might have been a little too much for their various guardians, though.

She stepped down from the coach, wondering what manner of boy Adam had been, and in what light he would have regarded a mere female at such a tender age. How she would have loved such a bold, bad son, she admitted dreamily to herself—before the full impact of that fantasy hit her and caused such pain to shaft through her that she actually paled and stumbled on the smooth gravel sweep.

'Whatever is it, Lady Serena?' Adam asked her, with a sharp anxiety in his deep voice that, had he but known it, only added to her distress.

Shaking her dark mood off with a shrug, she managed to meet his acute gaze serenely enough. 'Just a goose walking over my grave,' she said lightly, and smiled a friendly greeting at the Langthornes' butler.

'Hello, Morrow. How do your wife and the new baby go on?' she asked, as if totally unconscious that Adam's brooding gaze was still on her.

'Both are thriving, thank you, my lady,' he returned

with dignified pleasure at being asked, and bowed her into the family sitting room.

'I will leave you to put off your bonnets while I find something to sustain me until dinnertime,' Sir Adam told them.

'How you can be hungry so soon after eating an enormous breakfast I shall never know,' Rachel informed him tartly.

'I'm not ashamed of my manly appetites, sister dear.'

'No, you wouldn't be,' she replied sternly. 'Just be careful you don't end up fat as butter.'

'I will endeavour not to do so,' he replied blandly, and Serena wasn't at all surprised when her friend looked as if she would like to punch him in his non-existent paunch. She would quite like to do so herself on occasion.

'Go and eat something, then, and don't come back until you're bearable again,' his sister told him.

'About a week should serve,' Serena muttered, and Rachel chuckled as she led the way across the sunny room the family favoured over the grand staterooms so lavishly decorated by a former Langthorne with a mania for gold leaf and display.

'Adam is in a particularly organising mood at the moment, and I can't help but wonder why,' Rachel confided thoughtfully.

'I really have no idea,' Serena replied truthfully enough.

'And I don't suppose you have any idea how wearing it can be to be organised for your own good either,' she said exasperatedly.

'Oh, believe me, I have,' Serena replied fervently.

'Yes, of course you have,' Rachel admitted fairly. 'So who better to advise me how to outwit a managing gentleman?'

'Don't look at me. I never succeeded in turning George from any course he was set upon, and it's always harder to avoid being done good to when it's being done with love, I believe.'

'Being "done good to" describes it perfectly. Nothing I say will persuade Adam that I'm perfectly happy to become a doting maiden aunt to his own brood, when they finally come along.'

For some reason her earlier agony threatened to unsteady Serena once more, but she clamped down on it to regard her friend with a quizzical smile. 'You can't blame your brother for wanting to see you with one of your own instead, love. I should like to do so myself one day, if it comes to that, and dear Tom Hollard would never have wanted you to turn your back on a chance at happiness because it couldn't be with him,' she reasoned gently.

'I know,' Rachel admitted with a sigh, 'but I just can't imagine ever loving another man as deeply I did him. Anything else would seem like second-best.'

Knowing exactly how second-best felt, Serena was silenced.

'You two look very solemn,' Adam remarked airily as he strode into the room, full vigour apparently restored.

'Yes. We were planning to enjoy such an elegantly aimless, ladylike sort of a day, brother dear, until you threw that ridiculous scheme of yours into the ring,' Rachel informed him acerbically.

'Then why not carry on as you planned to? Nothing needs to be decided right now and a little idleness will do neither of you any harm.'

'You're up to something, aren't you?' she accused with a very suspicious look.

'Now, why should I be?' Adam said, sounding so wounded even Serena eyed him warily.

'Because you usually are,' his sister replied crossly.

'What a very odd impression you are giving Lady Serena of us both.'

'She's my friend; she should know the truth.'

'Thank you, sister dear. If I ever need a testimonial, pray remind me not to come to you for it,' he replied, with such an infuriatingly superior smile that Serena half wondered if her friend might really hit him this time.

'Oh, I'd give you one of those, all right,' she replied wrathfully instead, and rang for tea for herself and Serena, and to arrange for their sketchbooks to be brought in. 'We might as well leave you to get on with whatever you have planned, brother dear, as it's the only way I'll ever find out what it is.'

'Enjoy your afternoon,' he replied blandly, and left the room with all the honours of that particular battle.

'Exasperating, sly-tongued, managing, dictatorial man,' his loving sister muttered under her breath.

Serena laughed, and Rachel's frown disappeared as she smiled wryly. 'We could always follow him I suppose,' she suggested, half seriously.

'It would probably annoy him, and therefore be highly satisfying, but we wouldn't find out what's going on, for I'd challenge anyone to creep up on your brother without him knowing about it.'

'Then we'll forget him and do just as we planned,' Rachel asserted.

'We will?' Serena queried doubtfully.

'At least until he thinks we've forgotten all about him,' Rachel said resolutely. And as Morrow brought in their, and informed them their drawing boards had been set up in the dell garden as requested, they soon sallied forth to carry out her plan.

Once they were settled in the pretty dell garden, out of earshot of the house, Serena could ask after the stranger's well-being at last.

'Oh, him—he's going on very well,' Rachel replied airily.

'The poor man is finally fully conscious, I hope?'

'When he's not pretending otherwise to avoid inconvenient questions,' Rachel said, frowning at a nearby urn with irritation, as if it was an unworthy substitute for the unfortunate stranger.

'What makes you think he's pretending?'

'Because even *he* couldn't be that infuriatingly stubborn in his sleep.'

'Then he's being a difficult patient?' Serena asked incredulously, remembering the stranger's steady blue gaze and his gallant refusal to give in to the pain of his many injuries.

'Difficult? He's impossible!'

'Gentlemen *always* make the most appalling patients,' Serena soothed, with what she hoped was well-hidden amusement and unabashed curiosity. It seemed to her that Rachel was just a little too fervent in her condemnation for it to quite ring true. 'But has he given you any clue as to why he was thrown into the Canderton crypt like that?'

'Not him! He just pretends he can't remember, or changes the subject and fusses about his injuries whenever I ask him,' Rachel said disgustedly.

'Perhaps he truly has no memory of what happened after that blow on the head?' Serena offered weakly, remembering those steady, pain-filled blue eyes and silently agreeing with her friend that the man knew exactly who he was and always had done.

'He knows what happened to him. He just doesn't choose to trust me with the truth.' Rachel looked more confused and hurt than annoyed, as if the stranger's lack of trust mattered far more to her than she would ever let herself admit.

'Perhaps he thinks it would endanger you?' Serena offered warily.

'Which, if true, would only make me more certain that he's the most stubborn, infuriating and insufferably self-satisfied imbecile whom I ever had the misfortune to lay eyes on,' Rachel insisted.

From that Serena concluded Rachel was enjoying fighting with their mysterious guest far more than she was prepared to acknowledge.

'Has Wharton done anything that might give us a clue who it was who could have employed him?' she asked—partly because worrying at other people's problems was so much easier than brooding about her own, and partly because she truly wanted to know how and why the stranger had ended up in his macabre prison.

'He's done naught but drink himself into a stupor, as usual, and then sleep it off,' Rachel told her, all her indignation suddenly in her patient's cause.

Love, Serena decided with a heartfelt sigh, was unaccountable, and she very much feared Rachel was in danger of falling headlong into it without a clue as to her own fate. 'Then I pity his poor wife,' she said, deciding there was no point warning her friend against that traitor emotion. 'Wharton is so weakened by drink I doubt he can survive much longer.'

'Yet although she might be considered better off without him, she seems to pity him almost as much as she despises him,' Rachel said, as if brooding on the subject of love and marriage rather more than she was prepared to admit—not

that Serena had the least wish to see her wed such a broken
reed and then cling to him for the rest of their lives together,
as Mrs Wharton was doing.

'I expect she remembers the man he once was,' Serena
replied, and they both fell silent as they turned their attention to their drawing, pondering the perversity of the
human heart.

Chapter Twelve

Try as she might, Serena couldn't lose herself in an attempt to capture the moment on paper today. Sunlight and shadows were all one to her she decided with exasperation, as she stared down at the woeful sketch on her drawing board. Deciding there was little point attempting another study of the graceful cedar trees across the dell, or the bluebells that carpeted every available space in this enchanting spot at this time of year, she flicked over to a blank page and let her fingers fly without conscious thought.

Looking down at what they had produced some time later, she sighed deeply and shook her head at her own folly—for on the page in front of her was an altogether too accurate sketch of Sir Adam Langthorne. She had caught his smile, his air of supreme self-confidence, as well as the disturbing warmth that sometimes lit his complex eyes when he looked at her. Anyone who saw it would probably conclude it had been done by someone who knew him a little too well, and felt too much for the subject of her study for her own comfort.

Glad that nobody had, she hastily turned the page and

directed her fingers to produce something less personal and more conducive to her peace of mind. Once or twice she looked up and gazed about her, conscious of the feeling that she was being observed. There was no hint of movement when she did so and nothing to indicate she was under scrutiny either malicious or benign, but she found it impossible to centre herself on her drawing again. Finally she just sat in the dappled shade and let her thoughts drift aimlessly. She was lost in them when she heard the noise of a scuffle, then a rush of running feet and a confusion of hasty shouts as half the male staff of Marclecombe Hall converged on the dell and seemed to surround herself and Rachel in a protective circle that was at the same time reassuring and infuriating.

'For heaven's sake, let me through, Joseph!' Rachel demanded of Adam's personal groom, who stood stolidly in her path, managing to look as if he was quite unable to understand that Miss Langthorne wished to investigate the noises from the terrace personally.

'Whatever are you doing here, Toby?' Serena quizzed her own groom, as he too came dashing into the dell garden and took up position at Joseph's side, in a stern attitude that reminded Serena of a general at the side of his chief of staff in the heat of battle.

'Orders, Lady Serena,' he replied uncomfortably.

'I would know if I had told you to disappoint your affianced wife by following me about like a bloodhound all afternoon instead of keeping her company,' she informed him implacably, and Toby shifted under her stern gaze, but quite failed to move aside to let Rachel through.

Serena heard the sound of a lone horse galloping off, and remembered hearing the same sound after being shot at. She felt a fleeting moment of sympathy for the unfortunate animal, forced as it was to go from nothing to flat-out gallop so frequently for the convenience of its wretched owner. Then the full significance of that sound hit home, and she too became frantic to reach the house.

'Let them by,' Adam's voice ordered from above, and she and Rachel dashed forward to find a very frustrated baronet, Serena's brother-in-law Henry, Earl of Summerton, and Rachel's errant patient gathered on the terrace and glaring frustratedly in the direction from which the last echoes of those hoofbeats were still dying.

'Gone away, by God!' Henry growled, looking decidedly shamefaced.

'He suspected a trap from the off,' Sir Adam informed him shortly.

'Sorry, but I couldn't help sneezing, Langthorne,' Lord Summerton replied, shifting uncomfortably like a raw recruit under the stern eye of his troop sergeant.

'Of course not. But our task will be twice as difficult now,' Adam muttered absently, as if already brooding on his next move against the enemy.

'I know,' Henry acknowledged, with such crestfallen humility that Serena gazed at him in astonishment. 'Made a mull of it,' he admitted to his co-conspirators, but then shrugged back into his more usual role as lord of everything he surveyed—except his stubborn lady. 'Good day to you, Serena, Miss Langthorne. I'm for Windham before Amelia notices I'm gone,' he added, and with a nod and an abrupt farewell to Adam and the supposed invalid, he trudged off towards the stables, after collecting his own head groom from the melee still gathered in the garden below.

'Are we ever to be offered an explanation?' Rachel

demanded with icy dignity as Serena attempted to gather her senses and feel anything but terrified at the risk she was quite certain all three gentlemen had just taken.

'Inside,' Adam replied tersely, and signalled to Joseph to take the stranger's other side so they could assist him into the sitting room, where he subsided gratefully onto the sofa. 'Thank the others and see they're suitably rewarded,' Adam told his groom, then dismissed him with a terse word of thanks, telling him the ladies would be safe enough inside the house so long as they behaved themselves for a change.

Said ladies silently fumed over his arrogance, but Rachel fussed and soothed and scolded her patient while she did so, in a way that reminded Serena irresistibly of an indignant mother hen with one errant chick.

'I take it we are the only ones still ignorant of your identity and the nature of your plight, sir?' Serena asked the stranger, once Rachel was reassured he had done himself no harm by his reckless excursion.

'My apologies, Lady Summerton,' he offered, with a gallant attempt at a seated bow that probably impressed Serena more than it did his furious nurse.

'Thank you. But please will you tell us who you are, before we both expire of curiosity?'

'I'm Newbury,' he admitted, as if it was a sin he was all too conscious of. Obviously in Rachel's eyes he was quite right, for she immediately turned on her heel and stamped to the window, to stare unseeingly out of it as if her life depended on recalling every detail revealed on the other side of the glass.

'As in the Duke of?' Serena demanded clumsily, then blushed under Adam's distinctly unamused scrutiny.

'Afraid so,' the patient confessed ruefully, and Serena

wondered if he was the only one gaining the slightest amusement from this meeting as his smile widened at her lapse of good manners.

'Goodness,' Serena said inadequately, and plumped down on the nearest chair to consider the full ramifications of his announcement.

'That would be the Duke of Newbury who recently announced his engagement to Miss Garew the Incomparable, I take it?' Rachel asked in a cold, stilted voice from her position by the window.

'Indeed it would be, Miss Langthorne. The very same Duke whose sagacious and lovely fiancée even more recently eloped to Gretna with his younger and altogether more personable brother,' the Duke replied, as if telling a quietly amusing tale against himself.

'Good Lord—did she?' Rachel forgot her dignified fury long enough to turn away from her intent study of nature and exclaim incredulously.

'Thank you, Miss Langthorne. You have just soothed my battered pride to no end,' he returned with a self-deprecating smile. Rachel gave an involuntary chuckle—before she remembered how angry she was with him and turned it into a genteel cough and a determined frown.

'Then what on earth were you doing shut up in the Canderton vault in Thornfield churchyard?' she demanded, as if he had done it just to be perverse.

'Ah, now that is the question,' he said, with a thoughtful glance at his host.

'You had best tell them everything, Newbury. Before my sister decides to poison your tonic out of sheer irritation,' Sir Adam replied.

'And have Miss Langthorne give herself the job of

nursing me back to health all over again? I think not,' he replied, and Serena thought the gaze he turned briefly on her friend held more understanding and indeed tenderness than Rachel herself would credit—if only she had let herself meet it. 'I'm not sure either of us would survive the ordeal twice.'

'Then you had best confess all, had you not, your grace?' Serena said, to save Rachel any more teasing when she was evidently prey to very mixed emotions.

'Very well, Lady Summerton. But it is not a particularly edifying tale, I'm afraid.'

'I dare say we will weather it—possibly better than you have yourself, your grace,' she replied with gentle irony.

'You might easily do so, but very little of it covers me in any glory. I suppose it all began when Miss Garew and I grew well enough acquainted to agree that neither of us enjoyed being the catch of the season, so to speak. Please don't take that as an admission of vanity, by the way. A single duke of any age or persuasion is forever considered fair game by ambitious young ladies, and their even more ambitious mamas,' he said, with a self-deprecating smile even Rachel wasn't angry enough to deflect with a frown.

'And Miss Garew, being an incomparable, was automatically pursued by every gentleman with at least some of his right senses intact, I dare say?' Serena prompted shamelessly.

'Every one in full hunting cry,' the Duke agreed with fastidious distaste. 'Corinna is a lovely creature, perhaps all the rarer in being intelligent with it, and she soon decided she had no wish to go to the highest bidder for her hand, as her half-brother and guardian Alfred Garew fully intended. When I discovered her hiding from her more importunate suitors at various social occasions, we sympathised with each other and finally decided that, as we had no strong feelings about the matter either way, we might as well form a protective alliance and marry each other.'

'How very altruistic,' Rachel interrupted him rather sarcastically.

'Yes, wasn't it?' he agreed blandly. 'And she would have made a very fine duchess, I dare swear, except that—luckily for all three of us—she met my scapegrace brother at our betrothal ball rather than upon the occasion of our marriage.'

'In what way could that be considered lucky?' Rachel asked, obviously too intrigued now to hide her fascination with his tale.

'Because I like Corinna, and believe it or not I'm even quite fond of my disreputable brother,' he replied with a reminiscent grin. 'I never had the least faith in love at first encounter until they set eyes on each other that night, and just imagine the lifetime of unhappiness we would all three have suffered if my bride had tumbled head over ears with her new brother-in-law.'

Serena only had to imagine Adam appearing at her own ill-fated nuptials to shudder at the very idea of being wed to one man and longing uselessly for another. Just managing to ignore the implications of that tacit admission, she bent an enquiring look on his grace as they waited for the rest of his tale.

'None of us realised quite how seriously Garew needed to profit from his half-sister's extraordinary looks, and I suspect Corinna still has no idea how fast in the talons of the money-lenders he truly is. Her own portion comes from her mother's family, and he couldn't get his hands on it with various uncles and cousins appointed as her trustees and already suspicious of him. Even if he could have got at it, it would have been a mere drop in the ocean of money he needs to rescue his finances from the ten percents.'

'So what did he do next?' Rachel prompted.

'Garew insisted our betrothal continue. In fact he threatened to make Corinna disappear until all three of us agreed that it would do so. You can imagine how frantic my brother Daniel was when we got wind of the fact that Garew was negotiating with the least scrupulous of her former suitors to sell her to him, on whatever terms he could get, rather than see her wed a younger son with nothing more than his patrimony.'

'The wicked scoundrel,' Rachel exclaimed, too caught up in the story now to do aught but sympathise with the unfortunate Corinna, whatever her feelings toward that lady's former fiancé might or might not be.

'That is the least of the insults I would like to pile on him, believe me, Miss Langthorne,' the Duke agreed grimly. 'In the end Dan and I decided the only thing to do was plot Corinna's escape and a quick flight to the border, where they could wed. Once they had eloped, with the fastest change of horses money could buy, and with me in Gretna to stand as a witness, there seemed nothing her infernal brother could do but accept the inevitable.'

'I sincerely hope he didn't gain a penny-piece from their marriage,' Rachel said indignantly.

'Believe me, I made it very clear to him that he would not when I told him the news of it,' the Duke said, and none of them doubted it from his resolute expression. 'I underestimated the cunning of a cornered rat, however. When he wrote very ungraciously and offered to help release Corinna's dowry in return for part of it and his promise of silence, I lost my temper and went straight round to his lodgings alone to confront him. Which, of course, was exactly what he wanted me to do.'

'I suppose I can understand why he would kidnap you, in the circumstances, but how—and perhaps more importantly why—did you go from there to Herefordshire?' Rachel asked.

'Because he didn't know what else to do with me, I suspect. He had me in his power, but the money lenders had their talons so deep into him that I suspect London was too uncomfortable for him to linger. Thinking to outwit them, and me, he first drugged me and then got me out of the city at night, calling on the help of a man nobody would connect to him as it seems from various things they said to each other that they hadn't met since they were boys.'

'Wharton,' Serena said, thinking back to the conversation she and Sir Adam had heard outside the Duke's grim prison that night in Thornfield churchyard.

'Indeed. But I doubt if Garew realised what a faulty tool his old friend had become when he decided he would make the ideal confederate. He appears to have escaped his creditors only to fall in with a drunken fool, for all the ghastly ingenuity Wharton showed in finding a place to put me where nobody could possibly find me by accident,' his grace said, with a careful blankness of expression that told a great deal about how grim that imprisonment had truly been.

'But why take such a risk? We are a very long way from London, and your death would hardly profit him. I suppose your brother would inherit, and this Garew has hardly given Lord Daniel or his own half-sister any reason to love him, so he would have got nothing out of *them* if you had died,' Rachel observed hotly, to someone she would have them believe she disapproved of, if not actually disliked.

'He could try to blackmail them by implicating them in my death, I suppose, but I don't think he really intended to kill me—or I should surely be well and truly dead by now, as well as prematurely buried.'

'Then what on earth did he want?'

'Money, of course. He intended me to sign a deed of settlement on his sister that would tie up the vast fortune he decided I should bestow on her, and any children she might have, in his favour. In other words he would have everything and she nothing. Needless to say, I refused.'

'Of course,' Adam agreed, as if there had never been the slightest question he could do anything else.

Serena wondered how Corinna would have felt if the Duke had died protecting her from such a man, and decided it might be a fundamental difference between men and women that the former preferred death to dishonour and the latter would take the lives of those they were close to over honour every time.

'From the state you were in the night we discovered you, you must have refused to sign this deed quite often,' she observed, mildly enough.

'Time has little meaning in such a place. I had no idea when it was day or night. But it certainly felt like an eternity,' he replied ruefully.

'What would he have done with you if you had gone on refusing?'

'Killed me and forged my signature, I dare say,' his grace said without noticeable emotion, considering he was describing his own murder.

'He said he needed a body or your heir could not inherit,' Serena recalled, unable to hide her horror as she remembered those cold words and the even colder intent behind them.

'Did he, now? I was wrong about that, then,' the Duke said grimly. 'I suppose he is Dan's brother-in-law, like it or no, and perhaps he thought my little brother would make a more malleable duke. If so, he's sadly mistaken. According to my mother, stubbornness is bred in the bone of the entire Trent family, and will always out at the least convenient moment for anyone who underestimates them.'

'She is obviously a very perspicacious lady. I wish I could meet her,' Rachel muttered darkly, and the Duke laughed.

'Yes, she would like you extremely, Miss Langthorne. Being of a very decided cast of mind herself, she has little tolerance for milksops,' he told her, and grinned as she struggled for adequate words to crush him with.

'I can't see what Mr Garew has to gain by killing you now, your grace,' Serena said in the hope of averting an all out battle. 'Surely he would have done better to cut his losses and leave the country with whatever assets came most easily to hand?'

'He may be a rat, but even I have to admit that he's a tenacious one,' the Duke replied grimly. 'If I talk he will lose everything. But he knows I must be reluctant to do so, considering his relationship to my sister-in-law. I doubt if his hopes of blackmailing Dan and Corinna are quite dead either. He's certainly devious enough to fabricate some sort of case that they kidnapped and murdered me, if he finally manages to lay hands on me and do it. Anyway, I think he's very likely beyond logic now, and dreams only of taking some sort of twisted revenge. There's rumoured to be insanity in his maternal bloodline, and I admit I would never have considered marrying Corinna if she were his full sister. Luckily old Carmichael Garew chose common sense and a healthy fortune over aristocratic breeding when he married for a second time, and Corinna's as sane as you or I.'

'Possibly more so,' Rachel muttered, and the Duke grinned at her, as if reading her darkest thoughts about his own sense, or lack of it.

'Why would he think he has the right to take revenge on any of you, though?' Adam asked soberly. 'Garew is no more entitled to your money than he was to his sister's.'

'Yet such an admission is clearly beyond him,' the Duke admitted wryly.

'Then do you believe he has become unhinged?' Serena asked, with dawning horror that a man obsessed with taking some insane revenge on his imagined enemies might be roaming the countryside, trying to harm all those he considered responsible for robbing him of his prisoner and a fortune he had no right to whatsoever.

'Possibly. Even if he has not, there is a coldness in him that would probably justify murder if it removed an obstacle from his path, and I doubt he would feel a twinge of conscience while doing so. In more violent times such a man would either end up as king or the head of a ruthless criminal gang.'

'Or both,' Adam said cynically.

'Yet Mr Garew hasn't proved a very successful at his crimes thus far,' Rachel objected logically, but Serena could see that to an unstable rogue that might provide all the more reason for retribution.

'A man doesn't need to be particularly clever to be utterly ruthless,' the Duke pointed out.

'So, knowing all that, you still set yourself up as a target and waited for him to either step into your trap or shoot you, your grace?' Rachel countered incredulously.

'Would *you* meekly wait for such a man to impose his will on your life a second time, Miss Langthorne? And please do call me Luke. Considering you saved me from weeks of illness, if not actual death, I think we have gone beyond the formalities, do not you?' he challenged her right back.

'No, be damned if I would,' she fired straight back at him, her reply being to what she evidently considered the important part of his speech, and ignoring the rest by not calling him anything at all.

'Just what I told Langthorne, when he shared your objections,' he said, more in his usual self-contained manner.

'How very odd that you did not choose to share those misgivings with the rest of us, then, Sir Adam,' Serena remarked coldly, ignoring the Duke and Rachel, who were now staring at each other like wary gladiators.

'Not when you consider that you and my sister seemed determined to run your silly heads into whatever danger presents itself,' he replied unrepentantly, and Serena almost took Rachel's course of stalking over to the window and glaring out until she had her temper and her tongue under stern control once more.

Deciding it would give him far too much satisfaction if she betrayed her frustration, she merely gave him an ironic smile and waited for whatever weak excuse he could come up with.

'When he took aim at you the other day, I knew he was taking a warning shot across my bows, so to speak,' Adam finally admitted, very grudgingly. Serena still refused to speak and watched him steadily. 'It must have been obvious by then that I had Newbury in my care, and Garew sought to strike at me in the most potent manner possible. When I had the chance of having you both in a safe place, surrounded by stalwart protectors, how could I leave you or Rachel exposed to danger by letting the man roam the countryside at will?'

'You could have told us the full story and trusted us,' she informed him haughtily, refusing to soften despite the warmth that threatened to overwhelm her when he admitted hurting her would wound him.

'After your escapade that night in Thornfield churchyard, I would have been a complete fool to do that,' he argued implacably.

'Once we came to realise that a man's life was at stake, neither Rachel nor myself would have taken the slightest risk of endangering it further. Unlike yourself, Sir Adam,' she pointed out, with a significant look at Luke, who was now reclining on his sofa in the manner of an approved invalid. Not even his indomitable will could altogether disguise the lingering weakness left by his captivity and the beatings inflicted on him.

'Oh, don't blame my kind host, your ladyship,' he interceded. 'It was my plan to smoke Garew out, and Sir Adam went along with it very reluctantly.'

'I wonder he didn't lock you in your bedchamber. I would have done,' Serena informed him militantly.

'And risk leaving his household open to a nocturnal visit from Garew to smoke *me* out? I wouldn't dream of putting those I love in jeopardy in such a fashion myself, so there was never any risk of your neighbour doing so, Lady Summerton. We had to set a trap to halt Garew's ridiculous quest to profit from his sister's marriage, and this one was worth a try in order to deflect him from doing any more damage to the innocent. Even you must admit that it very nearly worked.'

'I suppose so,' she conceded reluctantly. 'But what do you propose to do now that it has failed?' she asked, intrigued despite her shock that they had taken such a risk.

'Therein lies the question,' Luke said, with a quizzical look at his host.

'Newbury wants me to hire him a fast post chaise and some outriders and send him back to London,' Adam revealed brusquely.

Chapter Thirteen

'Never!' Rachel protested fervently. 'I hope you informed his grace that Langthornes are as stubborn as the Trents ever were?' she demanded of Adam, while aiming a dagger look at her patient.

'Of course—and I warned him to expect the same of any Verlaine he ever came across, in case *you* are about to explode into stiff-necked protest as well, Lady Serena,' he added, with a smile that was half taunting and half tender and threatened to wholly melt Serena's heart.

'I already knew it, Lady Summerton,' Luke assured her, and Serena had no illusion that anything escaped his assessing blue gaze as he took in that intimate look Adam had done very little to hide. 'Your Cousin Helvelin is the most mulish fellow I ever came across.'

'I *knew* I had seen you before!' Serena gasped on a sudden moment of revelation. 'When you were still the Marquis of Ryedale you stayed with my cousin at Heron House once, did you not?'

'You were a very small girl at the time, so little wonder you don't remember me very well,' he said, with the self-deprecating smile that had made Serena like him so well from the first.

'But I do now. You rescued me from a very large cowpat and handed me to my nurse without even holding your nose. It was very gallant of you. Cousin Ian wouldn't have touched me with a long pole.'

'No, I distinctly remember his disgusted expression,' he agreed.

'So do I, now I think about it. And my nurse had just dressed me in my best in honour of a visit to my godmama. I don't suppose I sat down for a week once I was clean, nor saw Godmama for considerably longer.'

'Cosy as these reminiscences are proving, we have more urgent matters to consider,' Adam informed them, rather harshly.

'My apologies,' Luke offered, with another acute, amused glance from his host to Serena.

'Yes,' Rachel put in, with a remarkably similar suspicious glint in her eyes as she watched Serena and Luke reminisce. 'What do you plan to do next, now setting yourself up to be shot at hasn't worked as planned, your grace?'

His grace shrugged, then obviously regretted it as he paled and shifted his injured arm to an easier position. 'I'm at a stand, I fear,' he admitted.

'London,' Adam informed them, rather uninformatively. As they all turned to stare in surprise he deigned to elaborate. 'We need to take the fight to the enemy, and by forcing him to return to the place he least wants to be we will have the advantage from the outset.'

'But you just told Luke that you wouldn't think of sending him there,' Serena objected.

'Not alone, of course. But as we were all planning to

go there shortly ourselves, why should our guest not travel with us?'

'On the principle that Garew might as well have four people to shoot at as just one?' Luke asked irritably.

'No, on the surmise that only desperation will lead him back to London and that once there he won't dare show his face.'

'Which will gain us what, precisely?' Rachel asked impatiently, seeing two of Adam's schemes rolling conveniently into one and not much liking the result, from the look of her expression.

'The advantage—and a chance to choose where, when and how we take a stand against him. Wellington might be a naggy tempered curmudgeon at times, but he's a genius at picking out the best position from which to offer battle, and I did manage to learn the odd thing under his command.'

'Yes, that much is abundantly clear,' Rachel informed him tersely.

'Why not simply have Henry track him down and arrest him?' Serena asked reasonably.

'Because Garew's open disgrace will reflect on Corinna,' the Duke explained patiently, and suddenly Serena saw what looked almost like pain in Rachel's eyes as she swung her gaze from her brother back to her patient.

Could she be right about her friend entertaining warmer feelings than she knew for the Duke of Newbury? And what if Luke was indeed still in thrall to the lovely Corinna, despite all he said to the contrary? What an appalling tangle this promised to be, she decided despairingly, with all the wrong people in love with those who didn't reciprocate. Best if she left love out of the equation for now, and concentrated on Luke's enemies, she decided.

'And what *do* you plan to do when you catch him?' she asked.

'Buy up his debts and then buy him a one-way passage to the Americas. In such a new country he will either thrive or fall to his own level, and at least he can do so there without troubling his sister and my brother.'

'It seems a little inadequate, as revenge goes,' Rachel put in sceptically.

'Yet possibly better for all concerned,' he replied, with an understanding smile that agreed, yes, it was less than Garew deserved, but more than he could ever dare hope for.

'Family,' Rachel stated abruptly.

'Yes, family,' he agreed with a resigned shrug, and winced again.

'You'll have to cure yourself of that habit, Newbury,' Adam informed him with a sympathetic grimace.

'That I will. But as your family is to be involved as well, Langthorne, will you not reconsider your plan?'

'I long ago gave up making decisions on my sister's behalf. And Lady Serena will inform you if you try and gainsay her that she is an independent lady, quite capable of deciding her own course through life,' he said blandly.

Serena felt as if there was a sting in his words only she could fully understand—if she chose to. And she definitely did not.

'Then, speaking for myself, I shall go to London whether you take me with you or no,' Rachel informed both men, with a fierce look that forbade them to even try and leave her behind.

'You have achieved the impossible and persuaded my sister to change her mind once set against something,' Adam informed Luke, and Rachel and Serena exchanged exasperated glances. 'And what about Lady Summerton?' he added, with a direct challenge.

'She will do the same,' Serena replied, steadily enough.

'And since Cousin Estelle will have to come as well, for propriety's sake, we shall doubtless be travelling in easy stages quite suitable for an invalid,' Rachel added. 'Please don't suggest going ahead in my brother's curricle, your grace, or I might lock you in the Canderton crypt myself, until you show signs of developing a few traces of common sense.'

'Then all we have left to do is to plan our escape and a few weeks of pleasant dissipation,' Adam informed them, inexorably shepherding Luke towards his bedchamber. 'We'll leave you to break the glad tidings to Cousin Estelle,' he told Rachel blandly, and exited before she could think of a suitably pithy reply.

'My brother and the Duke of Newbury are each as insufferable as the other,' Rachel told Serena, who heartily agreed—especially when called on to back up her friend while she informed the elder Miss Langthorne of the treat in store for her.

'Is all well, Lady Summerton?' Adam asked her, when he met Serena carrying a selection of Miss Estelle Langthorne's vast collection of shawls downstairs, in an effort to restore that lady's comfort after the news of upheaval to come.

'Well enough, Sir Adam,' she replied steadily.

'Then to London we will go?' he asked, rather mockingly.

'Indeed—just as you always intended. And kindly stop making a May game of me at every opportunity, sir,' she retorted with chilly dignity.

'But you make such a delightful one, my lady,' he replied with an unrepentant grin.

'Then perhaps you should consider the perversity of laughing at other people's foibles and consider your own for a change?' she told him smartly.

'I leave that onerous task to you, Lady Summerton, as you seem to find it so fascinating.'

'You're mistaken,' she assured him haughtily, and saw heat flash and burn in his dark eyes before he controlled it.

'Indeed, I think I must be,' he said politely, just as if he wasn't recalling their meeting under the beech tree in Windham woods in vivid detail. But he was, if the wolfish smile he directed at her when she nervously licked her lips was anything to go by.

It wasn't as if they'd need to see much of each other in the next few months, she reassured herself rather desperately. It was perfectly possible even for a husband and wife to avoid each other amongst the balls and soirees of the London season. She and George had done so for several of them, after all. If she worked at it, no doubt she would see less of Adam than she would if they both stayed at home. So he had no need whatsoever to look so smugly victorious.

She met his dark eyes for a long moment, caught in some absurd daydream that between them nothing could be hidden for nothing needed to be. Ridiculous, and demonstrably untrue, she decided, as she swung on her heel and descended the stairs as quickly as she could without looking as if she was running away. Which would have been all very fine and dignified had he not followed her down them and into the wide marble hall below, looking as if he had no intention of allowing her to evade him, or whatever the emotion was that flared between them.

She could have no place in Sir Adam Langthorne's life, Serena reminded herself. He was a pleasant companion, with an informed mind and a wicked sense of humour, but that was all. Oh, yes—and he was the man who could also kiss her until her wits were adrift and flying with the stars. Which didn't mean they couldn't simply be friends, so long as they avoided churchyards and ditches from now on. Surely that shouldn't be so very difficult?

'If you will excuse me, your cousin really is feeling most put out,' she said, in pursuit of that laudable aim.

'I really don't think my esteemed Cousin Estelle is large enough for you to hide behind for long,' he told her, and there was a bitter quirk to his mouth that made her heart jar and then carry on, quick and light.

As he was just a friend she couldn't hurt him, could she? But what if he was intent on becoming more than that? Torn between the challenge in his eyes and a craven urge to prove him wrong by hiding from him in any and every way she could, Serena found that she had let herself be guided into his study, and she heard the door shut behind them before she realised he was intent on forcing some sort of confrontation between them—even if she couldn't tell if it was to be an argument or a seduction.

'This really is most improper, Sir Adam,' she told him rather desperately, and turned to bolt for safety.

His hand reached to cover hers, and she hit at it as if she had been stung. 'Considering some of our trysting places, I would class this one as almost respectable,' he denied smoothly, and drew her away from the door.

'Those were not assignations,' she told him. 'They were accidents.'

He looked down at her with a smile that contained far too much warmth for comfort. 'You have a way of humbling a gentleman's pretensions that is second to none,

Lady Summerton,' he informed her softly, and suddenly the airy room seemed very small, and he was taking up far too much of it.

'Useful in a lady on the receiving end of far too many dubious offers, sir, given her widowed status.'

'You think I shall offer you *carte blanche?*' he asked with revulsion.

'I have no idea,' she said, with a valiant attempt at weary sophistication that even to her own ears sounded more like panic.

'Then kindly try and remember I was at least *born* a gentleman,' he informed her angrily, and turned to pace the room as if he dared not lay a hand on her in case he forgot that fact and shook her until her teeth rattled.

'Tell me, Lady Summerton,' he demanded, when he had himself back under strict military discipline, 'why do you make ridiculous assumptions like that one? And what is it that Cambray did that sometimes makes you look as if you have survived a shipwreck?'

Somehow he had moved far closer to her while she was busy trying to convince herself life was wonderful just as it was.

Her breath stuttered briefly, and she refused to meet the hot, impatient look that gave the lie to his air of cool composure. 'I see no reason to dress in my best just to please my neighbours. I live a quiet country life, and it would be beyond ridiculous of me to go about in my finest when it would soon be ruined.'

'I'm not referring to your chosen mode of attire,' he replied brusquely.

'Then what can you mean?' she said haughtily, raising her eyebrows slightly in the hope of looking distant.

Unfortunately he refused to be put in his place. 'Perhaps I speak of that wistful look you get in your eyes when you accidentally leave yourself with nothing to do and have to think about your life for once? Or the way you run about doing the work of the other Summerton countesses for them? No!' he protested against the disclaimer already on her tongue, before she could so much as open her mouth. 'Don't pretend to have no idea what I'm talking about. Since you seem only to want some pallid sort of friendship from me, at least have the grace not to lie.'

There was a bitter tone underlying his words, and she felt tears sting as she contemplated hurting him. But better to disappoint him now than destroy him later, she decided stalwartly.

'I never claimed my life was one of unalloyed bliss,' she said bleakly.

'Then marry me, Serena, and we can at least add some to the mix,' he offered huskily, and there was no mistaking the warmth in his gold shot eyes as he watched her.

How hard he was to resist. The wry smile on his firm mouth, the muscled poise of his broad shouldered figure as he stood so close and so temptingly tall for a lady of her inches. She hoped he would never know what a struggle she had to fight with her baser self to resist him. After being a fool once, she reassured herself, she knew he *wasn't* the embodiment of her girlish dreams. Adam Langthorne was far too real for that, and more important to her than any man should be.

'I am deeply honoured, Sir Adam, and while I have no wish to cause you any hurt…'

'Then don't,' he snarled roughly, and countered all her rational arguments by dragging her into his arms and kissing her as if his very survival depended on it.

After a token struggle and an incoherent protest Serena melted into his embrace with a contented sigh, telling herself she had tried to refuse him and it wasn't her fault he wouldn't take her at her word. Kissing him back with all the ardent fire in her nature, she fought a battle with forbidden feelings that threatened her good intentions. Everywhere they touched—and there were so many places she couldn't spare time for an inventory of pleasure and arousal—she was reminded how different he was from her husband. Nowhere was Adam's touch brutal or perfunctory. Rather he was fiercely intent on her pleasure over his own, and that pleasure was breathtaking.

A cynical part of her whispered that he might be different if he was sure of her, might take instead of seducing, but she silenced it. She knew the difference between a man bent solely on his own needs and the attentions of a sensual lover of women—or at least she did now. Sometimes a man's true nature was beyond doubt, and this was one of them, she decided, as he tempered his needs to her more hesitant ones. Well, at least they ought to be hesitant, but her body was acting without reference to her dazed mind. She hardly had time to accustom herself to the astonishingly seductive feel of Adam's firm mouth on hers once again before he deepened his kiss and gently probed her eager mouth, and she couldn't pretend she wasn't loving every second.

'Uhm,' she heard herself murmur incoherently, as if she was savouring the most rare of treats—and wasn't that the plain truth?

His tongue invaded in the sweetest onslaught, and she was caught in a lovely dance as old and as new as time itself. Delight sang in an ardent fugue that ended in her shiver of pure joy and exultation. He ran a not altogether steady hand along the pure line of her jaw and tipped her head upward, so their mouths could become ever more intimate, and she just gave herself up to the moment.

While it would be ridiculous to feign maidenly blushes, must she be quite so wanton in his arms? she asked herself. A little of the enchantment dropped from her idyll at that unwelcome idea, but nothing on earth could make her stand back and pretend outrage. His hard body against hers told her a tale he had probably been trying to keep from her with that last distance she'd breached in her eagerness to get closer. Adam was so powerfully aroused, and she guiltily loved the idea that she inflamed him so rampantly that his desire for her was almost ungovernable.

When George had made it clear he wanted her she had felt no such heady excitement, even in the first flush of their marriage. What a hollow thing her so-called love-match had been, she decided, as her heart thudded with anticipation at the very thought of eagerly satisfying Adam's every need. She wasn't just a wanton, she was shameless, she realised in shock. Yet instead of stepping back she snuggled into him, making him even more aroused with the brush of her supple curves against his hard, masculine body. She let her tongue venture into his mouth, and was rewarded with a groan of need.

Impatient of the determined resistance offered by her velvet spencer, he swept his hands down her more lightly clad back and down to settle on the curve of her bottom. She suddenly found every workaday part of her body unimaginably erotic. Brought even more explicitly against his aroused manhood, she felt heat flash through every inch of her, and sighed in a much-needed gasp of air. All the strength seemed to seep out of bones and muscles she knew very well were toned by her unladylike preference for walking and riding and perfectly capable of holding her up.

Indeed, there was nothing passive about her as she keened protestingly when his mouth deserted hers. Adam incited her to ever greater need by feathering kisses down the vulnerable length of her neck, and she let her head fall back so he could teach her another heady pleasure as soon as she realised his intent. Flushed and unthinking of where they were and the way they were, so absorbed in each other, she murmured her approval at discovering another part of her was more responsive to his seduction than she had dreamed possible. His strong hand cupped one of her breasts, so full and aroused she was surprised it didn't show its eagerness through velvet spencer, lining *and* gown.

His mouth reached the base of her throat at last, and lingered over the pulse racing under his lips, betraying her eagerness, but his otherwise nimble fingers seemed to be confounded by the elaborate frogs on her spencer, and she smiled tenderly at nothing in particular. Adam should be *au fait* with frogs, given his propensity for driving other-wise sensible females out of their right senses by appearing in cavalry uniform in their presence, she decided. Deaf to the screams of her own common sense, as well as the dictates of propriety, she raised her hands to deal with what he suddenly found incomprehensible.

Even her fingers fumbled as she forgot to watch them and looked at her lover—her lover! Suddenly her mind took in the name, and bungled the frogs in overwhelming eagerness to embrace her fate as soon as possible. A very handsome fate he was too, she mused, as she finally found the wretched things again and pulled the first button roughly out of its braid eyelet. Somehow they managed the rest between them but she doubted her best spencer would ever be the same again, and wondered ridiculously how she could justify the purchase of a new one shortly before she went to town.

Then Adam's hands decided to obey him again, and he smoothed the jacket off her shoulders in one accomplished movement. She was out of it before she felt the loss of warmth. As he was already at her shoulders, he seemed to find it more convenient to carry on round her back and undo her gown while he was there. Feeling the glide and brief resistance of buttons leaving their fastenings, a shiver of pure pleasure rocked her at the brief touch of his bare fingers on her naked flesh. Warmth bloomed in a lovely shudder of desire, and suddenly the fact that it was broad daylight and they were ensconced in his study, the very heart of his house, with his household all about them, was about as unimportant to her as what the Grand Turk was expecting to eat for dinner today.

Serena loved the fact that he had forgotten it all too— that need of her inflamed him until nothing mattered but them and this and now. The recklessness only added to her pleasure and rampant curiosity.

'Hurry,' she urged softly, and sighed with relief as the last button yielded and her gown drifted open, as if even such respectable stuff had taken up the rhythm of life and was assisting in her downfall. Wriggling to help it on its way, she shrugged the puff of a sleeve off her shoulders and felt her breasts thrust against the pull of it, independent of her conscious thoughts. Not that she would have forbidden it, her more sensible self feared, taking control back for just a moment and trying to condemn this reckless banquet of the senses. No, this new Serena insisted—she welcomed it, needed it, and as soon as her inconvenient sleeves had been disposed of she pushed herself shamelessly against Adam's sleekly muscled torso and moaned her need of him.

Momentarily soothed by the brush of his silken waistcoat and the scent of the clean linen under it, she rubbed against the warmth of him and could tell, even with so much between them, that every muscle was clenched with the power of his need of her. Awed, she forgot herself in the wonder of it, and lifted heavy lids to stare up into his eyes. She found them all but taken over by the gold that always rayed his irises so fascinatingly. Something she had never wanted to want bloomed inside her in an irresistible tide and her last barrier against him fell. Mesmerised by him, she let him into every part of her and found there a new part of herself and of him. Love, she decided resignedly, as real and inescapable as the ground beneath their feet.

'Not the place or the time,' he protested indistinctly, as if the words were formed on lips that had forgotten all about eloquence. He was as lost in this wild loving as she was herself, but still valiantly attempting to recall the world, she realised with a tender smile.

'Our time,' she argued, and as he moaned and let himself sink into her pouting mouth with such eager abandon Serena thought she had put an end to such tiresome common sense for the time being.

'May it last for ever then,' he stubbornly managed, before he insisted on raising his head to savour her welcome, then plunged so deep into the eager depths of her waiting mouth that she flew beyond even the lovely novelty she had already experienced with him.

'Need you, Adam,' she informed him, when he paused for them to breathe, her mouth feeling as if it formed words reluctantly, as if in a language it hardly knew.

'Then for heaven's sake be quiet and let me love you,' he urged, with a chuckle that threatened to break.

After that he ousted any chance of speech by lowering his head and mouthing her frail lawn chemise aside to take a hard, hot nipple in his mouth. He suckled until she all but melted with the rush of heat that flowed over her and then settled, burning, at the very centre of her being.

Chapter Fourteen

'Uhmmm,' Serena mumbled incoherently, and vaguely wondered if she might swoon with pleasure as Adam cupped her breasts in his hands and gloated over them as if he had never seen the like.

She thrust her hands under his coat, smoothing mighty muscles and heated flesh under impatient, arousing strokes designed to make him as wild with need as she was herself. Evidently she succeeded, for he muttered something equally illogical and took up his explorations in a new and entirely satisfactory direction as far as Serena was concerned.

Feeling the pull of soft cambric against her legs, she spared a brief thought for the crumpled stuff under his seeking hands—then forgot it as he finally bunched enough of it about her waist to gain the freedom they both longed for. Urgent caresses rocked her out of her haze of need to wonder yet again that she could want any man so much that she felt she might expire if he didn't take her now—or preferably sooner! Protesting with reproachful eyes, and the downturned pout of lips swollen with kisses and desire, she felt him pull away from her with a judder of dread.

'You'll need this later,' he informed her tersely, and she wasn't sure whether to be indignant he could still think, or glad of his consideration.

Standing there, stripped of all but her short corset and her shift and stockings, while he kept even his neckcloth in place, she felt both wanton and suddenly a little apart from him—as if she was holding nothing back and yet he still had a layer of protection from this burning, demanding, humbling need. Then she met his eyes again and saw her mistake. If ever she'd doubted his feelings, that doubt was scouted as he let warmth and yearning and wolfish driven need blaze openly in his ardent gaze.

Serena recklessly let her sensual self run wild and flexed her body with siren-like allure. She gloried in it as yet another layer of Sir Adam's Langthorne's invulnerability revealed itself as a sham—at least when he was with her. Somehow he laid her gown aside with exaggerated care, as if he might rip it if he gave in to the hunger blatant in every pore of him, held back by the last threads of the deeply civilised man under the rakish exterior, and she loved him more than she had dreamt she could. She discovered, in awe, that she had never loved George, and the pretty, girlish infatuation she had once felt for her husband finally faded to nothing.

'Take me now,' she invited impatiently.

'Only if you take me too,' he replied, with that wonderful wolfish smile that had invited her to fall into his arms like a ripe plum from the first moment she laid eyes on him. She wondered how she had held out for so long.

Eagerly she closed the gap between them again and silently blessed him for letting her take that pace, make her own choice. 'Willingly, lover,' she whispered, and she reached up to pull his handsome head down and close her lips on his.

Now the full force of his passion rocked her, and she felt him turn her so he was the one backed against the hard edges of his mahogany desk, and she was warmed and surrounded by his aroused body. The heat at the heart of her was all but burning her up, and she felt a flush burn on her cheekbones, even where her breasts were once more cupped in his hands, as if she needed any more of his special brand of arousal to be ready for him. Knowing how mistaken he was, she fumbled with the fastening of his breeches.

'I want *you*, Adam,' she informed him imperiously.

'Then you shall have me,' he promised, and she shivered deliciously as he pushed her clumsy hands gently aside and dealt summarily with the last barrier between them.

A moment of hesitation, the last shadow cast by her marriage, and then she ran a hand down his velvet shaft in wonder, letting out a murmur of delight, exploring so gently. He seemed to hold his breath in fear of frightening her, or unmanning himself. She found him beautiful, wondrous, and the heat began to take her over again.

'Now!' she urged, and he ardently agreed by parting her thighs and thrusting into the hot, ready welcome she gave him with a pleasured sigh.

Vaguely wondering at how he was going to manage with their positions so unlike anything she had known before, she gasped with delight as he grasped her buttocks in his strong hands and urged her downward, then thrust into her at the same time in a rhythm that set her on the road to somewhere very new. Renouncing control to him with a trust she had never dreamt she could place in another human being, she eagerly paced herself to the movements of his powerful strokes and let her passion-heavy eyes and her eager mouth tell him he was vital to her, as urgent in her as she was for him, and that she was more alive and exultant than she had ever dreamt possible.

Waves of heavy, delightful heat ran through her as he let her take the full length of him at last, and the advantage of their position dawned on her as gravity let her feel the full, wondrous evidence of his potent arousal.

'Oh Adam,' she gasped, her back arched and her breasts thrusting shamelessly against his mouth as she felt his muscles work for her pleasure all over his impressive frame. 'Give me all of you,' she whispered, and she let her knees fall each side of him so they could both strive towards some magical, golden goal Serena was only beginning to guess at.

Open-eyed, they watched each other revel in the lack of all barriers between them, in the joining that meant so much more than any other had ever done. She felt as if this was the first time she had taken a man inside her. He made her new, and she tried to tell him so with the whole of her being. Maybe she succeeded, for a sudden flash in his golden-rayed brown eyes made them look almost on fire with need and ardour. She watched the blaze with an awe at his pleasure that probably revealed too much of her feelings, but reservations and caveats were not for now, and she thrust them away.

'Little chance of anything else, my darling,' he said, in a voice deep and rough with the force of his feelings, and the unmistakable craving of his body was explicit as he thrust with driven power and tenderness within her.

Feeling that blaze take hold of them both, as heat flashed through every inch of their joined bodies, Serena fought to restrain her moans as they rode each other towards the glowing ecstasy she could sense just out of reach, a breath this side of the beckoning radiance at the heart of life itself. Then her groan of pure satisfaction was muffled by his open mouthed, open-hearted kiss as they tumbled into extravagant delight together, clasped in a shining whole that was more than they ever could be apart. Shudders of unimaginable pleasure rocked through her as Serena met every last longed for thrust of his body within her, and felt his urgent, impassioned release even as she climaxed into a sunburst of sobbing, singing joy.

'Next time we'll take all *your* clothes off instead of mine,' she murmured against his heaving chest in a lazy glow of wonder, when she finally found the breath.

She felt him smile against her flushed cheek, and marvelled that afterwards it could be so different. George had rolled off her and into his own bed without so much as a word, and the one time she'd bothered to listen at his door she'd heard him snoring within moments of getting there. This lovemaking wasn't in the same world as what she had to shut her eyes and endure then, and she'd felt guilty even thinking of it.

'Next time will be in our bed, though I dare say it'll half kill me to wait three weeks while we have the banns read. So I'm afraid you'll have to save your wilder fantasies until after we're married, Lady Langthorne.'

Serena came down to earth with an uncomfortable thud. Shocked that he had interpreted her scandalous behaviour as consent, she struggled against his hold until she had put a distance between them.

'No,' she said stiffly, as she stood before him, trying not to cross her hands over her naked breasts in self-defence.

That might hurt him even more as she refused the future he had planned.

'No, you can't restrain yourself that long? Or just plain no?' he asked, shadows already stalking the golden heat in his dear eyes.

'Just plain no,' she whispered, and it took all the bravery she had in her to go on meeting his gaze as it cooled and then iced when he took in the steady determination in her own.

'Then you intend to give yourself to *any* personable gentleman who asks from now on, I suppose? Having given you a taste for the exercise, I suppose I should blame myself.'

'Of course I shall!' she blazed back at him, furious that he could believe such a thing, but guiltily sensing a coward's way out of explaining her refusal.

'Liar,' he informed her flatly, and coolly set about the task of putting them both to rights, while her mind reeled at the certainty in his gaze.

Serena let herself realise how much she loved him. Indeed, she had probably done so from the moment she'd set eyes on him in the elegant uniform of a subaltern. She acquitted herself of falling for any man in a uniform. In such troubled times she met officers all the time, and didn't fall at *their* elegantly booted feet. No, it had taken one very particular hero to fell her with a wicked smile and an acutely interested look. If she'd had any sense at all she would have left Windham Dower House that very day, but instead she had closed her eyes to the truth and stayed, telling herself she could do no harm if she kept her head—before losing it beyond her wildest imaginings.

'You're right,' she finally admitted.

'Then you love me?' he asked, as if confirming a dark suspicion.

Serena shrugged, then flinched as he cursed under his breath and looked as if he wanted to shake her. But he didn't dare lay hands on her lest he couldn't stop. She should walk away before they said anything irredeemably hurtful, but the idea was agony after their unforgettable lovemaking.

'I'll leave. Please make some excuse to your sister for my departure.'

She was turning to find her clothes and make a dignified departure when he grabbed her wrist and used her own momentum to swing her back. Staring at the long-fingered brown hand wrapped so securely about her slender wrist, she wondered how he had managed that manoeuvre without hurting her. And at the warm contact of flesh on flesh she felt an insidious softening, a seductive memory of such exquisite intimacy it made her heart race to think of it. Yet somehow she made herself trade a haughty look for his fiery one.

'Am I not to be granted a few polite excuses?' he asked, and any idea of leaving him with a few gentle words vanished as she took in the hurt he no longer even tried to conceal.

She couldn't fetch them onto her tongue when he looked as if he didn't know whether to kiss her or strangle her, or push her back down onto his desk and ravish her all over again. Instead she tried to confound him with affronted dignity. But what had worked occasionally on George had no effect whatsoever on her lover. Nor could she sustain it in the face of the frustration in his beloved gaze.

'I can't marry you, Adam,' she said bleakly.

'Why not, Serena?' he asked gently.

'Because I can't give you children,' she told him, refusing to meet his eyes and see them cool at the sense of what she said.

Yet they didn't, and she looked up at him almost against her will. The flare of heat and possessiveness looking back at her was hotter and more certain than ever. She wondered if she had been ambiguous. No, reviewing her words, she could find nothing but plain fact in them.

'Something we can doubtless overcome between us,' he replied arrogantly, as if the facts would change because *he* willed it so.

'I can't give you an heir,' Serena reiterated, and braced herself for pity and his hasty departure. Instead he looked faintly amused.

'Do you think me an addle-cove?' he asked, with the wry smile she had unconsciously come to look for.

'Well, no,' she answered, completely at sea, considering he was possibly the most intelligent man she had ever met. 'Of course not.'

'Good—although George Cambray richly deserved the epithet, and I should hate you to think we were cut from the same cloth. He wed a beautiful, noble, well-dowered lady, and nobody whispered scandal against you, which only left the lack of a tribe of revolting brats made in his image for Cambray to hold against you. I can't but think that a very good thing myself, as his children might have taken after him instead of you. The question remains why you let him convince you it was *your* fault?'

'It was obvious,' she replied, astonished by his scepticism.

'In what way?' he asked, gently relentless.

'The Cambrays are famously fertile,' she admitted at last, uncomfortable with the subject and wishing it done with.

'Which means he must have been? Try as I might, I can't see that as evidence that you are barren rather than he, and even if you are, I like my sister—her brats are welcome to Marclecombe if we don't have any.'

'Every Cambray bride for the last three centuries has conceived within six months of her wedding—you may trust Amelia to throw that fact at me at every opportunity, considering she did so within a month of hers. Anyway, *we* can't fail to have children, Sir Adam, because we won't be getting married in the first place,' she explained with exaggerated patience.

The very thought of even more wildly sensuous fulfilment made her clench her fists at her sides against the urge to give in and agree joyously. Adam would never treat her like an idiot just because she was born female; they could travel wherever they chose, and play host and hostess to the best and brightest company when at home… No! It was selfish to even dream of it.

'I never heard that lack of a wedding ring was a barrier to conceiving,' he informed her outrageously. 'But do you respond to all your suitors in such a manner?' he asked, one dark eyebrow raised in interested enquiry.

'No,' she snapped. 'I don't have any other suitors.'

'I *am* surprised. In pursuit of such a welcome, every sentient male in the county would willingly throw his hand and heart at your feet.'

'Since they would only gain a hearty box on the ears, I hope you won't encourage them to do so.'

'I?' he asked, with a fine pretence of affronted innocence. 'I would never behave in so unkind or ungentlemanly a manner.'

'Would you not? Then you consider *this* kind and gentlemanly?'

'No, I just think it a fitting response to a totty-headed

argument without any foundation, in fact,' he countered impatiently.

'Really? Then you will be doubly delighted at meeting with my refusal, since I doubt you wish to associate any further with such a want-wit.'

'Ah, but I do,' he assured her softly, and there was no mistaking the steely purpose in his intent expression now. 'I *shall* marry you, Lady Summerton, and no other. So don't insult me by suggesting I go and find myself an artless little debutante to impregnate. You suit me to the finest curl and last inch of your silky skin, and to every contrary thought in your lovely head, even when all vestige of common sense has flown it. The first time I set eyes on you I wanted you, Serena, but I was young and silly enough to listen to my conscience and I let you go. I won't do it twice.'

Somehow she knew it was only because he was exercising extraordinary restraint that she wasn't lying under him right now, being pleasured beyond her wildest dreams once more. He would meet with no resistance, she knew, as she looked back on their lovemaking and refused to regret a second. Yet the quick thud of her aching heart felt like a physical rather than mental anguish as it jarred with dread of an empty future.

How it would hurt if she ever came upon him and the wife he would surely take one day, despite his insistence that he would not. Such a meeting would tear her to pieces. So the best thing she could do was fly back to her family home and stay there until she was too old to care. Would she *ever* be old enough not to care who became Lady Langthorne, though? She wouldn't need to be old she decided; she would have to be dead!

'Nonsense,' she made herself say lightly. 'You never set eyes on me until six months ago.'

'I first saw you as a grown woman across a ridiculously crowded ballroom five years ago,' he informed her implacably, his mouth so grim it looked as if he fervently wished he hadn't. 'You stood out among those wilting debutantes so vividly that I carried the image of you to war with me, knowing it was unfair to ask you to wait, or to wed me and follow the drum. When I found you were engaged to George Cambray I nearly deserted and came back to snatch you off to Gretna, and to the devil with all else.'

Something told her she would have gone, once she had met those golden-brown eyes full of passionate sincerity and seen the devil lurking in his smile. Engaged to George, with his outward good looks and chilly slate-grey gaze, even silly Lady Serena Verlaine would have recognised the true warmth and wit and rightness of Adam Langthorne, whatever society had to say.

'I'm not the impulsive girl I was,' she informed him dully.

'No, you're a strong, passionate woman of extraordinary grace and style. If you will only let me, *I* will love and value you for the rest of our days,' he told her, and his urgent sincerity made her blink back tears.

'No,' she replied sturdily. 'You'll meet plenty of beautiful girls in London, and most of them have more character than you think. A year from now you could cradle your son in your arms and thank heaven I turned you down.'

'Little point in trying to convince you I would be raving at the gods for withholding you, if you really think me such a fickle and worthless fellow. How can you even *think* that within weeks of offering you my hand and heart I would wed a silly girl too young to be out of the schoolroom without a minder and make love to her instead?'

'I couldn't bear to watch you wait out the years without the children you would make such a wonderful father to, Adam. It would destroy me.'

'If you refuse me, then I shall have none anyway,' he assured her, and she felt even beyond the comfort of tears as his reckless declaration stabbed her like a knife.

'I do refuse you,' she told him solemnly, and hoped the steadiness of her gaze would make him realise she meant it and change his mind.

'I will wear you down, Serena, and when I do I'll demand a heavy price for this—one you'll gladly pay as long as we both live.' He met her eyes with implacable purpose in his, and she longed to let him put his handsome, stubborn head in the noose.

'I can't stop you asking,' she replied doggedly.

'Any more than I can stop you being a damned wilful idiot,' he informed her, his voice rough with impatience.

'Would that I could bar you from being an obdurate fool, then,' she told him crossly, astonished when it made him chuckle.

'And you say me nay? When our arguments prove how well matched we are, love?'

'Don't call me that,' she appealed.

'You may have a week or two to accustom yourself to the idea, Serena, but you can't stop me telling the truth in the meantime,' he challenged, stubbornness and the love she hadn't let herself believe in until now clear on his face and in his deep voice as he laid down his terms.

'And you can have the same time to come to your senses.'

'Never. I like being out of them far too well,' he teased,

as lightly as if they were discussing the weather, before marching her over to the nearest mirror to reorder her appearance. 'Any fool could see what we have been at on taking one look at you,' he informed her, with a male smugness she almost forgave him for when she recalled the last half hour.

The sight of herself—dishevelled, heavy eyed and still flushed with the aftermath of passion—made her forget her woes as she tried to banish the truth. Thank goodness he had too much honour to force her hand; all he need do was let her walk out of the room looking as well-loved as a woman could.

'I'll be your mistress if you want me, Adam, but I won't marry you.'

'I'll be damned if I will let the woman I love skulk about my house, Serena, so don't even think that again, let alone say it. I love you, you ridiculous woman—and you offer to be my mistress, as if that was a mere nothing to both of us?' He took a deep breath and visibly took control of his temper. She watched him with bewildered blue eyes and shook her head, bewildered by the depth and breadth of the emotions singing between them. Emotions that made her more certain than ever that she was right to refuse to wed him and condemn him to a childless future.

'I can't marry you,' she told him painfully, but she could see that he still didn't believe she would never yield to his demand she do so.

'And I can't marry any other woman. So one day I dare say you'll come to your right senses. Meantime, that door behind you leads onto the terrace, so I can berate you for lingering outside at such a time once you are safely back inside,' he told her, when she was neat and composed again. His self-mocking smile told her he was none too impressed by his own scrupulousness, especially when he pressed a quick, passionate kiss on her softly surprised mouth and pushed her out of the service door before he changed his mind.

'Well, really!' she muttered to herself, and stood still as a statue while her heartbeat settled and the rosy tint faded from cheeks she could feel still burning with temper and the need he had set alight in her. It felt as if it might not go out and leave her in peace if she lived to be ninety.

'A message from Sir Adam, Miss Rachel,' the butler announced some time later.

Rachel took the note and read it hastily, sending Serena a very thoughtful glance. 'Adam is helping birth one of the foals,' she informed Serena. 'Although he has grooms aplenty, and a stable manager employed to look after his precious racehorses' every need.'

Serena looked politely uninterested with an effort, and concentrated on the fashion plates her friend had produced in honour of the stay in town Serena now felt might test her sanity to its limits.

'Have you quarrelled, Serena?' Rachel asked at last.

Serena felt herself flush as she determinedly kept her eyes on a drawing of a young woman in a very daring gown more suited to the boudoir than the ballroom.

'Why should we argue?' she asked uncomfortably.

'If you need me to tell you that, then you're in deeper trouble than I thought,' Rachel replied, with a look that stripped away Serena's determination to pretend indifference.

'Maybe,' she conceded. 'But what leads you to think so?'

'Because the Duke and I fight all the time, and then

pretend the other doesn't exist while our tempers cool, just as you and Adam are doing,' Rachel admitted. 'For some reason the wretch infuriates me more than any man I ever came across—except Adam, who is my brother and put on earth to be infuriating.'

Rachel was fishing with a well-baited hook, but she had revealed far more of her own feelings than she realised. Serena had a suspicion they were both in danger of losing their hearts to gentlemen they were not destined to marry. The Duke of Newbury was a powerful aristocrat, had been engaged to a beauty, *and* possessed a desperate enemy. Loving him would lead Rachel into danger and expose her to heartache, and she so wanted her to be happy.

Rachel was pretty, of course; her velvet dark eyes were alight with intelligence and humour, when she wasn't blinded by her prejudice against the Duke of Newbury, but she was no incomparable. The Langthorne name was an old and honourable one, perhaps honoured for their refusal to seek headier honours. Yet his grace must be heartsore. Even if it had been a convenient arrangement, news of Corinna Garew's famous looks had reached rural Herefordshire—so how could Luke not regret losing such a woman?

'I wonder what we would have made of his grace if we had met him in a London drawing room instead of Thornfield Churchyard?' she asked lightly, furtively watching Rachel while she pretended to look at the fashion plates.

'That he was the most aggravating man ever to trouble polite society with his infuriating presence and unfounded conviction of his own superiority,' she snapped with a frown. 'Nothing will persuade me he was ever a polite and charming gentleman, Serena, even before he was reduced to enduring our hospitality. Hospitality he seems singularly ungrateful for. One would suppose the stupid man would rather we'd left him to his fate, so he wouldn't have to be grateful to us for saving him from an early grave.'

'Maybe he'll recover his temper with his health.'

'And maybe Bonaparte is still a corporal.' Rachel dismissed the possibility then laughed as Serena chuckled at her vehemence and cast her a quizzical look. 'I have no idea why we're spoiling this lovely afternoon when he's got the rest of the week to infuriate me,' she said, and turned to the topic of their wardrobes with a fascination Serena wished she could share.

Guiltily relieved that her friend was preoccupied with her own annoying gentleman, Serena let her thoughts roam. How turning down marriage to the one man on earth she longed to love, honour and perhaps even obey now and again made the time fly. As she had the rest of her life to regret his loss, it was probably time she paid more attention to the here and now.

'Shall you enjoy your second season, Rachel?' she asked at last, as if she had been musing on the subject for longer than the thirty seconds it had taken her to come up with it when her friend shut her book.

'Well, it can hardly be any worse than the first one, can it?' Rachel returned cheerfully enough, even if there was a watchful air about her that told Serena she knew a red herring when she smelt one.

Rachel seemed more resigned to the idea of a season in town than Serena, now Adam had proposed and been duly, dutifully, damnably refused. She shuddered at the idea of spending weeks trying to pretend the man she loved was no more than the brother of her best friend. The thought of watching him court another woman, despite his denial, made her stomach plunge with sick dread.

'If we could persuade your patient to behave, we could enjoy ourselves with a clear conscience,' she replied with forced lightness.

'He can come, or stay here and put himself in danger to his heart's content—if he actually has one, of course,' Rachel said militantly.

'He's ruffled your feathers, hasn't he?' Serena asked.

'An understatement,' Rachel conceded tersely. 'I suggest we tidy ourselves until we meet Cousin Estelle's less than exacting standards, and then we can enjoy the delicious dinner waiting for us without any male company. I for one have had more than enough of the breed for one day.'

'What a wonderful idea,' Serena replied.

Adam had absented himself from playing host, and didn't have the grace to reappear and hand her up into the Langthorne carriage when it was time for her to leave so she could studiously ignore him. Serena told herself she much preferred a quiet evening discussing fashion and putting their households in order before they left. Adam's presence would have created too much awkwardness over what now lay between them, so of course she preferred his room to his company. The fact that the Langthorne's coachman was accompanied by the head groom and one of the gamekeepers, both armed and dangerous-looking, reminded her just why she found Sir Adam over-protective and intensely aggravating. He was dictating her movements even in his absence, and she had borne enough of that during her marriage to George.

Just at that moment she perfectly understood Rachel's fury at her patient's similarly protective instincts, and wished the pair of them at Jericho. Both men wanted to treat them like decorations, so she fleetingly hoped they would marry the sort of females they richly deserved to be tied to. Maybe when they were draped in clinging ivy they would regret rational women.

Irrationally cross with one particular strong oak, she went straight to bed when she reached the dower house, pleading a headache. If Adam chose to indulge in nocturnal misadventures without her tonight he could, she informed herself furiously, even as her lie was in danger of becoming truth and her head began to pound. In time he would have deplored a barren wife who expected to be included in whatever adventures he was currently embroiled in, so wasn't it fortunate she had turned him down?

Chapter Fifteen

Adam had promised Serena a fortnight, but it came and went without any renewal of his passionate attentions. She told herself to be glad and to enjoy the whirlwind they were caught up in now they had re-entered polite society. Yet, despite the fairly honourable attentions of several very eligible gentlemen, Serena's aching heart refused to be soothed.

At least Rachel was enjoying her season, and Serena felt it was almost worth having to pretend Adam was just her best friend's brother to see Rachel gather a court of very discerning beaux like bees to honey everywhere she went. Serena had a suspicion the Duke of Newbury spent his time enduring her friend's popularity rather than rejoicing in it, and spared a moment from her own miseries to study that gentleman now, as he sat on the sidelines, nursing his broken ankle and watching Rachel glide by on the arm of a handsome young gentleman.

Luke managed to look impassive under the goad of their obvious enjoyment, but Serena knew the signs of a frustrated man by now, because she saw them whenever she looked at Adam and cursed him for a chivalrous, stubborn fool. Mind, if his grace made the same suggestion to Miss Langthorne as she had to her brother, he would very soon find himself facing a furious baronet over duelling pistols one chilly dawn. The idea made her shudder, then smile apologetically at one of her admirers who had asked her to dance after such absent-minded encouragement.

She tried to ape Rachel's easy manner and get through the business as best she could, but as she did so she wondered how long Luke and Adam would endure being on the sidelines. Not long, if the glimpse she caught of Luke's resolute expression as he neatly cut off Rachel's retreat as she moved towards Serena and safety meant anything. Ignoring the imploring look her friend cast her, Serena managed to look unaware that her so-called charge was being ruthlessly diverted, and decided Rachel could fight that battle herself.

Serena trusted the Duke, and was beginning to think him exactly the man Rachel needed after all. She had seen frustration, fury and sheer unadulterated longing cross his guarded face when he was with Rachel too often to be mistaken about his feelings for her, and Serena was willing to acknowledge, if only to herself, that she had been quite wrong. Instead of Rachel falling headlong for a rich, charming and compelling aristocrat, and pining for the unlikely, he had forestalled her and tumbled headlong into love while her friend was blissfully unaware of how deeply her own feelings were engaged. It would have had all the hallmarks of a farce if it didn't involve her dearest friend and a man she had come to admire for his courage and humour. As it was, she decided she was such a poor hand at love affairs that the best she could do was not to interfere. She trusted Luke to behave like a gentleman, and considered her own dilemmas while her dancing partner went to procure lemonade and left her in peace for a few moments.

She told herself it would have been easier if Adam was in Herefordshire, but part of her would rather be close to him than spared the pain of seeing him dance and flirt with the more exotic beauties of the ton night after night. Just now he was leading out a ravishing beauty she recognised as the young wife of a very old peer, and she fought to keep her expression impassive as a shaming rush of jealousy threatened to smash through her cool composure.

'My dance, I think, Lady Summerton,' a smooth-voiced beau Serena could not recall setting eyes on before claimed, and she supposed she would have to believe him.

Since it was one of the new and daring waltzes, they were soon spinning round the room as if in the deepest accord, and Serena unworthily hoped Adam was feeling as raw about seeing her dance so closely with another man as she was at seeing him bent attentively over the suddenly very irritating Lady Haverstone. She bestowed a dazzling smile on the handsome naval captain, who was watching her as they danced with a rather quizzical look, and noted with some satisfaction that he was indeed very good-looking—even if he was as fair as Adam was dark, and had the dangerous air of a very experienced charmer and lover of women. As a dancing partner destined to make a frustrated suitor gnash his teeth with frustration, instead of being too attentive to lovely young wives who should know better, he could not have been bettered if she had searched every drawing room in Mayfair.

'She can't hold a candle to you, Lady Summerton,' her dance partner informed her solemnly, and she tore her gaze away from Adam and his pouting peeress to eye him with increased respect. The gallant captain would make some lucky female a very handsome and acutely perceptive husband if he ever allowed himself to be caught in Cupid's web, she concluded. She could almost imagine Adam resembling this personable young man when he was younger, in air if not in essence, and once again she informed Fate that she didn't think much of her timing. How heady it would have been if she had been able to dance and flirt with dashing Lieutenant Langthorne in her come-out year, instead of meeting him again when it was too late for both of them!

'Thank you,' she said sincerely to her companion, and did her best to give him most of her attention for the remainder of their waltz.

'Sir Adam is a lucky devil,' Captain Afforde informed her when the heady music finally stopped and he was conducting her back to a thoroughly bored and deliberately oblivious Miss Estelle Langthorne.

'I have no idea what you mean, Captain,' Serena informed him, but there was knowledge of much she preferred to keep concealed in his bluest of blue eyes, and if she had met him before she had encountered Adam he might even have endangered her heart more than a little. Now she was immune to his charm and wit, and tried to let him know it in the cool look she sent him.

'I doubt it's obvious to all and sundry,' he went on blithely, 'but I should put him out of his misery and agree to wed him, if I were you, my lady. Apparently Langthorne was considered a fine officer by his own men, who don't give praise cheaply and should therefore be trusted.'

'I'm pleased to hear it, but you are not me, sir—luckily for both of us—and I don't see any signs of misery on that particular gentleman's countenance. Rather to the contrary, he looks very content with his lot,' she challenged him, but all he did was grin and melt ungallantly into the shadows as Adam approached and she was left with nowhere to hide.

'A word with you, if you please,' he demanded brusquely, and ushered her to the nearest unoccupied alcove.

Serena thought a few dark thoughts about the scheming Captain Afforde, who was obviously a rogue of the first order and therefore ought to know better than to matchmake, and then she promptly forgot all about him as Adam's presence blotted out every other man in the room. 'What about your sister?' she asked, rather desperately.

'She's busy,' Adam informed her.

'And that's supposed to make me feel better? I am supposed to be her chaperon.'

'No, you're supposed to be her dearest friend, who is honouring us with her company this season.'

'How very noble of me.'

'If she wasn't with Newbury, though, I admit I'd be loath to leave her to Cousin Estelle's tender mercies for long.'

'And the Duke's are so much better?' she asked severely, attempting to rise to her feet and seek Rachel out as propriety dictated.

'Since he's about to ask her to marry him, yes, I rather think they are,' he replied, and Serena let her legs have their way and flopped back onto the chaise.

'But how can he?' she gasped.

'It's quite easy when you face the alternative of a lifetime of loneliness,' he replied, with an ironic gleam in his eyes, and Serena watched her own feet shuffle like a schoolgirl's beneath the hem of her elegantly sophisticated cream silk gown.

'But she loved Tom Hollard so very dearly,' she murmured, almost to herself, as she mulled over the idea and wondered if there was a very good reason why Rachel had been so distracted lately after all. Did she really love Luke under that armour of impatience and exasperation? And, if she did, would that love lead to happiness or heartbreak for her best friend?

'Which means she can never be free to love again?' Adam asked, as if the idea were unthinkable—which of course it was. 'Having known Tom, I think you will acknowledge that would never be what he wanted for Rachel. He loved her far too well for that.'

'Of course that's not what I meant. It's just that she always seems so furious with the Duke,' she objected weakly.

'I can assure you that's no obstacle to loving someone,' he informed her, with a sardonic smile she understood a little too well.

'But does he love her?' she asked hollowly, wondering if she was referring to Rachel and her duke, or herself and her lover, so confused did she suddenly feel by these deep questions.

'Oh, you may be very sure of that,' he informed her loftily, and she rather thought he knew her question had had more than one possible meaning as well, and that his reply to it covered both spoken and unspoken ones.

'Why?'

'Because I would never let him propose to my sister if he hadn't gone to great lengths to convince me he loves her as he has never loved another female in his entire life.'

'Oh,' Serena heard herself say inadequately.

'Not that he needed to. I find myself remarkably acute at recognising the affliction in others now I have endured it myself.'

'Then he hides it very well,' she said, feeling as if she was defending herself against all his unspoken accusations of cowardice on her part, rather than referring to Rachel's future happiness.

'Do you expect him to wear his heart on his sleeve for everyone to see?' he demanded, as if she was intent on torturing him, rather than saving him from a very unhappy future.

'No, but he doesn't even seek her company.'

'Sensible fellow. He probably dislikes being tortured as much as any mad fool who wants and cannot have.'

'Yet at least it wouldn't be a torture of his own making,' she defended herself, flushing even as she remembered how boldly she had offered to be his lover.

'Half a loaf being better than no bread? Not for me, my lady,' he informed her tersely.

'Well, if what you say is right, his grace should very soon be in possession of a full loaf and have no need to make such a compromise for the sake of his lady,' she snapped back, feeling vaguely ashamed of herself for using Rachel's love affair to contrast her own, and discomfited by the tawdry one she was proposing. For his sake, she reminded herself, and somehow contrived to look only politely interested in this painful discussion for the benefit of such interested spectators as Lady Haverstone, who looked in danger of falling off her gilt chair in a vain attempt at eavesdropping upon their private conversation.

'I would call him a fortunate devil if not for the fact that he was incarcerated in the next best thing to hell before he met the woman he could love for life,' Adam observed, as coolly as if they were merely discussing the weather, but Serena was too caught up in their conversation to return the

compliment, and Lady Haverstone actually had the effrontery to grab her husband's arm in order to sidle a little closer.

'No, indeed, I should not wish that on my worst enemy,'
Serena said with a shudder, grateful to Lord Haverstone for
now giving his wife a commentary on the night and the
company in the strident tones of the very deaf.

'You're more merciful than me, then. I'd like to see
Garew spend a week in the Canderton vault—although
he'd be more insane than the poor king after an hour or two.
Which brings me to my second reason for seeking you out.'

'You plan to lock me in that terrible place instead?' she
forced herself to ask lightly.

'What a damnable opinion you have of me,' he replied,
refusing to be diverted. 'Once Newbury's engagement to my
sister is announced Garew's last hope of benefiting from his
sister's marriage will be at an end—unless he chooses to act.'

'You mean he might do something desperate?'

'Even more desperate than he has already?'

'I see what you mean. There is very little we can put
beyond him,' Serena conceded, unable to care that her face
probably showed her feelings all too clearly. Blackmail and
attempted murder put the ton in their place on the fringe
of reality quite wonderfully.

'So I can rely on you to see my sister is never left alone?
Or almost never, if we are to allow Newbury to retain a
semblance of sanity,' Adam said, with such an undercurrent of bitterness in his voice that Serena's hand rose to lie
upon his and offer comfort. Then she made it return to her
side, and shifted a little further from temptation.

'I presume she'll be safe indoors?' she enquired, wondering how she would withstand continuous exposure to
Adam's proximity if he said no.

'I believe we can take it in turns to plague the life out of her with our presence, my lady, so we two need hardly see each other,' he reassured her, and Serena felt as if her very heart wept.

'All of which presupposes Rachel will say yes,' she reminded him.

'It would be a fool who offered odds against Newbury wooing and winning her. But if you want to lose your shirt, Lady Serena, pray do so.'

'Thank you, but I would rather not bet against my dearest friend's happiness, Sir Adam.'

'Then let's see if we can find them before the tabbies whisper about their prolonged absence,' he invited and, rising to his feet, bowed and offered her his arm so she must publicly snub him in order to refuse it.

Slanting him an infuriated glare, Serena rose gracefully and laid the very tips of her gloved fingers on his arm. But she suffered such a charge of awareness at even so slight a contact that she wondered distractedly if it showed on her face.

'You are a very managing man,' she informed him stiffly, and looked haughtily down her nose at the hovering Lady Haverstone in quite the grand manner.

'Just as well, considering I am in love with an obstinate, mulish, self-sacrificing female who wouldn't know a sensible argument if it punched her on the nose,' he informed her, in a driven murmur that told her he had felt that leap of the pulses too.

'Since you think so, it's as well I said you nay,' she replied hardily.

'You wouldn't now, if I chose to test your resolution.'

'I told you I'd be your mistress,' she hissed in his ear,

and wondered what the company would make of this very improper conversation—if they could hear it over the noise of the latest dance.

'I should wait until you're asked, my lady. A gentleman does like to do his own hunting, you know.'

'I loathe you—you do know that, don't you?' she told him more distinctly.

'Then you make the most delightful enemy a man ever possessed,' he informed her, with an infuriating, confident grin that blinded her to the fact that they too had now left the ballroom and were heading in the direction of their host's library and potential compromise—if only the Duke of Newbury and Miss Rachel Langthorne were not already occupying it and compromising each other very satisfactorily.

'Well, I never!' Serena couldn't resist saying sternly as they started away from each other like a pair of guilty lovers when she and Adam entered the room loudly enough to dissipate the rosy haze in which they were lost to the world. 'As your chaperon, I must disapprove of this tryst in the strongest of terms, Rachel,' she informed her friend, with an excellent imitation of her own much tried chaperon from her debutante days.

'It's all right—he wants to marry me,' her friend told her, with such an idiotically besotted expression on her glowing face that Serena no longer doubted Rachel loved the Duke deeply. Even if it was such a surprise to her she barely believed it was really happening.

'Oh, that's perfectly fine, then,' she forced herself to say sarcastically, as she eyed Rachel's very ruffled appearance and Luke's flushed countenance. He looked like a duke who had just been caught raiding his own pantry at midnight, and Serena's liking for him only increased at this surprising lack of sophistication in so aristocratic and urbane a gentleman.

'Wish me happy, Serena?' her friend asked, rather wistfully.

'Of course I do, you goose,' she said, no longer able to keep up the pretence of being anything but delighted. 'With all my heart,' she added, and Luke had to let Rachel go as she hugged Serena and then her brother.

'I'm so deliriously happy I can hardly believe it,' she informed them incredulously. 'And I quite thought I detested him.'

'So did I,' his grace said with a self-deprecating grin. 'Right up to the moment you flung yourself into my arms and agreed to plague the life out of me for the rest of our days.'

'I felt it was my duty. If I refused you, heaven alone knows how arrogant and self-satisfied you might get,' Rachel informed him sternly.

'Then let's go and drink a toast to dutiful duchesses. I can't tell you how I look forward to disappointing those damned puppies you have gathered about you since we came to town.'

'I believe you're jealous, your grace,' Rachel purred delightedly.

'You can bet your dowry on it,' he informed her inelegantly, and should have scandalised Serena a lot more when he seized Rachel in an impulsive embrace and kissed her very soundly indeed.

'And no more waltzing until my fearsome nurse pronounces me fit to waltz with you,' he added, stealing yet another kiss.

Serena wondered if it might be her duty to inform them that that was quite enough of that, although it was perfectly evident both Rachel and Luke would disagree.

'No,' Rachel agreed with astonishing docility. 'It really was most unsatisfactory when I hadn't the least desire to be so close to anyone but you.'

'Do I really have to wait six weeks after that encouragement from my bride-to-be to march her up the aisle, Langthorne?' Luke pleaded.

'It'll be good for your soul and your broken arm,' Adam told him hard-heartedly, and it seemed to Serena that if he had no prospect of marching her up the aisle, he didn't see why they shouldn't all share his misery.

Guilt ate at her as she tried to convince herself she was doing the right thing in refusing to marry her lover, and sneakily informed her that she ought to regret her brazen offer to warm his bed without benefit of clergy. Yet how could she marry him and condemn him to a lifetime of childlessness?

'You will be wed at Marclecombe?' she asked, in the hope of diverting Adam from his frustration with her.

Much to her own evident shock, Rachel looked questioningly at her new fiancé. 'I should like to be married there, yes,' she said softly, and Serena could see dreams in her eyes as she turned from intruding on their privacy.

'Then you shall be—although I demand a better billet than I endured last time I came to stay in the area,' Luke replied with a wry, loving smile.

Rachel shuddered. 'Don't even think of it,' she protested, with a shiver that necessitated Luke holding her much closer.

'Marclecombe church is so tiny I doubt we'll get half the family in,' Adam warned, and Serena thought dreamily that it sounded wonderful.

Her marriage to George had been at Thornfield church,

which was big enough to hold a regiment, and by the time they had wed it had felt like everyone else's day but theirs. Appropriate in the light of their rather ill-starred union, she thought cynically now, and did her best to forget it by anticipating Rachel's wedding to her very particular duke.

'Will you attend me, Serena?' Rachel asked, and she had to blink a lot to prevent herself weeping openly.

'Of course—if you really want me to,' she replied, and tried not to meet Adam's eyes as desolation swept over her at the thought that it could have been such a happy day for both of them, if he'd been giving his sister away and she attending her, and they too had been waiting to marry.

'Who else?' Rachel said with a rather wobbly smile, and wrenched herself away from Luke to hug Serena again, as if her joy was too potent not to be spread around.

'Someone younger and more of a bridesmaid?' Serena replied lightly.

'No! And it's high time you returned the favour.'

'True,' Serena replied uncomfortably, relieved when Adam announced that they had scandalised the tabbies long enough, and it was time he found their host and made an announcement to give them more to gossip over.

It was a nine-day wonder, of course. Depending who was pronouncing upon the news of Miss Langthorne's betrothal to the most eligible duke on the marriage mart, she had either caught the unfortunate man when he was laid low by a riding accident that had landed him at the feet of a designing harpy, or he had somehow managed to engage himself to the delightfully unaffected Miss Langthorne before any other gentleman had had the temerity to cut him out.

With three weeks left in London before they must leave

for Herefordshire in time to have the banns read, Serena found herself involved in yet another whirlwind of shopping and fittings, as a trousseau fit for a duchess was added to Rachel's wardrobe. At times she caught a dazed, wearied look in her friend's eyes that shadowed her own wedding to George Cambray all those years ago, and her own feeling that the ceremony had taken on a life independent of her. But then Rachel would return home to find Luke waiting for her, with his usual impatience, and any resemblance to Serena's very correct marriage to her earl spun away like straw on the wind.

A whole week went by for Serena to indulge in wistful might-have-beens. At the end of it she waited on yet another elegantly uncomfortable chair for her friend to be fitted with yet another gown. Somehow she had made herself resist the silks and satins, the muslins and cambrics and velvets that would have perhaps been made up into such superbly seductive gowns that even the most dilatory lover would no longer have been able to resist her well-displayed charms. Yet even so, as she sat with too much time on her hands, and nodded sagely or shook her head doubtfully in response to what she gauged to be Rachel's feelings on each suggestion, her thoughts seemed to revolve inevitably back to Adam, and whether her life would ever be worth living again without him in it.

Perhaps once Rachel and Luke were safely married she should consider uprooting herself from the Dower House? Something told her she could never sit serenely by while every girl Adam danced with or spoke to was inspected by the dowagers, and either approved or rejected as an eligible bride. It would be torture, plain and simple. She couldn't do it, and even if it meant only ever seeing him again by the merest chance, she would go to the ends of the earth if it spared her the sight of him courting a more obliging female.

Yet never to see him from one year to the next, to perennially catch sight of tall, powerful, dark-haired men in the distance and hope against hope it was him, and then be so sad and broken when it wasn't, sounded a worthless existence. Wondering scandalously if she stood the slightest chance of changing his mind, when he was so arrogantly convinced that in time she would change hers and agree to become Lady Langthorne, she found herself nodding absently when Rachel suggested cerise trimmings on a purple walking dress, and came under severe scrutiny from her suddenly very critical best friend.

Chapter Sixteen

'You haven't listened to a word Celestine or I have said in the last half-hour, have you?' Rachel accused her, and Serena discovered she was quite right. Mr Garew might have snuck into this exclusively feminine establishment and wafted Rachel off from under her very nose and she would have gone on dreaming of Adam and her prospects of diverting him from his stern and honourable proposal to more scandalous activities.

'No,' she confessed.

'Then we will go home, take tea and then discuss the matter,' Rachel informed her severely.

'What? A purple gown with cerise braid? I rather think not.'

'Certainly not. I would rather put on sackcloth.'

'Well, that's a distinct improvement, then,' Serena offered, in an attempt to divert the coming inquisition.

'Don't try and change the subject,' Rachel murmured, and Serena found herself ruthlessly removed from shopping duties and back in Cavendish Square before she could insist there was too much to do to excuse such slacking.

'Sit there and don't move while I go and find the pins Celestine has left sticking in me somewhere,' Rachel ordered Serena as soon as they were back in their elegant hired sitting room.

'Not even to put off my bonnet?' she joked feebly, but just met with an exasperated look and an order not to be facetious as Rachel hurried off to undress.

Removing the exquisite bonnet Rachel had insisted she buy yesterday, as she was prodded into yet another milliner's establishment, Serena sat back on her chair and sighed. From the look of her, Rachel intended to prise a blow-by-blow account of her relationship with Adam out of her as soon as she returned, and Serena hadn't the heart to cling to her relentlessly cheerful façade much longer. When she contemplated being besieged with relentless arguments she shuddered, and wondered if her noble resolutions could hold out much longer.

'Oh, good day,' Adam greeted her, with a notable lack of enthusiasm, as he wandered into the room with a preoccupied frown on his face.

Why on earth had she just considered giving in and marrying him? Serena wondered, and felt her own temper snap. 'Good day, Sir Adam,' she replied repressively, and hoped vainly that he would wander out again.

'Where's my sister?' he demanded abruptly.

'Not here,' she snapped back.

'That is self-evident. I warned you to keep her close when she and Newbury became betrothed, I believe?' he asked—insufferably.

'You also told me it was unnecessary to dog her every footstep at home, did you not?'

'Yes,' he replied, looking as if he regretted his leniency.

'Garew is in London,' he finally rapped out, and Serena's heart lurched at the anxiety so evident in his eyes now she let herself look into them.

'She went upstairs to change her dress,' she told him, her anger at his abruptness forgotten.

'Then I dare say she's safe enough,' he conceded, and gave her a fleeting smile to acknowledge his temper and the urgency behind it too.

'Tilly would probably fight off Bonaparte's Imperial Guards if they tried to invade Rachel's bedchamber,' she told him, and they sat in uneasy silence for a while as they awaited Rachel's return.

'She's happy, isn't she?' he finally asked, as if doubts about Rachel's obvious delight in her coming marriage had been plaguing him for days.

'Of course. Love shines out of both of them when they're together,' she said, wondering how her friend's delighted incredulity at a second chance at happiness could have failed to impact on her brother.

'That doesn't necessarily mean they must be happy,' he muttered crossly, and Serena fought the sting of tears at that gruff announcement. How she had hurt him, she realised starkly, and temptation and uncertainty knocked against her stubborn belief that it was better to hurt him a little now than a lot later.

'Their love and trust in each other is there for anyone to see,' she said gently, hoping the assurance that at least Rachel and her Luke were happily in love might put their own lack of that happiness aside.

'As you all too obviously do not trust me, I suppose that will have to do.'

Too hurt by his words to even be angry at the moment,

she stared at him as if she had never properly seen him before. 'When have I ever implied I don't trust you, Adam?' she asked at last, finding it far too much of an effort to meet his eyes without flinching and somehow failing to do so.

'Every time you pretend you are nothing more to me than my sister's best friend, when even a five-year-old child would have more sense,' he said, as if finally driven to the end of his patience by her stubborn resistance. 'I have no wish to be done good to, my lady, least of all by you. I have been largely in command of my own destiny these fifteen years or more, so how do you think it feels when the woman I love thinks she can decide what's good for me, as if I were still in short-coats?'

'I have no desire to mother you,' she informed him haughtily.

'I'm very relieved to hear it. Then perhaps you should let me make my own decisions about whom I will or will not marry.'

'Oh, I will. But first you must find a woman foolish enough to wed you, and I wish you joy of her. Meanwhile, I dare say the Duke will arrive soon, and I have no desire to be discovered here arguing with you in this ridiculously over-gilded drawing room.'

'He doesn't want to marry you, I do.'

'Perhaps that's why I like him so well,' she said recklessly.

'You think you can laugh this off, Serena?' he rasped, in a voice now so coldly furious she had a job recognising it as his. 'Turn me off with a few shallow words and a joke? You have misjudged the matter if so.'

'Do I look as if I'm funning?' she faltered, her stomach sinking at the glint of fury in his eyes and the hurt behind it. That look of torment took away the edge of fury that had been keeping her warm and self-righteous up until now.

'Then kindly acknowledge that I'm a man and not a whipped boy, nor a spoiled earl without a single thought in his head for anyone but himself, my darling. I love you as I could never love another woman if I live to be a hundred. Can you put *that* in words of polite good sense and pretend it doesn't exist? I'm not sure that I can any more, and God alone knows I have tried to do so for your sake. For too long I've fought my very nature for you, Serena. I've concealed my feelings with stiff little courtesies and pretend indifference until I'm sickened by it all. No more. Either you take me or leave me, but I'm damned if I'll pretend indifference to you any longer. The whole world can know that I love you for all I care—and if you reject what we have, what we are, they can damn well know that as well.'

'But you know why I can't marry you,' she said weakly.

'Stop lying to me, even if you can't let yourself know the truth, Serena. You could marry me—if you had any faith in the strength and breadth of our feelings for each other at all.'

She stood staring at him, as if she expected lightning to strike at such a blatant misrepresentation of her motives. 'It would be selfish,' she told him earnestly.

'Not as selfish as you refusing to see reason and condemning us both to live in bitter loneliness for the rest of our days, my love,' he told her passionately, and Serena felt as if the earth trembled under her feet.

She took in the absolute certainty in his deep voice and his fervent gaze, and all she had thought so set and right became fluid and doubtful. *Could* he be right? *Was* it more self-serving to refuse to yield to this vast feeling between them just because she so badly wanted to?

'You might meet someone else,' she offered hesitantly, beginning to believe it as unthinkable as he apparently did—and hadn't her jealous heart been informing her of that same unshakeable certainty for weeks?

'I wouldn't insult another woman with the remnants of myself left over from loving you,' Adam told her grimly, as if the very idea revolted him.

Serena felt as if her heart had melted and reformed inside her, even as her thoughts caught up and raced along with it. It was there as surely as the sky above and nature's inevitable cycles, and in the face of it she felt a fool for trying to pretend this was a common or garden infatuation between them when it was love: real, deep, true love. All she had to do was reach to him and he would meet her, match her, complete her and complement her every time. She raised her hand towards him, a ridiculous, fatuous, loving smile lighting up her face as she did so, and...

'I hesitate to break in upon such a touching scene,' a cynical voice said from the French doors open onto the secluded courtyard garden beyond, and Serena started and tumbled back to earth with a terrible jarring thump of reality.

'Oh, and don't expect your estimable butler to summon help for you, will you? He's far too occupied with his own plight to care in the least about yours,' the thin figure in a ragged coat continued, with such chilling indifference that Serena heartily wished she had kept her pistol close to hand, instead of in her reticule on a side-table several yards away.

'You're late, Garew,' Adam told the newcomer nonchalantly.

'I would've arrived sooner if not for you,' the wretched

man replied, waving the long barrelled pistols he held in each hand as if they were aids to self-expression rather than deadly weapons. 'I had to take the stage and hide in the rookeries, thanks to your interference. Now I'm here, though, I shall offer a fair trade—although you don't deserve one.'

Garew sighted his right-hand pistol on Serena's heart, then slunk over and locked the door as they stood frozen in their tracks. Cocking the hammer with deadly efficiency, he met Adam's eyes with mockery in his icy, peculiarly colourless ones.

'Your queen for my rook,' he drawled, as if it was no more than a casual game of chess.

Serena thought his arrogance could be his downfall, if Adam had time to take advantage of it, so she fell back towards the nearest chair as if her legs wouldn't hold her. That elegantly lethal weapon never wavered from its target, but a look of contempt quirked Garew's thin-lipped mouth.

'The dear ladies,' he murmured with a shake of the head. 'So much sensibility and so very little sense, bless them all.'

'And your sister in particular?' Adam asked mockingly.

'If I'd known she was a goldmine I wouldn't have begrudged her keep.'

'I don't believe you have had the misfortune of meeting Mr Alfred Garew, Lady Summerton?' Adam countered, with a look of kingly contempt for the man that would have told Serena he hated him even if they had met in a ballroom as not very polite acquaintances.

'No, I had no idea I was so lucky in my ignorance,' she replied, and could have kicked herself when the wretched Mr Garew looked both surprised and annoyed that she could string such a sentence together without fainting. She sincerely pitied his unfortunate sister, and ducked her head submissively while furtively moving closer to her open reticule, hoping he couldn't see the deadly little weapon her fear of him had caused her to keep there.

'Mr Garew was guardian to his sister until she wed Lord Daniel Trent, my dear,' Adam explained, as if such knowledge must be new to her, and Serena wondered what he was about, to paint her as so unknowing. Then she realised he was trying to make her seem unworthy of a bullet, and felt a lurch of apprehension at what else he might risk to divert Garew's fire.

'It was devilish inconvenient,' the wretched man went on, as if discussing an unsatisfactory horse, 'but it put another weapon in my hands.'

'Murder *and* blackmail? How very gentlemanly,' Adam goaded.

'I don't understand,' Serena said plaintively, dropping her head onto one hand in an elegant pose the misogynistic Mr Garew would think suitably silly.

If she could only reach the lethal little pistol and somehow use it, they would have some chance of killing the evil leech before he could kill one of them. She knew now that he had been the cause of her unease that day in the woods. Since she had felt no such a premonition of evil earlier, Garew must have been watching the house and not following Rachel and herself after all. Of course he wouldn't dare show his face in public, lest his creditors found him, even disguised as a rather seedy-looking hack driver. She struggled to keep her contempt off her face and look suitably terrified.

'It's quite simple, my dear,' Adam said slowly and clearly, as if to a child or a want-wit, playing up to her pretence of feather-headed femininity. 'A younger son simply won't do for Garew. He's far too deep with the ten-percents for that. Only a very wealthy duke, so besotted with his new bride that he'll pay anything to keep her safe will do—or do you merely wish your half-sister to possess such an august title, devoted brother as you are?'

'Title be damned,' Garew spluttered, and Serena could see how well placed Adam's barbs were as temper glinted perilously close to madness in his soulless gaze.

'Only because you have no chance of ever inheriting one yourself, I suspect,' Adam observed contemptuously, and Serena wondered if he had gone too far as Garew nigh gobbled with fury.

'But how can that Trent boy become a duke when his brother is still alive?' Serena asked with a frown of bewilderment. 'And what has it got to do with *us*?'

Luckily Garew was now too busy watching Adam for potential tricks to take much notice of her. He steadied his aim on her every now and again, as if to remind the important part of his audience that he should do nothing to endanger her, but that was all. She waited for Garew's attention to wander again.

'A very telling observation, don't you think, Garew?' Adam asked. 'The answer, of course, being that he can't. Garew must remove the obstacle to his brother-in-law's succession before the current Duke can marry and beget an heir.'

'Then why didn't you just shoot him instead of coming here?' Serena asked, a little too acutely, then redeemed her wilting lily act by thrusting her hand into her reticule and pulling out a lacy handkerchief to sob into. 'That poor man—hurt and lying there in the dark. The thought makes me feel faint.'

'Quite,' Adam said, with a grimace Serena sincerely hoped was as much an act as her own snivels and trembles. 'But please calm yourself, dear Lady Summerton. Dwelling on an idea that distresses you so must be deleterious to your health,' he added, with the exaggerated masculine patience of a man threatened with feminine hysterics.

What? More deleterious than being shot in the chest? she was tempted to ask indignantly. But staying in role was too important for pride just now. She managed to squeeze out a tear or two to lull the repulsive Garew into thinking her a suitably broken reed. She only just managed to conceal her triumph when he shot her a look of contempt and let his aim waver as he averted his gaze. Evidently taunting Adam with their imminent death, or her exchange for a hostage Luke would do anything to reclaim, even at the cost of his own life, was much more fun. She decided Garew was a coward as well as a fool. Only a fool would think to get away with such a wild scheme.

'Do you have your burglars handy, Garew?' Adam asked, and Serena frowned into her handkerchief. Was he *trying* to get himself killed?

'Fools every one of them—and Wharton the worst of the lot,' Garew muttered, and Serena saw madness fighting with the dark purpose in his repellent gaze.

'Which makes you the fool for employing him in the first place, don't you think?'

Adam pushed at that glimmer of insane fury again, and Serena barely suppressed a shudder.

'And provides some answer as to why I have just received notice from Lord Summerton of the poor wretch's murder.'

Serena froze with genuine horror at this further proof

of the man's villainy. And as those long and deadly duelling pistols swung round to focus on Adam instead of her, she realised what he was doing by inflaming this cruel murderer. *No,* she silently pleaded with him. *Don't distract him from me by getting yourself shot instead.* And agony shot through every part of her as she imagined the terrible separation of death. Determined to thwart them both, she slid her hand into her reticule and thrust the pistol into the folds of her skirt in a lightning-fast move, while those oddly blank eyes flicked back to her coldly and dismissed her as irrelevant.

All she needed now was a suitable distraction to make him take his eyes and his aim from Adam, and she could shoot him. At such close range the little pistol should be deadly enough. There was no point in trying to disable him when he held a pistol in each hand.

'Sir Adam? Sir Adam—are you in there?' Rackstraw shouted from the other side of the door as the handle rattled and urgent fists hammered on the door.

'Garew! I know you're in there,' Luke's voice yelled manfully through the intervening inches of solid mahogany.

Garew let out a string of curses that almost led Serena to cover her ears at such virulence—proof that he kept the lowest company in the London stews. Instead she tightened her hand on the slender little pistol and furtively cocked it under cover of the noise their would-be rescuers made.

'Checkmate, I believe,' Adam said coolly. 'You will have to shoot my butler now. As well as the Duke, myself and her ladyship.'

Serena felt horror jar through every pore of her body, her every instinct screaming as Garew finally lost control of his careening mind and tightened his grip on the trigger of his pistols under that reckless goad. Damn Adam for deciding the man was too unstable to be trusted not to turn and shoot her out of sheer frustration.

Quicker than she could even think, Serena raised her pistol and shot Garew. Hard on the heels of her own shot both Garew's pistols discharged, and Serena waited for Adam to fall down in mortal agony, deciding her own life would come to an end with his. Instead Garew swayed, and she saw surprise clear the stony chill from his gaze in one last grasp at sanity before they closed and he slumped to the floor with a surprisingly loud thump.

Chapter Seventeen

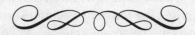

'**I**'ve killed him,' she said hollowly, and slowly subsided onto the sofa as if her bones had gone to water.

'And nearly killed me in the process,' Adam told her with a wry quirk of his mouth that might have passed for a smile in a dark alley at midnight. 'When I saw you pull that pistol out like a conjuror's trick card, my whole life flashed before me.'

The banging on the door reached thunderous levels as he stepped over the fallen Garew without bothering to see if he were alive or dead and gently prised the pistol out of Serena's frozen grip.

'Don't think of claiming *you* shot him,' she told him urgently.

'Why not? Afraid I'll get all the glory?'

'No—afraid you'll try and hang for me,' she wavered, and he looked as if he would have liked to wobble down onto the sofa beside her and hold her until they were both breathless, or more breathless—than they were already.

The thunder moved on to jarring thuds, as if someone was running at the stout door and trying to break through by sheer will-power and velocity. With a look that told her to stay exactly where she was and say nothing, Adam went over to the door and unlocked it, just as another charge battered against it. Wondering if she really was becoming hysterical, Serena struggled not to laugh as the Duke of Newbury barrelled into the room and straight into Adam's startled arms.

'Not quite the embrace I had in mind,' Adam informed his visitor suavely as he disentangled himself and headed back to Serena's sofa, where he stood behind her as if daring the world to comment.

'Adam—Adam, are you all right? And Serena; what on earth have you both been up to?' Rachel's voice sounded confused and urgent and exasperated as she stood in the doorway with half the household behind her.

'First things first, Rachel,' Adam said, as he reluctantly took his hand from Serena's shoulder at last and nodded towards Garew's prone body. 'Let's see if he's alive or no.'

A few seconds' awed silence and Serena held her breath, waiting for the full shock of what she had done to hit her.

'Just a ball in the shoulder,' Rachel said impatiently, as if the man lying on the rug bleeding had done it just to annoy her. 'He's fainted,' she added with an expression of disgust.

'Good—then he'll live to stand trial for murder,' Adam said grimly.

'Since I didn't know he had murdered anyone, would one of you like to tell me what is going on?' Rachel said with awesome patience.

'Hmm, in a minute,' Adam told her absently, and then rapped off a string of orders that snapped everyone into action instead of fascinated attention.

Very soon Garew had been carried off to the wine cellar

and left to recover what senses he possessed alone, after Rachel had bandaged his wound as roughly as she had it in her to treat any wounded soul. Bow Street was informed of their prisoner and his location, and Rackstraw's poor head tended rather more tenderly. Tea and brandy arrived at last, and the four of them sat down to recover from a very busy morning.

Rackstraw imperturbably shut the door on the quality and went off to inform his minions to mind their own business and do as they were bid. 'It'll make sense sooner or later,' he told them philosophically, and resorted to his pantry to settle his own ruffled feathers in peace until it did so.

'Now, am I to finally find out what you two have been up to?' Rachel broke the silence in the sitting room that had felt remarkably peaceful and comfortable once more after such startling events.

'We were innocent bystanders,' Adam informed his sister.

'You were never a blameless onlooker in your life,' she told him crossly, and Serena could see how shaken she was by their brush with danger.

'But for the death of that meagre tool he employed to put me in that vault in the first place, I would be inclined to let Garew go. Still, no doubt his other partners in crime will turn against him to save their necks,' Luke said, as his hand reached inevitably for Rachel's. She laid hers in it as if his was the only comfort against her remembered terror for her brother and Serena.

'When we find them,' Adam cautioned.

'I have more faith in Bow Street than you appear to have, Langthorne, and if they don't manage to catch his cohorts I dare say you will now Garew has threatened your lady,' the Duke said shrewdly.

'Aye, I'll do whatever needs to be done to prosecute the case,' Adam replied coldly, and Serena shivered at the hard determination in his eyes.

Seeing it, he reached his hand to hers in turn, and covered her cold one with his warm one, giving it a reassuring squeeze that she returned eagerly and openly—even if she wasn't as frightened by the memory of the last few minutes as the gentlemen gave her credit for.

'Is it true, then?' Rachel asked breathlessly, her fury and her curiosity toward any other subject forgotten in an instant.

'Is what true?' Adam responded infuriatingly.

'You know perfectly well what I mean,' she insisted, and then, deciding her brother was impossible, she turned to Serena, an eager question in her fine brown eyes. 'Are you his lady at long last?' she asked bluntly, and Serena felt the tension in Adam's long, strong fingers as he waited for her to speak.

'If Sir Adam wishes,' she admitted, with a joyous smile up into her lover's ardent and rather surprised gaze. Need and pride and relieved satisfaction blazed through it, and Serena felt her bones melt and her heart sing. She let her own pride in him, and her heady, tumultuous longing for her lover, show naked in her eyes as they met his with a smile of recognition that they were indeed going to be happy after all.

'Just as well, as you two being closeted in this room together for so long is sure to come out in court,' Rachel told them sternly, mischief and joyous satisfaction robbing her words of any censure.

'We were ably chaperoned by a murderer, don't forget,'

Adam drawled, with a grin for his sister that told her he didn't care if they *had* been caught alone in the most compromising circumstances. The woman he loved was going to marry him and, yes, he was as happy as the proverbial sand boy.

'True,' the Duke put in with a chuckle. 'I challenge even the wildest rake to compromise a lady whilst being held at gunpoint by a lunatic.'

Even Miss Estelle Langthorne dragged herself from her beloved books to take dinner with them all and toast Adam and Serena. She gave the happy couple a vague smile that told everyone she was as pleased by their romance as she could be by anything outside the covers of a book, and informed them that she fully intended to retire to the Langthorne Dower House and work on the treatise on botanical curiosities she had been longing to write for so long—if she could command Marclecombe's library whenever she needed it.

'You may denude it of every volume, if only you will dance at my wedding, Cousin,' Adam said with a smile Serena privately thought no sentient woman would manage to resist.

'Aye, gladly,' Miss Langthorne informed him, and for once her gaze was shrewd as it dwelt upon Serena and her lover. Indeed only her presence lent a sop to the proprieties as Adam had refused to let Serena go since she had finally promised to marry him, and Luke and Rachel were no help at all.

'I warn you, Serena, six months is quite long enough for any man to wait for a wife,' Adam told her as they climbed the stairs together, oblivious to Rachel and Luke kissing each other a lingering and regretful goodbye in front of whoever happened to cross the hall.

'Then we should elope, perhaps?' she asked serenely,

loving the feel of his muscular body moving so closely against hers, so openly intimate it felt as if the world was theirs for the asking. 'I could enjoy a long, romantic dash to the Border in the right company, Sir Adam,' she informed him, with an inviting smile she hoped he would find irresistible—because she really didn't want to spend another long and lonely night alone.

'I'd rather we used the special licence I've been taking out and brooding over so often I dare swear it is nearly illegible.'

'You were very sure of me, Adam.'

'We were born for each other, Serena, but I was afraid you'd never admit it.'

'I was determined not to.'

'Stubborn woman,' he muttered, and pulled her even closer, to kiss her as if he couldn't help himself now she had finally given in.

After that nothing else was decided except that they were not to be trusted to behave properly. Rachel marched up the stairs and found them locked in a passionate embrace where, as she informed them sternly, anyone could see them and very likely would. 'And here I am, an innocent and unmarried lady as well,' she chided them as they reluctantly disentangled themselves from each other's arms and eyed her reproachfully.

'And there's every likelihood you'll remain one if you don't learn a little tact,' her brother muttered darkly.

'Then I shall stay here and plague you for the rest of our natural lives, brother dear.'

'Heaven forbid. I must remember to tell Newbury I'll double the settlement if he weds you out of hand.'

'Don't trouble yourself. One over-hasty wedding in the family will prove quite enough scandal for now. And I have every intention of marrying him in my own good time, thank you very much.'

'Something I thank God for on my knees every night,' Adam informed her outrageously.

'Take no notice of him, Rachel,' Serena urged. 'The best way to silence his teasing is to ignore it.'

Rachel impulsively hugged as much of both of them as she could fairly reach. 'I do love you both, you know,' she said, and then turned and gave Adam a quizzical look. 'Even if I'm sometimes hard pressed to know quite why.'

'The feeling is altogether mutual,' he informed his sister with a lopsided smile, and hugged her back enthusiastically.

Half an hour later, Adam lay back against crisply clean linen pillows and luxuriated in the pristine sheets with a very contented sigh. All he needed to make his night perfect was the company of the woman he loved beyond life itself, and he shifted uncomfortably as the very thought of Serena sharing his bed rendered him painfully aroused.

'Three days!' he muttered into the shadows, and tried to tell himself that it wasn't very long at all. 'God, *I'll* be the lunatic by the end of them,' he told the bed curtains, with a lame attempt at a wry grin.

'It sounds to me as if you're well on the way to being one of those already,' Serena told him, amazing them both by tiptoeing into the room and boldly picking up a corner of the grand bedclothes on his grand bed, sliding into it before he had hardly caught his breath.

'You don't seem very pleased to see me, Adam,' she told him reproachfully. Maybe he was more strait-laced than she had thought, and would insist on chastity until they could finally wed; perhaps he was even horrified by her boldness?

'If you had any idea how glad I am, you would probably bolt for your room faster than I can say knife, so you'd best decide very quickly whether or not you mean it, Serena.'

Shifting against the snowy pillows with none of the satisfaction he had felt in them only minutes earlier, Adam met her eyes with a final attempt at coolness and self-control.

'Of course I do, you silly man,' she told him with un-ladylike impatience, and glared straight into his intent golden-brown eyes.

'What a henpecked husband I promise to be,' he told her in a dangerous tone that gave the lie to every word.

'Perhaps. But for now I want you as my lover,' she managed to tell him steadily. 'Husbands fill me with trepidation. But lovers…' She let her voice trail off and gave him what she sincerely hoped was a seductive look from under her eyelashes.

'Serena!' he protested harshly, his fingers contracting into impotent fists as he seemed to fight a battle with himself not to reach out and shake her. 'Don't even mention me in the same breath as Cambray when we lie together. If you're going to bring him to bed with us I'll wait to marry you until you can put him in the grave, where he belongs.'

'No!' she protested in return, horrified by his misunderstanding. 'I just want everything we do together to be different. I never had a lover before, so won't you be mine again tonight, my love, so I can dream of my wild soldier lover when I'm a sober married woman? Then you can be my wild husbandly lover, and I can dream about him as well.'

As she spoke the tension, or at least the angry part of it, drained out of his magnificent body—and come to think of it there was rather more of it on show than she had been expecting.

'Do you always sleep naked?' she asked, trying not to let her voice rise into a ridiculously maidenly squeak as she eyed him with a mix of awe and nervousness.

'We wild lovers never do anything else,' he informed her, in a velvety voice that promised her untold delights as he leaned ever closer and let his mighty chest rub against her respectably covered breasts. The sensation of his lightly haired chest gently abrading her silky-skinned nipples nearly made her sob with sheer wanton longing. 'I have heard it said that wild seductresses do likewise,' he informed her, with a grin that did nothing whatsoever to make her think he might prove a tame bedmate.

'Don't you know?' she gasped faintly.

'No, I never met a wild seductress quite like you, love. So do you think we could stop talking long enough to remove this thing?' he asked, with a dismissive wave of his hand at her nightgown.

'Yes, I think we might,' she agreed, but he won the race to reach for the myriad of buttons that seemed to frustrate every clumsy effort she made to undo them and wrench the wretched thing off.

'Bungler,' he accused, and took over the task. His own fingers shook just a little, and it took longer than Serena could have thought possible as she squirmed under the acres of cotton. 'D'you know, I think I could get to like this thing after all?' he drawled, as he made a deeper and deeper V with each slowly undone button.

'Urgh,' she answered lucidly, as cool air and Adam's softly circling finger stroked yet another inch of exquisitely sensitive skin.

'Precisely,' he muttered, as he bent his head to kiss along the growing gap, and Serena felt as if she might go mad if he didn't hurry.

Her hands rose to tug at the wretched buttons, and he clasped them in his and held them over her head as he brought his mouth down to press hot kisses against the soft skin between her breasts. He explored and feasted and adored as she fought to keep her body from bucking them eagerly off the bed. He raised his head and met her eyes through the shadows of the dying fire, and now all teasing had flown and urgency was hot in his gaze, yet it was almost as if he pleaded with her to loose something in herself she still hadn't yet dared let go, even with the love of her life.

'I want you so much I hurt,' she murmured, and his pupils flared. Yet still he waited, his fingers wandering deliciously under the now gaping cotton. 'I love you, Adam, so very much. When you are not by me I can't wait for you to return. When you're near I dare not look at you too often in case I behave like a trollop in front of whoever happens to be with us.'

'Why did you change your mind?' he asked, as if the question hurt him. 'I want you for my wife, Serena, even if tonight I'm raging with need of you as the only lover I'll ever have from now until my dying day. You're the only wife I have ever wanted, the only woman I ever will want.'

'Good—for if I ever found you were wanting another I might have to kill you both,' she joked, and then sobered as her deep blue eyes glowed with feelings she hardly had the words to articulate. 'You're the only man I ever want, Adam. Once upon a time I fell for a chimera of love—a shadow of what you are. I only knew where I had gone so wrong when I set eyes on you again and saw the man I had always dreamt of.'

'Six months,' he told her in a gravelly voice that even she had never heard from him before. 'Six whole, endless, tortured months and you kept me at arm's length because of Cambray's clumsiness?'

Serena wondered for a moment if he might really shake her this time, and she smoothed a loving hand over his wildly curling dark hair and brought it down to shape his lean cheek.

'Well, they do say love turns one's wits to water, don't they?'

'If they don't, then they certainly should,' he responded with a rueful smile, and suddenly everything was right between them.

Serena had a delightful suspicion it always would be.

'Speaking of which, why are we still talking?' she asked boldly, and smoothed that caressing hand over his tightly clasped jaw and down his neck, to flatten it out against his slightly hair-roughened chest and knead it as appreciatively as a purring cat.

'I don't know why we still can,' he muttered, and finally set about the business of undoing the last of her buttons and releasing her from all that propriety. 'Ah, lover, you're the most beautiful thing I ever saw,' he told her huskily, and moved until he was resting above her on his powerful arms and she was eager and desperate for more.

She sighed her pleasure as his mouth wandered her neck and downward, over her heaving chest, to settle at last and drive her to distraction with sweet flicks of his tongue on her hotly sensitised nipples. By now she was quite beyond rational thought, and her body was writhing and arching against his in emphatic demand. The feel of his fully aroused maleness against the vulnerable, needing heart of her was like nothing she had ever even dared dream of until he became her lover. But the only thing she wanted more than to feel him there was to take him into her again and make real love for the second time in her life.

'Love—Serena mine,' he responded disjointedly to her welcome, as if he too was beyond all but what they meant to each other.

He filled her until yielding and giving was a taking, and every thrust and glide of his mighty body within hers made the warmth and joy of it all grow until it seemed to have taken over the world. Even as they raced to fulfilment nothing could stop their exquisite unity of spirit, and his pleasure was almost as important to her as hers was to Adam. From now on, she thought with her last rags of rational thought, she would learn how to please him as mightily as he pleased her. Then he yelled out her name, as if he could only lose himself if she went with him, and suddenly they were convulsed with indescribable pleasure. Serena was rocked by joy and crying with bliss as they clung to each other through the wondrous storm of delight.

'Oh, Adam—oh, oh, oh!' she finally whispered into his sweat-glistened torso.

'Oh, good—or oh, not too bad?' he asked gruffly, and she couldn't believe he didn't know how radically he had just rearranged her entire world again.

'Oh, you idiot,' she said, and managed to find enough strength from somewhere to clench her fist weakly and thump him half-heartedly.

He chuckled, and she smiled contentedly against the broad chest that she was quite unable to relinquish using as a pillow for now. It had been the right thing to say, and she snuggled into the warmth of him, the fine smell of his salty skin, the irresistible intimacy of hearing his heartbeat so close to her ear. She licked her lips and savoured the taste of him on her tongue, and felt tension gather in the impressive muscles so sleek and delicious under her touch.

'I trust that as wild lovers go that was satisfactory, then, my lady?'

'Perfectly,' she murmured, and made the delightful discovery that the tiny male nipple under her bold tongue was as responsive to the right caress from the right lover as hers had been to him.

'Stop that, you houri,' he demanded, with very little urgency.

'I'm really not fit to wed a respectable baronet and former officer of His Majesty's dragoons,' she told him, with such blatant satisfaction that he laughed joyously.

'Any more than I match up to that very respectable widow woman the youngest Lady Summerton.'

'Then shall you look back on your wild, wanton lover and sigh for her when we are old and grey and nearly in our dotage, Sir Adam?' she asked with a cheeky smile as she looked up into his eyes at last, and wriggled curves that suddenly felt luscious and seductive against his harder planes and angles.

'I shall certainly do so for the three days I must live without you until we are a respectable married couple at long last,' he responded, with a wicked smile that told him he had no more finished exploring her than she had him. 'I might be driven to my dotage by sheer desperation when it takes so confoundedly long to arrange our wedding.'

'I have heard that clandestine meetings are the very

stuff of life for rakes and their wanton lovers,' she informed him with a tender, sultry look she hoped would drive any such notion out of his head for ever. 'After all, if we're to be saddled with each other for a lifetime, we might as well pack in as many illicit experiences as we can to sustain us during all those years of dull respectability.'

'That we might, my wicked lady—but just tell me one thing before we do, Serena,' he said and was suddenly all seriousness. 'Why did you relent and agree to marry me at last? If what you say is true, you have loved me nearly as long as I have you, and despite that you did everything you could not to wed me. What changed your mind?

'I realised love was the gift in itself, not the family I might or might not be able to give you. That would just have been a blessing we might have been granted if I had eloped with you as you signally failed to ask me to do five years ago. Instead I had to wed George and learn what love was not. So even before that wretched Garew creature came along and interrupted us, I knew that to turn away love was ignoring the greatest gift a man and woman could give each other. He didn't make me realise I couldn't live without you, Adam. I knew before that even dying without you would be agony.'

'Oh, Serena, my love, you humble me. Here I was, wondering if he'd blundered in and changed your mind with his theatricals and his lunacy and instead you had got to the heart of it before I did myself. It was only when he threatened to shoot you that I realised I didn't just want to marry you, I needed to wed you and love you and grow old with you more than I need to breathe.'

'Then three days should provide quite enough illicit pleasure to last us a lifetime, don't you think?' she asked.

'I doubt it. There's nothing in the marriage vows to say

married couples are forbidden illicit pleasures so long as they experience them together—or at least there wasn't the last time I looked.'

'How very remiss of them.'

'Or how very understanding,' he argued softly, and kissed her so soundly that it was a very long time before Serena could think of anything to say at all.

Epilogue

'So, are you finally going to admit it, Lady Langthorne?' Adam asked his wife, with a smile that almost took the edge off his distinct air of self-satisfaction.

'Admit what?' Serena asked him warily. Having been wed to the domestic tyrant at her side for a whole year now, she knew a lot better than to give him any encouragement to believe himself omnipotent.

'That I was right and you were wrong,' he replied, with a scorching look that could still make her knees feel as if they were about to melt and her insides do some very unlikely things, as if they had first met and loved only yesterday, instead of a little more than a whole memorable year ago.

'Oh, that. No, of course I'm not,' she replied, and leant much of her weight against his powerful body, luxuriating in the fact of him, the never-ending fascination of being his wife, and the downright pleasure of feeling him take her weight for a change.

'On principle, I suppose?' he murmured, enjoying the solid fact of her and their coming child against his muscular frame nearly as much as she was enjoying resting there, she decided.

'Of course. You would be unbearable for evermore,' she told him, resisting the temptation to tell him anything he wanted to hear so long as he took her inside and made love to her, despite her impressive girth and swollen ankles, neither of which he seemed to regard as a drawback in the face of her oft expressed opinion to the contrary.

'Whereas holding out for so long in the face of all logical argument was the epitome of common sense and cool consideration?'

'Of course it was,' she managed to murmur, despite the fact that his mouth was coming ever nearer and she wanted his kiss perhaps even more than she'd used to when she had been nearly convinced the right to them would be forever beyond her.

'Women!' he muttered, as he took her mouth in a rough caress that spoke everything of his desire and downright need of her and nothing of compulsion or irritation.

Although they had loved in harmony and in exasperation, in heated haste and slow, racked sweetness, this felt so right, so essential, that Serena knew each day and year they were together would just make it all seem even better. If loving each other had been easy, perhaps it wouldn't now be so rich and so endlessly exciting, she mused, before she felt the familiar conviction that she was about to slip under a cloud of hazy, golden delight and not come out until she had been well and truly made love to by her passionate, insistent, and very masculine husband.

'I know,' she muttered, in defiance of that phenomena as soon as she could summon up enough breath. 'We're quite wonderful, are we not?'

'Absolutely unbelievable,' he concurred, as he rubbed her pregnant belly absently. She almost purred under his ministrations, and the baby signalled its approval with a series of cartwheels that made her wince, despite her impatience to meet the little thug.

'I still think he's a potential dragoon captain,' she told him, as the acrobatics finally subsided.

'More likely she's going to be a graceful and charming lady, almost as lovely as her mama, and will drive me mad with her unsuitable suitors and contrary temper one day all too soon.'

'I look forward to it,' she said complacently, and protested volubly when he stopped rubbing in revenge and tried to look stern.

'You are a shrew, madam wife, and between you and the latest Miss Langthorne I shall lead a dog's life.'

'No, you won't. You'll be too busy fetching him down from trees and hiding your saddles so he doesn't ride off with your finest racehorse to have time to lead one of those.'

'I suppose she could be a hoyden, just like her mama used to be—still is, for that matter,' he told her infuriatingly, and Serena wasn't sure if she most wanted to kiss him or slap him.

'I'm not. I will have you know that I'm a respectable married woman—very nearly matronly, in fact.'

'And I'm the Emperor of China.'

'If you are, I have no desire whatsoever to be Empress.'

'Then you may be my chief concubine,' he allowed generously.

'Thank you for that.'

'Don't mention it.'

'Never fear, I won't. But I will take the little emperor-in-waiting off to rest without his father if you're not very careful indeed.'

'Oh, I'm always careful,' he lied outrageously, and Serena laughed up at him before giving him the beckoning look of blatant invitation she had been practising so diligently for the last twelvemonth and more. 'Fairly careful,' he amended huskily. 'If I was more cautious I might have had you to myself for a while longer.'

'I like this arrangement far too well to repine,' she murmured, and felt as if the sunlight and life and freshness of this late spring day had invaded her very soul with the delight of it all. 'In fact it seems to me almost the perfect arrangement.'

'Oh it is—and one I had every intent of bringing about the instant I laid eyes on you again, lady mine.'

'Arrogant, cocksure rogue of a cavalryman that you were.'

'Sensible, practical country squire as I am now, you mean?'

'No, Adam,' she gasped, as he proved the untruth of that statement all too easily by feathering kisses down her throat and lingering over the new abundance of her breasts, before closing oh-so-gently over her sensitised nipple through her wispy muslin gown.

'No, Adam—or *no* Adam?' he breathed as he reluctantly raised his head from the abundance nature was arranging for his coming child.

'No, Adam—never let me go and don't stop.'

'You may be very sure of that. But I think we had better go indoors, before we shock the noble Duke and his Duchess to their very core by making love on their ducal lawn, where anyone might see us.'

'I doubt it. I suspect they are too intent on causing a

scandal of their own,' Serena told him distractedly as his actions gave the lie to his prudent words.

'I dare say,' Adam informed her, indifferent to his sister's behaviour for once in their lives and defying Serena's protests that she was too tall and far too heavy with child to be carried upstairs to the grandest guest bedroom in the Duke of Newbury's grand mansion. 'All I know is that I scandalously love you, my darling Serena, and will do until there is no more now to do it in.'

'And I love you, Adam, so very much it hurts.'

'Then we must be doing it wrong,' he informed her outrageously, and Serena thumped him on a broad shoulder before he let her slide down his powerful frame and into his arms, just so he could prove to her one more time that they were in fact doing a great many things absolutely right, and had every intention of going on doing them for a very long time.

* * * * *

Texas Wedding for Their Baby's Sake

KATHRYN ALBRIGHT

Prologue

Charleston, South Carolina—February 1836

Caroline Benét searched through her basket of ribbons for the length of burgundy silk she had saved to decorate the veranda's front post. It had been here only moments before. She was getting flustered with all the last minute details she'd had to contend with before the start of the benefit social. Something tightened around her waist and suddenly warm lips pressed to her neck, just below her right ear, sending a shiver down her spine. "I believe I missed this spot the other night," whispered a rich, baritone voice. "Now, you're my hostage."

The strength in her knees wavered. *Brandon.* He'd finally arrived. Caroline checked her waist and found the burgundy ribbon wrapping her mid-section. With a tug, he spun her around to face him. His eyes, the deepest blue of the Charleston Bay water, twinkled with warmth. She wanted to return the kiss much more intimately than the present public site would allow. However, she settled for pretending to straighten the silk bow tie she'd given him for Christmas.

"I've missed you." His smile was for her alone as he pulled the ribbon at her waist to bring her closer yet.

She pushed halfheartedly against his chest. "Not here, Brandon. Anyone could see." Guests milled about the plantation's front lawn and through the gardens in the back. It was nearly time to start the festivities.

He didn't budge, but seemed to loom even closer. A proprietary smile eased his angular features. "Not until you admit you missed me, too."

The veranda railing pressed against her spine. She sniffed the air. "Is that liquor on your breath?" she asked, stalling, making him wait as he'd made her wait and wonder the past few days.

"You're avoiding my request."

She hadn't fooled him. He knew exactly what she was doing. "If you'll give me room, I'll answer."

He stepped back. Waiting. Confident. Downright cocky in fact and most likely due to her sudden lack of moral strength three nights past. The look on his face both thrilled her and worried her. Now that she had succumbed once, it surprised her to realize how easy it would be to do so again. It also alarmed her. A barrier had crumbled that she had no desire to rebuild. She wouldn't let it happen again. She had a reputation to uphold as a Benét.

She sighed. "You could have sent a note, something to reassure me. I…I thought you might be displeased."

His dark brows drew together. "I'll never understand women. Why in the world would I be displeased with you?"

"Well." She struggled to order her thoughts. "I haven't heard from you for days! And after we'd…" She couldn't say it out loud. Anyone could hear.

"You received my flowers?"

"Yes."

The crease in his forehead smoothed. He took her hand in his and pulled her around the corner, away from the eyes of her guests. "I thought of you every moment we were apart."

His admission released a coil in her gut that had been tense for days. "I missed you, too."

A smile played across his face—the mysterious one she loved. It conveyed an intimate promise for her future. He touched his lips lightly to hers. "I had no idea my proper fiancée would be so passionate. When I get you alone again…"

A thrill coursed through her at the thought his words conveyed, but with it came a stab of worry. "Brandon. No. You mustn't press me. Not until we are married."

"Then we had better announce our plans today, because I don't want to wait."

"I confess I feel the same way." Her cheeks warmed with the admission. "Are you shocked?"

Before he answered, a commotion on the lawn drew their attention. Brandon grimaced. "I see my brother has arrived."

"Your brother?" The black sheep. "When did he get in?"

"Three days ago. A full month late. Says he didn't receive word of Father's illness." A deep, buried anger seemed to boil up as Brandon spoke. His knuckles blanched with his grip on the porch railing.

"Do you believe him?" she asked.

He didn't answer for a moment. "It doesn't matter now."

But obviously, it did matter. Brandon had come to her the very night his brother had returned after a ten-year absence—and then he'd mentioned nothing about him.

Caroline watched as two of her friends blushed at something Brandon's brother said. So this was Jake. She studied the man who was seven years older than Brandon and who'd caused him so much ambivalence over the years. Most likely he was completely unaware of the pain he'd brought.

He wore dark trousers, a cotton shirt and a vest—yet still he looked more the rugged frontiersman than anything she'd ever seen in Charleston before. He didn't seem concerned that he was underdressed without a coat and tie for the occasion and decidedly out of his element. Indeed, he oozed self-assurance to the brim and, having seen and admired that same trait in Brandon, Caroline wondered if such was the trait of any Dumont man. She watched as a group of Brandon's friends cast interested glances at the newcomer and walked over to meet him.

"Looks like he has made a few conquests already." Brandon turned his back on the scene and faced her. "He keeps asking about the will. After being gone for ten years that's all he cares about—his share."

"It must be awkward for you."

"I can't welcome him home. It's just not in me. Besides, he already told me he's not staying. Just wants his money."

"He *said* that?" She hardened her heart toward the man. She couldn't believe he was so callous.

"It's the feeling I get."

"Has he owned up to why he left in the first place?" She knew Brandon had always wondered. It would be good if they could clear up some things between them.

"No. But Jake had every right to take off back then. I would have, too, if I'd been older."

"You showed stronger moral character by staying."

He huffed. "I was only twelve at the time—hardly old enough to run away. And Father had me under his thumb."

"He trained you well. You're the best surgeon on the coast." She unloosed the ribbon from her waist with a saucy smile, hoping to lighten his mood. "And just look where that's brought you—to my veranda."

He smiled. "I guess I do have him to thank for that." He tugged a tendril of hair that had escaped from her crocheted hairnet. "You always see the best in things."

"Is this Caroline?" A deep voice came from the stairs.

Brandon's jaw tightened. He stepped back indicating the tall man behind him. "Caroline Benét, may I present my brother, Jake Dumont."

Jake moved up the last two steps to the veranda and surprised her by taking her hand and bowing slightly. "A pleasure, miss."

She could understand her friends' sudden entrancement with this man. He had charisma to spare. However, she could read between the lines. Jake had caused Brandon grief and hurt over the years with his selfishness. Caroline wasn't about to openly accept him. He would have to prove himself to both of them. She pulled her hand away.

"Welcome, Mr. Dumont. I hope you'll enjoy yourself today. I imagine our little benefit is a far cry from the excitement you are used to."

He straightened at her reserved tone, his eyes narrowing. "Just wanted to spend time with my brother. Meet his friends. See which particular filly had caught his eye."

She didn't care to be equated with a horse. "Brandon tells me you are good with a rifle. Perhaps you would enjoy entering the shooting competition today. It's for a good cause."

"Thanks, but it wouldn't be a fair match. It's better that I just watch."

His lack of humility annoyed her. It would do him good to have a comeuppance. Several of the men here were quite accurate. And as far as she knew, Brandon was the best shot of all of them.

"You're that sure you would win?"

"I've made a living with my gun, scouting for wagons going west. It's an unfair advantage."

"Aren't you interested to learn what the prize will be?" She looked from one brother to the other.

"You're not…" Brandon began. She'd let him in on her plans a week ago.

"I am." She felt an impish grin forming. "The winning prize is a kiss from Abigail Satterly, the prettiest girl in the district."

"That privilege belongs to you," Brandon argued. "But you can be sure I won't have you giving away kisses to anyone."

Her heart thrummed. He was just too perfect, defending her looks that way.

"Are your parents going along with this? For that matter, are Abigail's?"

"It's all for a good cause. They understand that."

Brandon shook his head. "I don't like it."

The sound of polite clapping interrupted them. Brandon offered his elbow. "Sounds like your father's opening speech has started."

She took Brandon's arm to join the guests on the front lawn, conscious of Jake following behind her. Everything was going to be perfect in spite of his intrusion into their lives. She wouldn't allow it to be any other way.

The weather was just right—sunny and cool for the start of February. The Spanish moss draping the cypress trees swayed in the light breeze. It would be wonderful to meet the goal her fledgling organization had set of one thousand dollars. With the bake sale, the games of croquet, the shooting match and the generous amount of liquor, surely the guests would feel inclined to open their purse strings.

As her father's speech continued, Caroline considered what would be the best time today for Brandon to announce their engagement. Having already given their consent to the marriage, her parents wanted a date set. Mother had dropped hints that the governor would be invited along with Charleston's mayor and she was anxious to start the process of invitations, deciding on a caterer and all the other minutiae that went into creating the perfect wedding. Mother was at her best when planning and putting on extravagant parties—and as her only daughter, Caroline knew she would spare no expense. Caroline could just envision the guest list—the elite of the East Coast, the associates of Brandon's recently deceased father and her own parents' colleagues.

However, her parents were not nearly so anxious as she was. Just thinking of the passion she'd shared with Brandon…why it made her insides turn to liquid fire. She would not be able to stand a long engagement now that she'd sampled what life with him would be like. That same intense passion that he had directed toward his studies and then his career had suddenly been focused on her. It had been the most intoxicating experience of her life—so far.

After her father welcomed everyone, he turned their attention to Caroline. She was in charge of the baked goods auction. Brandon had promised to bid for her chocolate cake creation and win it no matter what. As anticipated, his friends increased the bid relentlessly to an outrageous sum. With a wide grin on his face, he stepped forward to claim the cake and then good-naturedly ordered that it be sliced and distributed among the guests.

At the end of the auction, Caroline covered the desserts and noting that the large punch bowls of mulled hot cider and brandy had been depleted, excused herself and went to the cookhouse to remedy the situation. She found the building deserted. Apparently the two maids were busy elsewhere.

She stirred the cider in the large caldron and then used a pitcher to dip out the liquid and fill two empty bowls.

"Would you like some help?"

She looked up to see Jake at the door. "No. I can manage. I'll be out in a moment."

Instead of leaving, he walked further into the room and removed his black felt hat. "I get the feeling you are managing very well. My brother is smitten with you."

Something about his tone cautioned her. She stopped pouring and set the pitcher down. "Is there something you want to say?"

"Guess I'm wondering where this relationship is headed. Brandon hasn't told me much about you, but I did hear he'd spoken for you."

"That's right. We're betrothed, although it hasn't been officially announced yet."

"Why is that? What's stopping him?"

"Look. I don't feel comfortable discussing my relationship with Brandon, with you. Why don't you ask him?"

"Because he's not talking to me. In my limited experience, most women are after only one thing."

She frowned, not liking his tone or his words. "And what would that be?"

"Money, of course. Although, I've got to admit it looks like your family is sitting well already."

She gasped. Had the man no manners at all? One didn't discuss finances like this—or speak of women so. "I happen to care deeply for Brandon. We've been good friends the past two years—not that you would have any idea since you haven't been around."

He shrugged. "Couldn't be helped, but I'm here now and I don't intend to see the Dumont estate fall into the hands of just *any* woman."

"You have a strong aversion to the opposite gender, Mr. Dumont? I find that hard to believe considering the way my friends have been throwing themselves at you since you arrived."

"Again, from my experience, women tend to be fickle."

"Then why did you come today if you are so ready to condemn half of the human race?"

"I told you. I wanted to meet the woman who had her sight set on my brother."

"To see if I measure up to your standards?"

"Yes."

Anger welled up inside, nearly choking her. How dare he talk to her like this? He had no idea how she felt about Brandon. Hands on hips, she squared off with him. "Since you are being quite frank, I will be, as well."

"That's how I like it."

"I don't know who gave you such a low opinion of women in your past, but some of us actually do have a heart. I happen to love Brandon, and I think my actions show it, which is more than I can say for you."

An amused smile played about his lips and eyes as he looked down at her.

She clenched her hands into fists, not liking at all the disadvantage of her shorter height. What was he up to?

A grin worked its way onto his face. "Just had to be sure, Miss Benét, and getting a woman riled up tends to make her say what's really on her mind. I needed to know my brother isn't being hoodwinked. I still plan to keep my eyes on you, but I think we understand each other better now."

"You're saying that in some strange way you have been looking out for Brandon by frustrating me?"

"Guess you could call it that. Brandon and I have the estate to settle. I'm sure he's made you aware of that. A stipulation in the will states that we have to be together to learn what it contains."

"All he has said is that you are interested in getting your share and that you planned to leave then."

"Seems like the best choice. I don't exactly feel welcomed—but then I never did. Doesn't mean I don't care what happens to him."

Apparently there was more to Jake's leaving than simply being selfish. If Brandon was aware of it, he certainly hadn't told her, but it was something they should address. The sooner the better. "Jake, I think you should talk to Brandon. You two need to talk before you leave."

His face hardened. "Don't you think I've tried?"

"Caroline!"

At Brandon's call, she turned quickly—and so did Jake. So quickly that they collided with each other. Jake grasped her shoulders, steadying her.

"Caro— What's going on?"

Brandon stood at the door, the surprise on his face transforming into a closed, guarded expression. He looked from Jake to Caroline.

Heat suffused her face despite the fact she wasn't guilty of anything. "Nothing. I'm getting more cider for the guests."

"Getting to know Caroline." Jake stepped back and tipped his hat to her. "I'll see you at the match."

She turned back to filling the bowl and took two deep breaths to calm herself. She couldn't very well tell him what his brother had said.

"Jake couldn't be satisfied with every other woman here today—he had to count you among his conquests?"

"Of course not. I have no interest in him other than as your brother."

"It didn't look that way."

She faced him. "Brandon…how can there be any doubt in your mind after the other night?"

He studied her face for an interminable time, and then finally his shoulders relaxed. "Guess it took my brother coming home to find out I was the jealous type."

"You're head and shoulders more than him."

He pointed at the cider with his chin. "Let's get that out on the table. I'm in need of a partner for the games."

The games on the lawn eventually wound to a close and the men headed toward the gardens and the canal in back where the shooting match would take place. Jake and Brandon stood like tall bookends on each side of her brother, Tom, who showed off the new pistol he'd just purchased. Her parents had tried to dissuade him, but Tom was determined to leave for Texas territory by the end of the week. He and another friend were anxious to prove themselves in the fight for freedom there. He'd tried to talk Brandon into going. Thank goodness, Brandon would rather heal people than shoot at them.

Jake studied the weapon with a practiced eye. He stroked down the cherrywood encased iron barrel, pausing to note the fancy stamped patterns in the brass casing, before checking the sighting.

"Try it out," Tom urged. "Won't hurt to break it in a little before I use it in a real skirmish."

Jake shook his head. "No, thanks. I'm satisfied with my own pistol. It's old, but it shoots straight."

"You should enter the match, Mr. Dumont. You'll make it much more exciting. Brandon here always whips us."

"He does, does he?" Jake looked at his brother with renewed interest. "I did teach him everything he knows about guns."

Brandon huffed. "That was a long time ago. I've learned a few tricks since then."

"That so? I might have to enter at that."

Brandon narrowed his gaze, first on his brother and then on Tom. "I'll give your pistol a try. That'll put me at a disadvantage—unfamiliar gun and all."

"What's the entry fee?" Jake asked.

"Three dollars."

Jake handed the pistol to Brandon. "Think I'll take you up after all. Haven't seen my brother shoot since he was twelve."

Ten men entered the shooting match. Bets were placed—all with the intention of a portion being dedicated to the new hospital addition.

Caroline joined the other ladies in the gazebo. From this vantage point she could see the shooting event in spite of the stovepipe hats worn by many of the men. Her unease grew as each of the local men eventually lost to either Jake or Brandon. It didn't take long. Within the hour, the match had been whittled down to the two brothers. The others good-naturedly bowed out.

Caroline seemed to be the only one to feel the underlying animosity that existed between the two men. They'd covered their emotions well, chiding each other, playing to the crowd. But now, although Brandon still seemed to be at ease, the tension had escalated to a palpable level. They stood, shoulder to shoulder, waiting while the target was moved back ten more paces for the final round. This was no longer a game.

Without speaking, they reloaded their guns, each man concentrating on their final shot and probably playing it out in their mind. A baby cried out among the crowd. At the sound, neither brother flinched.

Caroline could barely breathe. Brandon had to win. He just *had* to.

Brandon took his stance first. He loosened his tie and then set his legs wide, his right shoulder closest to the target two hundred yards down the dirt path that lined the canal. He raised his arm to shoulder level, aiming through the cross-hairs of Tom's new pistol. The crowd hushed. The only sound was that of the breeze rippling the cattails along the water.

He fired. A flash of smoke puffed up from the gun.

Tom raced to the target, checked the shot and turned back to the crowd. "One inch from center!"

Caroline let out her breath. Her heart started beating again. It would be near impossible for Jake to shoot any better at such a distance with such an old gun. Brandon had as much as won the match. He stepped back, his shoulders relaxing, his gaze centered on his brother.

Jake took his position—identical to his brother's stance. His right foot sank deep into the muddy bank, soaking his leather boots, but he seemed oblivious to the distraction. The crowd quieted.

With a loud crack, he discharged his pistol. Then he turned toward Brandon, meeting his eyes. Together they walked to the target while Tom ran from the tall grass to join them there. Everyone waited for the verdict.

Suddenly Tom grabbed Jake's arm and held it up.

Men closed in, clapping Jake on the shoulders and taunting Brandon, who held back, helping to gather the targets. Caroline was proud of him. He hid his tension remarkably well. It couldn't be easy for him to be bested in front of his friends and colleagues by his older brother.

"Now, about that prize you mentioned…" Jake said with a grin as he approached the gazebo. "Time to claim it. Where is this Abigail?"

"There's been a change," her mother said, coming to her side. "I'm afraid Abigail was unable to stay. Caroline will be handing out the prize."

Caroline's jaw dropped in shock. "Mother!"

Mother patted her arm. "Like you said, dear—it's for a good cause. You're the next logical choice among the ladies here."

"But Brandon…"

"This is an unforeseen emergency. He'll understand."

Someone in the crowd hooted. "Come on, Dumont. Take your prize. None of the rest of us has had the privilege."

From behind the crowd of onlookers, Brandon stopped gathering the targets and straightened to listen.

Her face warmed. This was getting out of hand. Perhaps it was best to get it over and done with. She put on her most gracious smile for the crowd. "I hope you have all paid up on your wagers."

"All but you, Caroline!" one of her married girlfriends called. "Pay up."

It's all in good fun, she told herself. All in good fun. But she couldn't bring herself to glance at Brandon. She stood her ground while Jake stepped inside the gazebo. With the exception of a boy under the mistletoe when she'd been ten, she'd never been kissed by anyone other than Brandon.

A good-natured grin split Jake's face when he stopped before her, but his eyes held concern. He must know he wasn't making his brother happy, but didn't quite know how to gracefully extricate himself from the situation, same as her. She nearly stamped her foot in frustration. If Brandon had announced his intentions toward her earlier no one would have expected her to kiss another man.

She raised her face, acutely aware of how Jake's lips matched Brandon's in design. Perhaps she could pretend it was Brandon kissing her...

The moment his lips touched hers, she knew there was no comparison. Where Brandon's lips had been soft and giving, Jake's were firm and stiff. They broke apart quickly.

"Ah! That isn't any kiss!" a man yelled. "Kiss her again and make it worth the three-dollar entry fee!"

Caroline's face flushed.

"You be quiet," the man's wife said, cuffing him on the shoulder. Soon everyone got involved, urging Jake and Caroline to kiss once more. At the edge of her vision, Brandon approached, looking perplexed at what was occuring.

Jake's Adam's apple floated up and then dropped in his throat as he swallowed hard. Beneath the brim of his suede hat, his eyes glinted in the hazy afternoon sunshine. "All right, Miss Benét. Let's give'm what they want."

He snaked his arms around her and pulled her flush against him. She gasped, her lips parting in surprise, unable to keep from comparing the two brothers. Where Jake's body was rock-hard from constant work out-of-doors, Brandon's, though firm, was more yielding. As their lips met, she heard a few twitters from the audience, and then she felt...

Nothing.

Oh, his lips were softer than she'd first thought. He plastered his mouth against hers and for a moment she was worried he might do something with his tongue, but instead he arched her backward, supporting her with his arms, and continued the chaste kiss.

Jake straightened and pulled away. He was no longer smiling. In fact, he looked confused just before his eyes hardened. He was mad as a hornet. "All for a good cause, right?" He released her abruptly and she stumbled a step.

Someone behind her giggled.

She regained her footing and as her brain cleared, her first thought was of Brandon. She glanced at him. His scowl dashed any hope that he might consider announcing their engagement now—after what had just occurred. Tom shouldered him good-naturedly but it did nothing to shake the shimmering anger in his eyes. Suddenly he spun on his heel and strode away.

Caroline wanted to chase after him, but her upbringing held her back. A genteel woman didn't just dash after a man—especially with all these guests watching.

Beside her, Jake grumbled something about hotheaded young men and then pinned her with his dark gaze. "I hope you are content. You just got the charity event of the season."

Dumbfounded, she watched as he, too, stormed off in the opposite direction.

Three days passed. Three days of her mother saying Brandon would eventually come to his senses, and three days of remorse. No one knew where he'd gone. Even Brandon's butler, Franklin, had been to her house asking if she knew his whereabouts.

During that time, her brother departed for Texas. Her parents didn't support him in this quest of his. Neither could Caroline, but she could understand it. Tom needed to separate from his parents and this was his way. At his age, he craved adventure before Father tried to mold him into a copy of himself.

Just after breakfast on the fourth day, a young boy came to the door bearing a message in Brandon's handwriting. Caroline snatched it from him and broke the wax seal.

Caroline—
Today you made it obvious you want a different kind of man than me. One more like my brother. I'm going to Texas with Tom. It will give us both time to think things through. The fight should only last a few months and then I'll be back. Who knows? Maybe I'll be a better shot—for both of us.
Always,
Brandon Dumont

Her knees gave way, and she sank to the floor.

"Miss!" The courier's eyes widened in alarm. "Miss!"

She glanced at the note—no date anywhere. Clutching his shirt, she waved the paper before him. "When did you get this?"

If it was possible, his eyes widened further. "I didn't do nuttin' wrong, miss. Man told me to wait three days. Just doin' what I was told."

Three days! Too late to stop him. She crushed the note in her fist. What was he thinking? He had no right to leave her like this!

It was all Jake's fault. She wished he'd never come to town. All that had happened since had led to this horrible moment—Brandon's unusual moodiness…the kiss. Her stomach clenched at what else Jake's appearance had led to—the night Brandon had made love to her. She held herself, rocking back and forth on the floor. How could Brandon do this to her? How could he leave after the promises he'd made?

As much as she hated the thought, she had to find Jake. He must go after Brandon and bring him back. She would beg if it came to that. Brandon had to return. He just had to.

Chapter One

Texas Territory—July 1836

Brandon whipped the rope above his head in a circle until it felt "right," leaned in cautiously on his weak leg, testing its ability to handle his full weight and then launched the rope toward the spindly pine thirty feet away.

Missed. For the third time.

He yanked off his hat and with his forearm wiped the sweat from his brow. A low chuckle sounded to his right.

Great. Witnesses.

He spun around and immediately regretted the quick move as a bolt of fire raced through his right ankle. Tall and solid, his brother sauntered up, an older, rougher version of himself—without the limp.

Brandon resettled his hat on his head. "Thought I was far enough from the hacienda to avoid an audience."

Jake dropped the reins to his horse. With a practiced hand, he whirled his rope overhead, letting loose at just the right moment. It sailed through the air and landed neatly around the young tree.

"Playin' to the gallery," Brandon mumbled. *As always.*

Jake shrugged his shoulders and dismounted. He strode to the tree to remove both lines and then tossed Brandon's back to him. "You're thinking too hard. Gotta get that big brain of yours out of the way."

Easier said than done in Brandon's case.

"Just takes repetition—doing it so much that your body takes over naturally."

"I can think of only one thing that comes to me like that—and it ain't lassoin' a tree."

Jake grinned. "Well now. That so? Didn't think that was a part of your medical education. Must be more to your past than I figured." He nodded at the pine. "Give it another go."

Brandon didn't want an audience. Not even his brother. He gathered in his line. "No, I'm finished. What are you doing back from Bexar so soon?"

"Got done early. Couldn't stand stayin' longer. Lot of sickness there."

Brandon pressed his lips together. He figured the doctor in town could use his help, but he couldn't bring himself to go. His doctorin' skills weren't what they used to be—not since the war. "So how'd you find me?"

"Followed your tracks," Jake said. "Gotta admit it was a hell of a lot easier than last time.

"A rabbit couldn't hide his tracks in all this mud."

"The rain did help," Jake admitted.

"Next time I'll give you more of a challenge."

Jake had come after him when he had taken off for Texas to fight with the freedom fighters. Now they were both stuck here—for different reasons. Jake's reason being infinitely better than Brandon's—and prettier.

"Picked up some ground mustard and laudanum in town."

Brandon frowned. "What for?"

Jake shrugged. "Just thought it might help you earn your keep."

"Who says I'll keep on doctorin'?"

Jake studied him with those penetrating blue eyes. "Well, while you're making up your mind, someone might need the medicine. Seems to help enough with your leg."

Laudanum took the pain away all right—of more things than just his injury.

"We need to make plans." Jake ignored his surliness. "Franklin will be here any day now."

"I figured he'd stay with us, although I can't quite imagine him using my table as a bed." Just the thought of his formal, impeccably dressed estate manager lying prostrate on the exam table gave Brandon the willies, his mind conjuring up the image of a funeral wake.

Jake looped his rope on his saddle horn. "He could stay in the cabin."

"Considering his feelings about dust and disorder…the cabin would be a disaster." Tidiness had never been one of Jake's virtues—he'd actually never owned enough things to bother with keeping tidy. Brandon, on the other hand, had grown up under Franklin's tutelage and knew everything had a place—a concept even further ingrained with his medical training. However, since coming to Texas, he'd let that compulsion slide quite a bit. "He'll be more comfortable at the big house."

"My thoughts, too," Jake said. "Juan has a lot going on with Victoria's family staying until the wedding. One more shouldn't break him."

"It's decided, then." Brandon strode to his horse and fixed the rope to the saddle. He didn't particularly want to talk about Franklin. He figured he'd hear more than his share of criticism when the man arrived. "I see you got your ears lowered in town."

"And a shave. A haircut wouldn't hurt you, too."

Brandon swiped a hand through his hair. He'd never worn it this long when he lived on the coast. It just didn't matter anymore, but apparently it was important to Jake that he clean up a bit for his big day.

"Being my brother and all, you're gonna have to think of a toast." Lines crinkled around Jake's blue eyes. "Say something great about me. Lie if you have to."

"Well, that makes it a whole lot easier," Brandon said sarcastically, but inside he was truly honored to be part of his brother's wedding. Eight months ago, at their father's funeral, he would have never thought it possible. They had both been too stubborn, too mule-headed to make the first move after a long line of subtle rejections.

He picked up Jake's hat from the ground, slapped it against his thigh to dislodge the dust and then tossed it to him. "Victoria has no idea what she's getting herself into."

Jake's smile widened. "One big adventure. That's me. Let's find Diego."

Brandon mounted his sorrel and once Jake was on his horse they headed west across the prairie to the hacienda. The air after the storm had lightened considerably, and the sun peeking through a hole in the clouds promised to dry things out.

"You given any thought to what you're gonna do after the wedding?" Jake asked.

"No." And he didn't want to think about it now.

"Considerin' going back with Franklin?"

Brandon shot a dark look at Jake. He couldn't return to the life he'd once had. Too many things had changed.

"Just wondering. You don't talk about it."

"I'll let you know when I sort it out myself."

"Suits me. Just thought you had a job waiting. Figured you'd take over Father's practice."

At one time, that had been Brandon's dream. Not now. Not ever. That life was officially over. "Nothing I have to get back to," he said, keeping his voice even.

"Aren't you curious about who Caroline married?" Jake persisted.

Brandon pressed his lips together. She'd had plenty of choices among his friends and colleagues. For her to accept another so quickly after he'd left for Texas…well, he still reeled from the news. He'd been stunned. Thought they had an understanding, especially since she'd sent Jake to find him. All the while he'd been fighting Mexicans in Texas he'd believed he had something to go back to once the territory was free. The entire thing left a sour feeling in his stomach. He'd trusted her and she'd thrown it back in his face—and hadn't even had the decency to write him a letter.

"Caroline and I…" Brandon started, and then stopped. No point spending time thinking on it. "It was over a long time ago."

"That's not the way it sounded to me."

"It's the way it was." He cast a sharp look at his brother. "Believe me."

"Humph."

"For the record, I'm glad she's married. She's someone else's worry now."

"Well, you're better off without her. If you can't trust her to wait a few months, you can't trust her at all."

"Just back off, Jake," he said, his voice hardening. He'd come to the same conclusion—especially now that he couldn't return to his old life. He was lucky to be rid of her.

In moments of lucid honesty, his conscience would

squeeze him, telling him that he'd played a part in losing Caroline. After all, he could have stayed in Charleston and swallowed his pride, could have confronted her. He didn't have to leave.

Like hell, he grumbled.

Turning away from his brother's probing, he concentrated on the slope of the hillside to the hacienda. From this distance the large U-shaped house looked inviting and well kept. It was only as they drew closer that evidence of the Mexican Army encampment there several months ago marred the landscape. Ruts from heavy artillery bisected the expanse of prairie to the east. Where the tents and campfires had been, weeds had grown up and choked out the prairie flowers. Nearer the house, trees had been destroyed for firewood.

He closed his eyes and took a deep breath of the sweet air, clean now since the rain had come. Here, for a brief moment, he felt at peace. If only it could stay like this. If only Franklin weren't coming and bringing remnants of his past life with him.

Brandon set his jaw. It would only be for a week or so. Just long enough to settle their father's will and get Jake hitched. He figured he could deal with it that long.

A shout sounded from the cluster of pines near the house. A rider appeared—white horse, big hat.

Jake whistled through his teeth, piercing the afternoon quiet with an ear-shattering noise. "Diego!" He stood in his stirrups, grabbed his hat and waved it over his head.

Diego spotted them on the ridge and kicked his mount into a gallop, riding bareback so fast that his hat slipped off his head and bounced against his back.

"He's riding hard. Something's wrong," Brandon murmured. He adjusted his seat, pressed his knees to his mount's flanks and urged his horse down the slope.

As soon as Diego pulled up on the reins in front of them, Brandon realized the man's cotton pants and shirt were soaked through. "What is it?"

"A wagon's stuck in the river."

"Anybody hurt?"

"An old man is caught up. His head is above water, but I don't know how long he will last."

"Water level is too high. It's made that crossing danger-ous." Jake glanced over at Brandon, his gaze resting mo-mentarily on Brandon's injured leg before turning once again to Diego.

A knot of anger lodged in Brandon's throat. It wasn't like Jake to hesitate because of him. Leaning forward in his saddle, he kicked his sorrel. The horse lurched into a gallop down the slope.

They raced toward the river. A mile north of the big house they rounded the bend in the dirt road and slowed. Through the cottonwoods, they caught sight of the wagon half-submerged in the water. The ears on the two lead horses flicked forward nervously as the newcomers approached.

From the high bank, Brandon surveyed the surround-ing hills, checking for signs of trouble—most notably Comanche or hostile Mexicans. He didn't fancy getting ambushed in the middle of the river where he and his brother would be easy targets. Reassured of their safety, he headed toward the wagon. Only it wasn't a wagon, but a black carriage tipped halfway on its side against a large boulder and held there by the pressure of the current.

He dismounted and strode to the shoreline. The water sluiced by, crashing over large boulders as it raced down-stream and created a terrific roar. The elegant crest on the carriage door lay half-submerged under the frothy surface and looked strangely out of place in this raw country.

Brandon swore suddenly under his breath as he recognized the fancy ornament. "That's Franklin out there!"

Jake's gaze shot to the crest on the carriage.

Brandon stepped into the rushing water, tensing against the slap of the current against his injured leg. Pain raced up his shin and stole his breath away in a gasp. A hundred white-hot needles jabbed at his ankle. He clenched his teeth together. Once he acclimated to the pain he'd be all right. At least he hoped so.

"Head back!" Jake growled in passing. "I can't worry about you, too."

"I'm not asking you to."

Slowly he made his way toward the carriage as Diego splashed into the water and raced ahead of him, catching up to Jake. The water coursed around Brandon as he maneuvered between a few boulders and sought to find stable footing on the smooth and slippery rocks in the riverbed. Although the day was warm, the water still felt as cold as ice.

Jake made it to the carriage first. A shriek echoed from inside the conveyance and bounced off the rock walls on the far bank. A woman's solitary enraged cry.

What the hell was a woman doing riding with Franklin? If in fact the man in the water was Franklin.

Brandon reached the carriage just as Jake thrust a bundle of wet sky-blue material and soggy blond hair at him. "Here! Take her! She's not making any sense with her ranting."

Momentum arched the woman halfway over his shoulder. Reacting in surprise, Brandon grabbed on as his weaker leg gave in and he lost his footing. They both slipped under the water. Her voluminous skirt tangled around his arms and face as he wrestled with the cloth, trying to establish a solid stance and get them both above the surface. His arm butted against a hard object. He grabbed the carriage wheel and steadied himself.

The minute their heads emerged above the surface another scream rent the air right next to his ear. The woman struggled and pummeled his back. "Put me down!"

"As soon as I get you to shore, ma'am," he said, trying to ignore the woman's hysterics and look for Franklin. He didn't have time to consider what the man was doing traveling with this she-cat, but he'd sure expect some answers later—banking on the fact that Franklin was all right.

Jake appeared on the far side of the carriage.

"Franklin?" Brandon asked.

"He's all right, but he's stuck under the carriage. Diego and I can get him."

Brandon nodded. "I'll head to shore." He turned, taking one step toward the strip of sand on the bank when something stopped him, nearly pulling him over backward.

"What the…"

The woman held tight to the cloth that disappeared under the coach.

"Let it go, ma'am."

"Noooo!"

"Let it go or we'll both go down again."

Still she wouldn't release the fabric.

"I gave you good warning," he said through gritted teeth. Quickly he whipped the knife from his belt and slashed through the cloth.

For a second her outraged gasp was all he heard—that and the roaring of the water. Then she found her tongue.

"How dare you! You don't know what you've done." She beat his back with her fists. "Put me down! You…you imbecile!"

"Don't tempt me," he muttered. It would serve her right.

But it just didn't seem the thing to do when he was trying to rescue her. He took an unsteady step toward the shore. This direction, the force of the water was stronger on his ankle. Thankfully by now both legs were nearly numb. The woman wasn't much weight, but her wiggling didn't make the going easy. He had half a mind to spank her since she was acting like a child. Too bad it wasn't in his nature. Heck, in the current situation, rather than quieting her, it might make her that much more of a wildcat.

Halfway to shore, he shifted her on his shoulder and off balance a moment, he stumbled. His foot came down crooked on a large stone. His ankle twisted and white-hot pain seared through him. His vision blurred. He forced himself to take three more unsteady steps. The small beach loomed close. He might make it. On his last step he teetered and went down face-first on top of the woman. Her extra layers of clothing along with what strength was left in his arms, softened the fall onto the sand—for him at least.

Momentarily stunned, she lay quiet—for the space of a second. Maybe, just maybe, he would get a thank-you out of her. Then she pushed at him with renewed strength. "Get off me you big oaf!"

In this horizontal position, the blood returned to his head in a rush and her high-pitched words registered. He rolled off and sprawled onto his back, letting his head drop back on the coarse sand. Slowly the throbbing pain in his leg subsided. Stars spun on the edge of his vision. When they stopped moving he opened his eyes.

The woman sat next to him, looking toward the carriage, her energy spent, gasping for new air. Pale golden hair hung in wet, snarled hanks down her back to her waist. Her satin dress, the color of the sky, clung to her bodice and twisted around her legs. Fool of a woman. She would have drowned in all that material. He'd saved her life and her screeching was the thanks he got.

"I have never been treated so deplorably!" she began.

He could tell she was gearing up for a considerable rant and mentally braced himself while an uneasy premonition built inside. The voice. The form. They were all too familiar.

She pushed the hair from her face and then turned, her green eyes snapping fire as she readied her arsenal of words.

"Hello, Caroline."

Her eyes widened and her cheeks, already pale from the cold water, drained further of color. "Oh, dear," she began awkwardly. "Oh…dear…"

In the two years he'd known her, he'd never seen her flustered. She'd always known the perfect thing to say on any occasion. He didn't think he'd find anything amusing about this situation, as mad as he felt, but there it was.

"What? No words for me?" The sarcasm rolled off his tongue easily enough.

She clamped her mouth shut and glared at him.

He'd forgotten how beautiful she was—the flawless skin, the straight nose and the generous rose-colored lips made for kissing. No, that wasn't correct. He'd tried hard to forget ever since he'd learned of her engagement, shoving her memory to the back of his mind. She belonged to another time, another life—in Charleston. Definitely not in Texas.

And as far as he knew, she belonged to another man now. What the hell was she doing here?

His chest tightened with anger. He'd come to the conclusion that he'd never cross paths with her again, that they'd gone their separate ways. After her betrayal, Texas had seemed like a safe bet that he'd never lay eyes on her again. This country was no place for the proper Miss Benét or whoever she was now. What had Franklin been thinking to bring her and where was her fool of a husband?

"What the hell are you doing here? Is Franklin all right?" he asked gruffly, purposely ignoring the fact that she'd started shivering.

At the mention of his butler's name, her anxious gaze flashed back to the river. "He's pinned on the other side. The carriage tipped over just as we tried to free the wheel and his foot got stuck. Those men…they need your help."

Brandon grimaced. Another trip through that water and he'd end up a casualty as sure as the carriage, but Franklin was more important than his own comfort. Franklin had seen him through all the good times and many of the rough times in his life. The one man he could always rely on. Shouts passed back and forth between Jake and Diego, their voices muffled by the water's rushing. He rose to his feet and headed toward the water, glancing back once at Caroline. Her censoring gaze didn't help matters.

Just then his brother and Diego emerged from the underbelly of the carriage carrying Franklin between them. They dragged him across the top of the water, keeping his head above the surface as they stumbled over submerged rocks and around boulders in their path toward the shore. Once there, they laid him, pale and shivering, at Brandon's feet.

"Might want to take a look at that right foot," Jake said. "It was wedged tight." He straightened, his gaze shifting to Caroline. His eyes narrowed and grew ten degrees colder. "Welcome to Texas territory, Miss Caroline."

She nodded cautiously, picking herself up from the ground and brushing the grainy sand from her palms. "Mr. Dumont."

She broke eye contact first and turned to Franklin. Wringing out a portion of her skirt, she knelt beside him and wiped the excess water from his face and neck.

Jake glanced at Brandon, his brows raised. Brandon had caught the fact that she hadn't corrected her name, but that didn't mean anything. Obviously she was shook up—the evidence being her ministrations to a man she had at one time considered beneath her station. A man she had gone out of her way to avoid.

"M-M-Master Brandon," Franklin said through chattering teeth. "How good to see you."

He clasped Franklin's large hand. "Hair's a bit grayer than the last time I saw you," he said gruffly.

"If that's the case," Franklin returned, glaring at him through his shivering, "it's your fault."

Brandon's eyes stung. "Let's get you into the sun to dry off."

He motioned to Diego and Jake and together they dragged him a few yards up the bank, out from the shadow of the cottonwoods. There Brandon knelt on one knee and examined the man's foot. "No swelling. No evidence of a break," he murmured. He checked the range of motion, flexing Franklin's foot. "Any pain when I do this?"

Franklin shook his head. "A little."

"Give it a day or two. You'll be fine."

"I tried to tell Master Jake that, but he wouldn't listen."

"He never does. And Franklin—out here it's just Jake and Brandon. We're not masters of anything."

"A hard habit to break, I'm afraid."

"Obviously since you never could adjust to addressing me as Doctor, either. Just Brandon. Please. Otherwise I'll be looking over my shoulder trying to figure out who you're talking to."

"To whom."

He'd heard the automatic corrections all his life from

this man. At one time it would have made him grin and he'd have riled Franklin all the more, just to egg him on. Now he ignored it and rose awkwardly to his feet.

He limped to his horse, conscious of both Franklin's and Caroline's gazes on him and removed the coiled rope. He handed one end to Jake. "Once you get your end secured and are ready behind the carriage, give me a shout."

He secured his end of the rope to his saddle and did the same with another line that he received from Diego. When the carriage was all trussed up and ready, Brandon called orders to the lead horse as Jake flicked a bullwhip at its rump. It started with a snort, tossing its head in surprise. With a concerted effort the carriage rocked from its position against the boulders. But they couldn't budge it further.

Noticing again the material caught in the wheel spoke, Brandon yelled to this brother. "That cloth is hooked on something."

Jake nodded in agreement and with the quicksilver flash of his knife, he cut through the fabric and let it float away.

Brandon ignored the moan at his side. No doubt the material was a favored shawl or some such nonsense. Well, out here you couldn't let such things stop you from acting. You did what was necessary. Sentiment got you nothing but misery.

The release of the material freed the carriage. On the men's fifth attempt, the conveyance righted all the way and the horses started, and then pulled it to the bank.

Once there, Brandon grabbed the old quilted bedroll from Jake's horse and spread it across the seat for a dry space. He held the door open. "I'll drive to the hacienda, Franklin. You rest that leg. And elevate it."

He tipped his hat to Caroline. She followed Franklin

into the coach, pausing at the door long enough to let her gaze sweep down to Brandon's leg. "When did it happen?"

He hadn't had the limp when he had left Charleston, so he'd expected the question eventually. It was the open concern in her green eyes that caught him off guard and made him remember her soft side, made him remember why he'd been drawn to her in the first place. He didn't want those memories—not after all that she'd done. She could just keep her concerns to herself from now on.

He grasped her elbow and helped her into the carriage. "It's not important."

For once, she didn't start another battle of wills. "Perhaps later then," she said and seated herself.

The acceptance that flashed in her eyes confused him. She'd always been one to push to get her own way. The whole fact that she was here now confused him. Just what was she up to?

He slammed the door after her and tied his horse to the back of the carriage. Jake watched him with a grim expression as he climbed into the driver's seat and took up the reins.

Brandon clamped his jaw together and jerked the reins, urging the matched pair forward. Whatever her reason for being here, it was over between him and Caroline. That's all there was to it. But it didn't take much to figure things were going to change with her around. Caroline would learn soon enough—it would be on his terms—not hers.

Chapter Two

The dark-haired Mexican who had first discovered their coach stuck in the river grabbed her trunk and escorted Caroline to the front door of the big house. Behind her, Brandon helped Franklin down from the coach, then with a shoulder under his arm and Jake supporting his other side, they assisted him slowly toward the house.

The size of the hacienda spoke of better times. Weeds and thistles choked the flower gardens near the door and the few struggling flowers did not look like they would survive unless nursed carefully.

She stepped inside the impressive structure. The floor tiles of the spacious front hall gleamed with a recent washing. It looked…vacant…she realized. No furniture at all. A few tiles were broken. The plaster on the walls had several large, spidery cracks.

"Diego? *¡Ven aqui!*" A pleasant soprano voice called from up the staircase.

Diego cocked his head. "Excuse me, *señorita.*" He flashed a smile and set her trunk on the tile floor. She judged him to be a bit younger than herself, despite the fact that he was taller by six inches. His loose cotton shirt and worn brown pants were still damp from river water, but not nearly as wet as her dress.

He took the stairs two at a time, stopping to speak in Spanish to the woman on the stairs. The woman glanced her way and then after another word to Diego, descended to meet her.

"Welcome. I am Victoria Torrez."

Petite and dark-haired with large, expressive brown eyes, Victoria Torrez had intrigued Caroline ever since Franklin had spoken of her on the journey west. Instead of the tough-as-leather, boots-and-spurs image she had pictured for a woman who'd battled alongside Jake at the Alamo, Victoria stood before her now in a flowing and very feminine pale yellow dress. She had twisted her shiny near-black hair off her neck into a fancy chignon and secured it with a silver comb.

Caroline remained still, acutely conscious of her own bedraggled appearance and the water dripping from her traveling dress into small puddles on the tiles. "Señorita Torrez. Thank you for your hospitality. I know you were not expecting me."

"I am happy to have you here." The sharp assessment in her eyes belied Victoria's gracious tone and voice. "However, this is my cousin's house—Señor Seguín's. He is the one to thank. He will greet you at supper. Is this all?" she asked, indicating the trunk.

"Yes."

"Then follow me and I'll show you to your room." She looked over Caroline's shoulder. "Jake, you can help Mr. Penderton to the room prepared for him on the west hall." She turned, and started back up the stairs.

Caroline followed her to a doorway that overlooked the

entry hall. She stepped inside the room and looked about, impressed with the beautiful Spanish architecture. The white plaster walls and arched doorways made the room feel spacious and cool, despite the heat of the late afternoon. Twisted ornamental iron hooks protruded from the wall by the door—Caroline could only guess at their use. A large cherrywood bed pressed against one wall. Next to it stood a matching stand with a pitcher and bowl for washing. On the opposite wall a small fireplace had been carved. The hearth was clean now and devoid of kindling. A simple, straight-backed chair sat in the corner.

No wardrobe cabinet, no desk.

Well, what did she expect? With her decision to come on the journey so rushed, she hadn't given any thought to where she would stay once she arrived. This was adequate—actually much better than a few of the inns she'd stayed at on the way here where she'd had to sleep on a pallet on the floor.

Victoria stepped to the window and surprised Caroline when she drew up her skirt and removed a small dagger from her garter. She cut a dead vine from the pink flowers on the wide sill, threw it outside and then replaced her knife. She turned back to Caroline as she adjusted her dress.

"You will be staying for the wedding?"

"Y-yes," Caroline stuttered, shocked at the casual display.

Diego arrived with Caroline's trunk and deposited it on the floor at the end of the bed.

"*Gracias,*" Victoria said to him. She turned to Caroline. "I'll let you get settled. Leave your damp things on the chair and I'll have them aired."

"Thank you." Caroline shut the door after her. She leaned back against the wood and closed her eyes, relieved to finally be alone.

What kind of barbaric place had she come to where women had to protect themselves with hidden knives? Hadn't the war taken care of any hostile situations?

And so much for the greeting she had hoped for from Brandon. Apparently their five-month separation had done nothing to ease his anger. Not once had she deluded herself into thinking he still cared for her, but truth be told, she had expected some civility on her arrival. His treatment bordered on rudeness. She shouldn't be surprised, though—the cad had deserted her.

She stamped her foot in frustration which only served to wrap her wet skirt about her legs and send a chill through her. Her teeth chattered, despite the warmth of the day. She opened her trunk and removed a dress. As her hand squeezed the fabric she gasped in dismay at the dampness. Tossing the dress aside she rummaged to the bottom of the trunk. Everything was wet!

It was bad enough she'd had to live without her usual toiletries for the duration of the journey. She'd made a point not to complain, but without her creams and special soaps, her skin had dried out and was darkened from the sun despite her constant use of a hat. Her bonnet, more ornamental and stylish, simply hadn't had the wide brim necessary to protect her face.

She plopped down on the bed. What more could go wrong? She'd wanted to make a good impression with Brandon. Actually she'd wanted to make him regret ever leaving her, to feel a fraction of the pain he'd caused her, although she'd never admit that to him. She sighed and turned her dry hands over in her lap, studying her ragged nails. She'd botched the entire thing already.

Spying her brush on the top of her clothes, she began the task of detangling her long hair. Voices drifted up from outside—one particularly familiar. She walked to the window and peered out, her strokes slowing when she spied Brandon speaking to Jake in the yard below.

She stood there unable to look away, absorbing every nuance of the man. No longer was Brandon the slender, ropy boy she'd met two summers ago at her father's encouragement. Now he seemed so much taller, so much wider at the shoulders. A day's growth of dark beard shadowed his face. The days in the sun had darkened his skin, much like the fishermen on the wharf back home. Odd, how on a man, that could be so appealing, whereas on a woman it was considered base and unrefined.

And his clothes! She was used to seeing him in dark woolen trousers with a waistcoat over his tailored shirt. The way he dressed now a person could not even tell he was a doctor. His buckskin pants hugged his legs, and his butternut cotton shirt, still damp and clinging, fell open at the neck. He looked more the frontiersman or cowboy than the doctor she knew him to be.

She frowned as he pulled a rifle from his horse's saddle boot. The array of weapons on his person was an even bigger change. At his waist he toted a gun similar to her brother's. And in a leather sheath at the small of his back rested a sinister-looking knife, the blade as wide and long as her forearm. She couldn't have been more surprised if she'd seen a bow and arrow in the assembly. What sort of uncivilized place had she come to where weapons were a person's constant companion?

She tried to put the disturbing thought from her mind. She was determined to view this trip—the entire ordeal—as an adventure that would eventually be over. Many people from the east had come to the Texas territory and stayed—women as well as men. Something here drew them. Whatever it was, she couldn't understand it and had no desire to. Her mind was made up. She would stay only as long as necessary and then return east.

Finishing their conversation, Jake mounted his horse and headed down the trail through a stand of pines. Brandon turned to gather the horses' reins, leaning upon a makeshift cane. He glanced once at the hacienda. She pulled back from the window.

Somehow, over the past months Brandon had become a man's man. She saw the difference in the way he held himself. She heard the difference in the quiet tone of authority when he spoke. When he'd carried her across the river, the muscles in his shoulders and arms had tensed firm and unyielding against her. Even now, just thinking of the solid feel of his body made something womanly curl in her center. Her cheeks flamed hot. Definitely a man.

And a stranger to her.

In the next second he turned away and favoring his right leg, led the horses, now free of the Dumont carriage, to the stable.

He'd never told her he was injured. Even her brother, Tom, had neglected to mention it. How had it happened? And when? Surely something so minor couldn't possibly have prevented him from returning home.

He might have denied it in his only letter to her, but all she could believe was that he hadn't forgiven her for her kiss with Jake. What a chain of events that had set in motion. Had she known at the time, she would have done everything in her power to avoid the charity shooting match. She would have begged illness—anything. The kiss had been for a good cause, but even so, she'd given up far more than one kiss.

They would have to talk of it. He had no excuse for his behavior. He was the one who had left her. Oh, his rationale at the time had been honorable enough—to help fight for Texas freedom. But it hadn't been his fight. And she had needed him to stay in Charleston more than he could possibly know. She was the one who should be angry with him. She had every right to be.

She huffed out a breath, trying to release some of her frustration. Well, it wouldn't be forever. She'd be careful to keep that in mind. All she had to do was convince him to come back to Charleston with her. It shouldn't be too hard. He'd always had an ambitious streak and her father had quite a carrot to dangle. Once Jake's wedding was over they could both return to the coast.

Another shiver trembled through her and she moved from the window and began to peel out of her wet dress. She couldn't think about it now. Exhaustion was taking its toll. Her arms and back ached as she poured water into the bowl from the pitcher. At first she couldn't remember why her arms were so sore and then she remembered she'd held Franklin's head above the water for a good amount of time before figuring a way to attach the cloth to the wheel. The makeshift sling had worked, thank goodness. She didn't want to think what would have become of Mr. Penderton if it hadn't.

Dipping her hands into the tepid water she began washing herself off. She wanted to be ready, refreshed and looking her best by suppertime. Mentally she began to prepare herself for the dialogue ahead. She would wait for a private moment. Brandon deserved that much. She would be calm, in control, and would have her say.

That evening, she dressed in her mint-green gown with the deep forest-green fitted bodice. Maria, the maid, had aired out the dress while Caroline napped. Although the bodice was still slightly damp, it was wearable for the evening. She waited in her room for Maria's knock announcing supper, pacing back and forth. Each time she neared the window she couldn't help checking to see if Brandon was in the drive below. She'd gathered that he wasn't staying at the hacienda, but somewhere nearby. The setting sun streaked purple and pink clouds across the sky and she was, for a moment, entranced by the landscape, the rolling hills to the south and the whispering stand of pines to the west.

At a knock, she opened her door and found Brandon standing there. He'd taken time to change into dry clothes—a white cotton shirt and black jeans. He'd also shaved. A wave of deep brown hair, still wet from a quick combing, dipped low on his forehead just above his blue eyes. She'd never seen his hair so long—had not realized it would curl slightly at this length. The sudden urge to reach up and touch a swirl of it on his shoulder annoyed her. She held the urge in check.

Brandon stood rigid. "I trust you had a good rest," he said formally. At her nod, he continued. "They are ready for us at supper."

His closed expression cut her to the quick. Why was he being this way? He wouldn't even look at her. "Brandon?"

The muscles in his jaw worked. "I know we have things to discuss. However, not tonight."

"My appearance has been something of a shock to you."

He didn't answer. Didn't do anything. He was hard as stone.

"What is wrong with you? Aren't you the least bit curious as to why I'm here?"

"Not now. What I want you to do for now is to put on a good face at the table. You should be able to do that much."

She frowned. "Meaning?"

"Meaning that what's between us isn't for anyone else's ears."

She bristled at his criticism. "I know how to conduct myself at a supper party."

His gaze was cool on her. "So I remember—parties and shooting matches in particular. Anywhere you have an audience."

She inhaled sharply. A retort formed on her tongue—

He silenced it with a dark stare. "I don't want to see my friends here caught between us."

Pressure built inside her chest. She hadn't come all this way for a dressing down. Her skills as a hostess in Charleston were sought after. Along with her parents, she'd entertained the governor for goodness' sake. People vied to be invited to a dinner party of hers. "I won't embarrass you, Brandon, if that's what you mean."

"Then we understand each other."

He offered his arm. Of course it was only for appearances—only because propriety dictated it, but after the things he'd just said, she hesitated before accepting his gesture.

"I won't bite."

"You have no idea," she shot back at him. She stifled her urge to continue the conversation. The slow burn in her chest had everything to do with how perturbed she was at him.

But he was right—now, while everyone waited supper on them was not the time to discuss things. She looped her arm through his. The warmth and strength of his muscle radiated into her. Unwittingly pleasure stole over her. She clamped down on the thought, blocking the sensation. It wouldn't do to let her feminine emotions overrule her head where he was concerned. She'd done that once before and look where it had brought her—to this rough, uncivilized territory. It would not happen again—ever.

They descended the stairs and continued down the hallway. When they stepped through the open doorway to the dining room, conversation stopped and every face turned toward her. It was then Brandon extricated himself and moved slightly away. She braced herself against the subtle rejection, refusing to look up at him.

A chair at the head of the table scraped against the tiled floor and an older gentleman stood and bowed formally. "Welcome to my home. I am Juan Seguín." He proceeded to introduce his wife and three children and Victoria's parents before indicating the two empty seats at the table for her and Brandon.

"Mr. Seguín—Señor Seguín, I must thank you for your hospitality," she said.

As she sat, Brandon slid the chair in under her. It was a small gesture and one he'd done countless times in the past. Why then did it seem intimate? Why did the slight tingle on her neck from his breath continue long after he'd taken the seat beside her? He was only performing a gentleman's duty, she told herself. He would have done the same for any woman.

During the dinner courses, Caroline gratefully accepted Franklin's domination of the conversation. He answered many questions from the others, describing his and Caroline's journey and speaking about the estate in Charleston. For her, it seemed her nerves were pulled taut. She noticed every movement of Brandon at her side, whether he picked up his fork or put it down. It was as though an invisible rope bound them together.

The very cadence of his deep-timbered voice the few times he spoke brought a rush of warm memories—the picnics at White Point Gardens, boating on the canal and his tender murmurs when she'd given herself to him in the boathouse. Thank God he'd survived the battles here. Thank God he still lived no matter their strained circumstances now.

Halfway through the meal, she inadvertently dropped her napkin. He reached for it with a swift motion, nearly bumping her head as he returned to a sitting position.

"Thank you," she said, taking it from him.

"You're not eating."

The way he said it, it was an accusation. She couldn't help herself. Although the food looked delicious, the strange spices made her stomach roil. She picked up her fork and moved the food about on her plate, looking for something bland.

The conversation continued without her participation as she tried to disguise her growing distress, looking anywhere but at the food in front of her. She gripped her hands together in her lap, her skin clammy, her stomach rebelling. Brandon had wanted this supper to be as uneventful as possible. She mustn't draw attention to herself.

However, it wasn't long before Victoria noticed. She spoke quietly to a servant who then removed Caroline's plate and brought a custard dessert.

Others at the table noticed, too. "You do not care for the flan?" Juan asked Caroline.

She would make light of it if it killed her. "I'm afraid my stomach is upset from all the traveling. I close my eyes and still feel as though I'm bouncing in that coach."

"A bit of ginger might help," Victoria said, motioning again to the servant. "Maria?"

"No," Caroline said quickly. "I don't want to trouble anyone. I'll be fine by tomorrow."

Jake, sitting across from her, leaned forward. "Caroline, now that we are all together. Tell us what brings you here?"

The challenge in his voice had the others glancing silently between themselves and then at Brandon. The dark look in Brandon's eyes countered any questions they might think of asking, but of course, that didn't stop Jake. Jake had never let etiquette keep him from what he wanted.

"I take it you didn't marry after all," he continued. "Or if you did, it must be to Franklin here."

Her gaze flew to Franklin, who had stopped eating. A frown marked his face. Over the course of the journey, Franklin had become quite dear to her. She would not have him talked about this way, especially by the very man who had asked him to come.

Victoria put her hand over Jake's forearm. "Perhaps now is not the time."

"Now is the perfect time, darlin'," he answered, placing his large hand over hers. "My pardon, Franklin, but we all want to know." He turned back to Caroline. "Last thing we heard was that you were halfway down the aisle at church."

Caroline put down her napkin. Married? How had that news traveled here? No one knew of her proposal outside of her social circle. She glanced at Brandon. Hadn't he said anything to his brother? Why was she being put on the spot like this?

"I take it you don't believe I have come to see you properly married, Jake," she said.

"Just didn't think we were on that good of terms when we parted. I'm tickled pink that you're here."

He said it politely—for the children's sake—she realized as she looked about the table, yet she heard the undercurrent of sarcasm. She hadn't come here to be badgered and she could give as good as she got. "No. I remember you promised me to bring your brother back to Charleston. Apparently that has gone by the wayside."

"I promised to try. I wasn't about to force him to do something he didn't want to do."

Brandon hadn't wanted *to return home?* The words were a slap in the face. He had a future there—his father's practice just waiting for him! More than that—*she* had waited for him! It couldn't be true.

Jake took advantage of her hesitation. "Besides, I wanted him at my wedding."

Awareness of the man at her side had her choosing her words carefully. "After Brandon left—after you both left— for Texas, my parents introduced me to an acquaintance of my father's. For some time they had been anxious to have me meet him. He is a lawyer presently, working with land development in and around Charleston."

"He sounds perfect for you."

She frowned at his comment. "He is a very nice man, but I never agreed to…I don't know how you received word that I was betrothed." She couldn't control the slight tremble in her voice.

Franklin cleared his throat. "I believe that message came inadvertently through me, miss."

He hadn't mentioned that in the four weeks they'd traveled together. His omission cut her to the quick. It spoke volumes of his earlier hope that her relationship with Brandon would be severed by his race to Texas.

"I regret not telling you. I should have said something. You see there was no point in sending another letter. We would be here ourselves in the time it took to get a note across the country. I knew we could straighten things out then. Now."

Her smile felt strained. "Well, of course. It was a wise decision."

Abruptly Brandon scraped back his chair and stood.

"This conversation can wait until later. Miss Benét and I deserve a chance to speak alone first."

Jake narrowed his gaze. "I don't think a few *honest* answers are uncalled for. We all want to know."

"Keep to your own business, Jake," Brandon ordered forcefully. "She's here for a wedding. She's here as our guest. Leave it at that unless she wants to say more."

Those sitting around the table looked to her—waiting. A stifling silence filled the room, so thick that she couldn't move for a moment. She took in a shaky breath, thankful for Brandon's intervention, albeit late. The best thing for now perhaps was retreat. As graciously as she could muster, she stood. "Excuse me. I'm not as hungry as I thought. Thank you for the delicious supper."

Chapter Three

Midmorning of the next day, Caroline joined Franklin in the courtyard. Sunlight dappled through the branches of the large oak in the center of the garden and sparkled on the water in the fishpond. The scent of mesquite from the kitchen fire wafted through the air. Before sitting down, she surveyed the two flower gardens—so ill kept compared to the vegetables growing in the other two plots.

Franklin put aside the legal notes he'd been reading while he sat on the long wooden bench. "You weren't at breakfast with us."

"No," she said, yawning in a most unladylike fashion. She didn't need to explain to him that she'd had trouble sleeping. He'd noticed it often on their overland journey. "I wasn't up for another interrogation from Jake."

"He was rough on you last night. I should have stepped in."

"He was unkind to you, as well."

"Don't trouble yourself about that. I know Jake—how he thinks. He didn't mean anything."

"No, just goading me any way he could to get an answer." She sat down beside him and smoothed out her chocolate-brown skirt. "I asked the cook for a bit of bread."

"You need more than that."

"At noon will be soon enough."

Franklin grunted.

A shout rose from the proximity of the stables along with the startled neighing of a horse. Jake shouted something—and then Brandon joined in, too.

"They're working a new horse," Franklin said, leaning his head back against the short adobe wall that surrounded an ornamental fishpond and crossing his arms over his chest. "Go on with you. I'm not moving so long as the shade keeps me cool. This foot needs another day to heal from the abuse it received yesterday."

"You're sure? I don't mind staying."

Franklin chuckled. "I'm content to stay in one spot today. And I'd think you would have had enough of my company after traveling together for the past month."

"Touché," she said, but there was a friendly lilt in her voice.

His face sobered. "I haven't thanked you for what you did at the river yesterday."

"No need." Her arms were stiff, but less sore today.

"You deserve more than a word of thanks. What you did took spirit."

Spirit. Most people would consider having spirit something to be commended. Her only regret of her actions yesterday was that it had resulted in the loss of her cloth when Jake slashed it free with his knife. She had been embroidering the design during the entire journey. "You would do the same for me. Actually you have—simply by bringing me with you."

"You gave me little choice in that matter, young lady. You were quite persuasive waving that pistol so nervously."

"Well, we're even."

"Not really. But I'll leave it alone for now. You have enough of other things on your mind at present."

She laced her fingers together in her lap, nervous how the morning would progress. "Now that I'm here. I don't know how to tell him."

"It will come to you."

"He doesn't care for me anymore. Maybe that's why he left in the first place—he just didn't know how to tell me." The words tumbled from her, her heart aching with their release. "He never did announce our engagement, even after…" *they'd made love.* "Jake was right last night. Brandon would have returned home after the war if he'd really wanted to. Hearing Jake say it out loud—well, it hurt."

"You don't know Brandon's mind."

"But his actions…"

"You don't know his mind," Franklin emphasized once more, his tone sharp. "He has a brilliant career waiting in Charleston if he chooses. Remind him of that."

She wasn't convinced. "He shouldn't need reminding or coercing. Like Jake said, he should *want* to return."

"He will. Once he learns of your condition he'll do the right thing."

She bit her bottom lip as a yearning started in the pit of her stomach wondering what the "right thing" entailed. Brandon could have quite a different concept than she did. "You can't be sure of that. I'm not."

"All you can do at this point is to say your piece. Offer him the job your father has prepared for him. After that, it's up to him."

She picked at the purple flower growing next to her, hardly aware that she held it. "He's changed."

"I warned you that might happen. War can do that to a man. It's not pretty."

"He's so hardened. So distant even when I'm right next to him. As though we never were close to begin with." She rose and paced the short path between the two flower beds. "Honestly, after all this time, I'm not sure how I feel about him anymore."

"I thought that didn't matter."

"It doesn't," she said defensively. Her hand tightened over the small mound of her abdomen. The whole purpose of this trip was to let Brandon know about their child. She needed his help. Desperately. Her parents would not let her return home with a baby and she wouldn't leave it to someone else to raise. At one time, she had hoped—naively—that Brandon loved her. That hope had been dashed when she received his letter saying he wouldn't be coming back to Charleston. No, she didn't have the luxury to believe in love anymore—on her part or his. She just hoped he would help her.

"Talk to him, Caroline. Better for it to come from you directly than to have him discover it from someone else later."

"You're right. As much as I'd like to, I can't control everything."

His gray eyes twinkled. "You try harder than most."

Bolstered to a degree by the man's matter-of-fact attitude, she squared her shoulders and walked to the tall gate at the end of the courtyard. Through the iron bars she could see Diego in the corral, working a horse. He snapped a line lightly on the animal's buttocks as it circled around him. Sweat glistened off the sleek black body of the horse.

At the railing Jake and Brandon called out directions

and advice. Brandon wore the same cotton shirt he'd had on yesterday, the sleeves rolled up past his elbows. A red bandanna circled his neck. His buckskin pants rode low on his hips, along with the gun and belt strapped there. He was Texan today. No trace of the East Coast Charlestonian remained.

She took a deep breath. He looked every bit as handsome this way. She felt a tug deep inside as she looked at him. If only they could go back to the way things had been before. If only...

She pushed the feeling aside. There was no room in her life for such emotions—not anymore. She opened the gate. The iron hinges creaked. With the sound, everyone turned and stared at her. She swallowed hard. "Good morning."

The horse snorted, tossing its head. Jake stared at her a moment and then turned back to the corral. A look passed between the men—some unsaid code. Brandon pulled away from the railing. "Thought I'd take you riding," he said stiffly. "Show you the lay of the ranch."

"I'd like that. I like to ride."

Under the brim of his deep brown hat, his eyes glittered, a midnight-blue against his tanned face. "I remember."

"But not as much now. I'm not quite so adventurous," she admitted.

A soft snort blew from him. "Then how do you account for the fact that you're here?" He studied her briefly. "Where's Franklin?"

"In the courtyard."

"Will he want to join us?"

She swallowed past the sudden lump in her throat. So Brandon wasn't interested in being alone with her—in talking. "He's resting. His foot still bothers him."

"I'll speak with him." Jake pushed away from the corral

railing. "I have some business to discuss with him before the wedding. Now is as good a time as any."

"Father's will?"

"No. Those details can wait for you. I have a few other things I need to speak to him about."

That Brandon even mentioned the will so easily told Caroline the brothers' relationship had indeed changed. In Charleston, he had refused to talk about it with Jake. What had happened to mend the rift they'd once had? she wondered. Things were definitely different between them now.

Brandon led the way to the stable where the pungent odor of straw, horse and leather nearly overwhelmed her. Several of the stalls were empty, but with evidence of use and in need of cleaning. Passing those, she came to another and recognized one of the carriage horses. Brandon gave the gelding a rub and pat on the neck before moving on to the next stall where he pointed out a pretty piebald mare for her use. "This one's lady broke. She'll do for you."

"You've made amends with your brother," she said. "Last night at the table, the things he said were as much for your benefit as for him."

"We're civil," Brandon answered.

"It's more than that."

He threw on a blanket and lady's saddle, cinching them tight. Turning to face her, he paused. "We've cleared up a few things."

"I'm glad."

His jaw tensed, but then he led the horse outside, gripped her waist and helped her mount. He was perfunctory and businesslike, with no lingering touches or glances.

Silently he adjusted the stirrups. His head bobbed close to her knee and the urge to reach out and push back the shock of brown-black hair from his eyes came over her again. She leaned down and raked her fingers through his hair. At her touch, he stilled for a moment, but then continued lengthening the stirrups for her use as if nothing had happened.

Silly. What had she expected? The intimate gesture, so commonplace during their courtship, no longer stirred him. The firm set of his mouth indicated he felt nothing.

Well and good, she told herself. She knew where she stood with him. Any illusions she'd had were just that—illusions. That helped smooth the course for her. The sooner she explained why she was here, the better for all of them. Then she could make plans for her future with a clear conscience.

He untied his horse from the corral rail and mounted.

Taking the lead, half a horse-length ahead of her, he started on the path through the pines. The summer air was warm and windy with just enough humidity to suggest that it was a benevolent respite from the normal amount. At the first bend in the trail, they passed a cabin nestled in the pines. A creek ran a short distance behind the log house, the sound of gurgling water both fanciful and calming at the same time.

"Jake and I stay here," Brandon said.

"May I take a look?"

He shrugged. "It's not much—a small, one-room office."

Obviously he didn't want to show her. "Perhaps later, then." His attitude perturbed her. In Charleston, he'd gone out of his way to accommodate her.

He kneed his mount and they headed toward the meadow beyond the trees. A sweet fragrance intermingled with the scent of pine drifted through the air. When they emerged into the sunlight, Caroline realized what it was—a field of flowers of every hue swayed in the light morning breeze. Bright red phlox dominated the landscape, inter-spersed with yellow primrose. Every so often breaking the monotony of the colorful carpet a thistle or milkweed bush sprouted up over the shoulders of the other flowers.

She watched Brandon riding ahead of her and wished the tenseness would drop from his shoulders. He held it around him like a shield. She had expected questions and demands for answers today and she was ready for them—anxious even to have the whole matter out in the open and done with. Yet she wondered now if she could penetrate his toughened exterior.

She studied his back, the way he sat his horse as though he were one with the animal. "You've taken to riding eas-ily enough."

He held himself rigid, not answering her, but he slowed his horse and waited for her to move up beside him.

"In Charleston you used a carriage. You said it was more fitting for a doctor."

"Those were your father's words."

"But you used one."

"I prefer to ride."

Why was he being so…so brusque with her? What had become of the young man she'd once loved? The easy-going boy who'd dared the other medical students to swim the channel just to win a chance to take her home. What had happened to him?

He'd become a man, the answer came to her. A man with secrets she no longer shared. A man closed off from her.

"Let's cut to the crux, Caroline. Why are you here?"

He said it so suddenly she nearly jumped in the saddle. She took a deep breath, ready to talk, but something didn't seem right. *He* didn't seem right. She couldn't bare her soul to this…this stranger.

"It's complicated," she said instead.

"Everything with you is complicated," he grumbled. "You leave a swath of complications behind you as long as the Rio Brazos."

"That's not so! You're being monstrously unfair. You want answers from me when you have yet to tell me how you were injured. How can you expect me to be frank and sociable when you bark at me like that?"

He stared at her coldly. "You are the one who came to see me, not the other way around."

"And what a wonderful welcome I received!" She urged her mount forward, angry at Brandon's rude behavior and angry with herself, too. Frustration pounded through her.

They rode on, neither one speaking for a time. Both of them trying to rein in their emotions.

Brandon broke the silence first. "Franklin guarded you like a cougar would her cub last night."

"You noticed."

"I noticed that he is not so bent on your removal from my life now. What happened?"

She darted another glance at him. "Perhaps he realizes he has no concerns on that point anymore. You and I are not the same impetuous couple we once were. We've matured."

"Sometimes that only makes things worse."

He couldn't know how close he was to the truth. "Franklin and I...we just became better acquainted with each other on the journey here. Did you know he was raised in New Orleans?"

"Yes, and you're changing the subject. How did it come about, Caroline? You coming here. I expected Franklin—not you."

In other words, *she* wasn't invited—or welcome. She'd

understood that all along, but to have it said out loud, and by Brandon, hurt. "Can't you just be pleased to see me?"

A scowl crossed his face. "I didn't mean that the way it sounded. It's just that you are a surprise."

"Six months ago, you would have welcomed such a surprise."

"Look, Caroline. The last I heard, you were set to marry someone else. By now, I figured the deed was done. I'll admit it took getting used to, especially after the things we promised each other." His thick, dark brows drew together and for a moment she caught a glimpse of vulnerability before his blue eyes hardened to stone. "Suddenly you show up here and you're not married at all. Seems like you're the one trying to twist me every which way and I'm supposed to accept whatever comes. Well, I don't."

Her piebald danced sideways, sensing the taut emotions. "I didn't realize the news propagated by my parents would extend all the way to Texas, although if I had known I doubt I would have tried to rectify it. At the time I was furious. You left so suddenly, Brandon, and without a proper goodbye! It was as though our betrothal meant nothing to you. Even though you hadn't announced it to our friends, between us it was real—or so I thought." Her eyes burned with tears she refused to shed. How dare he twist this around to be her fault. Hadn't she hurt enough because of him?

He had the grace to look away.

"My parents said you'd abandoned me, that any promises we'd once made to each other were null and void. That is why they tried so hard to dissuade me from waiting for you."

He reined in his horse and stared at her. "You waited?"

"I told you last night that I refused the proposal. Why do you think I said that?" Of course there was more, much more, to the story. She'd loved Brandon and him alone. To give herself to another man was beyond unthinkable—an ugly hypocrisy of the worse kind. "I realized after weeks of not hearing from you that I was being foolish—that I was hoping in vain for you to return. When Tom arrived home bearing your note, I finally understood once and for all that you would not be coming back."

They rode on in silence before Brandon spoke again.

"And Tom? What did he think?"

"He's your friend as much as my brother. He was disgusted with my father for forcing his own agenda."

His jaw tensed. "Your father didn't want me to come back?"

"With the news we received regarding the conflict here, he didn't *expect* you to come back. There's a difference. And he was looking out for me."

"His only daughter."

"You would do the same in his place."

"I might," Brandon conceded. "Can't fault him there."

He rode on another half mile before speaking again. "Tom gave you my note, then."

"Yes," she said quietly. She didn't tell him how the things he'd written had hurt her. How she'd had to harden her heart to keep it from breaking. How she'd lost all hope of ever seeing him again until she'd learned of Franklin's plans.

"So who was this man your parents wanted you to marry? Did I know him?"

"Does it really matter?"

His lips pressed into a thin line before he answered. "Perversely—yes."

"Graham Barstow."

"Barstow! He's ten years your senior!"

The way he said it, as though Graham were horse

fodder, annoyed her. "He's stable, respectable, and charming—and might I add rich."

"And dull as a game of Twenty Questions. You would have been miserable with him."

Secretly she agreed, but at the time, there had been other things to consider—such as Graham's financial solvency and his steadiness. "It makes no difference now. I refused him. It's over." Taking a deep breath, she nudged her horse forward.

They reached the far side of the meadow and Brandon took the lead once more, taking her to the top of a knoll that looked over the river. "This runs along the border of Juan's property. You can follow it until you come to that third hill."

The area that incorporated Juan's land was huge—farther than she could see. "What is that there at the base of those two hills, where the hawk circles?"

"That grouping of trees and boulders?"

She nodded.

"It's a natural spring. Good swimming place."

After all her traveling, a dip sounded heavenly—especially where the water was calm—much preferable to the river yesterday which had tried to tear her apart. "Can we go there?"

"Not now. It's too far," he said gruffly.

"We have all day, don't we?"

She was prepared to cajole him or argue with him, whichever would change his mind, but he turned from her and pointed out the dirt road leading away from the river on the far bank. "Yesterday, you crossed upstream. There."

A flash of white caught her eye. She urged her mount closer for a better look. Far out in the water, draped across a half-submerged tree, her swath of material floated. Perhaps it hadn't been lost to her. "Look! Brandon!"

He studied the river and the distance to the object.

"Can we retrieve it?"

"No, Caroline."

"But…but it's mine."

"Maybe in August when the water level is down—*if* the cloth is still there."

She glanced from his uncompromising face back to the river. "I won't be here in August." If she had her way, hopefully by then she and Brandon would be back in civilization, back in Charleston.

Without waiting for his assistance, she slipped from her saddle and hurried toward the bank. There had to be a way.

He caught up to her at the water's edge and grabbed her elbow. "Now hold on. I know that look in your eyes. Be sensible about this. We've had a bucket-load of rain. The river is too deep and too fast."

"But…"

"It's not worth it."

"It is to me," she insisted, frustrated at his practical manner. "I can swim. You remember what a good swimmer I am, don't you?"

"Not that good. You're crazy to even think it."

He didn't know what that cloth meant to her or he wouldn't say that. She'd spent hours working the stitches.

"What's so important about it anyway?"

When he would have turned away and mounted his horse again, she gripped his arms, improvising—

"If you must know…it is a wedding gift for Jake and Victoria."

"The thing is still not worth the risk involved," Brandon repeated, his voice hardening. "I'm sure it's dirty with mud by now and probably torn, too. Besides it's more than fifty feet out there."

"Bran—"

A twig snapped.

His head jerked up, his gaze sharp as he pulled her close. She held her breath, listening hard. "Was it a deer?"

"More likely a bear," he allowed. "Deer aren't noisy." He released her and took a few steps downstream, studying the surrounding foliage. When he turned back he drew the pistol from his holster and handed it to her. "Stay here. I want to check on it."

He grabbed his rifle from its boot, tore a cartridge with his teeth and poured the powder into the barrel. Then he fished a lead ball from his vest pocket and rammed it into the barrel.

Something had him worried. She was suddenly grateful for the arsenal of weapons he kept with him. Dumbly she nodded her head in agreement.

Chapter Four

He strode away, anxious to put a bit of distance between them. The minute he'd pulled her close, her light perfume had wafted over him. She'd clung to him, seeking protection. She couldn't know what a heady thing that was after all the months of feeling weak, feeling inadequate. How strong it made him feel.

Truth be told, it was hard facing her again. He'd done some pretty selfish things in his life—asking her to wait for him while he went off to fight in Texas territory being the worst. It wouldn't be right to hold her here—not someone like her.

When he'd pointed out that swimming hole a vision of her floating in the water like a water sprite filled his thoughts. He knew her too well. She would have been utterly feminine and tempting. And he'd be hard-pressed to keep his hands off. He'd want to touch her—a lot. That was *not* the direction he intended to take this little reunion. Jake's wedding couldn't come soon enough.

Not more than one hundred yards from where he'd stood with Caroline, he came across recent bear scat and paw prints in the dirt heading away. That didn't disturb him. What did was the campfire in the clearing—recently used since the heavy rains—and near it, the broken hull of a Brown Bess musket—evidence that Mexican renegades still roamed the land.

The sound could have been an animal or a trespasser. He should get back to Caroline. She was defenseless in this country. He turned and started back.

He couldn't have been gone more than five minutes—just long enough to satisfy himself that whatever had caused the sound was gone. Even so he wasn't prepared for the picture that greeted him when he broke through the brush.

Caroline straddled a fallen tree, halfway out over the water, reaching for all she was worth for that damn cloth.

"What the hell are you doing?" he shouted.

Startled she jerked back and then gripped the tree to keep from tumbling off into the river. "Brandon! You gave me a start."

"I gave you a start?" he said, incredulous. "You are willing to get washed away for that rag?"

Her chin jutted out. "It's important to me. And what do you care anyway? It's obvious you cannot stand the sight of me."

"That's not true."

"I'm not stupid. You don't want me here. You didn't want me to come. You're angry at everything I say."

Good grief. Here he was half scared out of his mind for her safety and she wanted to have a heart-to-heart. "Caroline. Come back here. We'll talk when you are on solid ground."

"I don't want to talk. You've been nothing but horrible to me. At the moment, I consider you quite a bore. I—I want to get that cloth."

He would have laughed had it not been for her precarious position over the water. She might be angry with him for what had transpired, but she certainly didn't think him a bore, not if that stroke of his forehead earlier meant anything.

"Caroline! You are going to get yourself killed if you're not careful and then where would I be?"

"Happier, I'm sure."

"You don't mean that."

"You wouldn't understand. Not that you really care to."

"Try me."

She quit reaching then and glared at him. She wasn't scared at all, he realized. She was angry with him and frustrated, but she wasn't scared.

"If you'll hand me a long stick," she said, "perhaps I can reach it."

"Why don't you come back here and I'll get it. My arms are longer than yours. I have a better chance. Besides, I'm the stronger swimmer."

"Even with your injured leg?"

He inhaled sharply. No one talked about his leg. No one. Only she would dare to, he realized. He fisted his hand and then slowly released it, meeting her gaze. "Yes," he said fiercely.

She studied the cloth once more. "Very well." Finally she pulled back.

The tension in his gut uncoiled a degree.

She started making her way, inch by inch, back to the bank. He wondered how she could move in her heavy skirt at all, the way the brown fabric twisted around her legs. He caught a flash of white cotton stockings and shapely ankle in her maneuvering. As soon as he could grab her he caught her waist and set her on solid ground.

The look on her face spoke less of being thankful than of mutiny. Quickly she pulled from his grasp and searched the surrounding ground. Finding a four-foot branch, she thrust it into his hands. "Don't set it loose to drift further downstream."

He was a bit more secure now that she was safe. "I wouldn't dream of it," he mumbled. Stubborn woman. Maybe he didn't know her as well as he thought he did. The thought, at first disconcerting, held a certain appeal. He hadn't expected her to climb out on a tree limb.

He took the stick and shimmied out onto the tree until he was within a few yards of the cloth. As he leaned out, he felt the tree give, bowing low over the water's surface—something Caroline, with her lighter frame, hadn't encountered. It would be just his luck to fall in. The water was freezing and fast enough to take him downstream for some time before he'd be able to make it to the safety of the bank.

"Oh! Do be careful!" Caroline called.

He gritted his teeth and reached again for the cloth, feeling the tree bend perilously close to the water. What was he doing? And all for a bit of fluff. She owed him after this.

He stretched further.

"You're nearly there! Don't give up!"

The tree limb dipped into the current. He hung on as his perch jostled dangerously. Getting his bearings once more, he reached again with the stick, but to no avail. A good three feet separated the end of the stick and the fabric.

He relaxed back onto the tree and sat upright. "It's too far out, Caroline. I'm coming back."

He slid backward on the trunk until he touched the dirt on the bank and stood. They were both ridiculous—her for risking herself for the silly cloth and him for doing the same thing. Luckily nobody else had come upon them. He threw the stick aside in disgust and started for her horse.

She stopped him with a hand on his arm. "I know you thought it was a fool's errand. Thank you for trying anyway."

This time he couldn't ignore the contact. He looked at her long-fingered hand on his arm. His skin tingled where she touched. Her touch had always done that to him. He studied her face—the high-boned cheeks, the sweep of her long, dark lashes against her flushed skin. "I'm sorry it's lost to you. I do remember how well you could swim. You were like a mermaid," he said quietly. "I remember… everything."

His gaze dropped to her lips.

She stilled, her green eyes big.

"How soft your skin was. How good you felt." Somehow, one arm ended up around her waist. "*Especially* how good we felt together." His heart beat faster. The image of her naked on the tarp in the boathouse was burned into his brain forever. He'd tried to eradicate it from his memory, but one touch from her was all it had taken to call it back full bore.

He stared at her full, half-parted lips, knowing how giving they were, how smooth the skin on her cheek felt. His body thrummed with the need to rub his mouth against her there, near her ear where he'd once pressed kisses that drove her wild. He'd been intoxicated with the power he felt at the time, drunk with the thought that he could make her shiver with merely a touch.

He grasped her upper arm. She watched him with a curious look in her eyes. If what she'd been saying was true, if she had denied Barstow and waited for him, she deserved a better man than he. Besides he couldn't just take up where they'd left off before he'd departed for Texas territory. It was impossible. Too much had happened and she didn't know the half of it. The war…the fighting…he'd seen too much. He was a broken man now with nothing left to give her.

He took a steadying breath, holding himself in check. Be quick and to the point, he told himself. Blunt. That was the only way to address this wisp of attraction that wouldn't let go. "You won't like the way this will end—and there is only one way it can—with you returning to Charleston alone. So let's not start anything we'll regret later."

She jerked from his grasp as if stung by a scorpion. Her bosom heaved under the crisp white blouse. "I have no trouble controlling myself. I merely said thank-you. You assumed anything further." She handed back his gun, which he holstered.

"Fine. Then we understand each other."

She was silent while he led the way back to the hacienda. He kept a watchful eye for any signs they might be followed and chose a different path than the way they'd come, skirting the meadow in favor of keeping to the cover of the trees near the small bluff. Safer for her.

He didn't want to worry her about what he'd seen. He wouldn't have given the campsite much thought if it hadn't been for that musket. Renegades—Mexicans who'd fought under Santa Anna. They'd caused all kinds of troubles since the war. He needed to tell Juan and Jake. Soon.

"Brandon!"

Adrenaline shot through him. He grabbed his pistol, ready to protect them both if necessary. At the same time, he heard the bellow of an animal to his left. Fifty feet away in the center of a pond they'd been rounding a longhorn struggled in his prison of mud. The beast's glazed, white-eyed stare spoke of its fear of them, but its weak movements spoke of exhaustion.

"What should we do?" Caroline asked, lifting her reins to move closer.

Brandon released his grip on his gun and grasped the bridle on her horse, holding her mount in place. "Don't go any closer, Caroline. That's not some milk cow from a farmer's meadow. He's wild."

"Then he's too dangerous to help?"

Brandon dismounted and ground-hitched his horse, studying the situation. "I didn't say that."

He grabbed his rope, moving closer. Seeing as how the bull was on Juan's spread made it Juan's. With the mess the rebellion had made of the land and Juan's livelihood, one bull could be a very valuable asset. He glanced back at Caroline. "Stay back out of the way. If he gets loose, he could run in any direction. Most likely will if he feels threatened."

He inched around the stand of cattails, going slow to keep from alarming the longhorn. He was crazy to try this, especially with his injured leg. He'd probably end up forfeiting his good rope—and that's if he was lucky.

His fingers curled around the looped cord in his hand. The buzz of dragonfly wings swooping over the brown, rucked-up water was drowned-out by the bull's occasional thrashing, followed by a snort that vibrated through the water. Lukewarm ripples lapped against his leg and sloshed into his boots. He slowed his movements…slowed his breathing…inched closer…

Glancing over his shoulder to make sure his horse waited quietly, he checked that Caroline had done as he asked and stayed back. His sorrel had lowered his head and munched on the tall summer grass at the base of an oak, whereas Caroline watched in breathless anticipation, her eyes alight with excitement.

He unwrapped a good fifteen feet of rope and checked his slipknot. "Now would be a good time to benefit from all my practice," he mumbled to himself. Vainly he didn't want to look bad in front of Caroline, didn't want her going back to Charleston with tales of his ineptitude, because she *was* going back. The evidence of the renegades had only strengthened his resolve. Texas was too dangerous for the likes of her.

He set his feet as best he could on the muddy pond bottom, then swung the rope overhead once, twice, and on its third journey let it go. It arched over the water's surface and landed around the longhorn's head and one horn.

He stared in surprise. How'd that happen?

Startled, the bull snorted and looked around, for a moment bewildered. Brandon slogged from the water and strode toward his horse. He knotted the rope over the saddle horn just as the longhorn, with one toss of his strong head, snapped the line taut. "Brace yourself," he murmured, for his own benefit as well as his horse's.

The bull thrashed in earnest in a gigantic attempt to be free of the restraining muck, brambles and rope. The stupid cuss didn't have a clue he was being rescued.

Striding forward, Brandon grabbed the line with his hands. "Back!" He jerked on the rope and lent his strength to that of his horse, pulling with all his might despite the way his sweaty hands slid along the rope.

The bull tossed his head and with his eyes rolling wildly jerked Brandon forward into the cattails. He landed, face-first, in the muck. "You pea-brained cow," he said, struggling to his feet with the water and mud streaming from him. "You'd buck a helping hand as soon as a coyote not knowing the difference."

Gripping the cord again, he pulled hard. The longhorn

rose in the water, and then his front legs, coated with mud, thrashed through the surface in an attempt to meet solid ground. Straining against the rope, Brandon whistled to his horse.

The rope tightened further and the young bull moved toward him. The animal struggled again, this time releasing his hindquarters and legs from the mud, but his strength was waning, his attempts to fight the rope weaker. At a sound behind him, he glanced back and found Caroline grasping his sorrel's bridle, urging his horse back.

"It's now or never, you cuss," Brandon said under his breath and strained with all of his might.

The beast thrashed one last time and suddenly all four legs came free of the bottom muck. The animal struggled forward awkwardly, confused at first to be out of the mud. Then, his hooves on solid ground, it stared straight at him.

Brandon swallowed. The stupid thing looked as if it might charge him.

Slowly Brandon stepped backward until he felt the warm hide of his horse at his back. In one quick motion, he pressed the rifle against his shoulder, sighting the longhorn in the crosshairs. "Don't do it…" he murmured under his breath, speaking to the bull. "Not after all that. You're free now. Don't do it."

He had sworn he'd never kill another living thing after the war. He'd been forced to modify his oath—once when a rattler had threatened Juan's daughter and another time when he and Jake had been hungry and came upon a deer. Never a person, though. And he didn't want to kill this bull if he could do otherwise, but there was no way he'd let it hurt Caroline.

He set his stance and targeted the irregular-shaped splash of white on the animal's chest. Mud smeared the area, but it was a vulnerable spot. Then he made the mistake of glancing into the bull's face.

A rivulet of blood trickled from the longhorn's nostril, so similar to the nightmare Brandon had had last night that it unnerved him. Then more blood came until all he saw was blood. It spurted from the beast's nostrils, coating its entire hide and then it kept on spreading, covering the ground in an ever-enlarging circle.

It couldn't be real. It wasn't real. Yet still his heart hammered in his chest. Suddenly he couldn't get enough air. He lowered the flintlock. The trees spun around him. The blood couldn't be real…but he stepped back as it flooded toward him in a thick carpet of dark red.

The animal charged.

Caroline's scream shattered the early-afternoon quiet, and reverberated through his head.

Startled, Brandon reacted without conscious thought. He focused on the longhorn racing toward him and fired. Mud flew everywhere as the beast collapsed at his feet, stunned, but not dead—and still dangerous. In fluid motion Brandon grabbed his knife and straddled the bull's thick shoulders. He pulled back on one horn to expose the soft underside of its neck and slashed its throat. The longhorn twitched once, twice, and then was quiet. As the jugular emptied out, the sticky blood ran in a small stream toward the pond, discoloring the muddy water's edge.

Brandon blinked. The pool of red had disappeared.

His heart thumped painfully in his chest, the adrenaline still churning through him, making his stomach roil. He leaned against a boulder and ripped the bandanna from his neck. *Just breathe. Relax.*

The spells were getting worse. This one happened in daylight. He checked his hands. They looked steady so far.

He didn't want Caroline to be here when the shakes came—and they always did as soon as his heartbeat slowed to normal.

"Brandon?"

Oh, God. Caroline. He mopped the sweat from his forehead and straightening, faced her. "Are you all ri—?"

The look of shock on her face told him otherwise. She looked like she might fall off her horse. He helped her dismount and walk to a small boulder. "Here, sit down."

Her lips were pale where usually they held a soft pink color. He crouched beside her, more concerned when she shrunk away from him. "You look like you're going into shock. What's the matter?"

"The way you handled that knife…like it was part of you. You've done this before, haven't you?"

"I've learned to do a lot of necessary things."

"But slitting a throat?"

He was getting anxious now. She had to leave. "Would you rather I waited for the beast to get up and attack again? I might not have had time to reload the rifle before that happened."

"You had a pistol."

"Which wouldn't even slow such a strong animal." Why was she questioning his methods? He'd gotten the job done.

He stared at the still form of the bull, wishing they hadn't come across it in the first place. "It's never comfortable—seeing something die. I'm sorry you had to witness it. But it's a fact of life. Maybe we saved the stupid animal from a worse fate, like slowly starving—or living."

Her eyes flashed to his, alarmed.

He'd crossed the line, said too much. He clamped his mouth shut. She had to leave.

"I want you to ride back to the hacienda and tell Jake or Diego to come help with the butcherin'."

His terse order bewildered her.

"Now. Not Sunday."

Hurt tightened her face, but she turned toward her horse.

He strode up behind her, grabbed her waist and set her on her mare. "It's just beyond that rise ahead."

She took the reins from him. "You could have been killed. Why did you wait to shoot?"

He wasn't about to discuss the real reason with her. "Just acting like a normal longhorn. I told you they were ornery. I hoped he'd turn away at the last minute."

She opened her mouth to say more but he interrupted. He didn't want any more questions. There wasn't time.

"Be careful heading back. Stay to the trees, not out in the open. And once you're there, stay there."

"Why?"

"Just do as I say, Caroline."

"But…"

He turned on her, suddenly angry at her constant pushing. "Is it necessary for you to challenge everything I say? Everything?"

Her eyes widened and unwittingly she pulled back on the reins, making her mount back-step. Good. He'd struck some fear in her. She might as well learn now that out here she'd have to be tough—and she wasn't tough enough— not with the way she'd reacted.

He turned back to the carcass, shutting her out. He didn't want to scare her with news of the renegades. He just wanted her safe—and away from him.

Resettling his rope around the animal's neck, his fingers started to tremble. He gripped the bull's horns, willing his hands to stop shaking, but it didn't help. He glanced up, hoping by now Caroline was long gone. She was just dis- appearing into the trees on the far side of the pond.

Relieved, he sank down on a nearby boulder and let the

shuddering overtake him. It always started in his hands and worked its way up his arms. No matter how hard he fought, nothing he did controlled it. He just had to wait for it to pass.

By the time Jake arrived Brandon had scouted out a patch of earth that hadn't turned to mud in the last three days. With the longhorn roped to their horses, they dragged it twenty feet to the grassy area. Jake knelt beside the carcass and whipped out his knife, quickly setting to the business of saving what meat and hide they could before the buzzards found them. Brandon watched for a moment, bracing himself, and then started in, too.

They stripped the hide and then packed the meat into it for ease of carrying. As they worked, Brandon told his brother about the cold campfire and the musket. "We should check on it—at least make sure they've moved on."

His brother nodded. "Is that why Caroline looked so shook up when she found me?"

Brandon paused in his work. Her mood could have been because of any number of things that had happened that morning. "I didn't tell her about the camp. She wouldn't have known."

"Wonder what had her bloomers inside out, then."

Brandon shrugged, keeping his eyes on his task. "This bull charged. That could have done it."

Once the horses were loaded, Jake looked Brandon over and a slow grin came to his face. "You could use a bath."

Suddenly on guard, Brandon stepped back. "No more'n you."

Jake sauntered toward him, a gleam in his eyes. Then he locked arms with Brandon and wrestled him to the water. Brandon fought back, but being of slighter build, he got the worst of it. In the end, they both ended up soaked—

but the tension that had coiled inside him all day like a snake had eased.

Jake yanked him from his seat in the water and together they sat against a boulder to empty their boots of the pond water. Brandon pointed with his chin at the bull's head lying in the grass. Buzzards or coyotes would strip it clean by morning. "Stupid animal," he mumbled. "He didn't have to die. Didn't have the sense to know I was trying to help."

"Yeah." Jake threw him a look. "I've met people like that, too."

It didn't take a genius to figure who he meant. Brandon chose to ignore him and mounted his horse, reining it toward the hacienda.

Chapter Five

After having told Jake where to find Brandon and why, Caroline entered the hacienda by the kitchen door. She was anxious to get to her room. The incident with the bull confounded her. The entire morning confounded her. Something was going on with Brandon—something he did not want to share with her. What had happened to him in the months since he'd left Charleston? What had the war done to him?

The kitchen wasn't empty, bringing her up short. Victoria and her mother watched expectantly while at the table Franklin used an iron bar to pry open a slatted crate. She recognized the crate as one that had traveled with them in the carriage boot.

With a loud creak, the lid toppled off. Victoria reached in and removed the delicate hand-painted teacup, brushing off the remains of straw packing. "These made it all the way here without breaking!" She examined the china with delight and then turned to hand the cup to her mother.

Caroline wondered how in the world Victoria handled the rough-hewn Jake with her petite frame and soft voice.

After Caroline's interrogation at supper last night, just speaking to him a moment ago had unnerved her.

Deep voices in the hall drew her attention. It couldn't be Brandon or Jake. They'd still be busy with the longhorn. These men spoke in rapid Spanish. One voice in particular was unique in its gravelly tone.

Victoria rose and stepped to the arched doorway. She listened a moment before returning. "Men looking for work. There are many drifters since the war. Juan is speaking with them."

"Did the Mexican soldiers come through here?" Caroline asked.

Victoria motioned about the room, her expressive eyes sad. "This was not the way the hacienda looked when I was younger. The *soldados* used the furniture for firewood. Books, too. They left scars everywhere—on the land, and on the people."

Caroline looked about with new understanding. "What a great loss for Juan and his family."

"It has been very hard for them. I don't know if they will ever recover completely."

"Are they happy to be living free of Santa Anna now?"

Victoria nodded. "I hope that preparing for my wedding has helped them look forward and not back." She pulled another teacup from the crate. "*Gracias,* Señor Penderton. I know it is because of your expert packing that they did not break. I will treasure these."

"They are from Jake's mother—an heirloom of the family."

"Then I will treasure them all the more."

He dusted his hands on his pants. "I'll leave you women to the rest."

"*Gracias.*"

After Franklin left, Victoria continued unpacking, talking to Caroline at the same time. "Tomorrow, I am going into town with Jake and my parents. There are a few things I must purchase for the wedding party. Perhaps you would like to accompany us?"

Caroline would rather get things worked out with Brandon. She still hadn't told him the real reason of her visit. "Actually I think I will stay here."

"As you wish."

"It's just that I am so tired of traveling," she hurried to explain. She also had to confront Brandon. She was sure that if she hadn't cried out, that longhorn would have trampled him. "As a matter of fact, I'm tired now. The ride this morning…"

"I understand completely, Señorita Benét. Please. Go. A *siesta* before supper is just what you need."

Caroline left the kitchen and climbed the stairs, glad that the men in the front entrance had gone. Just before closing the door to her room, she heard Brandon's uneven gait on the entry tiles and left it ajar to listen.

Victoria met him in the hall. "What do you think you are doing coming in here soaking wet?"

"Caroline all right?" Brandon replied brusquely.

"She is upstairs. Resting."

A pause followed Victoria's words.

"Should I announce that you wish to see her?"

Another pause. "No. I've got work to do."

Caroline closed the door softly. What was going on? One minute Brandon pushed her away, wanting nothing to do with her, and then the next he wondered if she was all right? She paced back and forth, unable to get the morning ride and Brandon's actions off her mind.

Her clothes had been removed from her trunk and taken

to be cleaned and aired. Thinking it would be good to air the inside of the trunk, too, she opened the lid and wedged a dowel in place.

In the corner a familiar piece of paper caught her eye. She took it out, carefully unfolding it, remembering the day her brother had returned from fighting in Texas and delivered it. She'd been so excited to finally hear something from Brandon, only to fall into despair after reading it. The page was wrinkled from frequent handling and now the indigo ink was smeared across the damp paper. Each time she read it she wished the words were different, that something more would appear.

Caroline,

I hope this letter finds you well. The fight is over. I'm as fit as can be expected. Jake explained to me about the kiss. It happened so long ago I hardly remember being angry, but I guess I was since I am here and you are there. Funny thing…after staring down a musket barrel with a bayonet pushed against my chest, that kiss seems like a pretty silly thing to get all fired up about.

I promised before that I'd be home after Texas won its freedom. I don't think much of a man who breaks his word—so you know I'm not high on my own list—but I won't be coming back. Sorry I can't say more than that. It's best if you forget about me. Take care of yourself.

Brandon Dumont

Caroline's fingers curled into fists as she read the note again. He must have written the letter after the war but before learning of her betrothal—a betrothal that never actually happened. The letter from Franklin must have crossed in the post. If Brandon had thought she was marrying another he probably wouldn't have bothered to write at all.

There was no mention of love, but the very fact that he'd taken the time to write said that he held some feelings for her or else he felt guilty for not coming back as he'd promised. At least at that time he did. He seemed to have gotten over it now.

There was no obvious emotion at all in the note—and this from a man who had been so passionate about helping the sick of Charleston at one time and then helping the Texans in their fight for freedom. He'd been a man of noble ambitions, vision and passion.

Where was that man now? Not once this morning had he mentioned anything about medicine or being a physician. It was as if he'd shut the door on his past life—including her. Then again, there'd been no talk at all about his future, either.

He'd been passionate in other ways, too. She smoothed her hand over her growing abdomen, remembering the warm slide of his body against hers, skin to skin, the one and only time they'd lain together. Passionate, attentive, tender—he was everything she'd ever dreamed of in a lover, in a husband. Her body resonated with the unforgettable sensations.

How would she live never knowing his touch again? At times her chest ached from wanting him even though at the same time she was angry at his abandonment. She would always remember that night even though the memory hurt in ways that cut deeply. Every time she felt the movement of his child inside, she was reminded of him.

She would not give this baby up. She couldn't. No

matter what her parents said. They couldn't be so cruel as to force her hand. She already loved the little one.

She had to convince Brandon to go back to Charleston with her. He was her only hope. Finding him so changed scared her. What would happen now? Could she depend on him at all?

She folded the note to put it away and suddenly the damp and worn paper ripped down the center. Her breathing stilled. She stared at the two halves while a strange sensation came over her. She had never been one to believe in superstition, yet an uncanny sense that this was an ill omen settled inside.

Chapter Six

Caroline knocked on the door to Brandon's cabin. A small sign boasted the word "Doc/Médico" painted on the wood.

"Is he expecting us?" Franklin asked, standing beside her and peering through the dirty front window.

"Actually. No. I haven't seen him since the ride yesterday." A fact that bothered her. After waking from her nap, she'd wondered where he'd disappeared.

"Were you able to talk to him?"

She paused in knocking a second time. Franklin was asking about the baby. "No." She tried the door. It opened easily. "Brandon?"

She wrinkled her nose as she stepped inside onto the puncheon floor. "This room needs a definite airing."

There was no sign of Brandon, but she could tell he used the place. A battered desk, the wood darkened with age, sat in the corner. Papers scattered the top of it along with a scale containing weights and measures. A near-empty cabinet stood against the wall shelving two tomes of questionable relevancy to medicine and five amber apothecary jars. Behind one cabinet door leaned a bone saw.

Opening a drawer, she found only long-handled scissors. There were no forceps, no scalpel and blades. Further searching established the absence of a mortar and pestle which were staples of her father's practice. She picked up a strange accordion-type iron implement and held it up for Franklin's inspection. "I wonder what this is used for." Considering the odd assortment of tools in the drawer, if this was all he had—ancient, rusty instruments and few at that— it was a far cry from what he'd worked with in Charleston.

A thick layer of dust and grime covered the top of the cabinet. She rubbed her fingers across and then stared at her fingertips in distaste. Clapping the dust from her hands, she met Franklin's gaze. "He has never accepted sloven- liness in the past."

She wandered toward the back of the one-room abode. Behind a curtain lay two straw pallets for sleeping. Not even a proper bed. After living at the estate in Charleston, how could he stand this for any length of time?

Sighing, she turned back to the center of the room and removed her bonnet, searching for a dust-free place to deposit it. Unable to find any clean horizontal spot, she finally spied a wall peg and hooked it there.

A scraping noise came from behind the cabin.

"Let me go first," Franklin said with a warning in his voice.

Before he could investigate, an expletive shot from the front of the cabin.

Brandon stepped through the door. He wore his buckskin pants and little else. Sweat gleamed on his torso, tanned from the sun and sculpted from hard work. He'd always had a decent physique before and had been a cut above the other men who'd vied for her hand, but now…now Caroline quite had the breath knocked out of her.

Awkward, especially with Franklin standing there, Caroline felt a blush start at her toes and work its way up her body. She really didn't know quite where to look when all she could think was how smooth and strong he looked, and of the one time she'd pressed against that chest quite intimately. She shouldn't look, for heaven's sake, but couldn't seem to drag her eyes away.

Brandon strode into the cabin—*his* cabin, he reminded himself—and looked for the pitcher of water he'd set on the counter. It was no longer there. His head pounded, reminding him he'd overindulged last night trying to keep the dreams at bay. Dreams of the war. Dreams of the nameless Mexican soldiers he'd patched up and ultimately buried. Dreams of Caroline. The liquor hadn't helped. He'd still woken at dawn, his mood foul from lack of sleep.

Turning back he looked directly at Franklin, whose lips pressed together in mute disapproval. Brandon growled another expletive and headed outside. He had work to do today and didn't need anyone criticizing him. And it was too damn hot to put on a shirt.

The impeccably dressed Franklin followed him.

Brandon grabbed the hoe and started in on the garden he'd been weeding behind the cabin. "What? Now you are suddenly her guardian?"

"I have always behaved as a gentleman. Despite my initial feelings, I was never rude, which, by the way, you just were to her. And it wasn't that I disliked her. You simply weren't ready to settle down."

"Didn't want to see me hog-tied before my time, is that it? Franklin, sometimes you are more like a parent to me than Father was."

Franklin studied him with an uncanny look in his gray eyes. "Caroline has grown up since you last saw her. She's been forced to."

Brandon mopped the sweat from his brow with a swipe of his forearm. He hadn't missed that she'd filled out nicely, curving in all the right places—especially her breasts. He'd noticed the snug fit of her bodice on the ride yesterday.

"While you were off playing soldier—"

"I wouldn't call it playing," he interrupted darkly, his voice full of warning. He attacked a particularly large weed with his hoe.

"My apologies. However, you still might try to consider her side of the situation."

"I haven't noticed much of a change. Considering that she finagled her way here, she still acts before she thinks, just like she did in Charleston. I'll bet jaws are flapping on the home front with both of your departures."

"She went to great lengths to avoid any social misstep. For your information, with the exception of one aunt, no one is aware that she's here."

"Guess there's no way of knowing until you return," Brandon said evenly. "You could be going back to a shotgun wedding for all you know."

Franklin's lips twitched. "I doubt it will come to that."

"So tell me—how did she corral you to her wishes? How did she end up coming in the first place? Her parents couldn't have approved."

A rueful smile came over Franklin's face. "I'm embarrassed by my part in it—or rather my lack of foresight."

Intrigued, Brandon leaned his hoe against the cabin.

"I've always prided myself in being more alert than the next man and more adept at anticipating situations before they occur. Preparation is the key, you see, to being ready for anything."

Now he really had Brandon's attention, confused as it was. "What in the deuce are you talking about?"

The man's face was a peculiar shade of crimson. "She stopped the coach and pulled a gun on me."

Brandon's mouth went dry. "What!"

"Impulsive, yes," Franklin hastened to say. "I'll concede that point. But apparently only where you are concerned."

Brandon snorted. Why Franklin was trying to explain away Caroline's action and take some of the responsibility off her shoulders was anybody's guess.

"She'd heard from her brother that I was traveling here for Jake's wedding and she was determined to see you. Taking me hostage was the only option she could think of to get her way. She has a good head on her shoulders. To tell the truth, I was impressed with her gumption."

"You could have been shot!" Brandon could throttle her! She had no experience with firearms and one slight bump of the carriage could have sent the blame thing off. It had to have been a ruse. "She wouldn't have used it. The entire idea is preposterous."

Franklin's brows shot up. "Surprisingly I believe she might have. She seemed a bit desperate in her actions. However I didn't give her much of a chance. She had the upper hand for only a few seconds."

"Long enough to have shot you through."

"In her defense, she aimed at my leg."

"Take it from me—it hurts no matter where the plug ends up," Brandon said sarcastically. But as he thought about Franklin, a man of goodly proportions, held hostage by Caroline, the image suddenly made him want to laugh. He didn't, though—that feeling being as foreign to him now as Charleston was. "The little chit. She does like to have her own way."

"Don't we all." Franklin's lips twitched again. "I found her to be quite resourceful and very determined. As I said—full of spirit."

Brandon had been drawn to that spirit from the first time they'd met. She took such delight in all things. As a doctor, he was constantly pushed against the ugly side of life. A physician's curse. He'd seen so much in his chosen profession of the sick, the sad, the lonely, the dying. Too often there was nothing he could do but provide comfort in place of a cure, a few hours of pain relief in place of eradication of the cause of the pain. While a student it had frustrated him. Knowing Caroline waited for him at the end of the day made it bearable. Believing that she waited while he'd been a captive in prison had made that bearable, too. But now even her presence couldn't hold back the nightmares. Nothing could.

Obviously there had to be more to her being here than just to visit him. If convincing him to return to Charleston was her mission, she'd soon learn that she couldn't have her way this time. He was more than up to the challenge of turning her right around and sending her back to Charleston after Jake's wedding.

Franklin cleared his throat, serious once again. "I came by to let you know that I am ready to go over your father's will with you and your brother."

"Good. I want to get things settled once and for all." He paused, considering. "But I thought you'd be going into town with them today."

"I've had enough of traveling for now. What did Jake say this morning? Ah, yes—the road to Bexar was a 'kidney-crusher.' It doesn't sound tolerable. Besides, I brought the things from Charleston that he wanted for the wedding."

"All right. I'll let him know when he gets back tonight. We'll go over the documents first thing tomorrow morning."

"I also left a small item for you on your desk."

Intrigued, Brandon started back to the house. Then Caroline stepped into view at the side of the cabin and he stopped. She held a tall mug for him. Of course she'd known what he'd been inside for. It didn't surprise him. She'd always been like that—able to anticipate his needs.

"I'll leave you two to talk," Franklin said, and then lowered his voice. "Clothe yourself, sir." He turned and headed down the path through the trees to the hacienda, but not before shooting Brandon another stern look.

Brandon straightened and leaned the hoe against the chopping block. Caroline wore a calico skirt and cream-colored blouse—much plainer when compared to her traveling suit. Probably cooler, too. A thin, deep red ribbon wove through the thick braid of blond hair which she had piled high on her head. Positively festive, Brandon thought, his mood turning surly.

With Franklin's words echoing in his head, he reached for the mug. Caroline's gaze flashed to his and then skittered off to contemplate the distant hills and oaks.

Perversely he enjoyed her flustered attempt not to ogle him. He *wanted* to make her uncomfortable—just like she made him feel by being here. Before she'd arrived, he had been successful at burying the life he'd had in Charleston. He didn't want to remember it. It was his past—part of his life that no longer existed. A life he could no longer return to. Not when the spells came upon him more and more.

And now he couldn't get the image of her holding a gun on Franklin out of his mind. She *was* impulsive—and daring—and…fun. Her unpredictability had been a source of excitement when they'd courted and once in a great while a source of embarrassment. All in good fun, though. With the exception of her braving the tree limb for that silly bit of cloth, he hadn't seen that side of her since her arrival.

"This is why you came inside in the first place, isn't it?" she asked. "For a drink?"

He snapped out of his reverie, gulped down the cool water and then handed the earthen mug back to her. He grabbed his shirt from the chopping block.

"You don't have to."

"Oh, but I do. Franklin made it clear to me I was in the wrong, presenting myself this way." He drew the cotton shirt over his head and shoved his arms into the sleeves. Glancing at her as he laced it up, he continued, "My only defense is that I didn't know you were here."

"It seems unnecessary…considering what has occurred between us."

At her words, a vision entered his mind that was not entirely innocent—her long, silky limbs, tangled in the boat's blanket and around him, her skin glowing in the slash of moonlight through the boathouse window. He shut the image from his mind and forced himself back to the present. "Maybe. But I don't want you compromised. Not in front of Franklin or anyone."

She stared at the ground where he worked as a blush stole over her cheeks and he wondered if she remembered that night as perfectly as he did. Her next words confirmed it.

"I believe in all honesty, I already am." She raised her green gaze to his. "Compromised."

She was right. Yet he didn't regret it. The memory of her had kept him alive, given him hope. Even if it all seemed pointless now. "I won't say I'm sorry for our one night together, Caroline. I can't be sorry."

Her lower lip trembled. "Nor I."

He swallowed hard and chucked his hoe into the hard earth. This line of talking had to stop. He'd clung to his anger like a shield, feeding it, making it grow. As long as he had believed she had betrayed him by marrying so soon after he'd left her, it had been possible to hate her and bury her memory.

But then she'd shown up.

"I wanted to speak to you about yesterday," she said.

He kept his head down, digging at the dirt, bracing himself. A fool would know what was bothering her.

"What made you hesitate with that longhorn?"

"I didn't," he lied. "I waited to see if the bull would turn. When I was sure shooting him was the only option left, I fired. You just happened to cry out at the same time."

Her brow furrowed. "That's not how it seemed to me."

"That's how it was." He straightened and held her gaze.

She seemed on the verge of saying more, but then surprised him by turning away. Walking the perimeter of his garden plot, she crouched to pull a small weed.

"I've wandered through the flower and vegetable gardens back home, but I've not seen the likes of some of these plants."

"They're herbs. For medicine."

She went still at his words.

"Some things I can gather wild—the onions for poultices, the foxglove for heart conditions, but there are others that are not readily available."

"Isn't it too late for planting?"

He shrugged.

A smile tilted the corner of her mouth. "Having a garden

is not something I would have expected of you. At least not in Charleston."

"Victoria is the one who started it. She badgered me about what kind of things I might need and then I found her out here one day, planting. She dared me to keep it going."

"That explains it, then. I guess there is a need."

"In Charleston all I had to do was stop at the apothecary. Here, there isn't one."

She shook her head. "Why would anyone want to live out here, Brandon? I really don't understand how Victoria manages. People lack the basic necessities and then to constantly worry about Indians and drought. It's all so scary—and so unnecessary when you can live somewhere like Charleston."

He took a deep breath. She'd very subtly turned the conversation and he had an idea where she was heading with it. "You wouldn't understand. You've had the life of a princess with a doting father and servants at your beck and call."

She frowned, defensively. "There's nothing wrong with the way I was raised."

"I didn't say there was. Only that you wouldn't make it in Texas. Life here is too harsh."

"And you haven't had difficulty? I realize that you weren't raised with a silver spoon in your mouth, but your family was quite comfortable."

"It's different for a man. We're tougher. We don't need the same trappings that women need. Women always make things complicated."

He didn't want any further complications in his life—no strings from the past to tie him down, no constant reminders of the life he could no longer have. She would leave and be none the wiser that he could no longer doctor.

He just had to keep his distance and make sure she understood things were over between them.

"I disagree." She motioned vaguely toward the cabin. "The addition of a rope bed and feather mattress rather than a straw mat on the ground seems like a complication most men would welcome. And a cookstove instead of a fireplace. Much more efficient. The same goes for medicinal supplies."

"You're entitled to your opinion. I won't argue with it."

She put a hand on her hip. "One of the things I have always admired about you is that you wanted to make the world a better place. You did it in a big way when you took off for this wilderness. Now you are doing it again, in a small way, with this garden."

"Don't deceive yourself, Caroline. Five months ago I might have felt that way. I was an idealistic fool, sure I could make a difference."

"But you ca—"

"Then I came up against Santa Anna's army and saw what happened when men had absolute power over others, or worse—when men were reduced to starving animals. The line vanishes between civilized and savage."

Her eyes were wide as she took in all he was saying.

"Trust, compassion and hope are luxuries a common man can't afford." Brandon remembered the moment the reality had shifted, become clearer—and much uglier. He'd seen it in his nightmares ever since.

"But Brandon…what of your plans?"

He could tell this was hard for her, but he couldn't back down. She had to know the truth. "What I do will have little effect on things. I can't fix the world's problems." Heck, he couldn't even fix his own problems.

Her green eyes clouded over.

"You're disappointed."

"It doesn't sound like you."

"I'm being realistic." His voice sounded harsh, even to his own ears. "It's better that way."

He turned his back on her and continued working, feeling the prickling sensation as she continued to stare at his back.

"Do you mind if I stay?"

Anyone else would have run away at the sourness of his mood. Not Caroline. "Suit yourself."

She brushed the wood shavings from the chopping block and settled herself there. After a while, she began speaking of their mutual friends—the cotillions, the weddings and the ones expecting babies. He thought about stopping her. He didn't want to hear any of it, but her soft, musical voice, the warmth of the sun on his back and the light breeze tickling his skin, converged to lull him into a peaceful rhythm as he chopped the hoe into the hard dirt.

When she began talking about the hospital and the new wing her father was building, Brandon stopped hoeing and straightened. "It's hard to reconcile that life with the one I have now."

"I suppose so, but when you return, it will seem like you never left. Father is looking forward to handing some of his responsibilities over to you. The west wing—just like you wanted."

He held her gaze. "I don't plan to work at the hospital."

"Whatever do you mean? You have your father's practice. His patients are asking for you."

He didn't answer.

"You can't have much opportunity to doctor here."

"I've patched up a few cuts, pulled a tooth or two."

"But I thought…once Jake's wedding is over you would be coming home. You are a brilliant surgeon. This can't be what you want. Not here. Not Texas."

When he didn't answer again, she stood.

Slowly comprehension filled her eyes. "Jake was right, then. You don't intend to return," she whispered. "You don't want to come home. Not to your work waiting for you. Not…not even to me."

The shattered look on her face nearly had him reaching for her. He clenched his fists tight at his sides. She'd come a long way to be disappointed, but there was no getting around it. Things were different now. "No."

She put her hand to her mouth, her eyes brimming with tears. "This is all because I kissed Jake, isn't it?"

He stared at her in surprise as she rushed on.

"It was foolish. I know that now. I should have refused to go through with it, but everyone was watching, expecting me to do something."

"I told you before that I don't have a problem with that." Which of course was a big, fat lie. The thought of that kiss had churned like acid in his stomach for months.

"It doesn't sound like you understand—or that you have forgiven me. How many ways must I say that I'm sorry?"

"Then why did you do it? I thought another girl was supposed to dole out the 'prize.'"

"Abigail Satterly was, but she hadn't told her parents. When they found out, they took her home."

"But why you?"

"It was my benefit—my responsibility. Practically everyone else there that day was married. How could I ask any of them? Besides, you were supposed to win the shooting match. You've always been the best shot."

He grimaced. "Until Jake showed up." He let out a long

breath. "I thought he had turned your head, like he had every other woman there that day. They were fascinated by him."

"I wasn't. Not ever."

He'd been angry with her for so long he found it hard to let go and believe her.

She pressed her fingers to her forehead. "You've obviously forgiven Jake. How is it you can forgive him and not me?"

Her question brought him up short. How could he indeed? "Jake proved a few things when he risked his life to save my hide and get me out of that Mexican prison."

"And I haven't proven anything. Is that what you're saying?"

"You're saying it."

A furrow formed between her brows.

He'd had enough. He wasn't going to examine something that happened so long ago any longer. "Drop it, Caroline. It's over now."

"Then is it someone else? Someone here?"

Lord save him from such a tenacious woman! The question was nearly laughable to him, but he didn't feel like laughing. Caroline had been the only woman for him since the moment they had been introduced on the beach. She'd been so enchanting and so out of reach that he'd wanted to impress her. Along with his friends, she'd teased him until he had swum the channel, surprising even himself, and arrived back half-drowned at her feet. Everyone there had deemed him crazy, but he was the one who had ended up taking her home.

She had changed over the past two years, in spite of what he'd told Franklin. Before she'd been pretty, but now she was beautiful and vibrant. With maturity her allure had deepened. He liked the way she looked, the honeyed hue of her skin, the sun-lightened gold of her hair. Despite what she might think, he liked being with her, liked hearing her voice and the excitement that always surrounded her.

He liked it too much.

He smoothed a crease in her collar. From there his finger brushed against the pale skin of her neck. Her pulse jumped under his touch. He dropped his hand away.

"You're not talking sense. Don't ever think that." His voice came out a growl. There had never been anyone but Caroline, but he couldn't say that. He couldn't give her that kind of power over him.

"Then why aren't you coming back with me?" She moved to stand in his path, forcing him to see her.

"Caroline…"

"Don't you feel anything anymore?" She placed her hand on his chest. "Your heart beats just as strong, just as steady as it once did. Do you feel nothing at all for me? What has become of the man I once knew?"

She stepped closer, circling his neck with her hand, drawing him to her. Her green eyes deepened to the color of the pines surrounding them. Mesmerized by the intensity of her gaze he stood rigid as she pressed her lips against his. They were warm and searching. And damn soft.

Unfortunately he'd been right. With her touch, he wanted more than a sweet kiss and he could feel himself going down for the count. He moved his hands to her waist and gripped her skirt, his fingers tangled in the material. He tried to remember his earlier resolve and restrain himself. He lasted about three seconds—a paltry attempt at resistance—and then gave in, wrapped his arms around her and pulled her close.

He deepened the kiss, sucking in her full lower lip before centering his mouth on hers. She molded her lips to his, soft and pliant, and tentatively touched her tongue to his. Heat flooded through him. He fisted his hand in her hair, destroying her fancy style and not caring one whit. Pins dropped to the dirt as her braid loosened and uncoiled down her back. Her touch ignited him beyond anything he'd been prepared for. His breathing came harder, faster.

"You'll come back with me, Brandon. I know you will."

Her words crashed through his mind, rocking him. He pushed her away. "You're playing with fire, Caroline."

He took a step back and raked his fingers through his hair feeling utterly disgusted with himself. His stomach churned. Acid washed up in his throat. He was tense with unsatisfied desire and the feelings she stirred up. He'd been successful at burying most of them and he'd promised himself he wouldn't allow them back to the surface no matter what she said to him.

"The man you once knew is gone. You can't bring him back."

She covered her swollen lips with her fingers.

"I just had to try," she mumbled.

He stared at her. He didn't like being manipulated. "Try? What are you trying to figure out?"

"It's foolish. I understand that now."

She had to understand once and for all that he wasn't ever going back. He gripped her upper arms, squaring her to him, forcing her to meet his gaze. "I won't be going home with you to Charleston. Believe me when I say there's nothing left for me there. Be satisfied with that." He took up his hoe for balance and strode into the cabin.

Standing there on the other side of the closed door, he waited for the tightness in his chest to ease and listened for the sound of her footsteps on the path to the hacienda. He looked around the small cabin—his makeshift office. It was all he could handle anymore. He'd told her he wouldn't be going back to the life waiting for him in Charleston. He snorted. That was a lie. The truth was he couldn't go back. The spells were getting worse. He couldn't stand to see his friends and his father's colleagues look on him with pity. With the shakes, the hallucinations, he didn't know how long he'd be able to practice—or even more importantly—how long he'd be of sound mind.

The thought of Caroline watching him while he came apart was unbearable. Just listening to her talk about the parties and cotillions—all the things that made life worth living to a woman like her—had embedded the realization even deeper. He couldn't give her any of that—didn't want any of that now. It was best for everyone concerned that he did not accompany her back to Charleston after Jake's wedding. If he were to go with her, sooner or later she'd come to hate him.

Chapter Seven

Long after Brandon had disappeared around the front corner of the cabin, Caroline stared at the path he'd taken. Now she covered her face with her hands as a strangled cry escaped. She'd ruined everything—in one impetuous moment. Her nerves on end, she drew in a shaky breath.

"That didn't go so good."

She spun around to see Jake leaning against a tree. "Wh—what are you doing here? I thought you'd gone to Bexar with the others?"

"I can see that," he drawled. "Just getting a late start. Kind of glad, though. Would have missed the show, otherwise. You do tend to do things in a big way, Miss Caroline."

She clenched her fists at her side, mortified at what he'd witnessed. "I had my reasons."

"You expecting to wrap him around your finger again? Is that your reason?" His voice lowered and she felt rather than heard the underlying tone of anger. "Can't you just accept the fact that he's his own man now and not someone you can push around?"

"You don't know what you are talking about," she said. She had wanted to do anything to shake Brandon out of the limbo he'd created for himself. Anything that might bring back the man she'd once known. "I had my reasons," she repeated.

"You always do," Jake said.

She inhaled sharply. It was true she had not gotten on well with him from the start but Jake obviously cared about his brother. Perhaps she could enlist his support despite his animosity toward her. "Please, for one moment, put aside your negative feelings for me and try to help."

"Why should I do that?"

"Because something isn't right, Jake. Something has happened to him."

He pushed off from the tree and sauntered toward her. "Of course something has happened to him. He survived a damn war. You don't go through something like that untouched. For all he's been through, he's doing fine."

"I don't think he is. I'm…I'm worried about him."

Jake's brows drew together. "Everything was great until you showed up."

"If you're saying that I'm the cause of his problems…"

His eyes were hard. "That's exactly what I'm saying. You're always wakin' snakes everywhere you go."

"I just wanted him to come back to Charleston. It's his home. All his friends are there. I thought he'd want to come back, too."

"He has friends here now."

Jake wasn't going to help. That much was obvious. He was as stubborn and opinionated as Brandon—even more so. "He has a much sought-after position waiting for him—working with my father."

"Texas needs doctors same as Charleston."

I need him, too, she wanted to say, but held her tongue. Jake studied her.

She plucked up her courage to try once more. "His talent is wasted here. He's a skilled surgeon, not a back-country rustic. He belongs where he can do the most good, take care of the most people."

"Which, of course, can only mean in Charleston." Jake snorted. "And with you. Lady you are one stubborn woman. *You* are the one beating him up."

"That has never been my intention. I want what's best for him. I...I care about him."

"Then you shouldn't have come—on both counts."

Hurt by his brash words, Caroline stared numbly at him, unable to formulate a sentence.

"Médico! Ayúdame!"

A Mexican woman rushed into the clearing, pulling a young boy behind her. One look at his tearstained face had Caroline putting aside her worries with Jake. "He's inside," she said quickly and led the way.

The boy held one hand gingerly as blood dripped from his thumb. A cactus needle? Snakebite? Caroline ran ahead to open the door, surprised when Jake scooped up the boy in his arms and followed her inside, depositing him on the exam table in the center of the room.

"Got a customer for you, Doc."

At the sudden commotion, Brandon rose from his seat at his desk. He knew the boy—Jaime—a son to one of the cowboys on the ranch. At ten years of age he was always getting himself into scrapes. What this time? He was about to ask what was wrong when he saw the hook protruding from the boy's thumb. His shoulders relaxed.

"Jaime, fish aren't interested in young boys for bait."

Jake grabbed up a canteen hanging on a peg in the

corner and headed for the door. "Looks like you can handle this on your own. I'll see you when I get back from town."

Brandon grunted, intent on examining Jaime's wound. He understood Jake's reasons for a quick departure. As much as his brother had been forced to doctor in the war, he'd only done it to stay alive. It wasn't something he wanted to do.

Brandon turned Jaime's thumb slightly, examining the type of hook and how large the size of the barb. The iron hook curled into the plump padding of the boy's thumb. Brandon trimmed off the piece of twine and then reached for his pliers. Jaime's dark eyes widened at the sight. A tremor ran through his thin body. "No! *Señor!* No!"

"It's the only way if you want it out," Brandon said to the boy, knowing he understood only half the words but probably the meaning was clear. To his mother, he said, "You'll have to hold him."

The woman moved in and did as he'd asked. It was then he noticed Caroline. She stood a few steps back, her eyes large, staring at the boy's wound. "You should go back to the house."

"P-perhaps I can help."

He took in her stance—her arms wrapped around her middle. She looked ready to bolt. "It won't be pleasant."

"I can, Brandon. I assisted my father on occasion. I'm not the least squeamish."

The pallor on her face said otherwise. He shook his head. He didn't need two patients. "I won't need any help. It's a simple extraction."

"But—"

"Don't argue with me on this, Caroline. I'll come up to the house soon. I promise. You're just making Jaime wait that much longer."

Her jaw clamped shut and her expression turned mutinous, but she headed for the door.

He relaxed slightly. Why had she even tried to stay? She didn't have the stomach for surgery—even something this mild. She was a society princess after all and certainly too delicate for this.

He was glad she had finally left. Such a small thing as an imbedded fishhook shouldn't fire up a spell, but he couldn't anticipate them anymore. They happened at the strangest times. It was just better all around if she wasn't here to see one.

He turned his attention back to Jaime and his injury. The tissue around the iron had already started to swell, the edges reddened. Blood dripped onto the floor. A wave of dizziness washed over him. The edges of his vision darkened. He couldn't let it happen. He dragged in a breath and steeled himself against the feeling, forcing himself to concentrate.

"Do you have a strong hold?" he asked the boy's mother.

She grasped the boy firmer in response, watching Brandon closely. A stoic resolve settled on her face. They both knew what was necessary.

Brandon gripped the pliers again. At his motion, every muscle in Jaime's small body tensed. Grasping the dull end of the iron hook with the pliers and working as carefully as possible, Brandon pushed the sharp, barbed end until it pierced through the skin and appeared again. Dizziness threatened as a vision came to him. Not the small stab of a fishhook breaking the skin, but the grotesque point of a bayonet emerging through flesh. He swallowed hard. He had to concentrate, had to finish this. His hands began to shake.

Jaime screamed and jerked his hand, his body stiffening. Tears streamed down his face.

Brandon shut out the sound, focusing on his work.

Using clippers to remove the barb, he withdrew the hook rapidly, then staunched the trickle of blood with a fresh cloth and applied pressure. Great hiccup-sobs racked the boy's small frame. Brandon waited, letting the pain ease, giving Jaime a chance to calm down. Giving himself a chance to calm down. He looked up and saw tears in the mother's brown eyes.

Abruptly he turned away, unable to bear her emotions on top of his own. She shouldn't share in her son's pain like that. It didn't serve a purpose. It didn't absorb and lessen the boy's pain. It only made her hurt, too—and ache all the more. He wondered if she would have nightmares like him. Maybe not over something this small, but then it was worse when you loved someone. Worse all around.

He took a deep breath and walked to the stove. Dipping a finger into the pan of bacon fat, he slathered it over Jaime's wound and then wrapped the thumb snugly with cloth. He took the piece of twine he'd cut from the hook and tied it around the bandage to secure it.

The boy's crying slowly subsided. "It'll be sore, but should heal in the next few days," Brandon said. He wasn't sure how much the boy or his mother understood.

"*Gracias,* Señor Doctor." Jaime's mother squeezed his hand gratefully as she dropped a leather pouch into his grasp. He murmured something—unsure what exactly it was—and waited until they left.

Only then did he toss the pouch on his desk and sink into his chair.

The shaking had started sooner than before—in the middle of the operation. He had suppressed it a small amount, but now he could feel a tingling sensation over-taking him. He tried to ignore it and busied himself, loosening the cinched top of the pouch to find it filled with ground corn. Still the tremors came. He pressed his palms to the desktop, trying by sheer will to make them stop. When they didn't, he watched his hands vibrate, half in medical fascination and half in horror. "No!" he ground out. Unable to control them, he linked his fingers and dropped his head in his hands.

How long would he be able to practice? The spells worsened each time he did anything that involved blood. With Jaime's wound, the amount of bleeding had been minimal, almost nonexistent compared to the soldiers he'd doctored and still he'd had a reaction. Soon he wouldn't be able to hide the spells. When that happened, no one would trust him to care for them or their loved ones. He'd be a laughingstock, the butt of jokes, the doctor who couldn't stand the sight of blood. What the hell would he do then?

A shadow fell across his desk and blocked the sunlight streaming through the window. Immediately he shoved his hands under the table. He knew without moving it was Caroline.

What was she doing still here? How much had she witnessed? he wondered. How much would her face and her eyes reveal when he looked up? "I thought you'd gone."

"What just happened, Brandon?" Her voice was low, cautious—curious.

She stood in front of the desk now. Instead of the disgust he'd anticipated, concern filled her eyes. Well, he didn't want pity, either. Especially from her. He shoved the sack of cornmeal aside. "Pay isn't much here. As you can see, not like in the city."

"That's not what I mean." She stepped closer. "It was the same as with the bull yesterday, wasn't it?"

"The injury? Of course not. It was a simple operation. I'm sure if the boy's father had been nearby he would have pulled out the hook. Women are easily sickened by such things. That is why I asked you to leave."

"You forget that I am the daughter of a surgeon," she said, frowning. "Although, I'll admit my stomach has been squeamish of late. You did a fine job removing the hook."

"So glad you approve." The moment the words were out he realized how petty they sounded. It wasn't like him to hide behind sarcasm. He'd like to say she was making him crazy, but it wouldn't be true. It was the spells and the nightmares that were pulling him toward insanity.

Her eyes clouded.

"My apologies. That was unfair. I learned a lot from your father, as I'm sure, growing up at his side, you must have, too."

"No, Brandon. You are purposely avoiding my question. Why?"

He didn't answer. Why couldn't she just let it go?

"I want to know what happened to you just now. Why were you shaking?"

He'd always respected her tenacity in the past, but then, it hadn't been directed at him. "Reaction to an empty stomach I suspect. I ate at daybreak and then worked all morning in the garden."

He stood and, leaning on his cane, made his way to the pantry. "I'd offer you something, but I'm sure you've eaten at the hacienda. What I have here is not adequate fare for you."

He felt her staring at his back as he cut a thick wedge of cheese from a half-eaten wheel. He was being a lousy host, but at this point he didn't care. He just wanted her gone. Now.

"Before the boy and his mother interrupted…"

"You misunderstood," he lashed at her. "The boy and the mother were not an interruption. They are my job— such as it is," he said harshly. "I don't have the luxury of scheduling my patients like your father does. This is Texas. I take what walks through that door."

She recoiled as if he'd hit her.

"I have some things to attend to today." He turned away from her and shuffled through the few papers on his desk. He didn't know what he looked at, didn't know what the papers said, he just couldn't look at her anymore. He felt her gaze on him, felt her censure with every movement he made. A cold, unfriendly silence stretched through the room.

"I'll just leave you to your meal, then." She plucked her fancy straw hat from the wall peg. "I'm sorry to have intruded."

Always the perfect response, he grumbled to himself as she left. His stomach churned with acid. Anger swelled inside—anger at her for intruding when he didn't want her to, anger at the betrayal of his body and the spells and hallucinations he couldn't control, and anger at himself for wanting beyond anything else the life he had once had with Caroline and knowing it was forever out of reach.

What vile things was she calling him now? he wondered. She couldn't get away fast enough. And wasn't that precisely what he'd been seeking? To have her leave?

Then why did he feel like such an ass?

Because he was one.

He picked up the cheese, stared at it and then threw it at the closing door.

Frustrated beyond rational thought, Caroline couldn't stand the idea of returning to the hacienda and facing Franklin or Juan. She entered the stable. Of the few horses left in the stable, the piebald from her ride yesterday stood waiting. She saddled her, anxious to get away. She had to leave this place and go somewhere to think. Thankfully the rest of the family had left for town. She wanted to avoid running into Jake or Victoria right now. She didn't feel like talking to anyone.

Something was wrong with Brandon. Something he didn't want her to know—maybe didn't want anyone knowing. He had frozen again while examining the boy's injury. It was barely discernible unless one watched closely. The episode was similar to the one he had with the bull, but at least this time it wasn't as dangerous—he didn't have a beast bearing down on him—and it didn't last as long. Was she the only one who saw it?

Jake's cruel words came back to her. If he knew anything about what Brandon was feeling or going through, he wasn't going to share it with her. Neither brother wanted her around. She upset their routine—challenged the areas they wanted left alone. And she was an outsider. Perhaps Jake was right. Perhaps the best thing for her to do was to leave.

Why, then, did she feel like she was deserting Brandon? At the errant thought, she sank down on a low bench. What was wrong with her? She shouldn't care anymore. But plain as day she'd argued with Jake and told him she did care. Was it just as a concerned friend?

Berating herself under her breath, she fixed her hair, haphazardly combing through the strands with her fingers and then plaiting it in one long, loose braid.

Although she'd acted on instinct and impulse, the reason for the kiss had been twofold. First, she'd wanted to shake Brandon up. She thought he'd lost all ability to feel anything for anyone. How wrong he'd proved her! Underneath his diffident attitude lay a sleeping cougar. She touched her swollen mouth. Her lips ached from his kiss. And, heaven help her, she had wanted more. Remembering the strength in his arms, the flare of desire in his eyes… Why, if he hadn't held her, she'd have swooned. Which wasn't like her at all. She blamed her heightened senses on the child she carried. His child. Her reaction couldn't be because she still loved him, could it?

Which brought her to the other reason she'd kissed him. She had wanted to know if a spark for him still existed. She had been so angry when he had headed off to help the Texians, and then again when he hadn't returned after the battle. She didn't *want* to care for him, didn't want to worry about him. He'd left her carrying his baby with nary a care for her. How could she even think or worry about him now when it was her own life that was in such turmoil? Her attention must be toward her own future and that of her baby. Brandon didn't deserve it and yet…and yet he was her baby's father, the man she had loved. How could she ignore what had changed him so?

She flipped her long braid back over her shoulder and stood. Leading the mare outside to the corral fencing, she found comfort in the beast's gentle plod, the sound of hooves against straw and dirt, the steady puff of warm breath on her shoulder. A ride would do her good. An hour or so at most and she'd feel better—perhaps then she could muddle through this situation more clearly. Using the low railing as a step, she mounted. With a last look at the path through the pines toward Brandon's cabin, she reined the horse away from the hacienda and urged it into a gentle lope.

Chapter Eight

Jake strode purposely into the cabin and came to a standstill at the sight of his brother holding a new physician's bag and stethoscope. "Where'd that come from?"

"Franklin brought it from Charleston."

With a grunt, Jake acknowledged he'd heard while at the same time surveying the room. "Is Caroline here?"

"She's at the house."

"No, she's not."

His brother's tone caught Brandon's attention. He stored the stethoscope in the bag. "Why? What's going on? And what are you doing back? I thought you were going to Bexar."

"We got as far as the Svendsons'. Their barn was burned last night. We thought it best to get back here and warn Juan, especially in light of the things you saw yesterday."

"Any signs of who it was? Comanche or the renegades?" He sucked in his breath at the thought. If Comanche were causing trouble, nothing would be left of Lars, and Ilse and the boys would be gone—taken.

"Renegades. There were signs of a struggle at the house."

"Lars?"

"Everyone is all right."

Brandon exhaled and followed as Jake headed to his sleeping pallet. Haphazardly Jake began stuffing his few belongings into his canvas duffel bag.

"What are you doing? You think they're headed this way?"

"Don't know. But you did say you saw something at the river."

"Near the crossing."

Jake rolled his straight razor, soap and comb in a cloth. "I'm staying at the house from now on. I don't care if I have to sleep in the pantry, I'm not leaving Victoria's side."

Brandon thought about Caroline in the house and whether he should do the same. Then he remembered their kiss. She was safer with him *out* of the house if that kiss was an indication of his self-control.

"We need to alert the neighbors," Jake continued. "Let them know the situation. Diego has already headed south. Damn! I shouldn't have let Victoria talk me into going to town. I hate going there. My gut has bothered me since I woke up and now this."

"At least you found out about the Svendsons. If trouble comes, we'll be prepared."

Jake rose and slung his duffel over his back. "They lost a horse and were scared pretty bad. Lars is taking his sons and Ilse into town to her sister's house for a few days while he cleans up the place."

Brandon only half listened as a new urgency came over him. "But you said Caroline isn't at the house?"

"No. How come she isn't here with you?"

He groaned. "Because I was an ass."

Jake pressed his lips together. "Well, you better find her. She shouldn't be on her own."

Brandon barely heard his words. He'd already grabbed

his cane and hat and was out the door, striding toward the hacienda. Of course she was there. She was probably burrowed in the library or in her room, nursing the cruel remarks he'd thrown at her. He'd been rough on her. The more insistent she'd gotten that he answer her questions, the deeper he'd dug his heels in and refused.

At the house he came no closer to finding her. She wasn't where he'd thought she'd be. No one knew where she'd gone. He strode back outside and surveyed the surrounding woods and the meadow. She couldn't have gone far. She had a lousy sense of direction. It was something he'd teased her about in the past, but she was smart enough to know not to wander off. Then again, in retaliation to her pressing his sore points, he'd made her as frustrated as he'd felt. It would be just his luck that he'd riled her until she took off without concern for her own well-being.

If anything happened to her, because of him…he'd never forgive himself.

In the stable, one of the horses was missing—as well as Victoria's saddle. All right, he'd have to track her. He'd learned a few tricks from Jake. Unfortunately if he could track her, so could the renegades. Moving faster, he bridled his mount.

"Señor Médico!"

He turned from cinching the saddle. The cook ran up wringing her hands on her apron.

"I don't have time, Maria. What is it?"

"You ask for Señorita Caroline? She take horse. Go." Maria pointed toward the foothills in the west.

"When?"

"A mediodía."

"At noon!"

"Si, señor."

She'd been gone two hours! His heart pounding, he mounted his horse and kicking him swiftly in the flanks, set him galloping from the stable.

He tried to second-guess where Caroline would venture, keeping his eyes open for newly trampled grass and hoof-prints. Across the meadow and just before the mud pit he veered north and headed toward the river. She'd been angry enough and frustrated enough that she just might try getting that rag from the water again. He came to the tree she'd shimmied. The cloth was still caught against the rock in the middle of the river. There was no sign of Caroline. No hoofprints. No sound but the water rushing over the rocks.

The scent of wildflowers and Mesquite brush permeated the blistering-hot afternoon. A barely nonexistent breeze stirred the leaves on the trees. He removed his neckerchief and mopped the sweat from his forehead, wishing he had time for quick dip in the river.

Suddenly he knew where he'd find her. The thought paralyzed him. She'd be at the pool. He turned his horse toward the hill country. What he would say when he found her, he didn't know. He'd treated her arrogantly in his hurry to avoid talking about his spells. She could be exasperating in her drive to get to the truth of all things and he hadn't been in the mood for her questions. Yet as short-tempered and condescending as he'd been, she hadn't backed down. She'd simply left, picking up that fancy bonnet of hers and sweeping out the door with a graceful flourish like she was some grand dame in a gentleman's supper club and being asked politely to leave. He had to admit, he did enjoy the color that had flushed across her cheeks when she got in such a state. The sooner he found her, the safer she'd be.

He dug his heels into the sorrel's flanks, spurring him into a gallop across the open grassland.

The scrub oaks thickened interspersed with cotton-woods and a pine or two. Rocks and boulders lay hidden in the tall grass. He broke through the oaks that lined the clear water pool. Across the water, he spotted something white against the backdrop of the green foliage. He reined toward it, urging his horse into a gentle lope. Another flutter—blues and reds and yellows—material, he realized, and then recognized Caroline's skirt and blouse draped over a low bush.

He surveyed the perimeter. The trees crowded close, but there was no sign of her.

Flat limestone banked the pool on three sides. He walked his horse to the edge. The water was so clear it was possible to see fifteen feet down to where the large rock slabs dovetailed together. A few contented trout circled lazily along the bottom.

He pulled away from the edge, telling himself he hadn't worried about her drowning even though his chest was tight for some reason. Like she had said—she was a strong swimmer. It just eased his mind to know she wasn't down there.

"Caroline!"

She couldn't have gone far—unless the marauders had already come across her. The thought of what could happen to her in a situation like that made his gut twist. He had to find her!

"Brandon? What is it?"

At the sound of her voice, he reined his horse back around. Fifty feet away, she rose up on one elbow from lying on a white slab of rock. She'd been so still, so pale against the stone formation, that he must have missed her the first time he looked.

His heartbeat settled into a quieter rhythm. She was obviously all right, obviously safe. Thank God. Dismounting, he strode to her and dropped to one knee.

She'd stripped to her cream-colored chemise which was still damp from a dip in the pool. Her eyelids were heavy with sleep. The nearby water seemed to sparkle in the depths of her green eyes. Blond hair hung in damp, wavy tendrils to her waist. Did she have any idea how beautiful she looked? He shook that thought from his mind. The important thing was that she was safe.

"What is it?" she repeated softly. "What are you doing here?"

I was worried about you, he thought to say and then didn't.

"It's you." His tongue stumbled over the simple words. He removed his hat, fingering the brim as he sent up a prayer of thanks that he'd found her and she was unharmed. He tried again. "You've been swimming."

"I didn't mean to fall asleep—it was just so peaceful here. So peaceful and warm."

He hadn't seen her this content and relaxed since she arrived. Maybe he should have brought her here sooner. His mind balked at the idea. Since her arrival, he hadn't been much in tune with her needs, only his own and the need to keep her as far away from him as possible. "You do know that snakes like to sun themselves on big warm rocks."

"Are you trying to scare me? Or are you calling me a snake?" Her lips curved upward. "Or yourself?"

He fingered the damp material on her shoulder. His knuckles brushed her soft skin. A shiver went through her. Could it be from the light breeze or was it his touch? It used to be his touch. "Myself," he murmured, remembering.

"I didn't mean to cause any worry. I was upset about this morning, about what happened. I just needed time alone. Away from the hacienda."

Away from me, he realized dismally. He'd succeeded, then.

A slow smile lit her face. "Can you believe that I lost my way only twice?"

"Proud of yourself?" he teased, again remembering how easily she could get turned around in a new area of Charleston. The fact that that deficiency hadn't stopped her from traveling across the country registered. Maybe she was braver than he'd given her credit for.

"Franklin told me about the rivers here."

"Did it help?"

"Not really. I'm still dismally inadequate without familiar streets."

"You shouldn't have ridden so far from the big house without me." His fingers brushed her skin once more. "How would you have found your way back on your own?"

"At the time, I didn't want to think of that."

"Irresponsible of you." His voice was gruff, but even he heard the touch of fond exasperation in it.

"I know. Chide me if you must, but I had to think. There is something I must tell you, Brandon, and I'm not sure how to go about it."

She looked vulnerable all of a sudden and unsure. How unlike the woman he was used to. It made him want to reassure her—comfort her. What was she doing to him? If he followed the tug he felt inside, it could only lead to problems. He drew his hand back. "Go on."

"I wanted to hate you," she whispered. "You have no idea what happened when you left."

She was talking about Charleston, he realized.

"You abandoned me when I needed you most. I—I do hate you."

"I can't change what happened."

She caught his fingers and drew them back to her, pressing his palm against her slender neck, holding his hand there and acting as though his touch was the most precious of things to her.

She didn't know, she couldn't know, what his hands had done. She wouldn't want them on her if she knew. Still, he couldn't drum up the strength of will to pull away again.

Her eyes held tears when she looked at him again. "What was so important that you had to leave?"

He studied her face. "I had to prove myself."

"To whom? Me? Jake?"

He shook his head, thinking back to that time when he'd left for Texas. "To myself."

"You? I don't understand."

Brandon sighed and sat down beside her. "Jake came home, strong and tough from living off the land for so long. Next to him, I felt like a green schoolboy. In spite of all my book knowledge and position as a surgeon, I couldn't measure up in his eyes. I saw the way women looked at him, like he was the answer to their dull lives. Everywhere we went, they vied for his attention. I guess I was jealous."

"Have you then? Proved yourself?"

He thought about that. Proving himself in battle had quickly changed with the need to survive. "Yes, but it's behind me. I don't want to talk about it. Not here. Not now."

She dipped her head and rubbed her cheek against his wrist. "I never looked at Jake that way."

Silvery tingles raced up his arm.

"Caroline…" he breathed. "Don't…"

But he couldn't finish his thought. His body thrummed

with feelings he'd long thought dead—feelings she'd awakened with her kiss. He moved his hand down, sliding his fingers slowly under the fabric's edge to the sloping curve of her breast.

Her breathing hitched. She leaned toward him and imperceptibly her breasts strained against the cotton fabric— a silent invitation for him to continue.

He was trespassing. He didn't deserve this. Yet he closed his eyes, concentrating on the feel of her smooth skin. He had always wanted her, would always want her. There was the crux of it. The battle between what he wanted and what he should do kept him from going any further, kept his hand poised there, at the soft rise of her breast.

She trembled, and this time he knew he'd caused it. A feeling of power surged through him, a power that wasn't right for him to use with her. He had to get control of himself, of the situation. He'd come here to make sure she was safe, not maul her like some randy cowboy that didn't know hay from locoweed. He closed his hand into a fist.

"Caroline, we need to talk."

She froze for a second, and then turned from him, batting his hand away. Sitting up, she drew her knees to her chest and pulled the hem of her chemise down to cover her ankles.

"We need to clear some things up between us."

Her lips pressed into a solid line. "I know, but I thought…I hoped you came to apologize for this morning's behavior."

He chose to ignore that. He wasn't going to apologize for what he'd had to do at the time.

"Fine, then." She scrambled to her feet. With her hands on her hips, she continued. "What is it you want now? Only three hours ago you shouted at me to go away."

He rose. "I didn't shout."

"You did! Why were you so angry?"

He knew what she was asking but he wasn't going to talk about it. He never wanted her to find out. "It's not safe for you to go off alone like this."

Her gaze narrowed. "No one has bothered me—except you. I feel perfectly safe. You may return to the hacienda reassured. Eventually I will find my way back." She turned her back on him and strode to where her skirt and blouse lay on the bush and gathered them up.

"Someone set fire to the Svendsons' barn."

She turned back to him, holding her clothes before her like a shield.

"It's in the valley just beyond the hacienda."

"Is everyone all right?"

"They're shook up. Mrs. Svendson and the boys especially." A honey bee buzzed around her head which he swatted away with his hat.

Her brows knit together. "What is going on, Brandon?"

"Things aren't settled here—haven't been since the rebellion. That's what I meant when I said it was too dangerous for you to be here, why I didn't want you to come. Mexican renegades, Comanche—they don't make friendly neighbors."

"I understood the risks, Brandon. They are the same for Franklin as they are for me."

"No, Caroline. They're not." He glanced down at her creamy exposed shoulders—the skin turning slightly pink. He wished she'd cover up a little. She was enticing enough with clothes on, let alone a thin cotton shift. "If you'll get dressed, we'll head back. It's safer for now if we both stay close to the ranch."

A stubborn look tilted her chin. "I'll return with you, but only after you explain what happened this morning at your cabin."

He swiped a hand through his hair. "Just leave it be, Caroline. I don't want to discuss it."

She met his gaze, studying him quietly. Then, rather than being upset, to his surprise she rose up on her tiptoes and kissed him lightly on the jaw.

"What's that for?" he said suspiciously.

"Apology accepted."

"I don't remember apologizing," he countered.

"Oh? You came after me, didn't you? And at least now you are not denying that something happened with the boy. It did. I saw it, and you know I did. I won't press you about it further. Just know that I'm here when you are ready to talk about what's going on. And…that I care."

The jut of her chin, the challenge in her eyes—she knew him better than he knew himself. She always had. He let out a long, slow breath. "I've always had feelings for you—since the first day your father introduced us."

"But?"

"But those feelings serve no purpose now. I can't go back with you, Caroline."

She paced the distance between him and the chaparral. "For two years I waited for you through your apprenticeship and I wasn't exactly idle. I did help out at the hospital. Remember?"

"Much to your father's chagrin. It's a wonder he approved our engagement after you started doing that."

"Well, when I learned of the conditions there, it was obvious something had to be done. Someone had to do it, so I did."

"I remember," he murmured. Once Caroline had made the poor conditions known to her friends, they'd taken it upon themselves to start the charity group in order to raise money for the hospital. She'd been instrumental in organizing it and seeing it through.

"While there at the hospital I saw things, learned things. What I'm saying is…perhaps I can help, if you'll only open up to me."

He didn't answer. He couldn't.

She waited. One minute stretched to two. She sighed then, and made a motion, indicating he should turn around while she dressed. Reluctantly he turned toward the water. Two bees buzzed across the surface while Caroline continued speaking.

"Whether you like it or not, Brandon, we are joined— by our regard for each other more than anything. You do remember our night together, don't you?"

"How could I forget? That was the one bright spot, the one thing that saw me through the blasted war. I'll always be thankful for that."

"I need more than for you to be thankful. I need you to understand something. That night—" she took a deep breath "—that night changed my life."

He turned back to her, understanding flooding him. "You were a virgin."

"Yes, of course, but not just because of that. Because— Ouch!"

"What wrong?"

"I just got stung!" She squeezed her forearm.

"Where? Let me see."

"Oh, it smarts!" Tears brimmed in her eyes as she brought her arm up for his inspection.

The reddened area near her elbow transformed into a welt the size of a cow's eye before his eyes. The offending stinger protruded, which he quickly pulled out. "We're near their hive. You must have disturbed them with all of your caterwauling."

"Me!" She glared at him.

He couldn't help chuckling—or touching her. He swept a lock of golden hair away from her cheek and tucked it behind her ear. "Knew that would rile you. I'll get some mud."

Before he'd gone two steps, a low drone invaded the quiet space.

He glanced toward the sound. A small, dark cloud quickly approached. Bees! Before he could react they swarmed him. He swatted two away from his neck only to get stung. "Caroline! Into the water! Now!"

Immediately, Caroline dropped the clothes she held. "You, too!"

"I'm right with you!" He pulled his gun from its holster and threw it into the brush. Then grabbing her hand, they jumped off the rock into the clear pool.

The water closed over his head in a whoosh, fresh and cold. The trout at the bottom raced away to a cranny in the rocks. The water was so clear that, looking up, he could see the swarm hovering just above the surface. Caroline had noticed them, too, for she didn't object when he continued to grasp her hand and hold her firmly under the water.

Her shift wrapped around her torso and clung, bulky, at her waist. She struggled to push it down, but it floated immediately back up, revealing her long legs. As she struggled with the material once more, Brandon couldn't help grinning, even though he lost some air in the process. He pulled her close, close enough to feel the tingle of arousal starting within him. Good Lord! Even in the water she could get to him.

Trying to ignore the sensation, he helped her push the fabric down, but then couldn't resist skating his palm down the curve of her derriere. Her muscles tightened firm and strong beneath his hand. She moved away slightly and looked at him, her eyes searching his face in confusion.

Her long blond hair floated around her head and everywhere the filtered sunlight touched, the strands gleamed silver. She became a water sprite, sleek and infinitely alluring. He kneaded his fingers in her flesh, gently at first, then as an answering tension in his gut strung taut, with more force.

He shouldn't be doing this. He knew that. But ever since she'd arrived, it was all he thought about—touching her, his skin on hers. He'd struggled against the urge but she had bewitched him all over again the same way she had that first summer they'd met.

Somewhere in the back of his mind, a voice told him to stop, that he didn't deserve her anymore. But he was tired of listening to his conscience, tired of doing what was right, what was expected. He wanted to feel alive again. Wanted to feel loved and desired in return. For this one moment, he wanted her. Selfishly. Completely.

Releasing her hand, he inched his palm slowly down to cup her bottom with his other hand. He pulled her flush against him and she ceased battling with her shift as it wrapped once more around her waist. She stilled against him.

Here in this strange sanctuary of quiet, where only the two of them existed, he felt whole again. He felt strong. And he wanted her with a desperate, burgeoning passion. He had denied it over and over again, succumbing only once before. He couldn't deny it any longer.

His heart hammered in his chest. Unable to resist, he nuzzled her jaw, her cheek. And then found her lips.

Chapter Nine

Heavens, but she needed to breathe! Her lungs burned, her muscles ached, and her heart thumped wildly in her chest. Brandon's touch was like liquid fire, making her senses come alive, pushing her body's need for air to the limit. She broke off the kiss and stretched for the surface.

Brandon understood immediately. Keeping a tight hold on her, he pushed off the bottom boulder and jettisoned them toward the sunlight. Breaking out into the warmth, they both gulped in huge amounts of air. A lone bee buzzed between them. She gasped and pulled back, preparing to duck under the water again when his lips found hers.

They slanted across her mouth, pressing, demanding. He adjusted the angle and his tongue touched hers, sending desire spiraling, crashing, through her. She grabbed his shirt and hung on, letting him keep them both afloat.

Slowly he drew back. Water drops sprinkled his tanned face and plastered his dark hair to his forehead and cheeks. The look on his face was that of a man determined to have his way, yet controlled enough to make sure it was what she wanted.

She inhaled. It was all wrong according to her upbring-ing, but she was already a fallen woman. She had trans-gressed and would forever pay the price. Blind love had been the reason the first time. This time it was different. She knew exactly what she was doing and love again had everything to do with it. With Brandon's first touch, he'd started a yearning inside that she couldn't control—didn't want to control.

It must have been the desire banked in his blue eyes that made her a bit reckless, a bit daring. "You'd better remove your boots then, cowboy." Even she was surprised at how husky her voice sounded.

A smile broke slowly across his face, spreading warmth all the way through her to the far corners of her soul. She'd not seen that smile since Charleston, since *before*. Her heart skipped a beat. He smiled at her as though she were the most treasured thing on earth.

"Don't disappear on me, woman," he growled, kissing her nose lightly.

Releasing her, he took four powerful strokes to the closest bank. Standing in waist-high water, one at a time he pulled off his boots and tossed them over his shoulder on the grassy mound by his gun. Next, he unbuttoned his shirt, flinging it after his boots.

She drifted on her back, treading water, as anticipa-tion built inside. A niggling thought occurred. She should tell him about the baby. She should, but it would ruin that look in his eyes—that soft, hooded look that said at this moment he thought she was the sun and moon and stars.

He lowered himself until the water lapped against his chin and then moved across the pool, barely disturbing the surface. Like a stealthy alligator, he floated toward her.

Ensnared by his steady blue gaze, the arguments they'd had melted to bits of nothing in her memory.

She glided her hands onto his strong shoulders as she felt his arms surround her waist and pull her close. The water lapped against his chest, straightening the dark curled hair.

"This isn't smart," he murmured.

She stopped his words with her palm. "Neither was traveling fifteen hundred miles to see you. I know how you are, Brandon. You can think yourself into or out of anything. You're clever that way. For once, please don't think."

She searched his eyes, feeling the need running through both of them. Her heart drummed a deep, abiding love for this man. She pressed her body against his—an invitation.

He groaned and finally gave in to his desire, dipping his head down to meet her mouth-to-mouth. He sucked her lower lip and then broke away to kiss her cheek, her neck and then behind her ear. She trembled, and felt his lips curve into a smile against her skin. So he remembered! A giddy feeling raced through her.

Whatever dark thoughts he'd been wrestling had departed, because now there was no hesitancy, no awkwardness in his movements. He came back to her mouth and, insistent, ran his tongue along the seam of her lips.

She welcomed him without hesitation, opening her mouth and accepting his thorough kiss. This was the Brandon she remembered—dogged, determined, his only thoughts on the goal ahead. And for this moment, that goal was her. Longing coiled deep in her center at the thought.

"I want you, too," she murmured in his ear. She brought her legs up to encircle his waist, her softness riding against his hardness. White-hot heat streaked to her core despite the cool water.

His nostrils flared. "You've grown bold. Not that I mind. With my weak leg, this position would be awkward for me were it not for the fact we are both in the water."

"Only for you, Brandon. Bold only for you," she said. It was the first time he'd mentioned his injury without the surliness he usually attached to it. She smoothed her fingers over his chest, rubbing over his nipples which were already hardened from the cool water.

He sucked in a gulp of air. "Glad to hear it."

With a firm grasp on her wrist, he lowered her hand. But he didn't touch her breast—at least not with his hand. Through her chemise, he took her hardened nipple into his hot mouth and desire streaked through her. Combined with the cold water she was completely lost in the sensations racing through her body. Her head lolled back and her breath came in short gasps as she wiggled against him.

He groaned again. "Caroline. Don't move."

She paused. Did he wish to stop? Now, when every part of her yearned for him? For his touch? "Why?"

"Because you make it impossible to go slowly."

"Then don't," she said, before kissing his chest. "I don't think I can bear it if you wait."

He moved with her toward the grassy bank. She lowered her feet, finding solid rock beneath her. If she'd allowed herself to dream of their reunion, here in the still waters of the pool is not where she would have ever imagined it, but she found the place suited him. Perhaps Texas suited him. Maybe this is where he truly belonged.

He spread his shirt over the sun-bleached bank and laid her down with her body still half-submerged in the water, her shift floating on the surface. Keeping one hand to her lower back, supporting her, he slid into her.

And, with his sigh mingling with hers, brought her home.

* * *

Later, much later, Caroline stirred in his arms, rubbing her bottom against him. Brandon woke instantly and tightened his arms around her. The sun had moved to the western sky, and cottonwoods shaded them now. They'd have to get back to the hacienda soon or a scouting party would be out looking for them. But for right now, he wanted to hold on to this moment.

He loved her. He hadn't told her, not since he'd asked for her hand months ago. He'd tried to deny it to himself—tried to stop from feeling anything. It was easier that way—and better for her not to know what was happening. He hadn't wanted to be there when the love he'd always seen in her eyes turned to fear, or worse—pity. When he could no longer keep the monsters at bay and the dreams and the visions took over—when he was no longer sane.

But he'd loved her just the same and always would.

Her hair was nearly dry, and hung tangled and wild down her back. The slope of her neck called to him and he rose on one elbow and kissed the silky, sensitive skin there. A shiver coursed through her as he'd known it would. Rising on one elbow, he realized she had goose bumps on her arm.

He squeezed her shoulder and watched her eyelids flutter open. "You're cold. We should get back."

A sigh made her breast rise and fall. "Can we come here again?"

The innocent question from her half-asleep lips made him smile. He kissed her neck once more, rolled to his back and stood. His pants from the knees down were still soaked through, and the skin on his toes were wrinkled from the water. "Come on, darlin'. Get moving." He walked across the slab of rock and gathered her clothes.

By the time he'd returned, she had repositioned herself

onto her back. He stopped for a moment to feast his eyes on her. Once she clothed herself, he'd have to rely on his memory. Her cotton shift, still damp, clung to her skin from her knees to her breasts.

It was the small rise to her midriff that suddenly caught his eye. The air evaporated in his lungs. What exactly was going on?

He glanced from her waist to her face and then back again. It couldn't be… "Caroline?" Her name came out on a choke.

Her eyes flew open and she sat up. Her face flooded with worry. "I wanted to tell you. Truly I did. But I didn't know how."

A baby! Good God! A baby! Stunned, he dropped her clothes, stumbling back a step. Slack-jawed, he stared at her, his mind racing over the events of the past months.

"When?" he finally managed to ground out.

She cupped her hand over her abdomen, as if that would protect the child from him, as if he would ever hurt her. "Autumn. Late October, I think."

A slow, deep anger began to churn in his gut. She'd deceived him! She'd lied to him!

"No need to hide it now." His tone was harsh.

Her shocked expression let him know his arrow had hit home. Well, so had hers.

He strode over and sat down to yank on his boot.

"Brandon, we should talk about this."

"Why now?" he said. "It wasn't important enough to tell me before."

"I just needed it to be the right time."

"Well, that time has come and gone. That time was before I left Charleston."

"I didn't know then. I only learned of the baby after you'd already gone."

He pulled on his other boot, his thoughts in too much of a jumble to think coherently. What the hell was he going to do with a baby?

"Look," she said. "I understand you're angry. I know this is a shock."

"Damn right it's a shock. You'll excuse me if I'm not playing the pleased father." He gripped the saddle to mount, but then paused. "That is the reason you came all this way."

She nodded. "Yes."

"Did you refuse Graham before or after you knew you were in a family way?"

"Both times."

That stopped him. "He asked you a second time? Even after your first refusal? A glutton for punishment."

"You're not being fair," she said, the volume of her voice rising in frustration.

He held up his hand, blocking her words, blocking the sight of her. "It's really none of my business."

"Of course it's your business. Otherwise, I wouldn't have come. I thought you should know."

He scowled. "Eventually."

Caroline glared at him.

He pressed his forehead against the smooth saddle in front of him, breathing in the familiar scent of leather. He should be happy but all he could think about was that she'd lied to him. And for the moment, he couldn't get past that. He dragged a hand through his hair and stared at the pool where they'd made love. How had he not noticed it earlier?

The answer was embarrassing. He'd been so consumed with passion, so aroused that nothing else had mattered. Had he been rough? He tried to remember, hoping he hadn't hurt her or the baby. Her breasts had seemed fuller, perhaps more sensitive. But then they'd both been overly sensitive to every nuance, every touch, every kiss. Even now, thinking of it again, his traitorous body pulsed with renewed wanting.

He grabbed his hat from the ground and settled it on his head. "Get dressed," he grumbled.

"Brandon…"

He turned his back on her. The cotton material of her shift rustled. He glanced back to see her rising awkwardly. Again he asked himself how he could not have noticed before. He took her arm and helped her to her feet.

"Thank you," she said, but jerked away as soon as she steadied herself. Her eyes flashed with banked anger.

He waited for her to finish dressing and then helped her mount her mare.

"Can we talk about this before we go back?" she asked.

He handed her the reins. "Not now, Caroline. You've given me a hell of a lot to think about." He mounted his horse without glancing at her again.

Good Lord. A baby.

Brandon maneuvered his horse down the steep hill and through the trees. The tightness in his jaw and the rigid set to his shoulders kept Caroline from trying again to speak to him. He helped her down at the corral, his eyes averted from her face, and led both horses into the stable.

She followed him. "We really must talk about this, Brandon. I don't want to part like this."

He turned from hanging the tack on the wall peg. "I take it Franklin knows." At her nod, he continued. "No wonder you have him in your pocket. He's always been a pushover for a woman in distress. My mother made good use of it."

He'd never spoken of his mother that way. Although curious, she was uneasy at his mood and held her tongue.

He removed the saddle and blanket from the piebald mare and set them on a bench outside the stall. "Who else is aware? Hopefully I am not the last to know."

"I think Victoria's mother suspects, but she hasn't said anything."

"Her mother? How would she know?"

"At dinner, I saw the look on her face when I could not tolerate the spicy food."

He snorted. "My power of observation, which as a physician should be razor-sharp, has failed." With his face set in stone, Brandon moved back to his horse and removed the saddle.

"No one else knows, Brandon. Truly."

He turned to face her, his eyes unreadable and shadowed beneath the brim of his black hat. "Other than having trouble with your digestion are you well?"

The question took her by surprise. He sounded more like a doctor than a worried father. She didn't know whether to smile or be angry and so she simply answered. "I'm sleepy all the time, but...yes. I'm well."

He nodded slowly, set the saddle on the bench and then walked out.

Chapter Ten

Brandon didn't join them for supper that evening. Curious glances came her way but no one treated her any differently so she was sure Brandon hadn't said anything to them. Soon they would know the true reason for her visit here and then she would have to bear their scrutiny in another, less pleasant way. But for now, talk at the table centered on helping the Svendsons.

Afterward, she didn't seek Brandon out. It wasn't every day a man learned he was going to be a father. He needed time to adjust. After all, she'd had months to consider the change along with the movement going on inside her body that confirmed a new life there.

As she headed to her room, Victoria called her from the open door of the library.

"Would you do a favor for me?" she asked. At Caroline's nod, Victoria continued. "Your trip today to the clear spring reminded me that we are low on honey. Would you ask Diego to go gather some? I need enough for the wedding guests and perhaps some for the Svendsons. He should be at the stable."

Caroline left the hacienda and walked across the expanse of packed ground to the corral. She stood at the gate waiting for a break in Diego's routine with the new horse. He wore a loose white shirt and buckskin pants. Instead of boots, he wore soft moccasins. With his long black hair tied back in a wide leather strip, he looked more Indian than Tejano. Standing in the center of the corral, he flicked a long whip that landed lightly on the filly's rump as it loped along the perimeter of the pen. At the same time he spoke softly, soothingly, letting the horse get used to his voice and his verbal commands.

When he noticed her, he slowed the horse to a walk and lowered his whip.

"Señorita Caroline. You wished to see me?"

"Yes. Victoria, uh, Señorita Torrez, has a request."

He smiled. "She has been Victoria to me since we were young. She is my cousin, so it is allowed."

"Oh. She would like you to gather honey up at the spring. She needs more for her wedding guests and some for the Svendsons."

"When the bees quiet. At dusk."

"That is nearly upon us. Do you need help?"

Diego's smile challenged her. "With the honey? Or with this filly?"

His teasing took her by surprise.

When she didn't answer he grinned good-naturedly and opened the gate. "Come in—the horse will not hurt you. She is nearly tame."

Caroline stepped tentatively inside the corral. The sleek, black animal pranced away from them, then put her nose up, sniffing the air for Caroline without coming too near.

"I think you are both nervous of each other," Diego said.

"I haven't been around unbroken horses. Father has a

horse for his patient visits but it is old and plodding." Caroline held out her hand to show the horse she had nothing to fear of her. "She is beautiful."

"She is to be bred to Juan's stallion. Victoria is very good with bloodlines and she and Jake are to have the first foal as a wedding present."

"I'd heard that. Tell me about this horse," she said, studying the animal. "What makes her better than the others?"

With a look of approval, Diego turned to whistle to the filly. She inched closer a few steps, and then skittish, she dashed away.

"Rosa!" Diego called softly, his voice calm and entreating. "Is that how you treat a guest? Come say hello." He walked toward the horse, which now shied away from him and circled the railing slowly, cautiously. Diego paused. "She is acting strange. Perhaps you had better—"

He stopped talking and, narrowing his gaze, peered into the stand of pines on the far side of the stable.

"What is it?" Caroline asked. Then a noise behind her made her turn.

Brandon stepped from the stable door and started toward them. He wouldn't be the reason for Rosa's nervousness.

Caroline looked back to Diego. With a brief shake of his head, he placed a finger to his lips. "Shh." Slowly, still watching the trees, he moved between her and the animal.

Suddenly the horse bucked, tossing its head, and then raced along the perimeter of the corral.

"Caroline!" Brandon yelled. "Get the hell out of there!"

She grabbed up her skirt and ran for the fence. Brandon raced toward her, his pace surprisingly fast despite his injury. He slipped through the wooden rails and rushed at the horse, waving his arms at the animal. "Ha! Ha!"

The filly skidded to a stop and reared, pranced backward a few steps and then dashed to the far side of the corral. With a knot in her throat, Caroline climbed through to safety on the other side of the fence, her chest heaving and her heart pounding.

Brandon strode toward her, his limp more pronounced than usual, his brows drawn together in a fierce frown. Once he'd slipped back through to the outside of the corral he turned to her. "What do you think you were doing?"

Caroline backed up. She'd never seen him so angry. Crystal sparks seemed to fly from his blue eyes.

"That horse is unpredictable. Didn't Diego tell you that? You could have been killed."

He'd gotten it all wrong. "It wasn't Diego's fault, Brandon. Something set her off."

"You shouldn't have been in there."

Diego climbed through the fence rails and looked from Brandon to her. "Are you all right, *señorita?* I am sorry for your scare."

"You ought to be," Brandon said, giving her no chance to answer. Caroline had never heard his voice so ugly.

Diego's eyes narrowed on him. "There was something in the woods making the filly nervous."

"I just came that way from the cabin. Nothing is there." Tension radiated off him in waves.

"You are calling me a liar?" Diego said with a sudden calm to his voice.

"Sounds like it." Brandon clenched his fists at his sides.

This wasn't the Brandon Caroline knew—a man spoiling for a fight. She put her hand on his shoulder.

He flinched and shook her off. "Back away. This is between Diego and me."

"Brandon, what are you doing?" she asked.

"Do as he says, *señorita*." Diego kept his gaze trained on Brandon.

Alarmed, she stepped backward.

"You will recall your accusation now, *hombre*."

"I'll do better than that!" Brandon swung his fist into Diego's jaw.

Shocked, Caroline screamed. "Brandon! No!"

Similarly stunned, Diego rubbed his chin. "You should not have done that, *amigo*." His eyes blazed as he rushed at Brandon, his head low, and slammed his fist into his opponent's gut. Air rushed from Brandon in a whoosh. He lost his balance and stumbled backward.

Diego rushed at him again, ready to plant another hard knock.

This time Brandon had the presence of mind to grip Diego's fist as it sailed toward his face. He grabbed onto the boy's arm, grappled with him and they both went down, dust flying.

On his back, with Diego on top of him, Brandon pushed and twisted until he straddled him and took the upper hand. He was the heavier of the two and Caroline cringed at what he might do to the boy. Then suddenly, Diego used leverage to knee Brandon in the back and push him over his head. Brandon landed with a thud, sprawled face-first in the dirt. He spit dust from his mouth, flipped over and found Diego's foot on his chest.

"Stop!" she cried out. "Stop!"

They didn't hear her—or more likely, they didn't care. Brandon grasped Diego's foot and pushed up, at the same time twisting it. Diego, the lighter of the two, dropped in a heap at his side.

She looked about the yard, hoping to find help on the way. No one was in sight. Her anger growing, she searched for a way to make them stop fighting. Spying the bucket at the well, she marched over, dropped it down to collect water and brought it back up, full. She stomped over to the two and dumped the water on them.

They barely noticed the splash. Blood dripped from Brandon's nose as he straddled Diego, rearing back with his arm, preparing to throw the next punch.

"I'll take over," Jake said, appearing at Caroline's side with Victoria just behind him. Victoria took her hand and pulled her out of the way.

Jake gripped Brandon's collar and hauled him backward, then let him drop, off balance, into the mud. Brandon lay there, stunned and breathing hard.

"I didn't save both your asses in battle just so you could kill each other here," Jake said, glowering over them. He turned to Brandon. "What are you trying to do? Knock him into a cocked hat? What's this all about?"

With a wary eye on Brandon, Diego stood. He fingered the cut on his lower lip gingerly, then turned his head and spat bloody saliva into the dirt.

"Well?" Jake waited.

Brandon sat up and dragged a hand through his hair. He'd have an awkward time getting up, Caroline realized, but she didn't move to help him. He deserved whatever he'd brought on himself this time. With a grunt, he slowly got to his feet. Still he didn't move to answer his brother.

"The horse spooked," Caroline said.

Jake raised a brow. "And that caused a fight?"

"No," Diego said. "He accused me of lying."

"You had no right to have her in there," Brandon ground out. "She could have been killed."

"I would not have let that happen," Diego countered.

"You know me well enough to know that. Something else has got you tied in knots."

Caroline had a suspicion she knew—it was about the baby. But please, he wouldn't announce it here, would he?

"You two," Diego said, looking from Brandon to her. "Settle your quarrel and leave me out of your troubles. I've got work to do." He stepped back into the corral to calm Rosa.

Numbly Caroline picked up the bucket and walked over to the well to set it down. She could feel Brandon staring at her, feel his stubborn glare burning into her back. Her heart constricted in her chest.

"I'm going to the house," she managed to say. She walked away but once she reached the gate, she glanced back. Jake and Brandon were headed toward the cabin, neither talking. Brandon held himself stiff, leaning once again on his cane, and kept his distance from his brother. Would he tell Jake about the baby now? Jake—who despised her? He would warn Brandon away from her.

Well, what had she expected? A declaration of love from Brandon? She wasn't foolish enough to think everything would magically be all right when he learned of the baby. He wasn't the same man she'd known in Charleston, but she had hoped he would want to help her, hoped he would eventually accept the baby.

She could almost convince herself leaving would be a relief. Franklin would take her to her aunt's house in Virginia where she'd stay until her confinement was over, and then…what then? She couldn't return home with the baby. Her parents had said as much. And she didn't think she could be separated from the child—Brandon's own flesh and blood. She placed her hand on her abdomen, unsure what she was going to do if he wouldn't help her, but she'd figure it out.

Yes, leaving this place would be a relief. The only problem was…she didn't believe it anymore.

Chapter Eleven

❧

Goliad

Brandon opened his eyes and stared through the window of his prison. A thick, early-morning fog hung in the air. Ice crystals sparkled on the new sycamore leaves beside the small house. His stomach growled, still hungry even after the meal he'd had late last night before the guard had shoved him into this room. It had been dark then and he had stumbled over the men sleeping on the floor.

He could see them now in the gray light of dawn—wounded Mexican soldiers lying any way that would keep them comfortable. Soldiers he was expected to heal with a miraculous wave of his hand—without enough bandages, without instruments, without hope. Hope being the main ingredient of survival. The one ingredient no one in the room possessed.

Paradoxically he'd made a name for himself among them. He was fast, which meant *less painful* when it came to the necessary amputations of his trade. An ironic way to heal a man—cut off what bothered him. If he was bitter, so be it. He'd seen too much of mangled arms and legs from shrapnel and bullets. A man couldn't see so much horror and come out unscathed. His mind would never be free of it again.

His personal guard saw him stir—a man of forty years, short and squat. The guard stepped near and booted him in the ribs. Brandon rolled away from the insult, finding small relief in the fact that yesterday's kick had been on the opposite side. At least his bruises were spread out over his body and not concentrated in one horrible spot. It was a normal beginning for the day and a repeat of the past twenty-five days he'd been in Goliad.

At least for now he still had his boots. Many of the Mexican soldiers had worn through theirs and had to wrap their feet in rags just to walk. He stood, his body aching in places he'd not known existed before his capture. With his movement the ropes that bound his ankles chafed against the raw skin there. He hissed in sharply.

At the sound, a slow, ugly grin came on the guard's face. He pointed to a wooden bucket in the corner used by the men for defecation. Brandon picked it up, nearly gagging as the contents sloshed and emitted the strong odor of urine and ammonia. He followed the guard to a pit behind the livery and threw out the contents of the bucket.

He took a moment to relieve himself in the pit, clinically amazed that his body could continue to make water when he seldom received any to drink. Perhaps when he returned to Charleston he would write a report on it and submit it to the medical group. The errant thought—one of many he had daily—only advanced the probability that he was losing his grip on reality. The truth was he'd never be free of this place alive, never go back to Charleston. Never see Caroline again.

The guard nudged him with his rifle, jostling him out of his reverie. Brandon buttoned his pants and followed the guard to the river where he rinsed out the bucket in the water.

On the far bank, a door opened in the tall stone fort. A line of ten men emerged, blinking and squinting into the bright sunlight. By their looks, they were Texians, not that he could tell by their clothes which hung in rags. One had red hair and appeared young—still just a boy. Another had dirty blond hair streaked with gray. The man glanced across the water, meeting Brandon's gaze. Brandon was shocked at the bleakness in his face. A few of the men were Tejano with dark hair and eyes. Half of them carried makeshift shovels. Prodded by the bayonets and rifle butts of their guards, the Texians marched away from the river and up over a knoll, moving from his line of sight.

The guard handed him a second bucket and they walked upstream a hundred yards through the grass. As they did every morning, the birds in the trees along the water called out to each other, creating a cacophony. Brandon stopped at his usual place and collected fresh water in the second bucket. Curious about the men he'd seen, he took his time, kneeling at the bank and splashing water on his face to help him wake up.

Suddenly shouts arose from beyond the hill—Spanish and then English alike. The swift, rapid cadence of gunfire split the morning silence. Then even the birds were quiet.

Something went berserk inside him. He had to see what had just happened, although he was terrified he knew. He lunged into the river and swam to the other side. On a sub-conscious level he felt the icy water and the drag of the current, but refused to consider it. All he felt was rage. Rage at the soldiers who'd kill unarmed men like dogs.

Rage at General López de Santa Anna who had most likely given the order. And rage at the inhumane carnage of war.

A rifle fired and his guard shouted at him to stop—then followed with a stream of obscenities in Spanish. Brandon didn't care and it didn't stop him. He reached the opposite bank and then half ran, half crawled up the grassy knoll to view what had happened. Some mad impulse urged him on to see it with his own eyes. Would there be any he could save—any he could help?

When he reached the top, he froze in horror at the sight. The Texians had been slaughtered, lying this way and that, their arms and legs bent at odd angles in grotesque shapes in a shallow mass grave. The men stared at the sky, their eyes unseeing, with blood splattered everywhere.

He doubled over and retched.

Suddenly white-hot fire cracked his right ankle and he collapsed to his knees, too startled to cry out. He twisted, falling further, and sprawled on the grass. His guard strode toward him, the musket in his hand still emitting smoke from the barrel. Pain would come soon. Brandon braced himself as daylight faltered and the edges of his vision grew dark.

"Now you will not try to escape, *Médico.*" The guard's voice rasped through his mind, harsh and guttural.

Escaping had been in his thoughts constantly since he'd been captured, but oddly, not at that moment. All he'd wanted was to know for sure what had happened. In a way, to witness it so that those men would not die in vain.

Pain pulsed through his leg and up to his knee. He turned over slowly, fighting the dizziness, and sat up to examine his leg. The ankle bone protruded through the skin. For now the bleeding was minimal. Apparently the plug remained inside, providing pressure to the small bleeders.

"I didn't intend to escape," he growled, tense, expecting a kick in the ribs or a musket jabbed into his back.

Why hadn't the guard finished him off? Seemed like the easiest thing to do now. He wouldn't be much good for doctoring the Mexican troops if he couldn't walk.

The man's musket suddenly landed on the ground beside Brandon. Since the one bullet had been spent and it did not sport a bayonet, the weapon was useless to Brandon, but it was odd the guard had dropped it—and within Brandon's reach. He glanced up. The guard's face had paled, immobilized into a horrified expression as he stared on the massacre below.

"No!" he cried out and then ran wildly down the hill toward a gathering of Mexican soldiers. Once there, he didn't stop but pushed the men aside to gain access to the one they surrounded—someone lying on the ground.

He'd lost someone special, then. Brandon couldn't dredge up the energy to care. He'd seen too much of death.

Alone for the moment, Brandon took the opportunity to withdraw the small, ivory-handled knife hidden in the lining of his boot. Gritting his teeth, he probed for the bullet. He felt strange, erratically hot and cold at the same time and knew he must be going into shock. Sweat poured from him as he struggled to wedge out the plug. It'd be so much easier with forceps, he thought, grimacing further as he moved the plug with the tip of his knife. The pain intensified. Finally he dislodged the bullet and popped it out onto the grass. Working quickly, he ripped off a portion of his sleeve and bound his ankle tight with the cloth.

He glanced down the hill once more. The guard had gathered his comrade in his arms and with the help of another soldier, they started back toward Brandon. He tried to stow the knife in his boot once more, but his vision blurred. No! He needed the weapon if he was ever going to escape. He had to hide it. He swallowed hard. He needed the weapon. He needed the…

Blinding pain at the side of his head shut out all thought and the ground swirled around him before going dark.

Light filtered through the dirty cabin windows and splashed across Brandon's eyelids. Morning! Disoriented, unsure for a moment where he was, the nightmare of Goliad slowly receded.

He opened his eyes and whipped the covers off, sitting up in one motion. Pain exploded through his head. His skull was going to split wide-open. He pressed against his ears with his hands, willing the pounding to stop. Dry mouth, scratchy throat, headache—all symptoms of drinking too much mescal last night.

The fight with Diego had ended the strangest day of his life. Jake had demanded to know what was going on but Brandon hadn't been ready to talk about it. Frustrated, Jake had stormed out of the cabin muttering something about Brandon being stupid and bullheaded.

There was that pounding again. A light breeze touched his chest as the front door opened. "Brandon?"

Caroline. No difficulty knowing what she was doing here. "I'm not good company this morning."

There was a pause. "It's noon."

"Same thing."

"Brandon. You can't continue to ignore me. I want to know how you feel about…things."

Me, too, he thought to himself. His thoughts went from one extreme to the other—one minute excited and amazed at knowing he and Caroline had started a new life, and the next minute scared to the point of incapacity that he would let her and the baby down. What the hell was he going to do?

"I'll be out in a moment."

He was glad that he'd closed the curtain to his small sleeping quarter when he'd fallen in bed. It gave him a moment now to gather his wits. He shoved his stocking feet in his boots and stood.

Too fast. His head swam. His vision blurred. Oh, yeah. This was going to be quite a day.

Yesterday, he'd hurt Caroline. He'd been rough, wanting to lash out at her because she'd deceived him—about the baby, about coming to Texas, about everything. He understood on one level that she'd been afraid of how he would react, but that didn't excuse her deception. Did she think he could walk away now? Is that what had her worried?

When he'd gotten himself pulled back together he shoved his straw pallet into the corner and peeked out through the curtain. Caroline had tied a kerchief over her hair and a white apron around her waist covered her calico skirt. He took a moment to study her. Now that he knew she carried a baby, he saw that her waist did appear slightly larger. Funny he hadn't noticed it before—like when he'd first carried her from the river. He'd chalk that up to his total shock at seeing her in Texas territory.

He pushed aside the curtains and stepped into the large room. "What are you doing?"

She whirled around. "Goodness, you're a mess! You look like a big, grouchy bear."

He glared and rubbed his day's growth of beard. "Good day to you, too."

She frowned at him in response and then continued searching through the cupboards and behind doors.

Methodically he tucked in his cotton shirt and looped his suspenders over his shoulders. "I asked what you are doing here?"

"I'm looking for a bucket." She opened a tall wooden cabinet behind his desk and rummaged through its contents. "I never knew you to be lazy. The day is half-gone and you are just waking?"

"If you must know—yes," he grumbled. He worked his leg, easing his weight down on his injured ankle. It was sore every morning before he stretched it out. He looked up to find she had ceased her search and instead, studied his movements.

"When you are ready to eat, I brought breakfast from the hacienda."

He stopped exercising abruptly. Just what was she up to? "Maria made it?"

She put her hands on her hips and faced him. "No. I can make a simple breakfast, Brandon."

He rubbed a hand over his face, eyeing her, and then walked across the room to the other side of his desk where he picked up the bucket from the space between the wall and the desk. "I'll go with you."

"I am capable of fetching water."

"That I know. Your aim was true when you doused me last evening."

"As I recall, it didn't help much. You must think I can't do anything on my own."

"I never thought that at all. I just figured I'd get a little water to wash my face while I'm at it." And he didn't want her carrying a full bucket anywhere in her condition.

"Why were you fighting Diego? I was safe."

"He shouldn't have put you at risk. It was unnecessary. It was stupid."

"But to *fight* about it? Sometimes I don't know you at all, Brandon. You were never one to resort to fisticuffs."

"Sorry to disappoint you, but you're talking about when I was back in Charleston—where it's civilized."

"You always said man should use his reasoning rather than to fight about something. I thought you believed it."

He snorted. "And I remember you telling me yesterday that I think too much. Some things just can't be talked away. Sometimes it takes action. And sometimes the lowest common denominator—passions and emotions—rule." He looked at her stomach as he said the last. "Your condition being a case in point."

She slid her hand over the small bulge. When she looked up at him, her eyes were glassy with unshed tears. "I would not call this baby conceived by the lowest common denominator. This baby—our child—is the result of mutual caring and love, not fighting."

"Are you so sure it was love, Caroline? Not just passion? The heat of the moment?"

Her lips pressed together. "At the time, it was both for me."

He was baiting her, purposely holding her at arm's length and saying things to hurt her and he didn't know why. Perhaps because she'd turned his world upside down in the past twenty-four hours.

"You came to this conclusion because of the rebellion," she accused him.

"Fighting for a free Texas fixed that in my mind, I won't deny it. It's human nature—something I've come to know more in the past five months than in all the years before."

"It has hardened you."

He didn't have anything to say to that. It was true. But he had to be hard. If he let down his guard, the memories came crashing back in to suffocate him. The ghosts of men he'd fought beside hovered just beyond his waking consciousness, calling to him in his sleep and when he was too tired to keep them away.

"Tell me about the war, Brandon. What happened? How did you get hurt?"

The question didn't take him by surprise. He'd expected it eventually. But she had no idea of what he'd seen, and he didn't want her knowing. No one should get that close.

He held out the bucket. "Let's get the water."

Sighing in disappointment, she reached for the handle. Too late he realized he stood too close to her.

She sniffed, her pert little nose wrinkling. "Brandon…?"

"Caroline?" he said mockingly.

"Are you liquor…"

"Liquored up?" he finished for her. Drinking wasn't a crime and he didn't need a lecture first thing on waking. What he needed were answers to the mess he suddenly found himself in.

She stepped back, her face registering dismay. "Does your leg hurt that much?"

He'd quit using alcohol—and laudanum—for the pain over a month ago. That's not why he'd been drinking last night. It had everything to do with him finding out he was going to be a father. "I'm fine as frog's hair," he said sarcastically.

That quieted her. Clamping her jaws tight together, she headed outside, taking the path through the trees to the well. He followed, letting her rinse out the bucket before he took it from her hands. "I'll get it now," he said and filled the bucket with fresh water. "You shouldn't be lifting it."

Once back in the office, Brandon divvied up the water—some in a basin for his morning ablutions and some for breakfast. It was colder than snowmelt, but he figured it would wake him up, especially after all he'd imbibed last night. He poured the remaining water in a large kettle which hung on an iron hook in the fireplace.

"Are you sure you can cook this way?"

"It can't be too difficult." She grabbed the flint stone that sat on the mantel.

Leaving her to the task, he moved to the small mirror that hung on the wall of his "room" and proceeded to shave his morning growth of beard. He took his time, wondering if she really knew what she was doing fixing breakfast. As far as he knew, she'd never prepared a meal in her life. She'd always had kitchen maids and cooks growing up—and a stove instead of an open fireplace. Through the angle of the glass, he saw her glance his way a time or two—when she thought he wasn't looking. He finished up with the razor and walked over to her.

"You don't cook for yourself much," she said. "The grime is thick here."

"Most days I go to the hacienda." He watched as she turned the flint over in her hand and then hesitated. "Sure you don't want any help?"

"I'm sure." The hearth had been prepared for a fire with kindling and dried pine needles the day he'd moved in, compliments of Juan's wife, Gertrudis. Warm as it was, he and Jake had never used it. Like he'd told Caroline, he took his meals at the big house.

She struck the flint, trying to gain a spark. It didn't work. She tried again without any more success than her first attempt.

He was careful not to ask if she wanted help again. This could take a while if her fumbling attempts were any indication. She seemed determined to do this on her own, so he pulled up his chair and sat down.

She studied the piece of flint as though it held some magic answer, and then, squatting down next to the kindling, tried again.

Nothing happened.

Brandon leaned near her left shoulder to watch and unconsciously breathed her in. Warmth radiated from her body and with it the honey perfume of her skin. He closed his eyes, wanting to hold in the scent and not let it go. Here she was, fixing him breakfast as intimate as any husband and wife. Her fumbling attempts at starting the fire only endeared her to him all the more. She was good at so many things—entertaining, organizing fundraisers, dancing— but none were of any use in Texas.

If only things could be different. If only they could try again. But it wouldn't work. She was right. He had changed and he couldn't go back to what he used to be. It was impossible. Still, he took another deep breath, dragging in that light, sweet scent that was hers alone. When he opened his eyes, she still hadn't set fire to the kindling.

"Let me," he said and gently took the flint from her hands. At his swift strike, a spark jumped from the stone and the needles began to smoke. He blew lightly on the kindling and slowly the red glow turned into a flame. "Just takes practice."

Her lashes fluttered down, but she didn't move away from him. He stared at her a moment, feeling the pull between them, wanting to close the gap and taste her lips. He didn't act on the impulse. Instead he sat back in the chair.

She rose and took the coffeepot from the mantel, scooping out enough water from the large pot to fill it. "Thank you. Franklin lit the fire most evenings. That is, the times we didn't stop at an inn." She threw a handful of coffee grounds into the pot.

Brandon watched every movement, noticing for the first time that her hands were dry and chapped. What else had she been doing on her journey? "You must have found sleeping on the ground uncomfortable."

"I usually slept in the coach and he took the ground. There was one night—" She hesitated.

"Yes?" He had a feeling he knew what she was going to say.

"One night that it rained and he stayed in the coach with me."

"That would have been the sensible thing to do."

The tension in her shoulders eased.

"Yes. I thought so, too. He was a gentleman the entire trip. Although—" she wrinkled her nose "—he did snore."

He felt the hint of a smile come to his lips. He trusted Franklin. What's more, he realized he trusted Caroline. She really hadn't deceived him; she'd just been afraid to tell him about the baby. Now that things were out in the open, perhaps they could deal with the situation.

"You mentioned that you stopped in New Orleans to stay with his family."

"Yes, we did."

"He used to talk about them a lot when I was young. I've never met them."

"We stayed two nights. I…I needed the rest."

"You don't need to explain, Caroline. I don't begrudge you the two days. Considering the bone-jarring roads and your condition, the trip must have been exhausting for you."

"It…it was. I believe Franklin is looking forward to stopping there again on our return to Charleston."

Silence followed her words, the weight of it heavy with unsaid words.

"I'm not going back, Caroline," he said. "We've already discussed that."

Her gaze held his. "I'm not asking you to. Not anymore. I only wanted to tell you about the baby."

Her cheeks flushed as she moved quickly back to the hearth and threw a slice of ham into the three-legged skillet. It sizzled and popped, the aroma making his stomach churn with hunger.

"You can turn it now." He looked up to see why she didn't move. She held her hand to her nose, her face pale.

"Are you all right?"

She swallowed convulsively. "Never better."

He grabbed the utensil from her hand. "I'll do it." He forked the ham and flipped it over. His eyes narrowed on her. "You sure you're all right? You look a little green."

"Yes. Of course. How will you take your eggs?"

"Any way you want to fix them." Slowly he sank down to a chair. She seemed determined to do this.

Removing the ham to a side plate, she cracked the eggs into the skillet.

Suddenly the coffee boiled up and over the side of the pot. She reached...

"Caroline! No!"

His warning came too late. She gripped the hot tin handle with her bare hand.

"Stars and garters!" She jumped back holding her hand. He started to rise...

"No. I'm all right. Stay there." She grabbed the spatula and flipped the eggs, only to have both the soft yolks break at the last second. "Now I've ruined them!"

"They'll taste the same."

"But I wanted them to be perfect. I wanted it all to be perfect."

"Nothing is."

She pressed her lips together at his words. Moving the eggs to his plate, she set it in front of him.

He paused in bringing the first bite to his mouth, his gaze narrowing on her fingers. "Let me see your hand."

"I can take care of a burn." She whipped her hand behind her back and rummaged through the few canisters in the cupboard. "How can a doctor not have something for a burn?" she asked crossly. "It is a basic remedy."

"Caroline," he said again, standing. "Give me your hand."

She sniffed. "Not on your life. You're unfit. You've been drinking." She backed away, and continued her search.

"That doesn't make me incapable of administering first aid. In spite of this blasted headache, I do remember something about burns."

"I don't want your help." She found a length of cloth, ripped it lengthwise and began wrapping her hand, her movements jerky. "I don't want your help," she repeated.

He gripped her wrist to stop her and force her to look him in the face. "Are we talking about the same thing?"

"It's obvious, isn't it? You don't want to help, you don't want a baby, you don't want me—"

He could barely keep up with her mercurial mood swings. "I think what happened yesterday makes a lie of that. Hold still. You are going to get my help. On both counts."

"You don't have any butter."

Irrational! She was being ridiculously irrational. Carefully he unwrapped the cloth. She hissed when the air hit the ravaged skin.

He examined her reddened palm and the blisters, his anger growing. "This is worse than you let on," he accused.

Pulling her away from the stove, he plunged her hand into the remaining cool water in the bucket. "Keep it there."

He held his hand over the frying pan, testing the temperature. When he was reassured that it had cooled sufficiently, he scooped up a dollop of grease from the ham and applied it to the blistered and reddened areas of her palm. Then, wrapping the cloth snuggly about her hand, he tied it off efficiently.

"Don't ever be afraid to ask me for what you need," he said, holding her gaze. "I can't always give you what you want, but if you need something, you know I'd do what I could." He'd been thinking of her burn, but hearing the words come from his mouth, he realized he meant much more.

He released her hand and turned away, unwilling to delve deeper into the feelings that had surfaced. "I should eat this before it gets cold. You went to a lot of work and pain to make it." He sat and took a long slug of his coffee.

"Brandon," she said, her back to him, "I never came here to coerce you back to Charleston. I thought you'd want to go—that perhaps you just needed a reminder of what waited for you there. I can tell now that I was wrong."

He heard the squeal of the iron hook as she positioned it away from the fire. This time she used a long poker to do the work, rather than her tender fingers.

"Tell me one thing," Brandon said.

"Yes?"

"Did Franklin know about the baby before you came? Is that why he brought you with him?"

"Not at first, but he fished it out of me soon enough. He didn't want to believe it. You know how he felt about me. But after I lost my breakfast a few times he realized I was telling the truth. Then he made it a point not to eat so early, but to wait until we'd traveled for a few hours."

"And your parents? They couldn't have gone along with this."

"No. As you remember they wished me to marry Graham—as quickly and as quietly as possible to prevent any gossip or counting of months when the baby came."

"What did you tell them about coming here?"

"They don't know. They sent me to Virginia to finish my confinement with my aunt. That's when I stopped Franklin and came here instead."

"In Virginia," he repeated slowly.

"Aunt Beth expected me weeks ago. I sent her a note explaining that I was coming here first and that I would arrive late at her place. Franklin has promised to take me there when we leave," she added softly.

His breathing slowed to nonexistent in his chest. She'd planned everything out without a thought to staying. He sat back in the chair. Where did that leave him?

"What is it you want from me?"

"Well, of course, at first I'd hoped you would return to Charleston with me. I can see that will not happen now." She spoke softly, carefully. "After the baby comes, my parents have arranged for Aunt Beth to raise it. They won't let me bring the baby home."

If he knew her at all, he knew that wouldn't sit well with her. "How do you feel about that?"

She met his gaze. "I can't leave my own child into someone else's keeping. I feel it moving inside me. I want to raise it. I had hoped you would be able to help me."

She needed his help. He dragged a hand through his hair as he weighed the possibilities.

A hesitant smile crossed her lips. "I mean, you were so honorable that you would fight for Texas. I hoped you would also honor this life you have started."

She turned back to her task of cleaning up the dishes she'd just used. Watching quietly, he mentally searched for an answer to her dilemma, trying for once to think beyond his own needs. There had to be an answer for her. When she untied the apron from her waist and hung it on the peg with her hat, he rose to his feet.

"Walk with me." He raised his hand, palm up, and waited for her to take it.

He led her through the grove of pines and then further on through the meadow without saying a word, using his cane over the uneven ground. She followed silently, afraid to break the strange truce that pulsed between them. His steps slowed as he neared a smattering of boulders under three ancient oaks.

"Would you rest?" she asked. They'd come a far distance from the cabin with the sun beating down. The shade felt wonderful.

He didn't answer.

"Then might I rest? It's hot." Without waiting for his approval, she sat on one of the shorter granite boulders and removed her hat, fanning herself with the brim. "I can tell when the wound aches, Brandon. There's no point in denying it."

"I didn't come here to talk about my leg. What's done is done on that account."

She stiffened at his tone but kept her voice pleasant. "I'm sorry if my asking annoys you. I happen to care."

He sat on a nearby boulder, stretching his leg out before him to work the ankle within his leather boot.

"We've walked over a mile and you haven't uttered a word. What is it you wanted to talk about that couldn't have been said at the cabin?"

"Just wanted some fresh air. Bear with me, Caroline. I'm sorting all this out."

At last. Perhaps now they would come to an understanding. Perhaps he would help her so that she could keep the baby. A light breeze rustled the leaves overhead. As much as she wanted to press him, she kept quiet, giving him the space to think. Whatever he decided would affect her future, and that of their child.

"Your parents knew you were with child," he said slowly. "That's why they were so eager to marry you off."

"Yes." She'd thought that much was obvious. Apparently he'd just figured it out.

"Did Graham know?"

"Not at first. When he proposed, my answer at that time was no. That I was waiting for you to return."

"But I didn't—return."

"No," she said, remembering the hurt, the overwhelming worry for him when he'd left her. And then to hear that he'd *chosen* to stay in Texas. She felt humiliated all over again when she thought of that.

"I can see how you would feel that I deserted you. I did."

She stared at him in surprise. His admission took the edginess out of her in one breath. "You didn't know. You...you thought I had married."

"I should have returned—at least to straighten things out."

"You were injured. You had no idea about the baby. And then Jake wanted you to stay for his wedding."

"You're trying to absolve me?"

"Not really. Just trying to be honest about things. You understand then how things were for me—at least a little."

"It couldn't have been easy. I'm sorry for that, Caroline."

An apology! That was more than she'd expected. He began to sound almost like the man she once knew—almost.

He took a deep breath, removed his hat and raked his hair back from his forehead. "So what happened after you refused Graham?"

"He thought giving me time would change my mind. That the longer you stayed away, I'd come to see what a 'catch' he was. When he proposed a second time, I nearly said yes but I couldn't deceive him like that. I couldn't bring a baby into this world in such a false situation. By that time, I was sure you weren't returning from Texas and I was so scared. Scared of what would become of me. Scared of what would become of the baby. But more than anything, scared that you'd been killed and if so, my life was over already."

At her raw admission, Brandon looked away. His throat worked as he swallowed hard before he turned back to her. "I wouldn't have blamed you for marrying him."

Unbelievable! Here she'd just poured out her heart to him, and he thought she should have made a different choice! "Wonderful! I'll just return now and see if he'll take me back!"

Brandon scowled. "I didn't mean it like that."

"Well, that's how it sounded."

"You were in a fix, with few choices." He stood and grasped her upper arms, forcing her to look at him. "Caroline. Listen. What I'm saying is I'm glad you waited for me—as difficult as that was for you. I'm glad you didn't marry Graham."

"Why, Brandon? You obviously are not ready to have a family."

"For three good reasons. If you had said yes, you wouldn't be here now. I'd still be angry with you for backing out on your promise to me. I'd have no idea about the baby. And I'd have no idea how much you really do love me."

She tensed, her thoughts frustrated and mutinous. "That's four."

"So it is." The soft hint of a smile played about his lips. "Caroline, give in. Give me this."

"I...I'm afraid to," she whispered. To let down her guard would be the same as relinquishing control, to allow herself to be vulnerable. She couldn't bear the hurt again, the anguish, if he should reject her again.

"You do, you know. Love me."

"I never said that."

"You didn't have to. Not in so many words."

"Then why do you think I love you?" The words came out breathier than she'd wanted them to.

He leaned his forehead against hers. "Stubborn woman. When you held Franklin hostage at gunpoint, you told me. When you came halfway across the continent to see me, you told me. And when, in spite of everything—" he stepped closer, nuzzling her hair "—you let me hold you and make love to you at the pool yesterday, you told me."

Her legs went weak.

"You never said so in words, but your actions said it every time." He leaned down and kissed her gently on the lips. "Every time."

She plopped down on the rock. "I intended only to let you know about the baby."

"That's all?"

"You...you hurt me." She looked down at her bonnet in her lap. She felt so exposed. "I never wanted to care again. I just need your help with the baby. I don't want to love anybody. Not ever again."

He tilted her face toward him, studying her face, seeing more there than perhaps she wanted him to. "You'll be a good mother," he murmured. "I've always known that."

His hand, gentle on her chin, made her tingle there. She wanted to turn and meet his fingers with a kiss, wanted to rub her lips against his palm and move into his arms, but she couldn't bear to have him see her so plainly. She turned from his probing, intense gaze.

He stepped back and straightened, drawing in a deep breath. "I have something to say."

Half curious, half scared, she waited.

"I don't like the thought of you being beholden to your parents or your aunt in any way. And I don't want my child growing up on the wrong side of the blanket, Caroline. I want him or her to have my name and every benefit that name might bring, including financial."

Her throat went dry. "What are you saying?"

"I want you to marry me."

She swallowed hard, barely able to breathe. It would take care of all her problems. "Are you asking me to stay here? In Texas?"

"I'm asking you to marry me. To be my wife."

She couldn't help remembering the first time he'd proposed, declaring he loved her. Then he'd left her. He hadn't said anything about loving her today although he'd admitted to understanding her dilemma—to a point. Still, he was offering her help and she would be grateful for that. In her situation she couldn't expect undying love. She had to take what he could give. Even though the proposal this time was less than romantic—no flowers, no boat ride on the canal, no moon. She opened her mouth to accept…

"There is something you should know before you accept—or reject—my offer," he said with a firmness to his voice she'd not heard before.

She waited for him to finish.

"I'm not going back to Charleston—"

So she *would* be staying in Texas. "That's all right. I—"

"—but I want you to."

Chapter Twelve

Her breath caught in her throat, and a coldness congealed in the pit of her stomach. "What—what are you saying?"

"We'll get married tomorrow—in Bexar," Brandon continued. "It'll be small. Quiet. I don't want to take anything away from Jake and Victoria's day. They should have their own wedding as they planned it. Then I want you to go home with Franklin and have the baby there. Your father and mother, with their connections will be able to hire a good midwife."

She couldn't believe it! What kind of strange marriage was he proposing? "And where would I live?"

"Wherever you wish. My home in Charleston, or if you prefer, you could live with your family. Their support will be important for you in your time of confinement."

It was the same thing as him leaving her. Only this time he was sending *her* away! She felt as though she might explode on the spot. "How could you!"

She had to move, had to release some of the agitation that overtook her. Standing, she strode out from under the oak into the heat of the day, then turned around and marched back until she stood before him. "I cannot believe you expect this of me."

He frowned. "I'm trying to consider this rationally. The child will have proper parentage and you will not be ostracized. It's the sensible course."

"Oh, it's quite sensible! With the exception of your sudden departure from Charleston, you have always been so careful to be rational."

He looked genuinely surprised at her outburst. "I thought you'd be happy. You'll be taken care of."

She tried to calm down. Didn't he realize he'd said nothing about love, nothing about his feelings for the baby—his baby?

"I thought you wanted to go back home."

Not without you, came the thought. "The pull isn't as strong as it was at first," she admitted. "I believe I could like it here."

"You can't mean that," he said cautiously. "Here in Texas?"

Her chest tightened with pain. "You don't want me here, do you? You're willing to give our child a name and money for support, but that is all you are willing to give."

His jaw tightened. "Now, Caroline, that's not true."

"Don't you wish to be at my side when the baby comes into this world and takes its first breath? Find out whether it's a boy or girl? Don't you want to see it grow, take its first steps, say its first words?" Her hands clenched into fists at her side. She'd never been so frustrated, so hurt in her life.

Brandon frowned. "Damn it all, of course I do! Seeing you ride away will be the hardest thing I'll ever do in my life."

"Then why are you insisting on it? Why can't we be together?"

"I have my reasons. Look. I'm being honest with you."

"No, you're not. Not completely." If he didn't really want her, didn't really love her, then he needed to say it. She wouldn't hate him for it, but she had a right to know where she stood with him.

"You want to know why?" he asked roughly.

"I deserve an answer—and so does your child."

He pressed his lips together. "You won't like it."

Hands on hips, she waited. She wasn't going anywhere until he explained himself.

"I know you've seen what is happening to me. The unsteady nerves, the shakes, the hallucinations."

She froze. *Hallucinations, too?* This wasn't what she'd expected him to say.

"It started when I was in prison. In Goliad. But it was only nightmares then."

"You have nightmares, as well?" Her thoughts churned back to earlier at the cabin.

He nodded.

"You use liquor to help you sleep, too? I thought it was to help with your leg pain."

The look he shot her way was dark and filled with frustration. "It's so I won't dream. The pain is nothing compared to the dreams." He removed his hat and sat on the boulder. "Every time I close my eyes I see them."

"Who?"

"The men I took care of…their injuries…" He paused a moment, then began again. "The last soldier I doctored in Goliad was a Mexican boy of sixteen. He'd been in the thick of the fighting when his arm was bayoneted."

"Did he survive?"

Brandon huffed. "I wrapped his arm so well that by the next day he was up and helping with the prisoners. By the second day he was back on the line working alongside the men. He was shot accidentally—as it turned out by one of his own comrades. Now tell me what good I did?"

Her heart ached for him. The pain he carried inside was real. "You didn't have a choice."

"When I was sixteen, I hadn't even heard of the Texas territory. I was swimming in the bay and fishing off the dock. That boy had never gone swimming—never seen the ocean."

"You did what you had to do."

"A smart man would have figured out how to save that boy."

"Brandon—stop. Don't torment yourself."

"What? Just let it go? Forget it?" He paced away a few steps and stared up at the sky. "Tell me—how in the hell do I do that?"

She didn't know how to answer, what to say to make it better. There wasn't anything that would help. She waited for him to turn back to her. "I don't know," she whispered. But he had to. It was killing him.

"There's more. You might as well hear the rest."

The way he said it scared her. So calm now.

He straightened his shoulders and finally met her gaze. "I'm going crazy. Not all at once, but little by little. The dreams, the spells—they're getting worse. I don't know how much longer I'll be able to doctor, how much longer I'll be able to function at all. You could have been killed with that bull. I...I don't want you or the baby hurt because I can't protect you. And I won't have you around watching me go slowly insane. That's why you have to leave."

Shocked to the core, her voice came out a mere whisper. "No."

"It's true. I've seen it enough since the war. A man isn't made to go through something like that and survive."

Awkwardly he rose to his feet and with the use of his wooden cane, stepped over and pulled her up. He touched her chin, raising her face so that her gaze met his. "My offer stands. I want to help, to do right by you, but you have to agree to go back to Charleston."

So this was her choice. A woman alone, raising a child. She wasn't that strong—not if her parents chose not to support her desire to raise the baby and she didn't have any reason to think they would. Brandon was right on that account. In the end, the baby would bear the brunt of their poverty and of being an outcast—this baby that she already loved.

She swallowed hard. He'd said nothing about love. At least now any romantic dreams she'd had would have to stay just that—as dreams.

It wasn't about herself anymore. She must think of the child now. "It is a generous offer. And, you have made a good argument. Your name and your money, but not you. A woman could do worse."

She stared up into his blue eyes while inside she broke apart. She felt brittle, as though the slightest breeze might shatter her into a million sharp-edged pieces. Choosing her words carefully, she answered him. "Under the circumstances, it's a reasonable offer. My parents are anxious for me to return, but they made it clear I was not to come back with the baby. I know I won't be able to leave it with my aunt. I already love this child."

"Then you'll agree? For the sake of our child?"

Our child. The words warmed her. She closed her eyes against the look of hope on his face. Agree? To a life without love? A life without him?

She blinked away the tears swimming in her eyes. "Yes. I…I'll agree to your terms."

The relief at her decision was plain on his face. "You won't regret it, Caroline. I promise."

She shrugged from his grasp. Inside, her heart continued to beat, but slowly, insidiously, it hardened and turned to stone. She'd have a marriage in name only. She'd been a fool to hope. Nothing felt right. Nothing at all.

The next morning, she dressed in her best gown—the mint-green one with gigot sleeves and the deep green bodice. She called for the maid to fix her hair high on her head, and thread it with a matching green ribbon. When she descended the stairs, a look of admiration passed over Brandon's face. He wore black pants and a white linen shirt. With his hair wet and slicked back, he was the handsomest man she'd ever seen.

Beside him, Victoria waited. "Dressed so elegantly, you two are sure to set people talking in town. Thank you for seeing to the things I need for my wedding."

Apparently Brandon hadn't told her the true reason for their trip into Bexar. Victoria looked curious, but held her questions, too well-mannered to pry.

The ride into Bexar on the rutted wagon trail was bumpy and rough. Caroline's insides were jarred into new positions and she wondered that the baby didn't come then and there.

Brandon pointed out the charred remains of the Svendsons' barn as they passed. The place looked deserted. Again, Caroline wondered what drove a man to try making a go of it in this desolate territory where no law and nothing could protect him. Finally, after two hours, the sun-bleached walls of the fort came into view.

They passed the Catholic church and Brandon pulled the wagon to a stop in front of a small, square adobe building. He helped her down from the buckboard.

"This is Catholic land. We would have to convert for the priest to marry us. I know you'd prefer a church wedding…"

A sinking sensation filled her. "Who will marry us then?"

"The colonel for the fort." Brandon tucked her hand in his arm, holding tight as though he suspected she might back out at the last moment, and escorted her into the office.

Colonel Parker was a slight, graying man who looked up from his desk when they entered the one-room building. He greeted their interruption with a distinct air of distraction.

It wasn't how she'd pictured her wedding. Her girlish heart had dreamed of a ceremony at the gazebo in White Point Gardens with a proliferation of blooming flowers and the blue waters of the harbor stretched out behind her. Here in this dusty town, with clucking chickens and rutting pigs just outside the door, she was surrounded by stucco walls. Her chest tightened. Everything here was foreign and strange from the pistol on Brandon's hip to the brusque manner of the colonel as he removed a worn leather Bible from his desk drawer.

She had never felt so out of place in all her life. Perhaps Brandon was right and she didn't belong here at all.

Brandon stepped closer and took her hands in his. Her world narrowed to his face, the serious look in his eyes and the tenseness in his jaw. To marry him is what she wanted—had always wanted. The rest—this awful room, her worries about his spells, the baby and their future—she would have to face later. "I am ready."

Was it possible, or did his shoulders relax with her words? Even at this late hour had he been worried she would change her mind?

There was no lecture on the sanctity of marriage, no questions on whether they should wait to make sure their love was real. The colonel simply began the vows.

"Do you, Brandon Dumont, take Caroline Benét as your lawful wedded wife, to have and to hold, from this day forward, for better or for worse, for richer or poorer, in sickness and in health, to love and cherish, until death do you part."

With the words *in sickness and in health,* Brandon squeezed her hands. The change was slight but she felt it—the small pressure of his thumbs against the back of her hands. His face remained as impassive as it had been before. "I do."

The traditional words were ones she'd heard often at the weddings of her friends, but now that it came to be her time to respond to them her heart filled with resolve. She would honor them, honor the love she had for Brandon, no matter that he might send her away. She answered, "I do."

Brandon released her one hand. He dug in his pocket a moment and withdrew a gold ring. Where had that come from?

"Caroline, take this ring as a sign of my love and faithfulness in the name of the Father, the Son and the Holy Ghost." He slipped it on her finger. It fit perfectly.

Still holding her hands, Brandon lowered his lips to hers, she tilted up to touch his—soft, warm, eloquent in tenderness. She trembled and opened her eyes.

He noticed, his lips pressing together almost imperceptibly.

"Remember your vows here today," Colonel Parker said from somewhere near.

She pulled back from the kiss.

"Ahem. Doctor Dumont, you'll need to sign the certificate."

Brandon turned toward the desk. They both signed their names and Brandon paid the colonel.

"Have you heard about the Svendsons' place?" When Parker shook his head, Brandon told him what he could about the renegades. Then, after shaking hands with the colonel and thanking him, Brandon escorted her outside.

"Where?" She held out her hand with the ring.

"It's yours. I had it made back in Charleston."

Then he'd had it over five months! "But how did it come to be here?"

"I asked Franklin to bring it. I thought Jake might want it for Victoria, but he had other ideas."

"So it really is mine," she murmured, stunned.

"It was meant for you from the beginning."

She fingered the ring, twisting it slightly.

"You are pleased with it?" His breath warmed her ear.

She nodded, not trusting her voice.

They walked down the street and ate at the cantina. Her wedding meal, rather than the smoked bacon-wrapped scallops and Johnny cakes with sweet milk she'd once envisioned, ended up being something called enchiladas and almost too spicy for her to choke down. She and Brandon didn't converse much, feeling the curious stares of the bartender and cook.

After their meal, they walked down the street to the parade square. There at the bazaar tents Brandon purchased the items Victoria had requested. When finished, he told her to wait while he retrieved the buckboard.

She watched him stride away as an intense feeling of loss came over her. She didn't want to be separated from him for one moment. How could she endure the rest of her life?

The ride back to the ranch was a quiet affair. Once, when the wagon jostled violently, Brandon reined the horses to a stop and helped her down so that she could stretch her legs. By late afternoon, they reached the hacienda.

Jake strode up to hold the horses while Brandon helped her down from the buckboard. Jake's gaze landed on her ring.

"Welcome to the family." There was no smile of welcome on his face or in his voice. "Guess this is what you wanted all along."

She didn't respond. She hadn't expected anything from Jake. And exhausted from the ride, she couldn't tell if his words were simply an observation or meant to hurt her.

Juan's wife, Gertrudis, had a light early meal waiting for everyone. At the table, everyone offered their congratulations. Victoria, especially, was full of questions that Brandon fielded expertly. Caroline could hardly eat. Her stomach was in knots from the trip and from what would happen next. Would she even have a traditional wedding night like any other bride or was that lost to her, too? Finally, begging fatigue from the trip, she started to head upstairs to take a short nap.

"Señorita?" Gertrudis said softly. "I will have fresh water sent up for you. Diego and Brandon can move your things to the cabin later when you wake."

"That won't be necessary," Brandon said.

Caroline's gaze flew to his.

"But, Brandon," Victoria said. "You will want privacy for a few days."

"Caroline will be sleeping in the same room until she leaves with Franklin."

At his announcement, everyone stopped eating and stared from him to her.

"What's this all about?" Jake demanded.

"It's no one's business but our own," Brandon said, his voice harsh. "Suffice it to say that Caroline will be returning to the coast after your wedding."

"And you?"

"Nothing will change. I'll stay here—in the cabin."

"Then why did you marry?" Jake asked suspiciously.

Brandon didn't answer, yet his hesitancy spoke volumes.

"Why?" Jake asked again, this time his voice more demanding as he rose to his feet and stared at her.

"Because," Caroline began, her gaze meeting Brandon's. Would he not help her? He didn't move or say anything, by his silence agreeing to whatever she would say next. She took a deep breath to continue. Everyone was staring at her. Straightening her shoulders, she willed her voice to be calm, steady. She would get through this. "Because I'm having a baby. His baby."

The sudden quiet in the room was deafening. She felt so alone, so incredibly vulnerable. She closed her eyes to the stares of the others. It was then she heard a chair scrape and felt strong arms go around her—his arms. Relief spread through her and she leaned against his chest.

"You are having his baby and yet you are leaving?" Victoria asked. Caroline opened her eyes to see the woman frowning. "Why must you go? This land, this place is not good enough for you?"

"No...that's not it." She didn't want Victoria to think that. Didn't want her to believe that it was her desire to leave. But she couldn't say anything about Brandon's problems. He was her husband now and that position demanded her loyalty.

"Enough!" Brandon said. "No more questions. Caroline and I have our reasons."

Tired beyond belief in body and in mind, Caroline shrugged from his hold. His eyes held hers a moment and in them she saw his concern for her. It didn't matter. He didn't care enough for her to stay with him, to make a life with him. He didn't think she was strong enough. She turned her back on them and trudged up the staircase to her room.

Chapter Thirteen

Just after sunset, Caroline rose refreshed from her nap and made her way down to the dining room where she heard soft conversation. She felt stronger—better able to withstand the questions now. When she entered the room, Victoria looked up from putting finishing touches on her wedding dress. Her lips pressed together in a thin line before she nodded to a nearby seat.

Caroline sat down and picked up Victoria's wedding slippers from a nearby basket. She had embroidered seed pearls in a delicate swirling pattern on the top of one slipper last evening and now started on the second slipper. Señora Torrez sat next to her, braiding silken cords and beads to make the wedding lasso—something Victoria had said was a Spanish custom.

"I saw Diego take mugs to the cabin," Victoria said, her words clipped. "The men are drinking a toast." She did not look up from sewing buckwheat into the hem of her wedding dress—a last-minute fix in case the day of her wedding was windy.

Caroline watched for a moment and could feel the animosity coming from the woman in waves. She couldn't let things between them continue like this. Still, she wasn't ready to talk about her unusual marriage arrangement with Brandon. Although to another it must look like Brandon had married her out of duty and that leaving was her choice, there was so much more to the situation. However there was one thing she could clear up.

"I don't hate it here, Victoria. I never meant to give you that impression."

Victoria lowered her needle and material.

"Texas is different. It takes some—adjusting."

"Is it that we are not so cultured, so elegant as this place called Charleston?"

"That is not what bothers me." And she realized she meant it. "Everything is rough here, coarser. The men wear guns and even you carry a knife."

"It is necessary."

"After passing the Svendsons' place today, I realized that. But that doesn't make it easy to understand. How will these marauders be stopped? There is no law here. No justice."

"We are the law. We take care of our own."

"But how can I bring a baby into this? Medicine is scarce. What if my child gets sick?"

Victoria's gaze was steady and cool. "Then you see why we wish Brandon to stay."

Afraid her next question would be about Caroline staying, too, Caroline changed the subject. "How many will be attending your wedding?"

Frowning, Victoria answered. "Not as many as I'd hoped for. If we could have had it at my home in Laredo there would be many more cousins attending. But the most important family will be here—Juan, Gertrudis and my parents."

Caroline smiled. "And Jake."

"*Si*. He is the most important of all." A dimple showed on her cheek. She lowered her voice. "It has been hard for him to wait—now even more so since he is staying in the house with us."

A sudden vision of Brandon, impatient with desire filling his eyes, nearly choked Caroline. If Jake was anything like his brother, Victoria could look forward to an exciting wedding night. She envied her that.

Victoria studied her shrewdly. "We are both passionate by nature. Would you say that Brandon is passionate?"

Caroline swallowed. She remembered Brandon's insistent kisses, his constant desire to touch her. Her face grew hot. She wasn't used to discussing such things.

Victoria's eyes suddenly sparkled. "Ah, I see your answer before you say it." Standing, she held the dress up to herself.

"It's beautiful!" Caroline said. And it was—a white silk creation with gold accent thread on the sleeves and bodice.

"It was my mother's wedding dress. I am so proud to wear it. It means much to me." She looked lovingly at her mother, said something in Spanish and then carefully handed it off to the maid with instructions.

The candlelight in the candelabra overhead flickered wildly. A door slammed and Juan shouted in Spanish from the front of the house.

"Something's wrong," Victoria said, rising.

Dropping her needle and thread on the table, Caroline followed her into the hallway along with Señora Torrez.

The door stood wide-open and the odor of smoke, carried by the wind, poured through the front door. Juan strode toward them, a rifle in each hand, his face grim. Drawing a long dueling pistol from his belt, he handed the weapon to Victoria. "The stable is on fire. Keep the women inside!"

Gunshots sounded near the corral. Caroline jumped.

The hair on the back of her neck stood on end. What was happening?

Maria hurried from the kitchen.

A donkey bellowed in the stable and then a horse neighed. The iron gate squealed as someone passed through.

Caroline's heart thudded with each new sound.

Victoria closed the door after Juan and turned to the women. "Into the library," she said. "It will be safest there in the chance that the fire spreads. Maria? Please bring the children and Gertrudis."

Victoria ushered her mother and Caroline into the enclosed room. "Into the corner. You'll be safer." She dragged a straight-back chair to the spot for her mother.

Caroline strained her ears, trying to make sense of the noises she heard outside in the yard. Even the stretches of silence sounded ominous. What was going on and where was Brandon? Was he safe?

"What is happening, Victoria?" she finally asked in a hushed voice.

"I know as much as you. Perhaps it is *Comancheros*, perhaps it is *bandidos.*"

Alarm heightened Caroline's senses. Her thoughts raced with the image of the burned barn they'd passed earlier that day and the desolation at the ranch. She might never understand why these people stayed here in the face of such danger, yet this waiting and wondering, this cowering in the dark library was worse than actually doing something. She had to find more protection than this.

"My gun is upstairs," she said suddenly.

Victoria read her thoughts. "No!"

Ignoring her, Caroline ran from the library and up the stairs to her room. She threw open her trunk and tossed the items within aside until she came to her brother's pistol. She checked to make sure it was loaded properly and then looked about the room for anything else she might use to protect herself and the other women. Picking up a tall candlestick holder from the bedside table, she then raced back down the wide staircase and into the library.

Victoria pulled her to the corner of the room with the others. "That was very foolish." But approval gleamed in her dark brown eyes.

"What do we do now?" Caroline asked, handing off the pewter candlestick holder to Maria.

"We keep watch."

"But the men!" Caroline worried that Brandon might be in his cabin, unaware that Juan needed help, or in need of help himself.

Victoria nodded, sharing in Caroline's worry. "Stay here. I will check the window." Staying low, and ignoring her mother's hiss of dissension, she maneuvered to the side of one of the two large windows in the library. No curtains covered the glass so that with the candles in the wall sconces flickering, anyone outside could easily see into the room. She blew out the candles near her head.

Caroline crouched low in the shadows and made her way behind the settee and two large chairs to extinguish the other candles. Then she moved to Victoria and peered outside. The night was black with but a sliver of moon.

"Can you see what is happening?"

"It's too dark out there. If only the moon were full."

"Do you see a fire?"

"No. But it could be inside the stable."

As they watched, a familiar figure moved stealthily across the yard.

Victoria gripped Caroline's arm. "That's Jake."

Two figures, unrecognizable to Caroline, emerged from the stand of pines that separated the main house from the cabin. She started to point them out, but Victoria already had her pistol trained on them. The tall one glanced at the hacienda and then watched as Jake slipped through the stable door. He motioned to the other and stealthily moved in behind Jake.

With her heart pounding in her chest, Caroline raised her pistol beside Victoria's. Victoria glanced down, seeing it, and whispered, "I'll go out through the courtyard and circle around the house to come up behind those men. You stay here."

"Juan told you the same."

Victoria's brown eyes flashed. "*¡Él es mi prometido!* He may need my help."

Caroline nodded, realizing she was seeing only a small part of what the woman must have been like during the rebellion. "Go then," she whispered. "Be careful. There may be more than two."

Victoria squeezed her hand and then moved silently from the room. After she left it seemed to Caroline that they waited an eternity in the dark although it could only have been a few more minutes. She wondered if the fire had been put out, wondered who the two men were and wondered if there were more.

A shot sounded. Her heart pounded triple time. A few seconds later the large door to the stable swung wide and two horses charged through ridden by men crouched low on their backs. Caroline saw a swish of deep gold from Victoria's skirt as she ran from the courtyard gates across the dirt yard and into the barn. Caught between keeping her word to Victoria and wanting to help, Caroline hesitated on the edge of the decision.

Victoria screamed.

Caroline ran from the room, threw open the front door and raced to the barn.

Smoke filled the interior.

"Victoria?" She coughed and waved her hand in front of her face in a vain attempt to reduce the amount she inhaled. Her eyes burned and watered.

"I'm here!" Victoria's frantic voice came from a point in the darkness. "Jake is hurt. I can't move him!"

"We need to get him out of this smoke," Caroline said. "Where are you? Keep talking so that I can find you!"

A moment later Caroline bumped against a boot and nearly tripped. Jake moaned. She crouched, feeling up his leg to his hip, to his waist and then his arm. "He needs fresh air. The smoke will kill him. If you can get under that arm we can drag him outside." Victoria's dress rustled while she positioned herself. "Now."

Together they turned Jake around and dragged him out into the clean night air. When Caroline let loose, something sticky coated her fingertips. She held them to her nose. The scent of blood filled her nostrils. "He's bleeding."

"Jake!" Victoria cried out frantically. "Jake. *Háblame!*"

No sound came from his still form. Caroline felt for a pulse as she'd seen her father do countless time before. There. In his neck. Rapid but steady. "He's alive, Victoria, but we must see better to know where he's hurt. I'll run to the house and get candles."

As she rose, a form dashed around the corner of the stable.

"Jake! I couldn't catch them!" Diego yelled.

"*¡Diego! ¡Ven aquí!*" Victoria cried. "Jake's here. He's been hurt."

Diego fell to one knee at Jake's side. "*¡Dios!*"

"Where is Juan?"

"He's smothering the fire on the far side of the barn."

A moan rose from Jake.

"We should take him to the house," Caroline said. "Can you move him? I'll go get Brandon."

"*Si,* Señorita Caroline."

"Do you have your gun?" Victoria asked. "Those men may still be near."

"Yes."

Victoria reached out and grasped her hand. A tremble shuddered through her.

"I'll hurry," Caroline said, and turned quickly away.

Moonlight slashed through the branches overhead as she ran down the path through the trees. The figure of a man loomed before her. Gasping for air, she stopped and clutched the gun in front of her with both hands, aiming at the shadow.

"Caroline. Wait! It's me."

She lowered the weapon. "Brandon. Thank God."

Immediately he was at her side, taking the gun from her shaking hands. "I heard a shot. What's going on?"

"Jake's been hurt!"

The curiosity on his face quickly dissolved into concern for his brother. "Where is he? What's happened?"

"He's bleeding. His chest, I think. Diego is carrying him to the house now. He tried to stop two men from stealing the horses."

Brandon grabbed her arm. "Stay near me. Whoever shot him may still be around." He crouched low and kept a firm grip on her until she was across the yard with him and safely inside the big house.

In the library, Diego laid Jake on the long settee that sat across from the fireplace. Victoria knelt beside him and, grabbing the knife from her garter, cut away Jake's shirt from his wound. Fresh blood ran from a hole in the skin, down his chest. She staunched it with her lace handkerchief which quickly turned from white to red.

Brandon stopped short when he saw his brother.

Jake lay quiet, pale and ashen. His breath was so shallow that the rise and fall of his chest as he breathed was barely discernible. Slowly he opened his eyes.

Victoria looked up at Brandon, meeting his gaze even as tears stained her cheeks. The fear Caroline saw in their depths gripped her heart like a cold band of steel.

Why wasn't Brandon doing something? Caroline glanced at him. He hadn't moved, but stared at his brother, caught up somewhere in his thoughts.

Diego stepped back. "I'll find Juan and see about the fire."

Brandon started, jarred at the sound of Diego's voice. He nodded, then knelt beside his brother and checked his pulse, much like Caroline had done. "Are you hurt anywhere besides your shoulder?"

Jake grimaced, his lips a tight line with the pain. "My head."

Brandon felt over his brother's scalp. "You have a lump the size of a walnut. This is the wrong angle for a fall. Someone struck you."

Carefully he peeled the shirt off Jake's shoulder, the sound of tearing fabric loud in the hushed library. He examined the bullet hole. Caroline remembered that oozing was good—pulsing blood would indicate an artery had been hit which could have been fatal.

"Can you move your arm? Grip?" He took Jake's hand from Victoria's hold. Caroline watched as Jake tried to squeeze Brandon's hand without success. A slight tremor shook Brandon's hand. Her imagination, surely. Or perhaps it was Jake that was shaking from the pain in his shoulder or the effort to squeeze Brandon's hand. Any number of reasons—

"Well, that's the pits," Jake said, training bleary eyes on his brother. "Can't have a wedding night without two good arms to hug my lady."

A sob escaped Victoria as she bent to kiss Jake on his temple. *"Te quiero."*

"You too, darlin'." His mouth quirked up in a smile and then he raised his gaze ever so slightly to Brandon. "Gotta come out."

Brandon took a deep breath. "Yes."

"Then get to it."

Brandon rose. "Franklin. Let's move him to the table in the kitchen. I'll work on him there."

Caroline pulled Victoria away and helped her stand. "Do you have any whiskey? Something to help blunt the pain?"

Victoria nodded numbly, and motioned to Maria to bring the liquor. Franklin and Brandon helped Jake to his feet and half walked, half dragged him to the kitchen. Once there he took a long gulp from the bottle of mescal and then stretched out on the long center table used for preparing meals. Señora Torrez placed a blanket beneath his head.

Brandon rummaged through the kitchen drawers, taking out a small knife, a spoon, two forks. "I need you to get your sewing basket, Victoria," he said, without looking up.

"But Brandon," Caroline said when she took stock of the things on the table. "What about your surgical instruments? Your father's instruments?"

"They were taken in the war. I'll have to improvise."

She saw nothing on the table that could be of service. "But your forceps, your retractors! How—"

"The bullet has to come out," he said. Frustration filled his voice. "I don't have a choice."

Caroline glanced back at Jake and found that what Brandon said was true—bleeding continued despite the pressure bandage Franklin applied to the wound. It was then she noticed Brandon was nearly as pale as his patient. A sheen of sweat coated his forehead.

He was nervous, she suddenly realized. She looked again at his hands.

And beginning to shake.

She couldn't deny it now. The tell-tale evidence was too obvious. A fine vibration seemed to hum through his entire body. In Charleston, his nerves had been as steady as the ticking of a grandfather clock. Steady and sure. He'd handled his cases with care and precision—and confidence. Perhaps his nervousness stemmed from the fact that this was someone close to him—his brother rather than a stranger.

She looked at the others in the room and saw that their concern was focused on Jake, not Brandon. That was good. There was no reason for them to have more worry heaped upon their fear for Jake. Somehow, Brandon must get through this. How could she help? She tried to think what her father had needed at times for his surgeries.

"Maria," she said, turning to the wide-eyed cook. "We'll need warm water to wash out the wound. Please put a pot on the stove. Gertrudis? We need bandages, cloths and towels to soak up the bl…to place beneath his arm and shoulder for support. Señora Torrez? If you could see to turning down a bed for him and lighting the lamp in a room. He'll need rest when Brandon is through."

The women left to do her bidding. As they were occupied, she turned to Victoria. "You'll have to hold his arm. Can you do it?"

Victoria nodded, her face grim but determined.

Caroline stood before Brandon. "What else do you need?"

He looked at her, his eyes clouded with confusion. "There's so much blood."

Caroline looked once more at Jake, assessing his wound. "Some," she said cautiously. "A normal amount for such a bullet I suspect. Less than the longhorn we encountered, a little more than the boy with the fishhook. I've seen similar when at my father's side." She moved closer, lowering her voice so only he could hear. "A normal amount, Brandon. What do you see?"

"A lake. It covers everything."

Shocked, Caroline tried to keep from letting it show in her expression. It was important to stay focused on what Jake needed at this moment.

"I tell myself it isn't real."

"You're right. It isn't. And your brother needs you."

He nodded, his eyes tormented pools of indecision beneath dark brows. "If I nick an artery, I could kill him."

"If you do nothing, he's already dead. The wound will fester."

"I know."

"That's Jake. Your only brother. He moved mountains to get to you here in Texas. You're a good doctor—the best I know and he needs you now."

She suddenly noticed Victoria listening intently and she rotated Brandon so that his back was to her. "You can do this, Brandon. You're a brilliant surgeon. I'm sure you've managed much worse situations than this. Now tell me, what is the first step?"

Still he hesitated and stared at Jake's shoulder, lost in a fog his mind had manufactured without his consent. "No more than the ordinary amount?" he whispered.

"No more," she said. She pinched his hand and forced a sharpness to her voice. "Now, Brandon."

His eyes cleared slightly.

She handed him a sharp knife and grasped his fingers once again, trying to infuse him with her confidence.

Brandon squeezed his eyes shut and when he opened them they seemed clearer, the purpose in them stronger. He moved close and poised the knife above the wound. Jake watched him steadily. "Brace yourself." At Jake's brief nod, Brandon motioned to Victoria. "Hold him tight—and don't faint on me, Señorita Torrez."

Caroline moved the lantern, holding it high to afford the best light for the operation. She dabbed the blood away from Jake's arm.

Brandon probed for the bullet. At the same time Jake stiffened with pain. Even though he'd been less than cordial to her, her heart went out to him. Jake kept his gaze trained on his brother, his jaw tightening with each new probe of the knife. Then she felt his gaze slide to her. The usual cynical look she had come to expect was displaced by his pain. However, she thought she saw something more. What—she wasn't sure.

More blood oozed up, blocking Brandon's view. Caroline dabbed the blood away. Whatever Jake thought of her, it didn't matter now. He had to come through this—for Victoria, and for Brandon, too. Brandon would never recover if something should happen here and Jake didn't pull through. She met Jake's gaze once more, watching him tense for a final time before his eyes closed and he went limp.

Victoria froze. "Is he…?"

Brandon pressed his bloodied fingers against Jake's neck. "He's passed out. A blessing for him. I'll need the spoon," he said to Caroline.

She handed it to him, wondering at its use. The bowled end was entirely too large to fit into Jake's wound. He flipped the spoon around and inserted the handle, scooping down with it. "I see the bullet," he said. "Got it!" He dragged the plug out quickly. "Pressure," he said.

Caroline wadded a clean cloth against the newly flowing blood.

"Needle."

Maria handed a threaded needle to him and he used it to tie off something deep inside the opening, then he sewed shut the edges of Jake's skin. He pressed a new wad of cloth against the wound and wrapped strips around Jake's shoulder to hold it firmly in place.

"Should we move him?" Franklin asked.

"Not now," Brandon said, moving to the stove to rinse the blood from his hands. "Give the blood a moment to clot. When he comes around will be soon enough. He's too heavy to get up the stairs at the moment.

"Stay with him," he told Victoria. "He shouldn't be left alone."

"Where else would I be?" She grabbed his hands in hers and pressed them to her wet cheek. "*Muchos gracias,* Brandon."

He took a deep breath. "I'm going to find out who did this." He left the room without so much as a glance at Caroline.

Startled at his abrupt exit, Caroline followed. She caught up to him in the library.

"I thought you were going to find Juan?"

Brandon ran a hand through his thick hair. "I had to get out of there," he admitted. "When I think about how close that bullet was to his heart vessels. Another inch…" He shuddered and sank down on the settee, staring at his hands. "Please, Caroline. Close the door."

She did as he asked, then stood at the door, guarding it from intruders, and watched the trembling overtake his hands. She wanted to run to him and grab his hands, forcing them to stop shaking, but didn't.

"It's nerves. I can't stop it from happening," he said, not meeting her eyes. He turned his hands palm up. "Ever since spending time in prison this happens. Guess I'd make a good subject to study."

She took a step toward him and then stopped. He didn't need mothering and wouldn't want it. "You did an excellent job."

"Maybe. I'll know more in a day or so, once Jake is up." He rose to his feet and took a deep breath. "It's better now. I need to see Juan and Diego." He started to say more and then thought better of it. Clamping his jaw tight, he strode through the door.

"Caroline!" Victoria called from the kitchen. "Help me, *por favor!*"

Caroline rushed into the kitchen. Jake moaned. He was coming to his senses. Victoria held down his shoulder, trying to keep him quiet as he thrashed about, the liquor still in his system. Maria and Señora Torrez held his legs so that he wouldn't wrench himself off the table.

"Franklin, let's get him up to his room," Caroline said. "Then we can give him more mescal. Take care not to pull the stitches."

Caroline, being larger than Victoria, moved to take Jake's injured left side and with Franklin on his right, they eased him into a sitting position. She spoke to him gently as he blearily came to, his face pale and pasty. Then ever so slowly, they helped him stand and make his way up to the bedroom upstairs. Victoria gave him another gulp of strong spirits, and then he sprawled onto the bed and closed his eyes once more.

Chapter Fourteen

The entryway door slammed open. Caroline stepped to the banister. Juan stood in the open foyer. "We're up here, Señor Seguín."

He looked up, his face dark with soot. It was then that Caroline remembered the smoke she'd smelled earlier and started down the stairs. "Is the fire out?"

"Sí," he said, taking out a cloth and wiping the black from his face. "Gertrudis? The children?"

"They are safe," Victoria said, coming from Jake's room and, along with Franklin, following Caroline down the stairs.

Diego and Brandon strode inside, rifles in their hands. The determined looks on their faces set her on edge.

"Ready, Juan," Diego said from the door.

Caroline frowned. "Ready for what?"

"To go after the men who did this. They can't be far," Diego answered.

"In the dark? How can you track them?" And hadn't there been enough excitement for one night?

"We'll do what we can." Brandon held Franklin's gaze. "Keep the house shut and pistols close at hand."

Franklin nodded, understanding his place in defending the ranch and keeping the women safe while they were gone.

The plan sounded ludicrous to Caroline. How could they possibly see anything? "Oh, no...those men could be waiting for you. They could easily ambush you in the dark. Why can't it wait until morning?"

"By morning they may be too far away," Brandon answered.

"Good! Let them stay there!" She didn't care if she was interfering. What they proposed was crazy.

"They took two good horses," Juan said. "I must try to get them back."

Caroline knew on a gut level that the men had to do something. They wouldn't sit and let this happen to them without a fight. That's how men were. But she didn't have to like it. Any one of them could be hurt—could be killed!

"It's not just about the horses," Brandon said. "It's about what they did to Jake. About what they could have done to any one of you or Juan's children. They have to be stopped. They can't go unchallenged or they'll do it again and again. As long as they get away with it, they will steal from and hurt good people. Our neighbors."

"Can't the law handle it now?" she asked, although her hope was growing dim that they'd put off this fool-hardy quest.

"There is no law close enough to help. And we're not going to cower in the house with the women," Brandon said. "It's how things are done here."

"In Texas," she said.

"Yes. In Texas." He stepped close to her and lowered his voice. "Enough discussion. Remember, you are only a guest here."

The hope that she could change their minds drained

from her body like sand through a sieve. She'd lost. "Go, then. Just go. You'll do what you want to anyway."

With one more glance at Franklin, Brandon spun around and joined the men.

Caroline slammed the door after them, clenched her fists and turned. Only then did she realize that Victoria had witnessed her lack of composure. The woman stood frozen to her spot at the base of the stairway, her gaze probing as she took in Caroline.

"They won't do anything foolish. You must remember that they've been through a lot together."

Caroline dragged in a deep breath and swiped at her eyes. Victoria's face blurred before her. How could she explain all that was inside her? Her chest tightened with emotion. She loved him. She hadn't meant to, didn't want to. It made everything so much more difficult, more complicated. But there it was. In spite of his problems, in spite of the fact he wanted her to leave, in spite of everything, she still loved him.

"I…" She tried to voice her thoughts and couldn't.

"I know," Victoria said with a small smile. "We have a long night ahead of us, you and I. Let's get some tea."

The bandits headed southwest. Brandon tracked them to the bend in the river near the crossing. He didn't want to think about what had happened with Caroline, but as time dragged on and there were no more signs of the renegades, thoughts of her invaded his mind.

She just didn't understand how things were here. You couldn't depend on anyone else helping you. You had to do things yourself and take the consequences as they came. Of all people, he knew that. Look at his injury—a consequence from running headlong into the Texian rebellion.

Caroline was smart and eventually would figure things

out. Now that she knew of his spells, she'd realize that he couldn't possibly be a husband to her, that he was probably going crazy and it would be too risky to have him around a baby or around her. She'd understand now that he couldn't doctor much longer. It was sheer luck that he hadn't hurt Jake during the surgery.

"I think we lost them," Diego said. He'd been walking rather than riding his horse for the past half hour and studying the ground for tracks.

"They were desperate enough to steal the horses from us while we were all at the hacienda, which means they are probably crazy enough to try to ford the river even though the water level is still high," Juan said. "They won't care if they kill the horses in the process."

"Hopefully they'll fall in and the horses will find their way back home," Brandon said.

Diego mounted. "Start again in the morning?"

Juan nodded and they turned their mounts toward the hacienda.

Near to midnight, they arrived at the ranch. After stabling their horses, Diego and Juan strode to the big house. Brandon stood at the corral and stared at the hacienda. The odor of smoke still lingered in the air although the fire had been put out hours ago. All the windows were dark with the exception of Jake's room where a candle burned, the flickering light dancing through the window. He imagined Victoria sat by Jake's side. They'd nearly lost each other during the rebellion. If their present course continued, their lives would never be smooth. Yet he still envied them. They clung to each other, put each other first in their lives. Their love would be well served.

It was a life he yearned for, a life he could never have. He looked up at Caroline's dark room and wondered if she

slept. This was her wedding night—*his* wedding night…
What would happen if he went to her? Would she welcome
him or turn him away? He had a feeling he could change
her mind easily enough—with a touch, with a kiss, her
body responded to him—but would it be the right thing to
do? And could he ever let her go afterward? He dragged
his hand through his hair, debating to himself. It was best
not to succumb to the temptation, best to keep his distance
until she left for good.

He started to close the stable door when something
flashed silver in the straw piled by the wall. Probably just
shine from a bridle that had fallen from its hook, he
figured, and stepped inside to hang it back up.

It wasn't a bridle, but a knife. He picked it up slowly and
brushed off the few straws that clung to the muddy blade,
studying the handle, the familiar carved crest in the ivory.

His knife—he'd carried it with him to Texas. What the
hell was it doing here? The memory of the prison rushed
back at him—the frigid cold, the constant hunger and the
ill treatment by his guards. A shiver went through him
even now, in the comfort of the warm July night.

He wiped the mud from the blade with his thumb. One
of the bandits must have dropped it. That seemed the only
explanation. He shuffled through the straw and dirt with
his foot, looking for clues as he tried to remember who had
taken the knife from him initially. Most likely it had
changed hands several times. Odd for it to show up here.

Finally, unable to come up with any more information,
he headed for his cabin. In the morning with daylight he'd
check again.

Chapter Fifteen

At dawn, Caroline rose, threw a light quilt over her shoulders and peeked in on Victoria. She sat in the rocking chair at Jake's bedside, her head lolling to the side, halfway between wakefulness and sleep. Jake slept on, his dark hair tousled about his head, his breathing deep and even.

"Señorita?" Caroline whispered.

Victoria roused.

"Victoria!" she said again and Victoria awoke with a start. At first disoriented, she focused on Caroline, but then her gaze swung to Jake. She leaned over and pulled the sheet up under his arms, carefully tucking it in and then checking his forehead for signs of fever.

"I'll sit with him awhile," Caroline said. "You should get some rest."

Victoria stretched, her hand to the back of her neck, and then rose from her chair. "I am tired." A look of concern passed over her delicate features. "But you…you are expecting a *bebé*. How did you sleep?"

"Not well." Caroline grimaced. "Some. I heard the men come back around midnight."

"As did I. They left again just now to look for signs of the bandits."

"Already? I didn't hear a thing."

"Good. Then you slept better than you realize."

"Did...did Brandon check on him? Has Jake been all right through the night?"

"*Si.* He was restless once, but has been sleeping now for a few hours."

Jake stirred and then quieted once more.

Victoria stood and motioned for Caroline to join her at the door. "You don't want to leave Brandon, do you? I see that now—in your eyes."

Caroline took a deep breath. "No."

"Then why must you?"

"It's complicated."

"Tell me," Victoria urged.

Caroline hesitated. She did want to talk about it... almost felt like she might explode if she didn't.

"Whatever Jake may think, I didn't come here to corner Brandon into marriage. I just thought he should know about the child, that it existed. And I needed his help." She struggled to collect her thoughts, to say what needed saying coherently.

"He left me, Victoria. If he'd loved me, he never would have gone. I found out that I was going to have a baby the day word arrived of the fall of the Alamo. I believed Brandon was dead."

Victoria waited quietly.

Her frustration ebbed and Caroline continued, calmer now. "I suppose, if I am to be honest about it, I did hope that on coming here that he would marry me. I was frightened of what others would say, how I'd be treated if I had the baby without being married."

"It is understandable."

"But I would never force him," she hurried to say. "How could I? It is not something a woman can do to a man."

"But surely you had a plan?"

"Yes—to persuade him to come back to Charleston, but I see now that that is impossible. He wants to make his home here." She tapped her hand on the banister, her thoughts going back a few days to when she first arrived, before she knew what was happening to Brandon.

"I want to keep this baby. Once it is born, my parents will not let me bring it home. They've already told me so. I...I didn't know how I would support it. That's why I came here—to see if Brandon would help me."

"Of course he would help! This *bebé* is his own flesh and blood! I don't understand why you must go, then. It is obvious he cares for you."

But not enough. "I don't belong here—at least according to him. You heard him last night. He doesn't think I'm strong enough to make a go of it in Texas."

Caroline couldn't explain about the spells or explain about the true reason Brandon didn't want her to stay, but perhaps Victoria had already noticed. Perhaps she could help.

"I know you did not know Brandon before the rebellion, but have you noticed anything...unusual...about him?"

"Other than his limp? No. He is different than Jake. More serious. Sometimes he thinks too much and it gets him in trouble." The corner of Victoria's mouth quirked up. "Sometimes Jake acts too quickly and that gets *him* in trouble."

Caroline smiled, thinking if the brothers' temperaments had been the opposite Brandon would have been the one who was shot and lying in the bed now. "Has Jake said anything?"

Victoria's eyes clouded. "No. But in many ways I am an outsider between those two."

"At his father's funeral Brandon felt like everyone in his family had deserted him—first his mother left, then Jake took off and then his father died. At the time, I was glad to be there for him."

Victoria met her gaze. "And now he has the chance for a family and he is sending you away."

Caroline nodded, miserable at the thought.

"Perhaps he is afraid to care again. Afraid he'll lose what he cares for."

"He can't lose what he never had."

Victoria's gaze swept down to Caroline's tummy. "Oh, I think he had you."

A blush heated her face. "You are not so proper as I first suspected, Señorita Torrez."

Victoria's eyes filled with merriment. "There are many things you do not know about me, but I think we understand each other better now."

Suddenly Caroline felt the baby kick. She straightened and cradled her stomach with her free hand. "He moved!"

Victoria's smile turned gentle. "Are you frightened?"

"Yes," Caroline answered truthfully. "And happy all at the same time."

"The baby will be here before you know it. Will you have a *dueña* to help at the birthing?"

"What is that?"

"A woman to help at the time the child comes."

"I—I don't know. I suppose a midwife will help."

"But you will have a friend…someone to care for you, to be there with you."

Caroline shook her head. She'd have strangers attending her at a time when she should have family and friends near—when she should have Brandon near. "My aunt will help, but I don't know her well. She's never had children."

Victoria frowned. "You must have—"

A low moan came from Jake as he shifted into a new position. Caroline lowered her voice. "Are you still planning to go through with the ceremony?"

"Yes. If it is what Jake wants."

Caroline nodded. "He's strong. He'll pull through."

Victoria yawned once more.

"Go and lay down." Caroline squeezed her hand. "You are the one who is exhausted. I'll sit with Jake awhile."

"Just a few hours. And you will call me if he wakes?"

"Of course."

"Gracias." Victoria gave a tired smile and tiptoed down the hall.

Caroline pulled the quilt about her tighter and slid into the rocking chair that Victoria had vacated. Jake seemed to be sleeping well, though his breathing sounded more rapid than previously and he'd changed positions—turning from his back to his side. With the amount of alcohol he'd ingested he'd likely sleep until noon. She watched him a moment. In his own way he was as handsome as Brandon—a bit rougher and unrefined perhaps. She wished she were on better terms with him.

She rocked back and forth slowly, the movement somehow comforting, her thoughts on all that Victoria had said. Daylight slowly changed the gray room to a sandwashed white color. The shadows in the corners grew lighter and made her wish the shadows in her life could evaporate as easily.

Drowsy with the rocking, she was nearly asleep when she felt another flutter low in her abdomen. Her hand flew to the spot to cradle it as a warm glow filled her. For a moment, for now, she would enjoy knowing she carried Brandon's child, enjoy knowing it kicked and squirmed inside, strengthening its little body. It would be smart, of course. There was no question regarding its intelligence with such a smart father.

And strong. She remembered how strong Brandon had been, swimming the channel to win the chance to take her home. His powerful arms had sliced through the water, hardly displacing a drop and yet he'd beaten the other two boys in the race by at least three lengths.

A light morning breeze tickled her cheek. She opened her eyes and stared at the curtains, fluttering at the window. Day was upon her again and with it her thoughts plummeted back to earth. She rose and blew out the candle at the window.

When she returned to her seat, she glanced at Jake.

He stared at her, his eyes open, quiet, assessing.

At least the sardonic look was gone from his face. If he'd started in on her, she wouldn't want to stay, but she would have so that Victoria could rest.

"Good morning," she said cautiously.

He didn't answer immediately, but continued to stare at her.

She tried again. "How do you feel? Is there anything I can get for you?"

"Water."

His voice was scratchy—most likely burned from inhaling smoke. She reached for the mug at his bedside and supported his head while he sipped. It seemed strange, the gesture almost motherly considering their ambivalent relationship. Her fingers scraped his day-old whiskers as she held the cup.

"More?" she asked when he'd downed the entire contents and didn't seem to care when some of it dribbled down his chin and chest.

"No. Thank you."

She set the mug aside and though she thought about using the sheet to absorb the small spill on his skin, couldn't bring herself to touch him so intimately. "Anything else?"

"No."

She searched her mind for something to say. "Victoria has just gone to her room to rest. Would you like me to call her?"

"No."

Unnerved by his continued study of her, his eyes so like Brandon's, she picked up the tray at his bedside. "I'll get fresh water."

"Stay, Caroline. I want to talk to you."

At the door, she halted.

"Tell me what happened last night. My head feels like it is caught in a vise."

"You don't remember?"

"I remember getting shot. After that, it's confusing. I remember everyone standing over me—Brandon, you, Victoria. I remember the pain in my shoulder—and my head."

"Yes." She replaced the tray on his table and took her seat again in the rocker. "Men started a fire by the stable. They were stealing the horses. Juan thinks there were only two. You tried to stop them in the stable. One of them shot you. Someone hit you on the head, too."

"Did they get away?"

She nodded. "After Brandon removed the bullet from you, the men went after the bandits. They took off again early this morning, just before dawn." It seemed a bit odd, having a fairly normal conversation with Jake. He'd been so antagonistic before. She leaned forward. "Are you in much pain?"

He tested his shoulder, moving it slightly. "Nothing I can't handle."

"You turned through the night, and the bleeding didn't

start again. That's a good sign. Brandon says you should be fine." *As long as infection didn't set in,* was what he'd said, but Caroline didn't want to load that on Jake now. With his hard life he was well aware of that possibility. "You had a lot of liquor."

Again he was watching her—contemplating her.

Did he need something? Perhaps—did he need to relieve himself? "If you need to use the chamber pot, I…I'll see if I can get Franklin to help." Her cheeks grew warm at the mention of the device.

An amused look passed over his face. "Not just now."

If he felt like talking, she was willing enough. She had never *wished* to be at odds with him.

"I saw it," he said finally. "What you mentioned the other day at the cabin."

She held her breath, letting him gather his thoughts to continue. She was certain Brandon didn't want anyone knowing about his problem, especially Jake, so she wouldn't be the one to blurt anything out.

His brow furrowed. "He hesitated. He's never done that before. Never. The few times I've seen him doctorin', he's always been sure and direct. Fast."

"That's one of the reasons my father offered him the position in Charleston. He's very good at what he does."

"I can see how that would come about. Matter of fact here in Texas he got a name for himself once the troops learned he was a doctor. They depended on him to be quick—especially with amputations. He could cut off a leg in less than a minute. Clean, too. There was less pain that way."

Just imagining what Brandon had had to go through made her stomach roil. Her face must have turned a shade of green, because Jake suddenly clamped his mouth shut. After a moment he continued.

"Sorry. I shouldn't have said that, not to someone in your condition. I just assumed you were used to such things with your father being a doctor and all."

"Does one get used to such things?" She shivered and hugged herself.

"Some things. But not all." His eyes narrowed. "Are you all right?"

She waved away his concern, even though it was the first show of compassion she'd had from him. At this point, figuring out what was going on with Brandon was more important than the nature of her interminably queasy stomach. "It may have been the fact that he was operating on you—his brother. I'm sure that would give anyone pause."

"Do you really believe that?"

She sighed. "No…no. I don't."

"Be honest with me, Caroline. You owe him—and me that much."

She blinked, and a tear escaped.

"Now don't go soft on me," Jake said gruffly. "I want to sort out what went on with Brandon last night. Apparently this has happened before. You've seen it. That's why you said something at the cabin. I just didn't want to hear you."

It wasn't exactly an apology. Few men were good at apologizing, but at least it was an acknowledgment that he'd been rude. "You and I have been at odds for most of our acquaintance."

"Chalk it up to not understanding women. Victoria says I have a long way to go but she's determined to teach me."

Caroline allowed herself a small smile. If anyone could tame this man, it was Victoria.

"Franklin is a good judge of character. I should have been suspicious when he suddenly changed his opinion of you. I'm beginning to see that he was right. There is more to you than just a pretty face. Especially now." He chuckled as his words took on new meaning, and then stopped abruptly when a cough erupted. He grimaced in pain. "Damn smoke. Water. Please."

He had to wait until he could speak without coughing.

"So the question is—why is my brother making you leave? And don't give me that 'I'm not strong enough mash.' You are tough or you wouldn't be here."

"You accept things so quickly. Why does Brandon have to be complicated?"

"Soon as I'm able, I'll knock some sense into him," he said gruffly. "In case you haven't noticed, he thinks way too much."

"I have noticed that tendency," she said teasingly, as though being smart was a deficiency. It is what made Brandon a good doctor. It is who he was. And it's what she loved about him—among other things.

"Don't give up on him, Caroline. He needs you whether he knows it or not. I don't understand exactly what is going on inside him, but I do know you are forcing him to figure it out—something he hasn't done since I found him in that prison."

Jake's expression grew serious. "Something happened in Goliad. He doesn't talk about it. Yet I know it weighs heavy on his mind."

"Victoria said you found him there."

"I found him sick and starving. He won't want to talk about it. But maybe he needs to."

Jake's words stayed with her after she relinquished his care to Franklin and went downstairs to breakfast. During her coffee with Gertrudis and her children, the men returned to the hacienda after searching for signs of the renegades. She heard the frustration in their voices as they left their mounts in the corral and strode up to the big house. Although Diego and Juan joined her, Brandon did not come inside.

Probably to avoid seeing her.

After eating, she walked outside to examine the damage to the stable. The fire, started by the bandits as a diversion, had worked. It was only due to the recent heavy rains that the fire hadn't flared out of control and whipped through the entire stable to destroy it. The bandits had struck it on the shaded northern side of the barn where it had smoldered and smoked more than it had burned. A cold blackened ring of pine needles marked the spot, which was muddy now from the water Juan had used to douse the fire last night.

She walked around the side of the barn. The path through the trees started to her right. She stared at it, mentally following each bend, each exposed root and low-hanging branch, to its end where the cabin stood in the small clearing. Brandon was there, probably eating his breakfast alone. Did he feel any urge to speak with her? Anything at all?

Well, she refused to seek him out. He'd left her alone on her wedding night. That spoke volumes.

With a frustrated sigh, she turned and walked around to the front of the stable. Slipping through the large door, she checked to see which horses remained. The two geldings from Charleston were in their stalls and Victoria's small mare, too. The young filly Diego had been working with was also in her stall. The thieves had escaped with the stallion Juan had hoped to use for stud and another large horse.

At least the stable hadn't burned to the ground. There was that.

The morning dishes had been cleared by the time she returned to the house, determined to help Victoria with the wedding preparations. With only two days left, there was still much to do. She sat down at the massive oak table, and took up Victoria's slipper. It would only take a few more stitches to finish it and then she would begin making favors for the guests that would attend the festivities.

Chapter Sixteen

Brandon rode to the Svendson ranch that afternoon. Lars Svendson was a Swede who had staked his claim here with his wife and young family three years ago. The place was much smaller than the Seguín ranch and Lars worked hard to sustain it, looking forward to the time his sons would be old enough to help him.

The place appeared deserted, but then he saw Lars striding from the direction of the hog pen with an empty bucket in one hand, a rifle in the other. He wore a cotton shirt that had sweat stains at the armpits, and dungarees, blackened from working among the soot and ashes.

Brandon dismounted and tied his horse to the front porch railing. He unfastened his cane from the saddle and walked out to meet him.

Lars deposited his bucket on the ground and shook Brandon's hand. "What brings you here, Doc?"

"Same trouble. Some men stole two of Seguín's horses last night."

"Everyone all right?"

"Jake was shot trying to stop them."

Lars shook his head. "How is he?"

"Mending. I got the bullet out." He glanced down at Lars's gun. "Not taking any chances."

"It's good I don't if they are still in the area."

"I'm pretty sure it was the same men. They went after the stable first, just like here. We ran them off before they got in the house. Did you get a good look at them?"

Lars shook his head. "My wife did. There were three. One older with gray hair, short, no meat on him. The other two were young—in their twenties—and tall as me. Black hair. One tied his back like a Comanche, but he was Mexican."

"They speak any English?"

"Some." He rubbed his jaw where a bruise was turning from purple to green. "I understood what they wanted enough."

"I can see that. What were they after?"

"Anything worth anything. First, they started the fire by the barn. When I ran out to check on it, they circled around and snuck into the house. Frightened my Ilse."

Brandon noticed for the first time that she hadn't come out to greet him. Usually she came quickly out the door when visitors arrived. He checked the house windows, but didn't see anyone peering from the dark interior.

Lars noticed. "She took the boys to Bexar. Wanted to be with family. Those men scared her. Grabbed her around the neck and pulled a knife."

"I'm sorry, Lars." He couldn't blame her for leaving.

"It's harder on women," Lars said. "But she'll be back with the boys. She is strong. She loves this ranch."

"What did the men take?"

"Food, blankets, canteens. What money I had. A gun. My rifle was hidden."

"What about your horses?"

"They left Betsy and Gerta alone, thank *Gott in himmel.* I don't know what I would have done if they'd taken my girls."

Brandon smiled. Lars's girls were his workhorses—shires that did the work of six saddle horses. "Your girls and their broad backs aren't easy to ride and are even harder to hide."

"*Gut* thing, too. But they did take my saddle horse." Lars chuckled, the skin crinkling at the corners of his gray eyes. "What happened at your place?"

"Juan saw two men. They used the same method—started a fire near the stable to draw the men away."

"Did they get in the house?"

Brandon shook his head. "Probably too many people. Victoria's parents are there for the wedding along with a few others. But they did take two horses."

"So, if these were the same men, they now each have a horse. They are probably far from here by now."

"Maybe. I'm not sure." From a sheath on his belt, Brandon pulled the knife he'd found in Juan's stable. "Is this the knife that threatened your wife?"

Lars took the blade and studied it. "I don't know." He turned it over in his palm. "I was trying to put out the fire when Ilse screamed. I ran in the house and one of the men hit me with a board. By the time I got to my feet, the men had gone."

"Your boys?"

"Ilse hid them in a cupboard. I tell you this, Doc…I'm just glad those men were bent on thievery and not on murderin' my family."

Brandon nodded in agreement, sure that Jake had been a sight more threatening than Lars's wife. That's why he got a bullet. Or perhaps the men were more desperate. He took the knife back from Lars. No need to tell the man the blade belonged to him. He most likely wouldn't care for that bit of news.

"Anything I can help you with here?"

A grin split the Swede's face. "Come with me."

He spent the greater part of the day helping Lars move the debris and rubble from the barn and make it habitable for his two shires again. Betsy and Gerta were a formidable team paired together to drag away the charred wood and made short work of the mess. The physical labor felt good and even with his bum leg, he felt like he pulled his weight in work. By the end of the day he was coated in sweat and fine straw dust from the new bed of straw he'd forked into the barn.

Lars walked him to his horse.

"That big brother of yours gonna be well enough to take a wife now?" Lars asked.

"I don't think anything, least of all a bullet, is going to stop Jake from marrying Victoria."

"Ya. She is a fine woman, like my Ilse. They make a good team."

"We'll see you at the house on Saturday."

"We'll be there, Doc."

With a wave, Brandon turned his horse toward the hacienda and kneed him into an easy lope. *They make a good team.* Lars's parting words echoed in his thoughts. To the big Swede, everything came in pairs and it was all about working together—his shires, his sons, and he and his wife. The confidence that Lars had in Ilse's ability to shake off the attack baffled Brandon. He'd never expect any woman to recover from something like that.

He veered west on his way to the ranch to wash the fine straw dust off in the clear pool. Thoughts of Caroline engulfed him as he dismounted and stepped to the edge of the water. She was everywhere here. He could see her rising sleepily from her rock bed, her blond hair tangled and falling down to her waist like some wood nymph from a fairy tale; her eyes widening in alarm at the descending swarm of bees and looking to him for protection; and then her hand grasping tight when he took it to jump into the clear pool.

Did they make a "good team"?

Obviously they did when it came to desires of the flesh. They couldn't seem to keep their hands off each other— at his home in Charleston or here at the pool. Even now, thinking of her, he wanted to feel her smooth skin again, feel him sliding into her warmth as he kissed away the doubts lingering in her eyes. Doubts he'd put there.

He kneeled and cupped water to splash over his arms and neck and face. The straw dust made him itch all over. Rethinking his decision to stay clothed, he removed his shirt and washed his chest and back. And then he sat down, stretching his legs out in front of him to wait for the last rays of the sun and the warm breeze to dry off his skin as he contemplated all that had happened in the past few days.

How he'd helped Jake last night was a miracle in itself. No instruments—no decent place to work. It's a wonder he hadn't pushed the plug further inside and caused more damage. Having Caroline beside him had helped. Even though his hands had started shaking sooner than usual he was able to focus. She'd somehow calmed that part of him that started his nerves to quiver.

They made a good team.

He thought of the moment he'd discovered the baby, of the soft, rounded curve of her tummy as she'd lain on her back. What was it like, he wondered, to feel it move. Would she let him put his hand on her? Let him feel it, too? Perhaps it was a silly thought, and selfish, but did having a part of himself growing inside scare her? Or…or appeal to her?

He pushed himself to his feet. *Get hold of yourself!* That he'd even had such thoughts irritated him. Of course she was scared. Any woman would be. She'd had as much choice in getting pregnant as he had in becoming a father. She'd just had longer to work through her feelings.

A father! He was going to be a father!

How could he support a family or protect them? With the visions, nightmares and shakes he had, how would he make a living? His chest constricted. So much blood on his hands. So many he couldn't save. Could he ever hope to have a normal life after what he'd been through? Did he even deserve one?

Good God—*a baby.* What the deuce was he going to do? It didn't matter whether or not they made a good team. Caroline had to leave. That hadn't changed. Was he strong enough to do what was necessary for the both of them?

A half hour later, when he rode into the ranch, the candlelight flickered through the tall windows of the dining room. Everyone was gathered at the table, finishing their meal under the wrought-iron candelabra. He stabled his horse and then entered the front door of the hacienda quietly. As he climbed the stairs to check on Jake, he listened to the animated conversation between Franklin and Juan, wishing he could join them.

Jake was sitting up in bed, sipping a hot mug of soup. Someone had concocted a sling for his arm to help keep his shoulder immobile.

"I see you are feeling better," Brandon said.

"That's a matter of perspective."

Brandon peeled back the bandage to check Jake's wound. The edges were slightly pink, but did not look inflamed. He placed a clean cloth against the skin and retied the bandage. "Looks like you might live to see your wedding."

"That's encouraging. Victoria will be pleased."

"I expect so."

Jake looked him up and down. "Haven't seen you around today. For a newly married man, you're not spending much time with your wife."

"She's not particularly happy with me."

Jake snorted. "Easy enough to see. Why don't you sit down a mite."

Brandon debated. Jake sounded ready to take him to task on a few things but Brandon didn't have anything better to do. "Guess we'll discuss things sooner or later."

"Darn right." Jake motioned to the rocker.

Brandon plopped down. "Look, she's the one who kept the small fact about her pregnancy from me until I stumbled on it for myself. You might excuse me for taking a second to adjust."

"She was nervous. You haven't exactly welcomed her with open arms. Just put it behind you."

"It's not that easy."

"Sure it is."

"Why are you suddenly defending her?"

Jake raised his brows. "I might ask you the reverse. It sounds to me like there is a lot more going on."

"What could be bigger than finding out you are going to be a father?"

"Finding out you are a mother without a ring on your finger," Jake said flatly.

Brandon rubbed his hand over his brow. "That particular problem is taken care of now."

Jake studied him. "Something is still not right here. How did you act when you got the news?"

"Like myself."

"Well, there's the mistake. You are difficult even at your best."

Brandon scowled. "Spoken like a true brother. I may have to change my toast to you and Victoria."

"You had something decent in mind?" Jake said. "Remarkable."

Brandon ignored the sarcasm and rubbed his brow. "We don't exactly come from great marriage material. I'm probably living up to our parents' expectations."

"That doesn't mean we'll repeat their mistakes. *I* don't plan to anyhow, but it looks like you are well on the way to messing things up."

"She's going back, Jake. Just leave it alone."

"Good God, Brandon! Her blue-blooded friends will destroy her back home."

"Not now. She has a ring and my last name."

"That won't stop people from talking. They're going to wonder why you didn't return with her or why she returned at all. It will create all kinds of gossip—gossip she'll have to deal with by herself."

"I'm hoping Franklin will help her there." Brandon didn't want her feelings hurt by those she considered her friends. She was angry with him now, but he was convinced that this was the best way for both of them.

"That's why her parents were so anxious to marry her off," Jake surmised. "It all makes sense now. There was no guarantee that you'd return from the fighting and as people learned of the baby, Caroline's unmarried state would be an embarrassment to them."

"From their point of view, they were just looking out for her."

"What she did—traveling all the way here—took guts.

She laid her feelings on the line with you whether you choose to acknowledge them or not. The least you can do is treat her with respect."

Guilt surfaced. He knew it hadn't been easy for Caroline and his demands had only made things worse. He dragged a hand through his hair. "I do respect her," he answered his brother. "I love her. But loving each other has never been the problem. From the first time we met, she's all I've thought about. The same can be said of her feelings for me."

"I still don't see what the problem is."

"I'm not what she needs!" Brandon gritted out the words. "I can't support a family, Jake. I can hardly support myself now."

His outburst startled Jake. "What do you mean? You have half of Father's estate waiting in Charleston for you. If you wanted, you could go back and take up father's place there. His patients were loyal to him. And you're the best doctor west of the Mississippi River. You're already making a name for yourself here. It's just a matter of time before you are earning your livelihood no matter where you live."

Before he'd finished, Brandon was shaking his head. "It's not about the money. You don't understand."

"Then explain it."

"I can't, Jake. Just leave it alone. Caroline is going to be all right. She'll be well taken care of once I get the will adjusted to include her and the baby."

His brother shifted in bed. "Did you know she saved Franklin's life? Made some kind of a sling to hold his head above water. There's a lot more to her than I thought at first."

Brandon remembered the cloth he'd slashed away from the wheel, the one that had washed downstream. "It doesn't change anything."

Jake stared at him a moment. "I'm done, Brandon. Figure

it out for yourself, then. You always have to make things more difficult when some things are just straightforward."

Brandon stood. "I'll see you in the morning. We can go over the will with Franklin."

"Does this have something to do with your spells?"

Brandon froze.

"Caroline didn't say anything, if that has you worried. But she did ask a few days ago if I'd noticed anything strange happening with you lately. She was worried about you. I brushed her off—actually I was downright mean with her."

"So why do you think something is going on?" he asked cautiously.

"Something happened when you took out my bullet." Jake paused. "Want to talk about it?"

"No."

"Does it have something to do with Caroline leaving?"

Brandon pressed his lips together. Jake would learn of his spells eventually, but Brandon didn't want that worry on his brother's shoulders—not now, right before his wedding.

"You're among people who care about you, Brandon."

"There's nothing that needs saying."

A furrow formed between Jake's brows. "I went through hell trying to get you out of that prison, but I'd do it all again if I had to. You're my brother. If you can't be straight with me…"

Brandon took a deep breath. He just couldn't talk about his problems. It wasn't something a man did. And it wasn't like Jake, of all people, to press him. The fact that he was, made Brandon realize his brother really was worried for him.

"I'm all right. Just leave it at that. Besides, there's something else we need to discuss."

"What's that?"

"I talked to Lars Svendson today. I have an idea of who shot you."

His brother raised his brows.

"It wasn't random." Brandon pulled the knife from its sheath and twisted it for Jake to see. "Do you recognize it?"

"Father's ivory knife," Jake murmured.

"I found this in the barn. The last time I had it on me was in Goliad."

Jake looked up from the blade to him.

"I think the man was gunning for me, but shot you by accident."

"Then if you're right…"

Brandon nodded. "He'll be back."

Chapter Seventeen

The day of the wedding dawned warm and sultry. The sunlight slashed in harsh relief through the window and across the bedsheets, too bright to ignore even with closed eyelids. With a frustrated sigh, Caroline pushed the sheet off and sat up. Sleep had been impossible anyway. She had tossed and turned until the early hours of the morning, only to rise and pace the floor for another two hours—all because of Brandon.

Why couldn't he see that they belonged together? Not in name only, but in all ways? If it were pride alone that stopped him, she would have argued against him, but it wasn't just his pride. He honestly believed he was slowly going insane. To live with such a burden was incomprehensible to her. To live with it alone…how could she let him do that? He thought it better they parted than for her to witness his spells. Well, maybe that was pride, but she loved him anyway. And she would love him through any illness he might have. Wasn't it better to be together and give each other comfort than to be alone? Trying to quell her frustration by sheer will, she rose from the bed.

A horse whinnied in the stable. She glanced out her window. Diego was up extra early, attending to his chores before the festivities of the day crowded everything else out. She watched him work the filly. The horse circled the corral at his command, dust from its hooves plumed up and shimmered in the morning light. A dog barked nearby, its call answered by the long yowl of a coyote in the distance.

Guests would start arriving in the early afternoon and before that she had promised Victoria to go out to the meadow to pick flowers for the tables and for decoration in the courtyard. She slipped on her cream-colored blouse and brown skirt. Later, she would change into the green dress she'd brought with her, the one she'd worn for her own wedding. For now, she plaited her hair loosely in one long braid down her back. Her parents would be appalled that she'd relaxed her standards so much, that she didn't call the maid to help with her hair every morning, but here in the country, it made more sense to be comfortable.

Today would be difficult. Brandon would be everywhere. But it was Jake and Victoria's day. If she could just focus on that, perhaps she would make it through.

The kitchen bustled with activity and excitement for the day. Two of Maria's cousins had arrived at daybreak from a neighboring ranch to help make the wedding cake, which now sat cooling on a side table. The sweet fragrance wafted through the large room and unsettled Caroline's stomach. Rather than bother Maria, who was already harried with what needed to be done for the day, Caroline grabbed a crust of leftover bread from the cutting board and took it into the dining room.

"That is hardly enough, *señorita,*" Gertrudis said as

Caroline sat next to her youngest child. "Let me have Maria fix an egg for you."

"No, but thank you," Caroline said. "Dry toast is more to my stomach's liking this early."

"Perhaps later. You will not be shy to ask for something? You must give the baby something to eat."

Surprised at the easy reference to her baby, Caroline searched her face. Gentle brown eyes stared back at her, waiting only for an answer.

"Thank you. I will be sure to ask if I feel hungry."

"Antonio! You must eat all of that!" Gertrudis said sharply to her eldest, then leaned over and kissed her son on his forehead to soften her words.

Watching the display of affection and glancing about the large oak table at the three children, Caroline decided that, yes, Gertrudis would be much like Victoria. Accepting of Caroline's state, but cautious at first, wanting to protect what was hers.

She heard heightened voices in the kitchen and wondered who entered from the courtyard. All of her senses were on edge as she finished her toast and sipped her coffee. Then Brandon walked into the room and took a seat across from her. Although she'd heard that he had often checked on Jake's progress, it was the first she'd seen of him since their wedding day.

"Mornin'," he said, and fell silent as he ate.

The children were unusually boisterous. To get a word in edgewise among the chattering, excited voices would have been difficult. Brandon's silence seemed almost natural, except for one searching glance her way.

She couldn't help that they'd be thrown together frequently throughout the day with the wedding, but to sit here now grew increasingly difficult. "Excuse me…" She stood.

Gertrudis looked up from wiping a drip of milk from her son's chin. "Victoria said you planned to gather the flowers this morning?"

Caroline nodded.

"Would you mind if the children and I joined you? I am afraid if they stay, they will only get underfoot. And they are eager to help with the preparations."

"Of course they may come."

"Gertrudis!" Victoria called from upstairs. "I need your help!"

The woman smiled apologetically at Caroline. "Perhaps we will join you later."

Up to now, Caroline had been treated as a guest in Juan's home. Her mind had been so preoccupied with what was happening between her and Brandon that she'd ignored much of what was going on around her. She did not want to be remembered by this kind woman and her family as a thankless imposer. She would be leaving soon. It was high time she joined in and helped more—especially on a day like today.

"I'll take the children with me," she heard herself say. "That is if you are comfortable with me watching them. I'm sure you have many things to attend to today and Victoria will need your help in much of it."

"You are sure?" Gertrudis said, a hopeful look on her face.

Caroline surveyed the three fidgety youngsters surrounding her. They ranged in age from two to seven years. Could she keep them together? "I'm not sure at all, but I'll do my best."

"Children," Gertrudis addressed her brood in a no-nonsense voice. When she had their attention, she spoke in a rapid stream of Spanish. After a moment, they glanced from their mother to Caroline. The four-year-old, Josefa, smiled shyly.

"I'll help."

Caroline looked up sharply at Brandon's voice.

"Won't you have things to do with Jake?" Caroline asked.

"At the moment he's with Franklin."

"Gertrudis!" Victoria called again.

"Thank you," Gertrudis said, looking at both of them as she stood. "I will leave them in your capable hands."

Caroline watched her leave and then turned to look askance at Brandon. She didn't know what to make of his offer. Didn't know what to make of him. "I'll…I'll just get my bonnet."

After a stop in her room, she headed to the kitchen, following the sound of laughter and good-natured scolding. The room was hot from the cookstove and the bustling women. "Is there something to gather flowers in?" she asked.

Maria handed her a wide, shallow basket and shooed her from the room with a wave of her arms.

The walk to the meadow took much longer than Caroline had suspected it would due to the shorter strides of the children. Before they'd gone a hundred feet, Brandon scooped up two-year-old Juan and carried him on his shoulders. Walking behind him with the other two children, Caroline noticed that the added weight did not seem to bother his injured leg.

They followed a deer trail in single file through the pines and then Brandon moved to her side once they broke through to the tall grass. They were careful not to touch, not to bump into each other. However, the silence was soon broken—and often—by warnings to Antonio to stop running ahead and to Josefa to quit dawdling.

The meadow, as it had been every day, burst with beautiful, colorful flowers. She used a small knife she'd confiscated from the kitchen to cut through the stems. Brandon returned to her from chasing after Josefa as she wrestled with a particularly fibrous stalk.

She sighed. "This will take all day at the rate I'm going. My knife is dull as butter."

He withdrew an ivory-handled knife, carefully handing her the handle. "Don't cut yourself."

Her work went faster after that.

Antonio picked a handful of tall red phlox before announcing his palms hurt from the thick stems and he wanted to quit. Brandon tried to coerce him to pick a few more flowers but soon gave up and challenged him to a throwing match. They meandered off in search of stones.

No matter that she'd lost her crew, Caroline soon had picked a basket brimming with red, yellow and white flowers. She continued adding to her collection, wanting plenty to choose from when she returned to the house. Josefa helped by picking anything with a petal, pretty or not, and running to show Caroline each and every one. Caroline kept the girl close, worried she'd pluck a weed with thorns or needles and hurt herself.

When she had another bundle of flowers, Caroline stopped to look for Brandon and the boys. She stretched her back and gazed across the rolling carpet to the hills in the distance dotted with oaks. The warm air rustled the tall grass, creating undulating patterns while honey bees droned over the tips of the clover.

She sighed. She wanted to stay here. She wanted to raise her child here, but she couldn't stay and face Brandon every day, knowing he did not want her here. She just couldn't do it.

"Josefa! No more!" she called. "We have enough."

She looked again for Brandon and the boys. They had wandered to the edge of the meadow and Brandon no longer laughed and wrestled with Antonio and little Juan. Instead he stared at something in the trees, then searched along the ground, walking slowly through the tall grass. Finally he looked up and she caught his gaze. She waved. It was time to start back to the hacienda.

He waved back and called to Antonio. The boy raced toward her, followed by Brandon. She picked up the basket in one hand and harnessed the second pile of flowers under the same arm, and then took hold of Josefa's hand. She started off, knowing that Brandon would easily catch up.

After she'd gone several paces an odd feeling overcame her—a prickling sensation at the nape of her neck, as if she was being watched and measured. She glanced toward the line of trees. It could be anything—a bear, or cougar, or a man. Or just a silly feeling and nothing more.

Nothing like this had ever happened to her before. She couldn't ignore it. She dropped the basket and flowers. Crouching down, she pulled Josefa to her and hoisted her on her hip. She wished for a gun as she grabbed Brandon's knife from the basket and held it against her skirt, her body tense, her senses alert.

She waited, anxious for Brandon to hurry. When he finally caught up to her, relief poured through her. His gaze narrowed on her grasp of the knife and he looked up sharply, into her eyes, then across the meadow to the trees.

"I shouldn't have drifted so far off."

"It's fine now," she said, holding out the knife.

"Keep it. It won't hurt for you to have a little protection out here."

"It was probably just a silly feeling, Brandon."

He studied her face and did not look convinced. "You carry Juan—he's lighter. And the basket. I'll carry Josefa and the flowers."

"All right. I'll be able to manage, then." She couldn't help glancing once more at the trees. Her heart still pounded. Once Juan was in her arms and Josefa in his, they struck through the meadow, Brandon keeping close to her back until they arrived safe at the hacienda.

Caroline dropped the children off with their mother and then set the flowers on the long dining table. Hat in hand, Brandon watched her from the doorway. "You'll stay at the house now?"

She heard the concern in his voice and saw it in his eyes.

"What did you see up there?" she asked, keeping her voice down so the women in the kitchen would not hear. "I saw you checking the ground and the trees on the edge of the woods."

When he stepped into the room, the walls seemed to shrink in comparison to his size. "Would you believe Antonio was chasing a toad?"

"No." But she smiled anyway.

"Didn't think so."

He stood in front of her now, close. Without touching her, she felt pinned against the table. She could smell his scent, a mixture of leather and soap. "What then?"

He withdrew a silver coin from his pocket and placed it in her hand. She turned it over.

"A Spanish silver dollar?"

"A peso. Also some spilled gunpowder and an area disturbed by men. I thought it might be those who'd shot at Jake."

"But you're not thinking that now?"

"It wasn't that recent. The gunpowder was half washed away from the rain we had. Did you see anything?"

"No. Just had a strange feeling."

"Maybe it was nothing."

It hadn't felt like nothing when it came over her. It was enough to make her grasp his knife.

"What are you going to do now?" he asked.

"I'll help here at the house. I need to trim these flowers and put them in vases." She turned her back to him and began sorting the flowers.

If it was possible, he moved nearer. "Stay close," he said in her ear. He watched a moment more. She heard him take a deep breath, as though breathing her in. "I like your hair this way. Loose."

Startled, she looked for him over her shoulder but he'd already left.

The first of the guests arrived late in the afternoon as Caroline climbed the stairs to her room to change into her best dress. Juan greeted the family and then ushered them through the house to the courtyard where the ceremony would take place. She searched through her trunk and withdrew the intricate ivory comb and lace handkerchief she'd purchased in New Orleans. Then wrapping the comb in the bit of lace and tying it up with a new ribbon, she knocked lightly on Victoria's door.

"*Si?* Please come in."

Opening the door, she stopped short at the sight of Victoria kneeling with her mother. "Have you lost something?" she asked, looking about the floor, and then stepped forward to help Señora Torrez to her feet.

Victoria stood. "It our way to say a special prayer before the wedding."

"I'm sorry to interrupt. I only wished to tell you that the guests have started arriving. And also, I have something for you." She handed over her gift.

"What is this? Oh!" Victoria cried out as she unwrapped the comb. With delight on her face, she tested it in her hair and checked herself in the mirror. "It is perfect for today! *¡Gracias!*"

Her gaze swept up Caroline's clothing. She plucked a cottonwood seed pod from Caroline's braid and handed it to her. "Gertrudis has left a gown for you to wear. She thought it might be more comfortable."

Caroline turned to go when Victoria grasped her hand. "I am glad you are here to witness my marriage. Whatever happens, I am glad you came. I think Brandon is, too."

She gave Victoria a swift hug. "Thank you. Now, don't concern yourself with my problems. Today is for you and Jake. Today is your day."

A rich smile transformed Victoria's face. "My heart is so full."

Caroline left Victoria and walked down the corridor to her room. A maid curtsied as she passed in the hall and then followed her into her bedchamber. "I was sent to do your hair, *señorita.*"

Suddenly she wanted to be alone, and in a most urgent fashion. "I'm sure Victoria or Gertrudis is more in need of your help. Thank you, but I'll take care of my hair, myself." She shut her door in the girl's surprised face.

My heart is so full. Victoria's words haunted her. Would she ever know that kind of happiness? That kind of love? She swallowed hard against the lump in her throat and dragged in a shaky breath. Hot tears brimmed in her eyes. Everything between her and Brandon had been complicated from the beginning. For her, such happiness would forever be out of reach.

More guests arrived. She could hear the exclamations of delight from Juan and Gertrudis, the children talking excitedly to other boys and girls their age, and the frequent creaking of the large iron gate in the courtyard. It would not be long now and she would have to make an appearance.

She drew her hair up high on her head, twisting it into a circular pattern and then pushed two carved ebony sticks through the mass of waves to hold it in place. The dress from Gertrudis had been pressed and now lay on the bed. Caroline stroked the deep royal-blue silk. It was looser through the middle and would be more forgiving of her expanding waistline than the dress she'd brought with her. The simple style was decorated by cream-colored lace at the neckline and on the sleeves.

"Señorita! It is nearly time to start! Early candlelight is upon us!" The maid called from the other side of her door.

"Coming!" Caroline removed her skirt and blouse and washed off her perspiration at the basin. Then, after powdering herself, she changed into the blue dress. It rustled down her body, the large bow in back perfectly positioned on the bustle. The kidskin slippers she'd packed for this day still fit and so she tucked her feet into them, pinched her cheeks for color and then headed down the stairs to the courtyard.

Beside the center fountain and next to the priest, Jake stood resplendent in a white linen shirt and black pants, with a large silver buckle on his belt. He'd polished his boots, wet-combed his hair and stood holding his black hat in his hand, looking for all the world like an anxious groom. He wore a black sling on his left arm to immobilize his shoulder. Noticing her entry into the courtyard, he winked.

Brandon stood beside his brother, nearly as tall, and with finer features but for the exception of his strong jaw. His dark hair had been trimmed since this morning and slicked back, with a few wayward curls that refused to be tamed at his neck. He wore clothes similar to Jake's—the white linen shirt, the black pants, black boots. No gun belt or gun this time. He was so handsome, he stole her breath away. In his hands he carried a small brass box.

Next to him, Diego whispered something and Brandon laughed in response. Amazingly he appeared relaxed and comfortable—much like he'd been in Charleston. He glanced up from the box and his gaze collided with hers.

He stopped laughing. He didn't seem to hear Diego talking at his side. She felt as though the entire breadth of people between them had disappeared. In his eyes she saw warm appreciation as he gazed from her face to her toes.

The priest spoke to him again, drawing his attention away from her.

"You look lovely, Miss Caroline," Franklin said, coming to her side.

She tucked her hand into the crook of his arm, looking over his dark gray suit. "And you, as well. You're not sitting?"

"Not today. But let us move closer. It's not every day I see a Dumont married off. Remember, I knew Jake when he was a boy."

"Was he as independent and stubborn then as he is now?"

"Absolutely."

"What about Brandon?" she asked, thinking of the child within her.

"Ah, yes. He was much more the 'pleaser' of the two."

"I believe that is something he's gotten over." If he'd cared anything about pleasing her, she'd be staying in Texas.

"Considering his present course, I would have to agree with you." He squeezed her hand on his arm. "There are a few more days for him to come to his senses. Don't give up."

"I won't, but I am losing hope," she admitted.

Caroline looked over the people that had arrived. There were more than Victoria had expected—at least seventy men, women and children gathered under the spreading boughs of the oak. A warm, dry wind swept through the garden and rustled its leaves. Chairs from the house had been placed near the fountain for Victoria's parents and the older guests.

The priest stepped forward and those assembled quieted. A look came into Jake's eyes such as Caroline had never witnessed before and she knew that Victoria had stepped to the open gate. Turning with the others present, she beheld a vision.

Victoria walked slowly forward in the flowing cream-colored gown. Her black hair, artfully coiled on her head was set off by the ivory comb Caroline had given her and half-hidden by the long lace mantilla veil. She carried a delicate white fan edged in gold, a prayer book and a rosary, as well as a colorful bouquet of the flowers gathered that morning. Her steps sure, her eyes glowing with love and seeing only Jake, she joined him.

They knelt on a pillow as the priest made the sign of the cross over Jake's head. Gertrudis stepped forward and dropped a handful of gold coins into the priest's hands. He blessed the coins, and then gave them to Victoria, who, in turn, gave them to Jake. Jake placed them in the box that Brandon held.

The customs were unfamiliar to Caroline. She tried to follow along, but unused to the priest's Latin words, especially with the Spanish accent, she soon found her thoughts and gaze drifting inexorably to Brandon. He would see to it that she was taken care of—and the child. He'd always had a responsible nature. It showed in his relationship to his father and to his profession. He didn't do anything halfway. Pride for him, and a fierce, possessive love enveloped her. *Here*, she told her unborn child in her mind, *here is the man who is your father. He is handsome, stronger than even he can imagine, and intelligent. But more than that, he has a good heart.* She sighed, if only he would let go of his stubbornness and see that they were meant to be together.

Enjoying her unhindered view of Brandon, she realized she would carry this image with her when she left.

Juan and Gertrudis stepped forward and looped the beaded lasso around Jake's shoulders and then Victoria in a figure-eight shape. Jake said his vows in English.

The priest took the box of coins from Brandon's hands. Jake accepted the box, and in turn, presented it to Victoria, pouring the coins into her cupped hands and saying: "I pledge all my present and future goods into your care for your safekeeping." Then he set the brass box on top of the small pile of coins.

Victoria smiled and began her vows. "I, Victoria Torrez, take you, Jake Dumont, to be my husband. I promise to be true to you in good times and in bad, in sickness and in health. I will love and honor you all the days of my life." The words took on deeper meaning in light of Jake's recent injury. Caroline glanced at Brandon and caught him staring at her.

The priest removed the lasso from their shoulders and handed it to Victoria. "This cord is a symbol of the love which binds you and the vows you have made today, that you may share equally in the responsibility of marriage for the rest of your lives. You may kiss now and seal your pledge."

Jake took Victoria into his arms. The kiss, so tender and deep, made Caroline hold her breath. It was right to celebrate their love. She glanced once more at Brandon, wishing that he could see what could be theirs. He gazed on the couple, his jaw tight as the kiss ended. He was the first to step forward and offer his congratulations as the mariachi band started to play.

While Jake and Victoria received the congratulations of the closest guests, the servants began moving the chairs to the perimeter of the courtyard to create a space for dancing. With a twinkle in his eye, Diego dragged one chair into the center and motioned to Jake. Jake helped Victoria stand upon the chair. Gathering the end of her veil together, she handed the end to her husband and directed him to raise it high to form a bridge between them.

As the band began a lively tune, the children rushed forward and, holding hands to make a long, snakelike chain, danced under the bridge. They were followed by the women, and though Caroline felt a strong urge to join in, she still felt like an outsider and so held back. When the music stopped, the women stopped in place also. Victoria threw the bouquet over her head. It was caught by a young woman that Caroline did not know, who, with a wide smile, waved it in the air.

At Diego's urging, Brandon stepped forward and helped steady Victoria while Jake dived under her wedding dress. Caroline watched along with the rest of the guests, surprised that Victoria allowed the intimate thing in front of everybody. She looked at Franklin, wondering what he thought of the display and found him laughing along with the other men. Amid the good-natured taunting of the guests, Jake emerged with a rakish grin on his face and Victoria's ribbon garter between his teeth.

The men fell into line to the beat of the small band and danced between the couple. Brandon did not participate but walked over to a small table and poured himself a glass of mescal. Then he made his way around the perimeter of the guests to her.

"May I get you a drink?"

She shook her head. It was the wafting odor of food

from the kitchen that enticed her. She hadn't eaten since morning, and then only that crust of bread. She was hungry, not thirsty.

While Victoria's father gave a short speech, Caroline fought off a wave of dizziness. But when Victoria and Jake moved out to the dance floor for their first dance as a married couple, the music and their twirling bodies converged until she saw black at the edge of her vision.

"Caroline? What's wrong?" Brandon grasped her arm, steadying her.

"I…don't feel well."

"When did you last eat?"

She shook her head, trying to dislodge the cobwebs that had taken up residence in her brain.

"Franklin," Brandon said, his voice sharp as he helped her to a chair. "Bring a glass of wine and a bit of cheese."

"I'll be fine. Just give me a minute."

"Of course you will. As soon as you eat. You have to take care of yourself, Caroline."

"I do take care of myself," she said, not caring for the censure in his voice. "It's only that today has been a different sort of day with the wedding and all." She sipped the glass of wine that had materialized in front of her.

"Cheese, too," Brandon ordered. He crouched down and held a small square to her lips.

She took his offering and chewed it slowly and then swallowed. Leaning in toward his shoulder, she closed her eyes and breathed in his scent.

"Here," he said, jostling her slightly. "Have a piece of bread."

"You're being attentive tonight."

"I think the wine has gone straight to your head."

His voice was gruff, but then he slipped his arm around her shoulder. She snuggled in closer. They were married, after all.

Opening her eyes, she found that her surroundings were a bit hazy.

His gaze softened. "You look beautiful tonight. Will you save me a dance?"

"Yes," she whispered. Her entire body hummed with his nearness.

"Victoria is dancing with her father now. Juan will go next and then I am expected to dance with her," Brandon said, the corner of his mouth lifting. "I hope she is not expecting graceful."

"You are a good dancer. You'll outshine Jake."

"Can't do that." His eyes twinkled. "Not at his own wedding."

He was teasing! It had been so long since she'd heard that tone of voice from him.

"Are you feeling better now?"

"Yes. You don't need to hover."

"Maybe I want to."

He stayed beside her, quiet, until his turn came to dance. A curious emptiness filled her at his departure. She would have to get used to it, she told herself. Soon, she would be on her own.

Caroline watched him dance, envious of Victoria, remembering how it had once felt to be in his arms, to be led around the dance floor until she was deliriously dizzy, always trusting in his strong arms to keep her from falling. She had always trusted him, she realized. If only he could do the same with her now.

A shadow came between her and her view of Brandon. Jake stepped in front of her. "I think it's time we had our dance. It's traditional for relatives and your recent wedding makes you one."

"Are you feeling up to it?" she asked, worried about his wound.

He shrugged in a way that reminded her of Brandon. "Are you?" A quick grin split his face as he held out his hand. "Right now I want to talk to you—while we dance."

Charmed, she stood.

Jake whispered wickedly in her ear. "If it is a boy, you will name him after me. Right?"

To hear him say it so easily, with a trace of pride in his voice, made her relax as she placed her hand in his. "Absolutely not. Should I bear a son, he will carry Brandon's name."

Jake grinned. "I suppose that's tolerable." He turned her about the floor in the steps of the slow waltz. He was a strong dancer, but not as strong as Brandon.

Knowing she would soon be leaving the ranch, Caroline had one more thing to clear up between herself and Jake.

"If a kiss sent Brandon halfway across the country, what would giving your name to his son spur him to do?"

"You got a strong point there."

"Yes. I shudder to think on it."

Jake's expression turned serious. "Well, I imagine that reaction had a lot to do with his strong feelings for you."

"I want you to know that I am… I never meant to hurt either one of you. I'm so sorry."

His eyes clouded over. He remembered it, too. "Neither one of us knew what that would set in motion. At the time it was a lark—nothing more."

"Is there any way that you can…?"

He studied her face. "Let's put it behind us. I think we've all paid our dues."

"I would take it back if I could."

"Hey! It was a great kiss. Just the wrong man."

They finished the dance and Jake bowed. Coming up from her curtsy, Caroline said, "I misjudged you, Jake. You can be kind."

He grinned. "Don't tell anyone. I have a reputation to uphold."

"Oh, I think Victoria has seen through your reputation."

"Only the parts I let her see."

"Keep dreaming," she said with sugary sweetness. She turned to see Brandon staring at her from across the courtyard. "Thank you for the dance, Jake. Thank you for everything."

His face sobered. "Franklin plans to leave the day after tomorrow."

The sense of hope that had started building inside came crashing down. "So soon?" She couldn't keep the disappointment from her voice. That was not enough time to convince Brandon to let her stay.

"He is nervous to be alone with you in your condition," Jake continued. "He wants to make sure to get you to Virginia before traveling gets too difficult."

"I suppose I understand his position. It's just that I should like to stay longer." *As long as possible.*

"Whatever happens, Caroline, if you ever need anything, you can count on me."

"Then please talk some sense into Brandon. That's what I need." She could barely choke out the last. She was near hysteria herself, not caring if the maids heard or not.

Slightly dizzy, whether from the dancing or lack of food, she hurried from Jake's scrutiny and dashed into the kitchen. What was she going to do? Only one day left for her to change Brandon's mind!

The maids were busy making tortillas, trying to keep up

with the demands of the wedding guests. Caroline kept going, into the hall and out the front door, away from the party and music, away from the prying eyes and ears.

Moonlight illuminated the drive between the hacienda and the corral, bright enough for the pines to cast shadows. Hearing Brandon's uneven footsteps behind her, she stopped and took a deep breath of the night air. One of the horses in the stable whinnied nervously and stomped a hoof.

"You followed me," she said, turning toward him.

"Where are you off to in such a rush? Thought we had a dance."

"Oh." She'd forgotten.

"What did Jake say? Was he giving you a difficult time?"

"That Franklin plans to leave in two days, which of course means I am leaving in two days." She pressed her fingertips to her forehead. "It's just so soon."

He didn't meet her eyes.

"Please, Brandon. Don't send me away. Trust me. Trust us."

"I…can't. Caroline, be rational. The situation is complicated."

"Of course it's complicated. Life is complicated, and I want to share all of it, ups and downs, with you."

He hesitated a moment, but then shook his head. "No," he said. "You aren't facing facts."

It was hopeless. He wouldn't listen. She couldn't change his mind. She walked to the corral where Rosa trotted along the railing. "I've lost you, haven't I?"

"The person you lost died in that prison. But you'll have my name and the funds you need to raise the baby. I spoke with Franklin about it this morning. You're all set."

"But I won't have you," she said quietly, turning to face him.

Brandon raked his fingers through his hair. "Are you coming back to the party? You don't have to dance if you don't want to."

"I need a minute."

"It will be all right, Caroline."

No. It won't, she wanted to cry out.

"Do you want me to wait?"

"No. You go on. They'll wonder where you are."

She crossed her arms in front of her and turned away, waiting for him to leave. Finally she heard his boots against the packed dirt as he strode to the courtyard gate. She wouldn't go back to the party. With her emotions so brittle, she couldn't face the people there.

A horse in the stable nickered softly. The moon was already high in the eastern sky and somewhere beneath it was Charleston. Could she be happy taking up her old life? In the few days she'd been here, she knew she'd changed. Not just because of the baby, but because she looked at life in a different way. What mattered most were the people she loved. In Charleston, her life had consisted of parties and society, of picnics and charity work. Could she go back to any of that now? It all seemed so foreign to her.

She started across the dirt drive. A twig snapped behind her. She glanced toward the sound and came to an abrupt stop. A man stood at the stable door. The moonlight gleamed off the gun barrel he raised and aimed straight at her chest.

She couldn't move, couldn't breathe, couldn't scream even though that's what her mind told her to do. Fear sucked the air from her lungs. His shirt hung dirty and lopsided on his bony frame like the rags of a derelict. A mean smile showed yellow teeth half-hidden by strands of his straggly gray hair.

She glanced about and realized they were alone. All the

others were in the courtyard. The fact that he had been inside the stable while she and Brandon talked unnerved her. It was almost as though he'd been waiting for her. "What is it you want?"

"Cállatte!" he growled, and notched the pistol higher, aiming at her face. He held out his hand, palm up. "Your blade, *por favor.*"

Where had she heard his voice before? "Blade?"

His eyes narrowed. "The one you carry on yourself. Give it to me."

How did he know about the knife Brandon had given her? Unless…she went cold inside. "You were at the meadow this morning."

He didn't answer, but extended his hand impatiently. "Now. Or do you prefer I take it myself?"

The thought of his dirty hands pawing her spurred her to action. She removed the knife positioned in her garter. He grabbed it away before she could straighten.

"Your voice…you spoke to Juan about work." She glanced over his shoulder. "You and another man."

"He is waiting for me. And now for you, too." He stabbed the knife into the stable door at eye level, then motioned for her to go ahead of him. "Do not call out. I have killed many. I am not afraid to shoot one more."

"You wouldn't want to bring everyone running at the noise of a gunshot," she said with bravado.

He sneered and grabbed her arm. "Señorita. You are not in a position to question me. We go." He shoved her forward, into the woods.

Chapter Eighteen

Brandon filled his bowl with *mole,* grabbed a warm tortilla and joined Diego on the ledge that surrounded the fishpond.

"Amigo. You don't look so good."

"I'm good," he said, and shoveled a spoonful of the soup into his mouth, hoping to halt any further conversation.

"¿Dónde está tu esposa?"

"She's inside," he answered.

"I have considered asking her for a dance. Would that bother you?"

Brandon stopped eating and dropped his spoon into the bowl. "As a matter of fact, it might." First Jake and now Diego. Heck if he let Caroline dance with someone else before him.

"She is a relative after all." Diego's dark brows rose, and then Brandon caught the twinkle in his eyes.

Brandon ignored him and finished his *mole* and tortilla. A servant bearing mescal on a tray walked by, and he grabbed a mug for himself. Listening to the beat of the mariachi band and watching the dancers swaying to the music made him think of Caroline all the more. He'd gotten what he wanted, so why wasn't he happy? What was wrong with him?

She would keep to her part of the bargain—he could tell by how frustrated she was. It still amazed him that she was willing to stay here with him. He had never expected that. He'd thought she'd be glad to go home to her parents and friends. Love sure made a person do crazy things.

"Isn't it past your bedtime?" he asked Diego. "How long do these weddings last anyway?"

"Often until dawn. And even the little ones like me get to stay up."

Brandon grunted, watching the couples on the dance area. Jake blew softly on Victoria's neck. "Somehow I don't think my brother is going to wait that long."

Diego smirked and Brandon had the feeling that Diego knew a bit about women.

Victoria reached up to cup Jake behind his neck and pull him down to taste his lips. Brandon couldn't keep from staring at the intimacy of the act. The trust he witnessed in Victoria's eyes made him wish for the same—from Caroline. It was his fault she guarded herself around him. His condition on their marriage had hurt her. Unfortunately he saw no way around it. It was for her own good.

He stood and tugged his hat low on his forehead. "I'm not hanging around. See you in the morning."

"Buenas noches, Anglo."

He walked through the house and stopped at the bottom of the stairway. Resting his hand on the banister, he considered going upstairs, at least checking to see if candlelight flickered under her doorway. He hated leaving things the way he had. Caroline hadn't been herself and it was his fault.

He took one step up and stopped. This was foolish. He was only deluding himself that he just meant to check on her. Once he entered her room he'd desire a whole lot more than that—he'd take her body and soul.

He did want her to stay with him. Here. In Texas terri- tory. And for some unconscionable reason, she was willing. So why couldn't he just relax and let them both be happy?

He climbed the rest of the stairs to the second level. No light spilled from under her doorway. No sound came from within. Probably asleep by now.

A young couple tripped through the entryway, the girl whispering and laughing softly as the man she was with escorted her into the library. They shut the door softly.

Brandon turned once again to Caroline's room. Instead of knocking, he opened it carefully, slowly. If she was asleep, he'd leave her alone.

He waited for his sight to adjust to the darkened room. She wasn't in her bed. He glanced about the room, thinking she must be sitting in a chair. "Caroline?" he whispered, and swung the door open further, stepping into the room. "Caroline!" Not here—that was plain. She must have rejoined the party.

He strode downstairs, through the kitchen and out into the courtyard looking for her among the guests. Still he couldn't find her. A sliver of alarm snaked its way up his spine. He tamped it down. As he walked through the gate heading for the stable, Diego joined him.

"What is it?"

"Probably nothing. Just looking for Caroline." But he couldn't let go of a growing feeling of dread inside him. The corral was empty. "Rosa's gone."

He nearly missed it—nearly entered the stable but for the sudden gleam of white at the door. He stopped. There, pinned to the wood at eye level, was the ivory-handled knife he'd given her.

His gut clenched.

"What's this about?" Diego asked.

"She wouldn't have left it here like this. Something is wrong." He wedged the knife free.

"Should I get Jake and Juan?"

"No." Brandon had a feeling this was personal. Somehow, this knife held the key.

"Maybe it is only a lover's quarrel?"

Brandon shook his head, convinced that was not the case. He checked inside the stable—no other horses were missing. "Caroline knows Rosa is only green-broke. She wouldn't chance riding her—not if she had a choice."

He studied the vague footprints in the dirt. In the moonlight, Caroline's small prints were recognizable going toward the pines, but now she was probably on horseback. "I think she's been kidnapped. Get your rifle and meet me at the cabin."

It'd take a miracle to find her at night. He was banking on the fact that the person who had taken her wanted him, not her. She was the bait.

At the cabin, he grabbed his rifle and a powder horn. By the time he'd stepped outside again, Diego had joined him.

Diego's gaze flicked to Brandon's rifle. Brandon ignored him. This was Caroline who'd been caught in the crosshairs. She was in trouble because of him. He couldn't let her get hurt, couldn't let their baby be hurt.

"We are looking for the same person who shot Jake," he told Diego. "He was aiming for me."

Diego took the information matter-of-fact, his young face grim and determined. He gripped his own rifle. "I'm ready."

"We won't have far to go. He wants me to find him—on his terms."

They tracked the horse until they lost sight of the hoof-prints in the thick pine needles. That gave him a direction at least—toward the river.

"Rosa is unpredictable," Diego murmured. "Especially with strangers. I hope the *señorita* is not riding her."

Brandon placed a finger to his lips, signaling Diego to keep quiet. He'd heard something as they neared the rushing water. On the alert, he pressed forward slowly, cautiously.

The whinny of a horse sounded, upwind and much further away. At the same time Brandon saw trampled grass in front of him. Were there two men? Had they separated or was this a trick?

It made sense for Brandon, being the slower of the two, to stay on his original course and let Diego chase after the faster bandit. He hoped Caroline would slow her captor and could only trust that he would find her in time. He motioned to Diego to follow the sound. Diego nodded once and disappeared silently into the brush.

Brandon waited. Listening.

The sound of a hoof pawing the ground caught his attention. Slow and stealthy, he parted the branches of the mesquite brush. He surveyed the area just beyond where the trees lined the river. Rosa stood in a small clearing. She snorted once, stomped her hoof and turned in a circle, straining against her reins which were tied to a low branch. He couldn't see Caroline anywhere.

"So you found us, *Médico*."

Fear prickled up his spine. He jerked his head around recognizing the voice. Where? Where had he heard it before?

And then he saw her. Caroline stood with her back against the trunk of an oak, her wrists lashed behind it. Relief shot through him. At least she was alive. Her blue party dress was torn at the shoulder now. With the exception of her light blond hair and that one white shoulder, it was difficult to see her in the dark.

Next to her stood a man with gray straggly hair and clothes that hung loosely on him. Brandon squinted, trying to make out his features better, trying to read what he saw in his eyes.

"An old friend has come to call," said the man, and raised his pistol to wedge it in Caroline's ribs.

His stomach knotted with fear. He had to do something, anything to help Caroline. The man looked vaguely familiar. He had to keep him talking if possible. The raspy voice—Brandon was sure he'd heard it before. He racked his brain trying to place it. Not a neighbor. Not a friend.

"You have me at a loss, sir," he began and took a cautious step forward.

"Move no closer, *señor!* Drop your rifle."

Suddenly it all rushed back at him. He let out a long breath. "Goliad."

"*Si, Médico.* You remember now."

A chill went through him. His guard. The man who'd shot him.

"The rifle. I said drop it."

Brandon lowered the gun slowly to the ground and then straightened.

"You are not so proud now, I see. You must use a stick when you walk." He narrowed his eyes.

"Thanks to you."

"Still you walk—which is more than my boy can do. I will not miss again."

Brandon's thoughts jolted into place. The knife. The last time he'd seen it he'd used it to dig out the plug in his ankle.

He'd tried to hide it again but had passed out. "It was you in the stable. You are the one who shot my brother."

"The bullet was meant for you. I will not make that mistake again."

"You blame me still?"

Malevolence blazed in the man's old eyes. "Because of you my Luis is dead. Because of you, I have no one to care for me in my old age. No one to carry on my name."

"Your son's name was Luis."

"*Si*—as is mine."

"What do you want with me?" He asked, but he had an ominous feeling he knew.

"I want to take from you what you took from me—someone you care for."

The hatred in the man's face—a malice bordering on insane—struck fear in Brandon. Luis's eyes bulged, his neck veins protruded. Where the heck was Diego? Brandon couldn't take his eyes off the renegade for a second to check the surrounding foliage. "The war is over now. We all lost things important to us. Why would you want to take anything more?"

"Because you have it all and I have nothing!" Luis raged, waggling the gun carelessly in his direction.

Everything inside Brandon screamed to leap forward and wrestle the gun from the man's grasp, but to do so would surely mean his own death. Not that he cared so much about himself. It was Caroline he didn't want hurt. He took a step forward.

The renegade stiffened. "Stop. I will not wait to shoot."

Brandon held himself in check.

"I have eyes. This woman—she is your woman. She carries your child. You deserve nothing—no woman, no *bebé*. Not when you have killed my son."

Fear lodged in Brandon's chest. "She deserves to die as much as your son did, which is not at all. Infection killed Luis. Infection brought on by his wound—a wound I did not give."

"The wound came from a soldier."

"True." He took a deep breath. He would not remind Luis it had been a Mexican soldier who shot the boy by accident. "If you must have your revenge, your retribution, then someone must die. It should be me—a soldier. Not this woman."

"Killing you is not enough. That will not make you hurt the way that I hurt. Every day I must carry this pain. I want you to know the pain that I feel from the loss of my son."

Brandon glanced at Caroline while Luis spoke. She watched wide-eyed. In them he saw fear—a controlled fear—the kind that made a person's thoughts and reflexes fast. He marveled that she wasn't reduced to begging or crying as some women—and men—would be. He *would* see her clear of this, he vowed.

"How old was your son?" Brandon asked, stalling for more time, hoping Diego was nearby—or coming.

"Sixteen."

"I remember him. He was very brave."

The bandit quieted, as if he, too, were thinking back, remembering.

"He did not want to die there in that cabin, but he faced it like a man. He asked…" Brandon took a shaky breath as his throat thickened. He'd done everything in his power not to remember, not to care about that boy…about Luis. He had a name now. Brandon forced himself to continue.

"Luis had trouble breathing in the cabin with all the smoke and the stench of old blood. He asked me to take him outside. It was a clear night like it is now. Cool.

Scarcely a breeze. I was weak from my own wound but found the strength to help him."

Brandon closed his eyes, remembering it more closely than he wanted to. The boy's wound had putrefied. Even now, Brandon remembered the odor of the rotting flesh. "His body burned with fever. I took him to the riverbank. The guards tried to stop me once, but on seeing that Luis had a uniform like them, they simply followed to see what was happening. When I laid him on the ground, he opened his eyes and stared at the night sky."

The pistol hung limp in the man's hand. "My son liked the stars."

Brandon stepped closer as he spoke. "A smile came to his face. A look of peace. He asked if I saw the big dipper. He said it in Spanish and it took me a minute to understand him. He gripped my hand, said *gracias* and died."

Brandon stood before the man now, near enough to reach out and jerk the gun from his hand. The renegade realized it, too, and stepped back, grasping the handle firmly with both hands, again aiming it at Caroline's chest.

Brandon's heart lurched. "You don't want to do that."

"But I do." An unhealthy light came into Luis's eyes.

"It will not honor your son and it will not bring him back."

The man's lower lip trembled. The gun wavered in his hands. Brandon saw that now the end pointed down—at the baby within her. His luck was going from bad to worse.

"Luis would not want this of you. He was brave. Is what you are doing brave?"

The man's shoulders slumped.

Brandon moved swiftly, ripping the gun from the man's hand and turning it on him.

Luis, his eyes wild, yanked a knife from his waistband. He knocked the rifle to the side and lunged toward Brandon.

They grappled and went down with a heavy thud, rolling in the dirt, straining against each other for control. Despite his size, Luis wielded the knife with an unnatural strength. Like a maniac he bore down on Brandon, one hand gripping Brandon's throat and pressing his windpipe, the other hand grasping the knife and hovering inches from his jugular.

Would it matter if he died? The thought came to Brandon in the flash of a second. What future did he have with the madness slowly taking him? His life could be over so quickly and then he would have peace. No more worrying about how he would make a living, no more striving to fight a sickness that couldn't be stopped, no more pain. The thought paralyzed him in its intoxication. In its simplicity. Inside, a low, insistent voice urged: *Just let Luis finish this. Let it happen. Let this be over.*

Jake would understand eventually. He had Victoria now. He would be angry, but he'd get over it. Better that than the worry Brandon had last seen in his eyes. He was beginning to suspect the spells Brandon had although he wasn't completely sure. Brandon didn't want him finding out for sure. He was already the weaker brother—the one who'd gotten himself captured. Jake shouldn't have to keep rescuing him, but he would unless Brandon was out of his life completely.

All Brandon had to do was relax his grip on Luis's wrist, let him slide the knife closer. The man's rotten breath made him gag and in that instant the knife dipped and nicked his skin. It could all be over in one flash of silver. So easy. Perhaps cowardly, but he wouldn't be around to see Jake's disappointment—or even Caroline's. He wouldn't be around…

To see his child. To help him or her into this world, God willing. To watch him grow and teach him about life.

Intense longing filled him, replacing the despair. And Caroline—Caroline most of all. Lord knew he loved her. He didn't know what his future held, but she had to be in it. Somehow he wanted her safe, even if it was across a thousand miles.

The heel of Luis's hand pressed down on his windpipe. Blackness formed at the edge of his vision. Lack of oxygen, Brandon thought clinically. Even in the middle of a knockdown fight, his education, his mind, invaded his thoughts. What a fool.

From somewhere beyond the small circle that had become him and Luis, Brandon heard Caroline cry. She sobbed his name, the anguish and fear thick in her voice.

She was still tied to the tree, he realized. Still a prisoner to whoever won this match. He couldn't let Luis have her. She needed him to best this maniac. She needed him to be strong. Letting Luis kill him was the coward's way out. He'd been thinking like a coward, and damn it, he'd never been a coward in the past. He wasn't about to start now.

A low growl rumbled in his throat. With his thumb, he pressed the man's inner wrist hard—right there where the nerves supplied the hand. Harder…harder still.

Pinpoints of fear entered Luis's eyes and the possibility formed that he might not win, might not be able to carry out his plan. He tensed, the veins in his neck bulging; with renewed force he pushed harder yet.

"Don't do this, Luis. Your son would not want this."

"You know nothing about my son!" Luis grit out the words.

The blade dropped from Luis's hand, slicing Brandon's neck as it landed point down in the dirt. In that second, Brandon jerked up his knee and sent the man toppling over his head. He dragged in a deep breath and pushed to his feet, turning to face Luis again. Somehow, Luis had regained the blade and now strode toward Caroline with a wild, determined look in his eyes.

Brandon reacted without thinking. In a flash of movement, he grabbed the rifle from the dirt and pulled the trigger.

Luis jerked midstride. His eyes went wide. He lunged toward Caroline and then collapsed, the knife scoring down her dress on his descent. He fell with his head against her foot, his eyes blank—the stare of a dead man.

A scream pierced the air. Caroline's scream.

Brandon threw the rifle aside. "It's all right now. Caroline, it's over."

"Oh, God. Oh, God," she cried, her breath coming in jerky sobs as she stared in wide-eyed horror at the man on her feet. "Brandon, please, get him off me."

He grabbed Luis under both armpits and dragged him a few feet away. Then he found the knife in the dirt and cut the ties that bound Caroline. She fell into his arms and clung to him, her body shaking uncontrollably.

"It's all right now," he said again, trying to soothe her. "You are safe."

"I was so scared!" She sniffled. "You could have been killed."

"The thought crossed my mind. Maybe…maybe God wants me around awhile longer."

"Don't make light of it, Brandon. I want you around. I need you around." The words came out jerky and halting.

"Now who is the one with the shakes," he said, rubbing her arms. "Come here. Sit down." He helped her to the ground, her back against the oak, and sat beside her. As he did, the tear in her dress opened and a fresh smear of blood caught his attention.

He pushed the material aside, examining her leg. "He

cut you!" An angry slash from her thigh to her knee oozed bright drops of red.

"It stings, but it is no more than what happened to your neck."

"Quite a bit longer and deeper. I'll have to watch that it doesn't get infected."

She reached out and touched his chin, pulling his gaze to her face. "Always the physician."

He grimaced. "I should have been faster. You wouldn't have been hurt, then."

"Don't try to analyze it this time. It's over and you...you were wonderful." Her eyes brimmed with unshed tears and held such a look he'd never seen before, as if he were a hero—her hero.

"Is the baby...?"

In answer, she moved his hand to her abdomen. He stilled at the intimate gesture. Swallowed. Through the silk layer of her dress he could feel her changing contour. The baby pushed against his hand's added weight. Relief washed over him.

"By the way," she said softly. "You believed you couldn't take care of me."

Slowly he pulled his hand away.

"Tonight you proved yourself wrong."

"This doesn't change anything. It can't."

She sighed. "Just hold me. Till the shaking stops. Please."

His ankle ached. He shifted to move closer to her. "I should get you back to the hacienda." But already he was wrapping his arms around her shoulders, pulling her to him, his mouth pressing a kiss to her temple.

He could hold her like this forever, he realized. Keeping her safe, protecting her. He breathed in her scent, remembering it all over again, and slowly trailed his lips down her cheek until he met the corner of her mouth. He hovered there, waiting, wanting to kiss her—wanting her to want it, too.

She turned her face toward his, her eyes searching his, their breath mingling. It seemed so natural to kiss her. He molded his lips against hers and felt them tremble. If he could, he would give her what strength he possessed—anything to help her get through this.

She opened her mouth and he touched her tongue with his—tentatively at first, and then bolder. Hold her like this forever? Who was he trying to convince? The stirring in his groin made him realize he'd only last so long. He was a young, relatively healthy male and holding led to other things, especially with a woman as giving as Caroline. She didn't need that now. She was probably on the edge of shock from all that had happened. He moved his lips away from hers and kissed her lightly on the forehead. With a sigh, she relaxed against his chest.

Twenty minutes later, Diego found them. He took in the situation in a glance, his gaze moving from them to the man laying dead on the ground. *"Híjole,"* he said as he surveyed the scene and blew out a breath. "Are you all right? Señorita Caroline—are you well?"

She pushed away from Brandon and brushed a strand of hair from her face.

Reluctantly Brandon let go and brought his mind back to the present. Caroline was no longer shaking. He covered up her wounded leg with the edge of her dress and turned to Diego. "Where have you been?"

"I chased the other *bandito* across the river."

"Did you catch him?"

Diego shook his head. "But I found his camp and our

horses. When I heard the gunshot I headed back. I thought you might need help. Doesn't look like you did."

"It could have gone either way for a time," Brandon said, taking his proffered hand for help up.

"It took a while to find you." Diego gave him a quick slap on the back and then turned to help Caroline, but Brandon brushed him aside and grabbed Caroline's hand. Diego took the hint in a flash. He grinned. "I'll get the horse."

"What now?" Caroline said. "We can't leave Luis to the buzzards."

"No," Brandon said, staring at the body. "He was crazy with grief. He didn't deserve to die."

Her brow furrowed. "But he would have killed you or me if you hadn't stopped him."

"I know."

She leaned against his chest and he felt an overpowering urge to keep her there, pressed safely against him. He circled her with his arm.

Diego brought the horse around. Together, he and Diego lifted the body over the horse's back. Rosa shied a bit, and then quieted under Diego's hand.

"Are you able to walk?" Brandon asked.

In answer, she slipped her hand in his.

He gave her fingers a squeeze, pulling her along as they started back to the hacienda.

Chapter Nineteen

Caroline heard a faint knocking through her dream. She'd slept poorly, reliving the events of last evening over and over. Now someone dared to wake her up?

The knocking came again. "Caroline?" Brandon said.

"I'm not awake."

"I'm coming in."

"No!" she cried, sitting up against the oak headboard. "I'm still abed!"

He cracked open the door. "I want to check your leg."

He stepped into the room looking as though he'd been up and working for some time. His body radiated heat. A sheen of sweat covered his face and drops trickled down his neck, wetting his cotton shirt.

She drew up the sheet feeling modest in spite of the fact they were married now. It wasn't a true marriage by her definition. "What have you been doing?"

"Digging."

She thought at first he meant in his garden and it struck her as an odd thing to do after last night, but then realized he probably had been seeing to a grave.

He sat on her bed, careful to keep clear of her legs.

She flexed her ankle. The laceration burned as she stretched. A line of fire raced up her leg.

"Does it hurt much?"

She remembered asking him the same question about his leg and getting a snarl for an answer. That had been days ago—when he'd just learned of her pregnancy and was angry. Much had happened since then.

"Some. I'll be ready to travel in a day or so as long as infection doesn't set in."

His jaw tensed. He swept his gaze down her length and as he did so, his mien became all doctor. "Let me have a look." He readjusted on the bed and rolled the sheets back, taking care not to expose anything more than her leg. A dark red scab ran the length of it, the edges of her skin puckered at places, pink but not unusually reddened. He spread his hand over the cut, checking methodically up her leg for heat and the telltale sign of induration or redness that would herald infection.

Slowly he moved his hand up her thigh. Her heartbeat quickened. Knowing his intent didn't stop the tendrils of desire that curled in her abdomen at his gentle touch. He reached the top of her cut, so close to the apex of her legs. His fingers trembled, hovering over the last bit of scabbing.

She looked up into his face, inches from her own. A question lingered in his blue eyes, along with a look of intense wanting.

He expelled a ragged breath. "Caroline…?"

He leaned close, his lips hovering near hers and she remembered how soft they were, how they sent chills through her body and left her begging with need. It broke her heart to deny him. She closed her eyes and willed herself to be strong and resist the temptation that was and always would be—Brandon.

"You want an answer I can't give. Not if you are still set on sending me away," she murmured, wishing her voice was stronger. Only if he asked her to stay would she say yes. And he didn't want that.

"You know I want you, Caroline. It's always been you and only you. Last night when I thought I might lose you and the baby..." His voice trailed off as he searched for the right words. "I've never known such a deep fear."

"Not even in the prison?"

"No. Not there. I've never worried much about myself, but you—you have to live. You are what keeps me going. Thinking of you has always given me hope."

"Yet not enough to ask me to stay."

"You know why I can't let you."

"I've heard your reasons. You're afraid I'll think less of you when the nightmares get worse, when the spells rob you of your mind." She struggled with her thoughts. They were harsh. But it was how she felt. "But you are a coward, Brandon. No matter that you survived last night's ordeal. No matter that you saved me from Luis. You are a coward because you won't trust me. Not with your whole heart. You won't trust me to stand by you through the good days and the bad."

"I've been through bad days—with my father and my mother. I don't want that for you—for us."

"But, Brandon—" She grasped his hands. "Your name will not keep me warm in bed at night. It will not stop me from...from loving you as, God help me, I still do. Beyond reason, beyond life itself, I still love you. And I want to be with you. I believe in you, Brandon. I believe in the strength of the love we share, but only if we are together."

He was shaking his head while she spoke. Unwilling—

or afraid—to believe her words. His face blurred before her. She blinked away the tear.

"I need someone who believes as much as I do. I need someone who will be there for me and for the baby. Someone I can count on." She struggled against the thickness clogging her throat. She had to get this out, had to make him understand that she wasn't giving up on him, but what he asked—to leave him—was near impossible for her.

"I'm not turning my back on you or the child. You'll be taken care of."

She shook her head. "That's not enough for me anymore."

"It's all I have to give."

"I don't believe that. Whatever happened in prison changed you, Brandon. I don't understand you anymore. Perhaps I never did. You had better leave now." She said it to hurt him even though she didn't really mean it. She would always love him.

He didn't go—but remained sitting on the bed. "Have I told you how I got my position in Santa Anna's army?"

She stilled. He'd never spoken of his time in the battle. As far as she knew, he'd never told anyone. She shook her head.

"I was heading toward Goliad with another soldier, Richard Blalock. I carried orders in my pack for Colonel Fannin from General Houston. On the road the Santanistas captured us. Richard knew we didn't stand a chance but he knew the orders had to get through. He pointed at me and yelled, *'Médico! Médico!'*"

"I don't understand."

"Santa Anna gave orders to kill everyone but doctors. Those he needed to tend the Mexican wounded. Richard knew of it. I didn't. The Santanistas shot him and let me live."

"Oh, Brandon! What a horrible thing to witness, but it

was brave of him. If not for him and his quick words, you would have both died."

"Richard had a wife and two children waiting for him in Washington-on-the-Brazos."

"Have you contacted her? Does she know?" It would help, she thought, and not just the woman. It would help Brandon to speak to her, explain how her husband had died and how the man had been a hero to the end.

"I tried, but she'd moved on by the time I was well enough to travel."

"He saved your life. I…I will always be grateful to him."

Brandon didn't comment.

"What happened after that?"

"The soldiers took me to Goliad to doctor their troops. There was nothing to work with—no stethoscope, no bandages. Infection set in constantly. At first I figured that if one of the men died in my care, the soldiers would shoot me. When that didn't happen, I couldn't decide whether I should be relieved or whether death would have been the better choice."

It hurt to hear him talk like this. She reached out and put her hand over his.

He stared at it. "There wasn't enough to eat. If I was lucky, I'd get a bowl of beef broth once a day. Sometimes the broth would have pieces of raw meat in it. Wormy, gamey—I won't speak to what that did to my gut. But it was all I had so I ate it."

Caroline held her midsection. "Please, Brandon. No more. I can't stand to hear it."

"I lost weight. It's a wonder Jake recognized me when he found me."

She swallowed convulsively, trying to quell her rising stomach contents. He was finally opening up to her—if she could bear to listen. "How did that happen? How did Jake find you?"

"My guard thought I was trying to escape and shot me in the ankle."

"Luis?" The words the bandit had said last night rushed back to her.

"After his son died, I wasn't any use to him anymore. Luis moved me to a room with the other Texian soldiers. We were pretty much forgotten there. We'd get water if we were lucky. My wound festered. I grew delirious. Victoria happened to see me as I was being transferred and got word to Jake. That's how he found me—burning up with fever and half out of my mind."

She couldn't help it. She was crying now. Crying for the innocence he'd lost in that prison, crying for the inhumanity of man, and crying with relief that he'd survived at all. She knew war was ugly, but she'd never been this close to it. "I had no idea…" she murmured. "No idea at all."

"I'm glad you don't. No one should."

He fell silent, his gaze on her hand covering his.

"About last night," she said. "I was proud of you. You were amazing in your strength—and in your capacity to forgive a grieving man."

"He shouldn't have died. Shouldn't have charged me."

"You did the only thing you could. Luis was worn-out with grief for his son. I hope that now he is in a better place."

Brandon didn't comment, but continued to look at his hand in a way that she suspected he was seeing something else—either last night or his time in Goliad.

A new thought came to her and she leaned forward. "Afterward, there was blood—on my leg and dress, and on Luis's chest. Brandon, did you see anything?"

"You mean another hallucination?" he asked cautiously.

She nodded.

"I was only concerned with you."

"Have you noticed that the spells are less, not worse since I've arrived? You don't dare admit it, but it is happening before my eyes. Last night, I was the one shaking after the attack, not you."

He shook his head, refusing to believe her.

"And when you removed the bullet from Jake, you started to shake, but it wasn't like the time with the fishhook. You controlled it, Brandon."

"It still happened."

The more she thought about it, the more she was convinced she was right. "Perhaps it means you are healing—at least you have some control over the symptoms. You focused. You did what had to be done. Don't you see? You are getting better, not worse."

For a moment, she thought he believed her, but then he frowned. "You're grasping at straws. It doesn't mean anything." His voice sounded harsh, strained, as if he couldn't bring himself to think it—to believe it.

She felt hollow inside. Why was it so hard for him to believe anything good about himself? "You don't want to heal, do you? It would change all your plans."

"Caroline, you're not making any sense."

"I know exactly what I'm saying. If you were to heal on the inside, you might actually have a future. Trouble is—you don't believe you deserve one."

He pulled his hand away.

She'd tried her best. There was nothing more she could say. Turning her attention back to her leg, she asked, "Do you note anything to worry about?"

He cleared his throat. "No. It's healing well."

"Will it scar?"

"Probably." He huffed. "You're worried about a scar in a place no one will ever see?"

"Only my husband."

His gaze flew to hers. He sat straighter on the edge of the bed, remote. "You've had no cramping? No bleeding? The baby moves?"

She drew the sheet back over her leg. She felt betrayed by her own body, by the way it yearned for him even now. "The baby is fine. If you'll leave now, I'll get dressed."

He stood and took a step back. "Of course." When he got to the door, he didn't walk through.

"What is it?" she asked.

"It is past noon. The last of the wedding guests are leaving." He sighed. "I buried Luis this morning. Juan is having the priest say words over the grave before he departs."

She swallowed hard.

"We don't have the luxury of waiting for another day, Caroline. The priest is here now."

"I understand," she murmured. But understanding couldn't hold back the conflicting emotions rolling through her. To have the funeral so close to Jake and Victoria's wedding seemed somehow to taint the day.

"I'm sorry it has to be like this," Brandon said.

"It needs to be done. If things had turned out differently last night…" She didn't finish. The words were too difficult to say, too horrid to even consider.

"It would have been me lying out there in the meadow," Brandon finished for her.

"Yes."

"You needn't worry. I've already talked to Franklin. My will has been altered to provide for you."

Anguish ripped through her. "Oh, Brandon. It's not about the money. It's you I need. Only you."

His jaw tightened while his face closed into a mask. "Gertrudis is worried about you. She's made tea and is waiting downstairs. I'll be back later."

He turned on his heel and left. Through the window she saw him join Juan and the priest. Of course he needed to be there, needed to hear the words of absolution for Luis—absolution perhaps for himself, too.

Brandon headed for Luis's grave, shutting out Caroline's words. He knew she'd try to change his mind about making her leave Texas, but he couldn't think about that now. Thoughts of her were too tangled, and he needed to see to Luis.

That morning he'd buried the man who was guard, soldier, renegade…and father and put a simple cross at the head of the grave. Juan and Diego waited for him there.

The few words the priest said brought a sense of finality to Luis's life. At the end, Brandon grabbed a handful of dirt, dropped it on the grave and said, "Have peace, Luis. Go with God."

The others headed back to the hacienda, but Brandon couldn't bring himself to join them. He stared at the grave awhile, thinking about Luis and his son. Thinking about all he'd been through since coming to Texas. He sat down and rested his arms on his legs.

He should take comfort in the unending sameness of this land, the permanence of it, but when he let down his guard, the thoughts that came to him were not peaceful, but chaotic. They were the sounds of men who had at first yelled out their battle cry only to have it end in a wild-eyed scream of pain, watching them fall as a lead plug found a vital organ—or a bayonet penetrated their flesh. The blood. The loss of life. The cries of agony.

He closed his eyes, dropping his head between his arms, no longer willing the images to retreat but examining each one in his mind, holding them up to the light of day and accepting them for what they were—horrific and ugly. He'd asked for it when he came to Texas to fight. He knew there'd be death. That was the price of Texas' independence. He thought he could handle it. After all he'd been around death before as a doctor. How different to see it from the perspective of a soldier. He hadn't counted on the sheer numbers lost in the rebellion or the unnecessary loss of life because of lack of food and water, or bandages, or medicine.

He'd believed there was nothing left of himself to give Caroline. The war had taken his hopes, his dreams and his health. He'd felt hard on the outside, unable to feel anything anymore. And here she'd shown up and proved him wrong, breaking through his shell until being near her, holding her, was all he wanted. He needed her softness, her light, in his life.

In spite of all his worries, last night he *had* protected her. The blood from the fighting and from her leg hadn't triggered a spell. She'd been right about that.

Telling her about his time in Goliad had been hard, but once he started, he couldn't stop. The words poured out of him from deep inside where they'd been locked. Knowing that she would sit there and listen and accept whatever he said without judging him somehow made him want to keep talking. The more he said, the more it felt like a weight fell from his shoulders.

Could he trust that he was getting better? Could he trust that the spells were subsiding? Or would he live forever in fear of them coming back worse than before.

He stood and looked down the small knoll to the hacienda in the distance. From here he could see Diego starting to work Rosa in the corral. Smoke from the chimney spiraled up and drifted north in the light breeze. By now, Caroline would be finished with her tea. She'd probably be ready for another nap after all that had happened. Would she look out the window and wonder what kept him away? He dragged his hands through his hair.

He wanted her. In her room today, he had wanted to pull her body against his and kiss her soundly, completely, until she gasped for air—until she drove every last memory of the war away and left only her love in its place. What would happen if he went back to the house now, knowing they were married and he had every right to touch her, to hold her…

Would she let him stay with her tonight? Would her heart have softened toward him since earlier when she turned him away? He hadn't pressed her before, but perhaps now he would. He wouldn't force her—yet he didn't want her to accept him as though it were her duty. He'd sampled the fire in her and that's the only way he wanted her—burning for him as he burned for her. Anything less would be a corruption of their feelings for each other. Yet could he enjoy her body as a husband could and then send her away?

He turned away, his back to the hacienda, and started walking, putting one foot in front of the other. He strode through the meadow and entered the woods on the far side before he realized he hadn't brought his cane with him. He tested his weight on his leg at a different angle. Except for being sore from the fight with Luis, it didn't hurt much today.

He continued through the woods. If he couldn't put distance between himself and Caroline in his thoughts at least he could do so in space. Until he had a grip on his emotions, on his thoughts, he couldn't be near her.

He had told her that Texas was too tough for her, that

she wouldn't survive here, yet she was the one who had held Franklin hostage to force her way here. She was the one who had climbed out on that tree limb, turning back only when he'd insisted. And it was she who had withstood kidnapping with more spirit than he believed possible. All while her baby—his baby—grew inside her.

Trouble was, some of her ideas made sense. He did want to be around to help when the baby came. He did want to know if he had a son or daughter—and not just from a letter. He wanted to hold the baby, be there for the first smile, the first word. If he truly was getting better why was he forcing her to leave? It was beginning to make no sense—even to him.

The woods became denser and he heard the sound of water over stones. The river. He'd walked a far distance and without his cane. He picked his way through the foliage along the bank and stood for a moment, watching the water race past. The level had decreased in the past few days. The current flowed and eddied over boulders along the bank. Toward the center it was deep enough to mask the swift speed. Only a person unaware of the river's distinctive personality would knowingly challenge it.

He glanced downstream, his eye drawn to the white cloth Caroline had been so adamant about rescuing. It remained tangled on the half-submerged branch in the middle of the river. What was it about the material that triggered such a strong response in her? A wedding present for Jake and Victoria—that's all she'd said about it. Franklin was the one who had admitted she used it to gird him up when he'd been caught under the coach.

He was amazed the cloth hadn't washed away by now. He considered the pros and cons of going after it. He'd like to get it for her. Was he being a complete fool? Last night, his past had challenged him and he'd survived. Perhaps, he thought as he stared at the cloth, perhaps today he would challenge the river.

He walked along the bank, studying the current, the distance to the branch, and the flow of the water in the curve upstream. A snake slithered out from a decaying log by his foot. He ignored it, caught up as he was in the possibility of retrieving the fabric. He would have to enter the river a generous one hundred yards upstream from the branch if he were to make his way to it and not get swept past.

Enough thinking! If he was going to do this before nightfall—or winter—he'd just better do it.

He made his way to the calculated entry point and pushed through the thick brush. Bracing for the moment his injured leg would feel the sting, he stepped into the drink. The water swirled around his thighs, pushing him. He took an unsteady step. His ankle held, and he took another step, and another—the water up to his waist now. He pushed off, his strokes strong and hard as he swam, overcorrecting his path to allow for the pull of the current.

He was adjacent to and nearly past the cloth in a flash. His leg caught on part of the branch and he went under. His heart pounded. He struggled and freed himself, then floated beyond the cloth, only to grab the top of the tree branches to hang on. Dragging in great gulps of air, he paused a moment to let his heart return to normal.

Slowly, against the current, he inched his way back to the fabric. Holding on to the branch, he carefully untangled the cloth. Then folding it so that it didn't trail and catch on anything else, he pushed off into the center of the river.

In comparison, it had been easy to swim toward the cloth. The river flowed fastest in the center and the current sucked him there. To get out of the pull—the very grip of the river—

proved to be the difficult part. He swam hard, gaining only small success in making his way back to the bank. The water swept him onward. His limbs became leaden weights as he tired, but still he struggled. He gasped for air, and then gave up the fight, letting the current take him.

Chapter Twenty

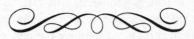

"Señora Dumont? Is Brandon back yet?" Diego called from outside the cabin.

It was the first time she had heard herself addressed that way. A pleasant warmth spread through her, much like drinking hot chocolate on a cold winter's night. She cracked the cabin door. "He hasn't returned."

"Should I look for him?"

"Not yet."

His dark eyes flashed. "It isn't right for him to leave you. Are you sure this is what you want?"

She was glad twilight had come and Diego couldn't see her blush of embarrassment. She wasn't sure how to answer him.

"You have the *pistola*?"

She glanced at her brother's gun on the mantel. After what had happened last night, she felt better having it near, loaded for protection. "Yes. Don't worry. I…I'll come to the house if he doesn't return soon."

"*Si*. Or I will return to check on you again." He headed back to the hacienda.

She closed the door and paced the length of the floor. Where was Brandon? Had something happened to him? After he'd left with Juan and the priest, she had berated herself for turning him away. What kind of foolish pride was it that made her refuse him earlier? If, as his wife, all she would have to remember was one night in his arms, then she would make it count.

Her gaze fell on the wooden bed in the corner where once the straw pallets had been. This afternoon when she had announced her decision to move to the cabin, Victoria had asked Juan and Diego to move the bed and her trunk from the hacienda. A braided cord held aside the curtain, revealing the bed and the wedding bouquet on the pillow. She had been touched by their gift and thanked them, although she wondered now if she would even have a wedding night.

She looked out the window for the millionth time. The full moon painted the landscape in shades of gray. A dying wind rustled the pines and the tall prairie grass beyond them. The red flowers swayed, their petals already closed up for the night. In the distance, a man walked toward the hacienda, his stride steady, yet favoring his right leg. He glanced at the cabin and paused, and she knew he was taking in the smoke coming from the chimney and the candle flickering in the window.

Caroline held her breath.

She grabbed the door latch, but couldn't bring herself to open it. Although she wanted to go to him, something inside told her no. She should stay. Wait.

Wait for him to come to her. After all, she'd been the one to travel fifteen hundred miles to see him. Now it was his turn.

She waited.

She spun on her heel and paced—to the bed to readjust

the bouquet for the hundredth time, then to the hearth to stir the soup in the kettle. She stopped moving about and held her hands clasped before her, waiting by the small fire she'd started.

He didn't knock. He simply strode in and shut the door. And dropped the latch.

Something had changed. She could feel it as sure as fresh rain coming in on the afternoon breeze. The air was charged with a current running between them. She could tell by the way he looked at her—a fierce tenderness in his eyes. Her breath caught in her throat.

He crossed the distance in four strides and pulled her to him, his mouth swooping down on hers, firm and demanding. His fingers tangled in her hair, sending tingles over her scalp and down her spine. In the back of her mind she realized his clothes were cool and damp. It mattered little since heat emanated off his body in waves.

Her muscles turned to liquid. How had she denied him this morning? She could deny him nothing. Not when every part of her yearned for his touch.

He released her lips and stared down at her, his face now unreadable, his deep blue eyes boring into hers. "I have something for you."

He turned back to the door. It was then she noticed a cloth hanging from the latch. Something white and dirty and wet. She went still, knowing without further examination what it was.

He held it up for her. "It's not for Victoria and Jake."

"No."

"It never was."

"It's for the baby's cradle and later, the bed." She turned the fabric over, examining the holes and the destroyed edges.

Brandon turned her hand, bringing a portion she'd embroidered to her view and read out loud the words she'd stitched around the perimeter in gold thread. "Love is patient and kind. Love is not proud. Love bears all things, believes all things, hopes all things and endures all things. Love never fails."

She spread her hand over the fancy cursive letters, some a little crooked, but each painstakingly made. "I've never been much of a seamstress. I don't have the patience for sewing, but I wanted our child to always know he or she was loved."

He stepped closer—so close she felt his breath on her cheek. "There's no doubt the little mite will know he's loved with you for a mother."

She tried to absorb his closeness, afraid it might be all she would get. Tonight of all nights that would be horrible. She wanted a wedding night.

"I've been doing some thinking."

Oh, dear. "I don't know if I can handle much more of your thinking, Brandon," she warned, bracing herself.

"Now hear me out. I figure that if I can survive what happened in Goliad, perform surgery on my brother despite one of my spells, best a deranged renegade bent on killing the both of us and swim the river at its peak for a piece of cloth, then I can handle just about anything I get served in this life. And crazy as it sounds, for some reason you seem to want to share it with me."

"Of course I do. I love you."

"Simple as that?"

"It is for me."

"Then stay with me, Caroline." His voice was insistent, urgent in her ear. "Don't leave."

"Don't leave?" she repeated. She had to be sure she understood. "You mean for tonight?"

He shook his head. "I mean ever. Don't leave ever. I want you at my side when I'm working. I want to help bring our baby into the world. And I want to hold you in my arms every night starting with tonight, starting with now. I'll never let you go."

She hesitated, wanting so badly to trust his words.

"You said some things this morning, things I hadn't faced before. You were right—I was able to remove that bullet from Jake's shoulder because of your help. And the spells, they are easing up since you came."

Her vision blurred.

"I don't know if they'll go away completely," he warned.

"Whether they do or not, you have to trust that I'll be here for you. You can't send me away."

His gaze burned into hers. "In *sickness* and in *health,* from this day forward…"

"I meant those vows," she whispered.

"I do, too, Caroline."

He captured her lips with his. If there were any lingering doubts, his kiss brushed them away. He *was* strong—strong enough to confront the demons that had haunted him.

She pulled back and studied his face once more, finally letting herself believe his words.

The corner of his mouth quirked up in that smile she loved. His blue eyes twinkled. "Guess you're my hostage."

She took a deep breath, letting the joy spread through and fill her. "No. You're mine. And just think—I didn't even have to hold a gun on you."

She released herself from his embrace and stepped back. Turning to the hearth, she took the pistol from the mantel and carefully released the cocked lever before setting it back down. She spun around to face him, enjoying the slightly stunned look on his face.

"Now, Dr. Dumont, I believe I'm ready to start my life in Texas with you."

* * * * *

REGENCY
Silk & Scandal

*A season of secrets, scandal and
seduction in high society!*

Volume 1 – 7th May 2010
The Lord and the Wayward Lady
by Louise Allen

Volume 2 – 4th June 2010
Paying the Virgin's Price
by Christine Merrill

Volume 3 – 2nd July 2010
The Smuggler and the Society Bride
by Julia Justiss

Volume 4 – 6th August 2010
Claiming the Forbidden Bride
by Gayle Wilson

8 VOLUMES IN ALL TO COLLECT!

www.millsandboon.co.uk   M&B

A wanton widow

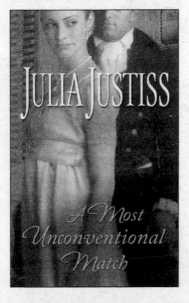

Hal Waterman has secretly adored newly widowed Elizabeth Lowery for years. When he calls upon Elizabeth to offer his help, his silent, protective presence awakens feelings in her that she does not understand.

Elizabeth knows that society would condemn her, but Hal's attractions may well prove too much to resist!

Available 16th April 2010

M&B

Sparkling ballrooms and wealthy glamour in Regency London

Orphaned Miss Georgiana Hartley fled to a neighbouring estate, hoping the lady of the house would rescue her. But its owner, Lord Alton, was unmarried!

When the scandalous viscount introduced Georgiana to his sister's influence, Georgiana was soon transformed into a charming lady, cultivating a bevy of suitors. But then Dominic realised he wanted Georgiana for his own!

www.mirabooks.co.uk

Sparkling ballrooms and wealthy glamour in Regency London

Kidnapped in the small hours,
Miss Helen Walford was rescued by the
infamous rakehell, the Earl of Merton!

Her only defence lay in anonymity. But captured
by her beauty and bravery, the Earl of Merton
knew that he had to find his mysterious lady.
He'd move heaven and earth to track down the
woman he knew to be his destiny.

Sparkling ballrooms and wealthy glamour in Regency London

Content with her humdrum country life, Miss Dorothea Darent had no intention of marrying. But one kiss from a dashing stranger changed everything.

When the scandalous Marquis of Hazelmere encountered Dorothea, he was entranced. The lady was surrounded by suitors – and now the confirmed rake must fight for his beautiful prize!

www.mirabooks.co.uk

Immerse yourself in the glitter of Regency times and follow the lives and romantic escapades of Stephanie Laurens' Lester family

www.mirabooks.co.uk

millsandboon.co.uk Community

Join Us!

The Community is the perfect place to meet and chat to kindred spirits who love books and reading as much as you do, but it's also the place to:

- ◼ **Get the inside scoop from authors about their latest books**
- ◼ **Learn how to write a romance book with advice from our editors**
- ◼ **Help us to continue publishing the best in women's fiction**
- ◼ **Share your thoughts on the books we publish**
- ◼ **Befriend other users**

Forums: Interact with each other as well as authors, editors and a whole host of other users worldwide.

Blogs: Every registered community member has their own blog to tell the world what they're up to and what's on their mind.

Book Challenge: We're aiming to read 5,000 books and have joined forces with The Reading Agency in our inaugural Book Challenge.

Profile Page: Showcase yourself and keep a record of your recent community activity.

Social Networking: We've added buttons at the end of every post to share via digg, Facebook, Google, Yahoo, technorati and de.licio.us.

www.millsandboon.co.uk